#3 in the August Riordan Series

CANDY FROM $TRANGERS

Mark Coggins

Carol,

Best wishes,

Mark Coggins

BLEAK HOUSE BOOKS

MADISON | WISCONSIN

Published by Bleak House Books,
an imprint of Big Earth Publishing
923 Williamson St.
Madison, WI 53703

ISBN: 1-932557-16-4

Cover and book design: Peter Streicher
Cover photographs by Andrea Gerard

Library of Congress Cataloging-in-Publication Data

Coggins, Mark, 1957-
Candy from strangers / Mark Coggins.
p. cm.
ISBN 1-932557-16-4
1. Private investigators--California--San Francisco--Fiction. 2. Missing persons--Fiction.
3. Teenage girls--Crimes against--Fiction. 4. Web sites--Fiction. 5. Computer sex--Fiction.
6. San Francisco (Calif.)--Fiction. I. Title.

PS3553.O41555C36 2006
813'.54--dc22
2006023449

献给周琳
(to Linda)

Acknowledgements

The author wishes to thank his fellow writers Sheila Scobba Banning, John Billheimer, Bob Brownstein, Anne Cheilek, Ann Hillesland and Mike Padilla for helping him to make Candy from Strangers the best he can make it. Thanks are also due to Larry and Ed Berger for lending their expertise in all things jazz-related, and to my editor, Alison Janssen, who kept me and my characters honest (and taught me a thing or two I didn't know about tattoos), and finally to my agent and teacher, Donna Levin, who not only placed the third book in a series with a new publisher (impossible!), but has generously applied her own very considerable editorial and development skills to all the books I have written.

"Take gifts with a sigh: most men give to be paid."
—John Boyle O'Reilly, *Rules of the Road*

"Everybody wants to see the pictures, and yet nobody wants to see them."
—Ray Bradbury, *The Illustrated Man*

"Many a man digs his grave with his teeth."
— *Golden Dawn of the New Epiphany*

CANDY FROM $TRANGERS

IT *WAS* THE MEAT

W HEN HENRY GLOVER WROTE *It Ain't the Meat (It's the Mo-tion)* in 1952 for the King Records R&B group The Swallows, I'm sure he never anticipated the trouble it would cause. The Swallows had made a modest hit of the song, but the risqué lyrics and the fact that white kids weren't buying many records from black groups limited its play. It took Chris Duckworth belting it half-century later to really do some damage.

It was Fleet Week in San Francisco and Chris and I were playing our regular Tuesday night gig at House of Shields on New Montgomery. With his shimmering, form-fitting gown, pearl necklace, dangling sea horse earrings and the blond hair from his wig piled high with a scallop shell and gold chopsticks to fix it in place, he looked like a hottie from the mermaid escort service. And while the maritime theme had not gone unnoticed or unappreciated by the nearly three dozen whistling, caterwauling sailors on shore leave, what had been completely missed by all but a few regulars wearing smug expressions of barely suppressed glee was the fact that the singer was a man.

We were a pickup quartet that night—and a ragged one at that. Tristin Sinclair was hammering ivory on the beat-up—and always out of tune—house upright, Nick Dundee was doubling on muted cornet and valve trombone, but was having problems with his embouchure, and I was playing a borrowed upright bass that was painted acrylic white and sounded even worse than it looked. Equipment problems aside, we had gotten through the first set without much trouble, but when we took our places on the miniscule bandstand for the second, I could tell we were in for a rougher ride.

Between trips to the bathroom to freshen his makeup and flitting around the sailors' tables and booths to sign autographs ("All my love, Cassandra"), Chris had managed to down three Cosmopolitans purchased by his seafaring fans. Now he was swaying to an imaginary tune as he came up the steps, and when he lunged for the microphone, hugged it like a fire pole and flicked it on to slur, "I hope you boys are going to serve out your full tour … because there's nothing sadder than a bunch of prematurely discharged seamen," the hooting, whistling and stamping from the crowd fell on us like a naval bombardment.

I'd become friends with Chris on my "day job" as a private investigator while looking into a software theft. But if a straight, curmudgeonly private eye and a gay—and chronically unemployed—computer engineer were an unlikely match for friendship, even more unlikely was the warped father/son tenor the relationship had assumed. I felt myself slipping into the father role again as I took a quick step forward to tug at his gown. "A little less cheese for the mousetrap."

This earned me nothing more than a broad wink from Chris and a shouted, "Leave the lady alone, Liberace," from a hefty, sunburned kid with pig eyes. The Liberace crack came from a joke Chris had made about my white bass when he introduced the band.

Impatient with the byplay, Sinclair mashed his trademark pork pie hat further down on his bald head and called, "Devil and the Deep Blue Sea." He counted off the tempo and cued Dundee, who brought his trombone to his mustached lips to lead us through an eight bar intro. Chris moved his hips in time to the music and when we got to the head, he began Ted Koehler's lyric, "I don't want you … " in a rich contralto. He sounded phenomenal. So phenomenal, in fact, that if I squinted at him as he sashayed around the mike, I didn't have any trouble believing I was listening to a beautiful woman singing the Harlem Cotton Club classic.

The sailors had even less trouble. At the end of the tune, they rose as one man to give Chris a standing ovation. One wholesome-looking nineteen-year-old farmer's son from Nebraska or Wisconsin—or someplace where the phrase "gender bending" was not in regular use—snagged a bouquet from a Hispanic woman selling flowers and laid it lovingly at Chris's feet. Chris blew a kiss at him as he returned to his seat near the front of the stage, and the combination of the attention from Chris and the cheers from his compatriots caused the kid's face to light up like he'd won the 4-H Club ribbon.

Chris looked back at me with a power-drunk expression that was one part exaltation and two parts mischief. He had them in the palm of his hand, his expression seemed to say, and now he was going to squeeze. He turned to Sinclair. "It's time," he said. "Play *Meat*."

Sinclair rolled his eyes and mumbled something in a derisive tone, but it was too loud in the bar for me to hear exactly what. When I put my hand to my ear to indicate I'd missed it, he waved me off and began counting the tempo like he was shouting commands to a firing squad. At the end of the four count, Dundee came in to do a solo of the first chorus on cornet. Chris danced around the stage through the bridge, rolling his shoulders and making little pointing motions in the air in time to the beat. Then he brought his hands to his hips, sidled up to the microphone and sang almost coyly, "It ain't the meat, it's the *m-o-t-i-o-n*," emphasizing the word "motion" with a growl and a galvanic thrust of the pelvis.

Such noise-making as the sailors had done to that point was the whispered chanting of Buddhist monks in far away Tibetan valleys compared to what they did then. The remainder of the chorus was completely drowned out and the vibrations from their stomping and pounding knocked over several of the bottles at the back of the mirrored bar. Chris grabbed the microphone off the stand and belted out the third and fourth choruses, teasing the sailors into a frenzy with a bawdy pantomime that involved rubbing his backside with the microphone cord as he sang the line about wrapping around "her" man like a rubber band.

He put the microphone back as Sinclair began a solo on piano and then beckoned to his farmer boy. The kid came running up to the stage with a dizzy eagerness. I saw Chris bend to greet him and then reach for the neckline of his gown. There was a sudden movement that his torso blocked, and then one of Chris' falsies sprang from his chest region and flopped onto the floor in front of the kid.

Chris had decided to show his fans he had more in common with them than they realized.

The kid's face registered bewilderment and then shock, and as the noise from the audience drained away like water in a dirty bathtub, Sinclair's piano solo began to sound very loud and very lonely. Chris straightened and moved back from the edge of the stage, a manic grin on his face as he continued to flash his nipple—and his oh-so-flat-chest—to all who wanted to see them. There were not many.

Sinclair finished his solo and Dundee started bravely in on cornet, but someone in the audience shouted, "faggot," and another, drunker voice yelled, "Hambert, why don't you give your cutie a kiss?"

I presumed Hambert was the farmer's son, and when he wheeled angrily in the direction his tormentor, I knew it. "Shut the fuck up," he shouted, his voice breaking with emotion.

"Don't ask, don't tell," came the rejoinder.

Hambert tore the white cap from his head and flung it to the ground. He turned back to the stage and stood rooted with his fists clenched as he watched Chris release the material of his gown, take several tentative steps back and wave placatingly in his direction.

"Chris—" I shouted, but it was too late. Hambert flashed onto the stage with his fist cocked and landed a tremendous shot to Chris' right eye. The sailors in the audience gave a collective whoop. Chris' blond wig flopped forward to reveal his own blond locks under a hair net and he dropped to the floor like a clubbed seal. There were more shouts, and before I could move out from behind the bass, a beer bottle came sailing across the stage where it shattered against the bell of Dundee's cornet. Fortunately, Dundee had pulled the instrument away from his lips, but the force of the impact drove it back, and he yelped in pain as he hunched instinctively to avoid the flying glass.

I threw the bass to one side and took a skipping step forward to where Hambert stood over Chris, still blinking with surprise at the results of his assault. I'm sure he was nice to the dairy cows in Wisconsin, but I didn't hesitate an instant before burying a left uppercut in his midsection. I followed it with a right hook to the side of his neck as he bent over the first punch, and he bounced off my knee on a quick ride to the floor.

If I thought I was getting away with anything, a swinging beer bottle aimed for my ear persuaded me to the contrary. It missed my ear and tenderized my shoulder instead. The stage was now swarming with sailors and I twisted to find the bottle in the hand of the kid with pig eyes. I grabbed him by his little black kerchief and yanked him and his groin into speaking distance with my left knee. It was a short conversation.

Almost immediately an arm came around my throat and started choking me from behind. A horse-faced guy with an overbite and three stripes on his sleeve who didn't bother himself with vague concepts like "fair fight," took the opportunity to start pounding my midsection while I grappled with the choke hold. It wasn't looking any too good for me, but for two things: a short burp of siren from a SFPD cruiser that pulled up outside, and Nick Dundee's trombone coming down on the head of the sailor behind me with a jarring clang.

The choke hold loosened immediately, and the stevedore or cabin boy or whatever rank is associated with three stripes turned to look out the plate glass window of the bar. When he turned back, I gave him a fistful of treatment for overbite. He took two tottering steps back and fell off the stage.

"For a guy who's not wearing his own front teeth, you're awful quick to smash other people in the mouth," said a voice I recognized as Dundee's.

"Just trying to make the world over in my image."

Dundee had a fat lip of his own where the cornet had jammed him and there was a cut next to his soul patch from the flying glass. He shoved the trombone into my hands. "Get the instruments. I'll get Sleeping Beauty."

I nodded my agreement and took a quick step over to the piano bench where his cornet was lying. By the time I turned back, all the sailors who were conscious had abandoned the stage and were trying to wedge themselves through the swinging front doors before the cops came in. Chris was still on the ground, but was struggling to lever himself up on one elbow.

"Where's Sinclair?" I asked.

"Long gone," said Dundee. "He ducked out before the first swabbie hit the bandstand."

Dundee pulled Chris roughly to his feet and I saw that his eye was already swollen shut. "Jesus," he said in a petulant tone. "Haven't these guys ever heard of performance art?"

I grinned in spite of myself. "After that stunt, they're probably thinking more along the lines of counterfeit art."

"Come on, you," said Dundee. He pulled Chris toward the rear of the stage.

I put a horn under each arm and bent for the string bass. When I looked up again, Chris had managed to twist out of Dundee's grasp. "Not so fast," he said. "I need my wig and falsie. Those silicon-filled babies with the erect nipple cost a fortune."

"You're lucky to get out of here with your head attached—much less your falsie," sneered Dundee. "Just hurry the fuck up, will you?"

Chris trod a wavering path back towards the front of the stage, but then gasped at the sight of Hambert smeared across the floor. He dropped to a place by his shoulders and reached down to smooth the hair on his forehead, eliciting a low groan from the sailor. He snapped his gaze up at me, tears glistening in his one good eye. "What did you do to him, August?"

"I punched his lights out. What the hell else did you expect me to do? The guy took a swing at you."

"He was just confused and embarrassed. There was no need to brutalize him. Will you look at the mark on his neck?"

Cursing under his breath, Dundee moved past me to snag the wig and the falsie from the littered stage. On his way back, he yanked Chris to his feet again and dragged him up to me. "This will teach you not to get involved in domestic disputes, August."

"Amen to that."

Juggling the horns and the bass, I negotiated the drop off the back of the bandstand and Dundee followed with Chris in tow. We went down a dim, heavily-paneled corridor, past a stuffed deer with a constipated expression and disapproving glass eyes and out a door that opened on an alley running between New Montgomery and 2nd Street.

The night air was heavy with fog and the emergency lights from two patrol cars at the mouth of the alley stabbed through it with red and blue flashes. A sailor bent on getting clear of the cops pounded by us on the sidewalk without so much as a glance in our direction. Many more of them stampeded down New Montgomery towards Mission, but the one cop I could actually see by the cars seemed more concerned about staying out of their way than catching them.

Dundee nudged my arm to get my attention and jerked his chin toward 2nd Street. A late-model Mercedes with tinted windows seeped into the alley and rolled to a stop beside us. The power windows on the passenger side slid down and all of us bent to look in at the driver.

"Hello jolly fellows," said a smirking Tristin Sinclair from behind the wheel. "Anyone here needing rescue?"

I ignored Sinclair and straightened to look at Dundee. "What's with the car?"

Dundee sighed. "His wife inherited money," he said simply. He took the cornet from under my arm and passed it in to Sinclair. He took the trombone, but then paused to examine the tuning slide where it had beaned the sailor.

"Any damage?" I asked.

"Nothing serious—just a little dent. Maybe it will give me a new sound—like Dizzy's bent trumpet. How's the bass?"

"Constructed as it is of the finest plywood from the forests of Newark, New Jersey, I'd say it would take more than a boatload of sailors to hurt it."

"Yes, I suppose so." Dundee handed the trombone into the car and then passed me the wadded up bunch of wig and falsie that he still held. He pulled open the door and situated himself in the passenger seat.

I closed the door behind him and leaned into the window. I finally said the thing we both were thinking the whole time we were talking about the instruments. "Hope your lip's okay."

"It'll be fine. I needed to rest it anyway." I nodded and then moved to step back from the car, but he took hold of my wrist. "I don't have to tell you that I'm not playing any more gigs with Cassandra here."

"You don't have to tell me."

"Take care, August."

He released my wrist and punched the button to roll up the window. Sinclair put the car in reverse and backed slowly out the way he had come. When he reached 2nd Street, he turned and went south towards Mission.

"Are you mad at me?" said a voice at my shoulder.

I frowned and looked at Chris. "What do you think?"

"I think you're mad, but not so mad that you won't loan me 40 bucks."

"I'll give you a ride home. You don't need to take a cab."

"I'm not going home. I'm going back in there." He pointed at the door of the bar.

I suppose I should have been surprised, but somehow I knew it was coming. "It's that kid, Hambert, isn't it?"

He nodded slightly, causing his sea horse earrings to swing wildly out of proportion to the original movement.

I stood there with my jaw clamped, watching them swing for a long moment, then threw down the falsie and wig, manhandled the bass up against the brick wall of the building and yanked out my wallet. I scooped out all the cash—a hundred bucks at least—and shoved it down the neckline of his gown on his flat side. "There," I spat. "Take it. Now maybe you won't look so lopsided when the ambulance attendant lays you out on the stretcher."

I had already picked up the bass before he managed to blurt something inarticulate, and I was all the way to the cop cars at New Montgomery before I heard him shout, "Wait. August. You don't understand."

I threaded between the cars and came up to the officer I'd seen earlier. He stood at the back of the second car holding the microphone to his portable radio. I smiled and nodded at the flashing red emergency lights.

"Red sky at night," I said. "Sailor's delight."

He gave me a bored look, glanced down at his watch, then shook his head. "It's already past midnight, chum. Sailor take warning."

MADAME BUTTERFLY

I ALMOST TRIPPED OVER HER WHEN I FOUND her. I'd turned off New Montgomery to the alley where I'd parked my car, and the fog, the darkness and the bulky bass made it hard to see the ground in front of me.

She lay facedown on the asphalt as if she were embracing it. She had a white sailor's cap perched on the back of her head and a silken cascade of ebony hair tumbled out from beneath it. She wore an over-sized Navy uniform jumper with a flap in the back, tight-fitting jeans and a pair of red "fuck-me" pumps with four-inch heels. Even with the shoes, she wouldn't stand more than five-foot-one, and if she weighed over a hundred, somebody's big fat thumb was on the scale. But I had a feeling that the next place those statistics would be appearing was a police report, because she was lying very still and it probably didn't have to do anything with sleep.

I shoved the bass against a chain link fence that closed a gap between two buildings along the alley, and squatted beside her. Pulling her hair away from her neck, I laid a finger along her carotid artery. I might as well have taken the pulse of the Venus di Milo. I took hold of her left arm, which was stretched out above her head, and brought it back to her side. Then I gently turned her over. She was young and Asian—I guessed Japanese or Korean—and her face was heavily made-up. She'd ringed her eyes with thick liner, giving herself the Egyptian "cat eye" look that Elizabeth Taylor had in *Cleopatra*.

Her eye shadow was the garish electric blue of peacock feathers and her lips the glistening red of molten sealing wax.

The uniform jumper was much too large for her and she wasn't wearing anything underneath. An adolescent breast peeked through the V-neck, its pale innocence a stark contrast to the overreaching sophistication of her makeup. I caught a flash of color along her collarbone and eased the material of the jumper off her shoulder to get a better look. It was the tattoo of a butterfly—not a simple, cartoonish-looking butterfly, but a beautifully executed image of an iridescent green and yellow Swallowtail that I wouldn't have thought possible to render on skin with just a tattoo needle and ink. An odd pink band or ribbon wrapped around the butterfly, flowed a few inches beneath it and then abruptly stopped. I couldn't tell for certain in the poor light, but it seemed as if the artist intended to do more with the band and had postponed the work for a future session.

There were no marks or signs of violence that would indicate how she had died. I tugged the material of the jumper back over her shoulder and stood up to look at her. I had no connection to the girl at all—she was from a different generation and quite possibly a different country—but somehow I felt like I'd stumbled across the body of my younger sister. I took in a ragged breath and let it out slowly. At least I didn't have to go far to find the police.

The ride to the San Francisco Hall of Justice on Bryant Street was a short one, and in less than thirty minutes I found myself in a squalid little interrogation room in the basement. The only things in it were a scarred wooden table that had crushed soda cans under two of the four legs, a pair of metal chairs with torn vinyl upholstery and a trash can overflowing with empty coffee cups, greasy pink donut boxes and cigarette butts. There were plenty more butts scattered around the concrete floor, as well as several rusty puddles of water the size of beer mats. A uniformed officer sat me down in the chair on the far side of the table and sauntered out of the room with a knowing smirk on his face. He locked the door behind him.

Minutes plowed by like migrating glaciers. I looked at the cigarette butts on the floor and longed for a fresh pack. I ran my thumbnail along initials carved in the table and longed for a knife (they'd taken mine at the door). I sorted the old movie tickets I found in my pockets and longed for the shows—even the horrible one starring a certain Latin bombshell and her on-again off-again fiancé. I had just laid my head on the table to try and get some shut-eye when a noise like the space shuttle taking off reverberated overhead. I looked up in time to get smacked in the forehead by a drip of freezing water.

A rusty five-inch pipe loomed high above me, dripping grimy, scaly-looking water from several places that exactly corresponded to the puddles on the floor. I blotted my forehead with my sleeve and yanked my chair over to the side, uncovering the puddle that went with my own personal leak directly above. I didn't have much doubt that the cops had put the chair there on purpose, and when "Smiling Jack" Kittredge came through the door wiping his hands on a paper towel, all remaining doubt vanished.

"Sorry to hold you up, Riordan," he said, "but first things first. I've been needing to pinch a loaf all night." He threw the wadded up towel at the trash can, but it bounced off the mound of refuse already there.

I'd never met Kittredge before, but I recognized him from his press coverage. He was an up-and-comer in the department, a smart, flashy-dressing cop whose arrest record was exceeded only by his publicity sense. I knew intuitively he was the kind of showboating prima donna I hated most: a guy who wasn't afraid to put "product" in his hair, who carried around a hanger in his car to keep his suit coat from getting wrinkled and who wore flip-flops in the locker room shower to protect against athlete's foot. I said:

"Is the department resorting to Chinese water torture to soften up witnesses before questioning?"

Kittredge laughed and went through the motions of straightening his already straight tie. It was a shiny silk number that looked like it cost more than I paid for rent. "Oh, did you get hit?" he said. "We've been on the city to fix that pipe for years. The men's room is right upstairs, but it only leaks when you use one particular stall."

"A chilling coincidence."

Kittredge pulled off his jacket and carefully placed it on the back of the other chair. He sat down on the last three inches of it and rested his elbows delicately on the table. Diamond chips in his cuff links gleamed and the smell of designer cologne wafted over. "Are you suggesting that I caused waste water from a sewer pipe to drip on you on purpose?"

"Ask me when I'm not in the city dungeon and my answer doesn't put your Armani duds in jeopardy."

Kittredge flashed the perfect white choppers that had earned him his nickname. "This is Boss. Armani is for swishy hair dressers who polish their fingernails."

"You're a young man—don't sell yourself short. There's still time for a beautician's license."

Kittredge clamped his jaw shut. He pulled his arms from the table and crossed them over his chest. "I heard you were a wise ass."

"Only when someone pokes a stick in my cage. What's with the juvenile intimidation techniques anyway? You can't possibly think I had anything to do with the girl's murder. A hundred people saw me in the bar and I talked to a police officer not five minutes before I found the body."

"It doesn't take long to kill someone. Maybe the girl was hooking, maybe she propositioned you, and maybe you have some hang-up about women because of the way your mother dressed you in frilly bloomers. You strangled her and then told the patrol cop that you stumbled onto the body."

I felt my face go slack with a look that must have contained a sort of surprised wonder. "Man, oh Manischewitz. You saw right through me. I'm not saying another word until I talk to my lawyer."

Kittredge brought a hand up to rub his chin. Heavy stubble on skin made a rasping noise I could hear across the table. He said nothing.

"But if I were going to talk, I'd say that it was darn clever of me to strangle her without leaving a mark. And while I don't know exactly how the coroner's report will read, I'm betting it won't say she died within five minutes of the time I talked to the patrol officer. She was too cold."

Kittredge shrugged. "Then you killed her at your apartment before going to the bar. You transported her in your trunk to the alley, and rolled her out on the asphalt after the riot. You were going to just leave her there, but you decided to get clever and play the concerned citizen."

"This just gets better and better. I suppose your next move will be to get a subpoena to search my trunk for fibers to match to ones taken from the body."

"Well," said Kittredge, "it would be easier for all concerned if you would just agree to the search."

I snorted. "It didn't strike you as the least bit suggestive that—during Fleet Week with a thousand sailors in town—the girl just happens to be wearing the hat and jumper from what looks like a U.S. Navy uniform?"

"Cracker Jacks, they call them. Like the kid on the Cracker Jacks box."

"Call it whatever you like. It shouldn't be difficult to determine if it's government issue. If it is, then it seems likely your killer is a Navy guy. And since they only wear that kind of uniform on ceremonial occasions, I'm willing to bet your average swabbie only has one. You just need to go around to the ships in port and find out who is missing the jumper and hat from their dress uniform."

He smiled in a patronizing way. "Interesting suggestion. Any other advice you'd care to pass on? You being the hot shot private dick and all."

"I'd check the tattoo. It doesn't seem like it's finished. Maybe the girl and her sailor friend went to a tattoo parlor to get his and hers tattoos while he was on shore leave and they had a spat or something. Anyway, one of the parlor operators might have seen them together."

Kittredge narrowed his eyes at me.

"What?"

"Nice of you to pull her shirt off to examine the tattoo when you stumbled over her. Next you're going to tell me that the brand of underwear she had on was special."

I pointed at him. "You just said, 'when I stumbled over her.' You didn't say when I pulled her from my trunk."

"Yeah, well, it could be you don't work that good as the doer. But a street sweeper went through the alley at 11:40—you were the lucky recipient of a $60 parking ticket, in case you didn't notice—and she wasn't in the road at that time. The patrol cop says you came by at 12:25, so that only leaves a window of about 45 minutes for someone to have dumped the body."

"Well, it wasn't me."

"And you don't know the girl?"

"Never set eyes on her."

Kittredge nodded and toyed with one of his cuff links. He flared the nostrils on his big beak of a nose and sniffed violently. "Turns out I wasn't kidding about her panties. The label on them is in Japanese. The coroner hasn't looked at her yet, but one of the guys on the meat wagon has taken a few forensic dentistry classes. He says the fillings in her mouth aren't typical of U.S. dental work, either. She's probably from Japan."

"I take it you didn't find any ID on the body?"

"Nope. We'll talk to the Feds in the morning about Japanese women who are here on a visa and see what it gets us."

"To call her a woman would be pushing it. She didn't seem like she was much more than 16 to me."

"The paramedic says she's older. Two of her wisdom teeth have come in for one thing." He paused and looked over at me with cool, penetrating eyes. "You asked me why we were giving you a hard time. I'll tell you. It's to prepare you for this message: butt out. I can accept that a guy with a private detective's license just happened to stumble on a dead body in a dark alley in San Francisco. But what I will not accept is that same guy sticking his nose in the case to make money or generate publicity for himself."

"You're one to talk about headline grabbing, Kittredge."

"Shove it, Riordan. I read those articles about you and the venture capital guy Valmont. About how you played the hero in that winery up in Napa and saved his bacon. But don't tell me you would have had a three-month stay in the hospital if you had involved the authorities at the right time instead of going it solo."

"You don't know what we were up against. There were lives at stake."

"Lives at stake? Does that include the guy you shot and the one you beat senseless with a phone book? I hear what you say about the Navy uniform and the tattoo. It so happens I agree with your conclusions and we'll be acting on them tomorrow morning. But if I so much as catch a whiff of you in or around this investigation from this moment forward, I will put the lie to your crack about damaging my suit and tear you from limb to limb—and then I'll throw the book at you. And I'm not talking about the Yellow Pages."

His face reddened and he was breathing hard by the time he finished. I stared at him for a moment and then held up my hands. I heard myself say, "This is one I'll be very happy to stay out of, Kittredge. You can have my word on that." And I knew that I meant it.

He seemed faintly disappointed, but he nodded just the same. "Right. Next stop is the impound lot, where you damn well better give me permission to search your car."

IT TAKES ONE TO KNOW ONE

THERE WAS NO RED IN THE SKY the following morning—just a lot of gray. I'd put in a few sleepless hours of mattress time and now was heading downtown along Post Street from my apartment on Hyde. It was about 9:30. The fog still hung heavy in the air, and it was thick enough that it fooled a handful of seagulls into flying inland the three-plus miles from the bay. They were gliding in a corkscrew pattern well above the sidewalk when one of them gave a shrill cry, broke formation and tried to dive-bomb me from twelve o'clock high. But unlike Jack Kittredge, the seagull missed.

To avoid further terror from the sky, I made a dash across the street to the haven of Saeed al-Sahhaf's corner grocery. Wearing his usual black beret and olive green sweater, Saeed looked like a Republican Guard commander from the last war, but he was actually a former college professor who had gotten fed up with the lazy, ill-prepared graduate students who populated his 19th-century literature classes. "If I'd had to grade one more paper with improper or missing footnotes," he told me, "I would have slit my throat and scratched out the corrections in my own blood. I'd rather hawk greasy donuts and bad coffee."

I purchased two of the former and a large cup of the latter and continued down Post. Grease from the donuts had spotted the bag by the time I turned right onto Powell, and by the time I reached

Market, the spot had grown to a translucent stain the size and shape
of the Indian Subcontinent.

I shouldered my way though the line of tourists at the cable car
turn-around, slopping some of the bad coffee on a middle-aged guy
wearing a Fisherman's Wharf T-shirt with the tag line "Got Crabs?",
and went up to the Samuel's Jeweler's street clock in front of my
building to indulge in a superstitious ritual of mine: I never walked
by without tapping it. The old clock had been refurbished recently
and the new blue and gold paint on it shone brightly, but just then
an emaciated character in army fatigues and a sweatshirt with cut-off
sleeves was slumped against it.

He had a wispy black mustache that stuck out like cat's whiskers,
and from beneath a stocking cap that looked like the reservoir tip of
a Trojan condom, a wash of lank, badly dyed blond hair flowed to
his shoulders. When I reached around him to tap the clock, he fixed
me with a glazed look and said:

"Wanna buy some dope, man?"

I grinned and shook my head. "No, thanks. I get mine from
1-800-PET-MEDS."

I covered the distance to the cavernous entryway of the Flood
Building before he managed a shouted, "Does that really work,
man?"

My rooms were on the 12th floor and came fully equipped with
pebble glass windows, superannuated potted plants and two office
mates, both of whom were there. Ben Bonacker, an insurance salesman with the biggest capped teeth this side of the Mississippi and the
worst jokes on either side, was standing by the fax machine with an
exasperated expression on his face. He was dressed in his interpreta-
tion of "business casual": a golf shirt with the logo of his insurance
company on the breast pocket and a pair of the always fashionable
Sansabelt slacks. I gestured at his considerable waistline. "You missed
a loop there."

He reached instinctively for his belt line, then stopped short. "Nice, August. Very nice. Kick a man when he's down. Can't you see I'm in crisis mode here?"

"What's the problem?"

"I've got to get this quote to a client by ten, but every time I fax it, it comes out blank on the other side."

I set my coffee on the table next to the fax machine and grabbed the stack of papers in the exit tray. I flipped them face up and plunked them back in the feeder tray. "Pages go face up. See the little icon with the writing on top?"

Bonacker stared at the icon for a long moment, the air in his nose making a whistling noise as he breathed. "Oh. Yeah. I was just going to try that."

I gave a curt nod, picked up my coffee and headed back to my office. Gretchen Sabintini, my second office mate, part-time secretary and one-time fianceé was standing in the hallway with a smirk on her face. "I do love a man who's handy around the workplace."

Gretchen was wearing black—like always. Business casual to her was a slim-cut pants suit with a silver zipper down the middle and double darts in front that cinched the fabric of the jacket tight around her improbably narrow waist. She finished the ensemble with black Italian boots and a black ribbon choker with an antique cameo that I had given her when we were still engaged.

I looked her up and down from her luxuriant auburn locks to the toes of her pointy boots and smacked my lips. "You look good enough to marry."

She smirked some more. "Too late for you, buster. You missed your chance."

"Then you leave me no choice but to seek solace with these donuts in my lonely office." I elbowed on the light switch as I entered and plunked myself in the decrepit wooden swivel chair behind the desk. It squeaked like a weasel in electroshock therapy.

Gretchen appeared in the doorway. "Still, I do like the choker."

I pushed the detritus of my private detective business from my desk blotter to make room for the donuts and then tore open the bag. "That's nice," I said between bites. "A wistful statement of regret would have been nicer."

"I do like the choker."

I sighed—wistfully. "I guess that's to be expected since you picked it out. Something about not liking the turquoise bolo tie I originally selected. Now why didn't you help Bonacker with the fax? He can barely work the elevator, for Christ's sake."

Gretchen advanced to a spot in front of my desk. "I'm on strike."

"Why?"

"Because he told one of those awful jokes of his to my boyfriend when he came by for lunch yesterday."

I paused in my annihilation of the first donut. This was going to be good. "You mean your boyfriend, the *urologist*?"

Gretchen frowned and picked up one of the many half-empty paper cups that littered my desk. She held it under my nose so that I could see the island of green mold floating in the black sea of coffee sludge. "When are you going to mow the lawn?" she snapped. "Of course that's who I mean. And no more of your snide comments about his chosen profession, thank you very much."

I popped the last piece of the donut in my mouth and made a zip-my-lips gesture while I chewed. "What's the joke, then?" I asked finally.

"I'm not going to repeat it. Let's just say that Dennis was very offended and—"

Bonacker must have been listening in the other office because he chose that exact moment to stick his head through the door. "By the way, August, what *did* the urologist's vanity plate say?"

"I don't know Ben," I said, not believing I was actually encouraging him. "What did it say?"

"2 P C ME"

I forced a belly laugh, not because I found the joke funny, but because I wanted to needle Gretchen. She didn't needle very well.

She grabbed a ruler from the desk and whacked it near the blotter, making pieces of donut glazing jump like trained fleas. "That's it. It's a general strike now. I'm not lifting a finger to help either of you."

Bonacker gave me a broad wink and disappeared from the doorway. I looked back at Gretchen and found her glaring down at me, still holding the ruler in a threatening manner. "I believe you said something about a lonely office. Let me oblige you." She chucked the ruler on the desk and charged out of the room, pulling the door closed hard enough to make the pebble glass rattle.

After mistakenly grabbing a cupful of mold from earlier in the week, I sipped some of today's coffee and then worked hard on finding solace with the second donut. I was down to crumbs of comfort with the glazing chips when a timid knock sounded at the door.

If my "come in" sounded a little smug, it was only because I was expecting a contrite Gretchen returning to apologize. What I got instead was a not-so-contrite Chris Duckworth. The mermaid outfit had been replaced by jeans and a colorful sort of half-blouse, half-smock that grave robbers must have filched from Carmen Miranda's casket. His eye, however, was still swollen shut and was now competing with the blouse for the "best use of discordant colors" award, hues of green, blue and black being the most conspicuous.

"Nice to see you back in men's clothes—sort of."

Chris gave a weird, cyclops-like leer and stepped into the office. He arranged himself and his flowing blouse thing in one of the clients' chairs. "You got that line from Woody Allen."

I wadded up the donut bag and tossed it into the trash can. "The 'sort of' part was mine."

"There's innovation."

I stood up with a squeak and took two of the paper cups from the desk to the sink at the back wall. I dumped the coffee and mold down the drain and then tossed the cups in the garbage. I was halfway through the process with a second pair when Chris spoke behind me:

"Aren't you going to ask me what happened?"

"Well," I said over my shoulder, "you're alive. That's the most important thing."

"I'm more than alive, I'm positively teeming."

I turned to look back at him. "Oh, yeah. A couple of more shots like the one you took to the eye and you wouldn't be teeming. You'd be in the hospital—or worse."

"You're exaggerating. I knew what I was doing."

I slung the second pair of cups into the trash, splattering liquid all over the can and the floor. "Knew what you were doing?" I said. "If you knew you were going to start a riot, you might have let the rest of us in on it."

He put two fingertips to his damaged eye and winced. "I am sorry about that part. I didn't think that was going to happen."

"Chris, when that crowd of sailors came into the room, it changed from a liberal, tolerant bar in San Francisco to a place where diversity—particularly diversity in sexual orientation—was not welcomed. Didn't you read about that kid in Wyoming that was killed? Or the transsexual in the East Bay? You can't do a gender bait and switch with those kind of guys and not expect them be very threatened, and consequently, very angry."

Chris looked at me soberly for a moment and then bust out laughing. It was not the reaction I expected. "He's gay," he said finally. "He's gay."

"What?"

"The sailor at the bar. Hambert. He's gay."

I slid into my chair. "The guy who hit you because he found out you weren't a girl is gay?"

"That's right." Chris nodded eagerly. "As gay as a french horn."

"When did you find out?"

"I knew it as soon as I saw him. That's why I popped my falsie. To show him what was what."

I slumped back into my chair to the accompaniment of a long, low creak like the opening of the door on the old "Inner Sanctum" radio hour. "Couldn't you have sort of pulled him over to the side during a break and given him your big news in private?"

Chris looked down and rearranged the folds of his blouse. "I guess I was a little drunk. I wanted to do it with flair and panache."

"Panache? Pardon my ignorance, but is panache French for bonehead?" I paused for a moment. "There's still more to this, isn't there? What happened after I left?"

Chris leaned forward to put his elbows on the desk and then propped his chin on a bridge he made with his hands. He looked at me coyly. "I went back to the bar, pulled the young admiral from the wreckage, and then took him straight back to my apartment to provide comfort and succor."

I waved my hands in a squeamish gesture. "I don't want to hear anything about the succor part."

"Why ever not, August? Can't one friend tell another about his love life? It was all very romantic. We lit candles, put on the appropriate mood music—"

"What'd you pick? Something by Enya?"

Chris said, "No, we ", then the dime dropped. "Very funny, August. There might have been more of the old in-ya and out-ya if you hadn't mauled him so badly. He could barely perform."

"Okay, I think that's about all *this* friend wants to hear about your love life. What happened this morning? Did you drive him to the docks and wave a silk handkerchief as he sailed heroically through the Golden Gate?"

"Heck no. He's here for another two weeks. We had a wonderful breakfast at a restaurant with a patio terrace and then he bought me this little number at a Castro Street boutique." Chris leaned back from the desk and held a pinch of fabric from his blouse. "Very fetching, don't you think?"

"Too bad you didn't get the matching turban covered with pineapples and pomegranates."

Chris wrinkled his nose at me. "If I thought you had any fashion sense—or a modicum of concern for your own appearance—I might be offended."

"And if I knew what a modicum was, *I* might be offended."

Chris stood up. "Well, a modicum of concern might be giving a damn when you're walking around with a piece of donut sticking out of your uppers."

I had recently been fitted with a partial denture to replace two front teeth that had been knocked out and I very was sensitive about it. I brought my hand up to cover my mouth. "Thanks," I mumbled.

He stepped back from the chair and fluffed out his blouse. "I forgot to ask. Did you make it home okay?"

I briefly considered telling him about the girl and then remembered my vow to steer clear of it. "Yeah," I said with my hand still over my mouth. "Got home fine."

"Well, you've got some personal hygiene to attend to and I need to catch a little shut eye to make up for last night."

"Wait a minute."

"Yes?"

"Where's the money I loaned you?"

Chris gave an airy wave of the hand. "Oh that. Well, Hambert didn't have enough cash for the top, so I had to give him your money to pay for it. He's good for it, I'm sure."

"You mean I paid for *that*?"

Chris moved to the door. "Yes, that's right. You see now why it's all the more important that you appreciate it. Cheers." He slipped through the door and was gone.

I got up to look in the mirror over the sink, and sure enough, there was a chunk of donut sticking out from the denture. I pulled the plate out of my mouth and was running water over it when Gretchen barged in.

"I'm still on strike, but—" She stopped short at the sight of me turning to look at her. "That's disgusting, August. Put that thing back in. You look like the ghost of Leon Spinks."

Startled and more than a little embarrassed, I hunched over the sink to return the plate to my mouth. It took a lot of fiddling to get it seated, and I felt myself going redder and redder as I struggled. "What," I said when I finally succeeded. "What do you want?"

Gretchen held her face stiff to keep from smiling. She said: "You have a client."

CAESAR'S WIFE

A PRIVATE DETECTIVE AGENCY IS NOT LIKE A barber shop: walk-ins are very rare. I get most of my business from lawyers and other self-important types who expect me to make house calls, so I hardly ever meet clients at my own office—and when I do, they almost always have an appointment.

In the time it took Gretchen to bring my walk-in from the reception area, I dried my hands on the back of my pants and hurried to clear the rest of the paper cups from the desktop. If I thought it would help, I would have put a spit curl in my forelock.

Gretchen introduced her as Ellen Stockwell, and as improbable as it seems, the name didn't ring any bells for me at the time. She was lithe and thin and moved with an economic grace, like a gymnast or ballet dancer. She had a handsome, open face with prominent cheekbones, and when she smiled I noticed a slight gap between her front teeth. The flaw endeared her to me immediately—either because I felt a kinship from my own dental challenges or because I read her decision not to have it fixed as a sign of confidence and comfort with herself. She wore simple clothes—navy blue slacks and a crisp white blouse with french cuffs—but she wore them with style. I put her in her mid-40's.

"We don't get much walk-in traffic," I felt obliged to say after I got her settled into one of the client chairs.

We looked at each across the desk. She seemed to be waiting for me to say something, but I didn't know what. "You do know who I am, don't you?" she asked.

"A lady in distress?"

"Yes, certainly that, but I thought you would recognize my name. You worked with my husband, Lieutenant Stockwell."

That was the problem: Stockwell without the "Lieutenant" was not sufficiently memorable, but taken together, they were unforgettable—like a devastating illness or a high school humiliation. He was the hard-nosed East Palo Alto police officer assigned to investigate the murder of Roland Teller, and I was the San Francisco PI who was dumb enough to get hit from behind and wake up on the floor next to the body. It was not the beginning of a beautiful friendship.

I felt my lips forming an insincere smile. "Of course, the Lieutenant. How is he?"

"Not very well, actually. We've both been under a lot of strain."

"I see."

"Yes, a lot of strain." She sighed and she seemed to go away for a moment. When she came back, her voice was harder, more determined: "So much so, that he's moved out of the house. That's why I'm here. Our—"

I bent forward in my chair with a loud squeak and nearly pawed my way across the desk. I didn't like the direction this was headed. "Excuse me, Mrs. Stockwell. You may not know this, but California is a no-fault state. There's no need to hire a private detective to prove that the other party committed some, ah, unsavory act."

"Unsavory act?"

"You know, like physical abuse or adultery or ... " My voice trailed off under the weight of her stare.

"You misunderstand me, Mr. Riordan." She reached for her purse and brought it into her lap. From it she took a 4x6 color photograph and placed it on the desk blotter. "This is our daughter, Caroline. She's been missing for three weeks."

The photo was a waist-high shot of an attractive teenage girl in a black synthetic top with feathers at the wrists and collar. The material of her top gave out around her solar plexus and I could see that she had a stud in her belly button. There appeared to be another above her left nostril. She held her arms akimbo in a haughty, exasperated stance that seemed to signal an impatience with the picture-taking process. She had her mother's dark eyes and prominent cheekbones, but I didn't see anything in the picture that came from her father, unless the Lieutenant's hair color had once been purple.

"She seems very nice," I said, trying to put some mileage between me and my earlier remark.

"She's nice enough when she wants to be, although I'm not sure how one could tell from a photograph."

The rebuke, though gentle, was enough to restore my God-given gift of gruffness. "Look, Mrs. Stockwell, I jumped the gun with the divorce business, but I still don't see what you're doing here. In the first place, your husband is a cop. Even if you don't live in East Palo Alto, the police wherever you do live are bound to go the extra mile for a brother officer. Second, if your husband ever thinks of me—and there's no reason why he should—I'm certain he doesn't think of me as the person he would hire to find his daughter. He may not have mentioned it to you, but we did not exactly see eye-to-eye on the Teller investigation."

"He told me you were a horse's ass."

I held my hands out, palms up. "I rest my case."

Ellen smiled, the little gap between her teeth making her look for a moment like a mischievous child. "Please don't be offended. My husband thinks everyone is a horse's ass. But he also said that you had a special knack for stirring the pot and making things happen. That's exactly what we need."

"But he doesn't know you're here, does he?"

"Quentin doesn't know much of anything these days. He's been drinking. He's living in a residence hotel. And he's been placed on administrative leave. I'm on my own now and I have to do what I think is best to find my daughter."

Hearing Stockwell called Quentin made me slow—and rather lame—in my response. "I'm sorry. He's taken this hard, then."

Ellen ran her hands along slender thighs and then clutched at her knees. "It's more than Caroline's disappearance. Our oldest died last year of a drug overdose. Quentin feels like he didn't give either child enough of his time when they were younger and he can't bear the thought of losing another." She let go of her knees and slumped back in her chair. "Neither can I."

As bad as I might feel about the situation, I did not want to be involved with Lieutenant Stockwell and his family. I tried to sneak around it. "What I said earlier about the police helping a brother officer—they must be doing everything they can."

"We live in the East Bay, in Union City. Quentin has always had a chip on his shoulder about working on the force of a poor town like East Palo Alto. I'm afraid he made some rather unfortunate remarks to the investigating officer regarding her competence and her personal habits."

"The investigating officer is a—is a woman?"

Ellen gave a sort of grim, half smile. "Yes, I know what you're thinking. It didn't help that the officer was female. My husband doesn't hold the most progressive views about women on the force. He told me his idea of pecking order once—white males, followed by black males, followed by males of any other minority. Then come white females, and at the bottom, black females. Except for the gay males—they're at the very bottom. The Union City officer is a black female."

"At least she isn't gay."

"Gay or straight, he still called her a dyke."

"Ouch."

"There's much more to Quentin than these terrible biases and prejudices, but especially when he's under pressure, they seep from him like poison. The other problem is Caroline's age—she turned 18 last month. Since she's no longer a minor and there's no evidence of a crime, the police won't place a priority on the search."

She pulled her chair closer to the desk and grasped the edge of it. "You see the situation I'm in. My husband is very depressed, almost completely incapacitated. He can't do anything to find her. The Union City police were helping very little before Quentin talked to them, and now that he has, they won't even return phone calls. I really don't have anywhere else to turn. You are my last, best hope."

So much for sneaking around it—I felt like I stepped right into it. I played my final card. "I really can't take the case unless your husband agrees to it. He's bound to catch wind of my involvement, and I can't do an effective job without his cooperation, to say nothing of the difficulties I'll have if he tries to hinder me."

"Quentin's in no shape to hinder anyone. But my impression is he has a grudging respect for you. Given the circumstances, I don't think it will be hard to get his agreement. Won't you please take the case?"

I swept the blotter clear of a few glazing chips I missed earlier. Ellen watched me intently, her whole body erect and rigid in anticipation. It was like being watched by a hungry dog waiting for table scraps. "Okay," I said slowly. "If the Lieutenant agrees."

She released the edge of the desk and folded her hands demurely in her lap. "Thank you. I know it's uncomfortable for you, but it means everything to me. Shall I give you a retainer? What's the appropriate amount?"

I drew in a deep breath and blew it out through my nose. "I charge $55 an hour for general investigations, and I usually ask for a third of the anticipated charges up front. I guess $2,000 would be plenty. I would also need a signed client retainer form."

Ellen had snapped open her bag and was fishing around inside it. She found her checkbook and held it up for me to see, then caught the nuance in what I'd said. "Why are you putting it that way? You don't sound as if you're really committed."

"I think under the circumstances you and your husband should both sign the retainer form, Mrs. Stockwell. The money, too, should probably come from both of you. Can we set a time for all of us to meet and discuss it?"

She frowned. "I suppose you could come to our house this evening. I could arrange for Quentin to be there."

"All right."

She nodded slightly, and when I didn't say anything further, urged, "Hadn't you better get some preliminary information?"

Suppressing a groan, I extracted a warped yellow legal pad and a stubby number two pencil from my desk. I tore off the top sheet off of the pad—which had a juvenile drawing of a naked woman astride a string bass—and signaled I was ready to take notes. "Okay," I said. "Let's start with the basics."

I copied down her address and various telephone numbers, got the name of the investigating officer in Union City, and then asked:

"Does Caroline live at home?"

"Yes, she's going to art school."

"Which one?"

"The San Francisco Lyceum of Art."

"San Francisco and art I can spell. What was the other word?" I tried to pronounce Lyceum, but it came out like, "lye-swim."

Ellen laughed in a pleasant way. "I guess you never got hooked on phonics, Mr. Riordan."

"That's one addiction I avoided, thank God. And you can call me August."

"Please call me Ellen." She spelled Lyceum for me, then added, "It's a very good school. They might even be able to help with your drawing." She nodded at the sheet of paper I had torn from the pad.

"Thanks," I said. "But that's just the way I want it." I glommed the paper from the desk and slid it into the top drawer. "I guess I better ask when you last saw Caroline."

Ellen looked down into her lap and absently snapped and un-snapped the catch to her purse. "The last time we saw her was three weeks ago Wednesday. I dropped her at the BART station so she could catch the train into the City."

"Did anyone see her in class that day?"

"No, she doesn't have class on Wednesday. She was going to her job in Noe Valley—she works at a Starbucks."

Noe Valley is a yuppie neighborhood in the southern third of town, but I didn't think there were any art colleges nearby. "Did they see her at Starbucks, then?"

"Yes, she worked her full shift and left around 5:30. She didn't say whether she was going home or had other plans."

"Why Noe Valley? Isn't the art school downtown somewhere?"

"It is, but her best friend lives in the Mission District and she wanted to work close to her. They are both going to the Lyceum and they sometimes do their projects together at her apartment."

"I take it the friend didn't see her after work."

Ellen shook her head slowly, causing the tips of her short chestnut hair to sway together at a point beneath her chin. She looked up at me with an intent expression, and just in that moment, I flashed on Jacqueline Kennedy. There was something elegant and completely feminine about her that conjured up the image I had of Jackie. "No," she said. "Monica says she hadn't seen Caroline for several days. She didn't—well, she said she hadn't seen her."

"You don't sound very certain. Do you think Monica is lying?"

"I'm not sure. It's not so much that I think she's lying as I was bothered by her attitude. She didn't seem the least little bit concerned that Caroline was missing."

"Do you mean she just didn't care or she didn't think there was reason to be concerned for Caroline's safety?"

"I guess the latter. Monica is different than Caroline. Much more of a free spirit. Perhaps what I took for unconcern is just a reflection of her laissez-faire approach to life." She gave one of her gap-toothed smiles. "Or perhaps I don't know what the heck I'm talking about."

"As someone who doesn't know Lyceums from Lysol, I may not either, but my sense is further conversation with Monica is definitely warranted. In fact, I'd appreciate it if you would make a list of all Caroline's friends—including all boyfriends, past or present. I'll get it from you tonight."

"I already put one together for the police, but I'll review it to make sure I didn't miss anyone."

"That will be a big help."

Ellen waited for me to ask more questions. When I didn't, she snapped her bag shut with a sudden finality and came to her feet in a smooth motion. "I shouldn't take any more of your time. Can you drop by around five? I'm sure I can have Quentin over by then."

I stood up and meandered around the end of the desk. "Five would be fine."

She put her hand out and I took it. It was small and pliant and it felt pleasantly cool. "Thank you again," she said. "I can't tell you how much this means to me."

"I just hope it means half as much to your husband."

"Don't worry. He'll see the light."

I walked her to the door and pulled it open, but she stopped to look at the black-and-white photograph beside the door frame. "Who is that?" she asked.

"That's Paul Chambers, a famous jazz bassist. He's one of my heros."

She studied my face as if making up her mind and reached across to touch my arm. "I hope you'll be one of my heros, August."

Her touch and the way she looked at me made me hope it too—for at least as long as she stood there.

GUM FOR THE GUMSHOE

I HAD THE HANGTOWN FRY FOR LUNCH AT Sam's Grill on Bush and read the morning Chronicle while I massacred the dish of fried breaded oysters, eggs and bacon that was supposedly invented during the Gold Rush in a rowdy burg called Hangtown—now Placerville. It's gratifying to know that the very first California cuisine did not feature jicama, baby basil or mango chutney, but instead combined two of my favorites: bacon grease and fried breaded seafood.

I was nearly through the paper before I spotted the article I was both dreading and strangely anxious to see. It was nothing more than a two-inch squib on the second-to-last page of the Bay Area section—probably thrown in by the night editor right before the edition closed. It said the body of an unidentified Asian woman had been discovered in an alley near the 100 block of New Montgomery and asked anyone with information about the case to contact detectives or call the anonymous Crime Stoppers line. There was no mention of cause of death and no mention of me. I felt tension go out of my shoulders and realized my anxiety had been about seeing the girl's discovery linked to me. For once, I told myself again, I really did want to stay out of somebody else's troubles.

I quartered the paper neatly, placed it on the table and piled 22 bucks on top, knowing from experience that the Fry, an Anchor Steam beer and decent tip could all be covered by that amount. I backed out of the booth, elbowed my way past the crowd of businessmen waiting at the small bar for a table and heard John, the maitre d', tell a newcomer that "if he wasn't happy about the wait, maybe a McDonald's Happy Meal would suit him better" as I went through the door. *Gourmet* magazine had called John "insolent and arrogant beyond belief," so I guessed he was working to keep his reputation intact.

I walked the dozen or so blocks to the garage on Turk Street in the seedy Tenderloin district where I kept my car. It was actually an inexpensive repair shop for German makes, but I gave the owner a hundred bucks a month for the privilege of parking my 1968 Ford Galaxie 500 in the basement next to the ailing Mercedes and BMWs that were his stock in trade. I had to crank the Galaxie hard to get it started and this elicited the usual snickers and smart remarks from the Latino mechanics who worked there. "Hey man," said one, "I had a car just like that in high school—until my dad got a job."

I threw a wadded up paper bag from Popeyes Chicken and Biscuits that I just happened to have in the car at him and barreled out of the basement. When I got to street level, I went down Turk to Gough and from there to Highway 80 and the Bay Bridge. I was heading to the East Bay for my meeting with the Stockwells in Union City, but since I had the time, I thought I would stop and chat with the police officer who had been so charmed by Lieutenant Stockwell. Given my own relationship with the Lieutenant, I figured we couldn't help but get along.

The Union City Police Headquarters was in one of those multi-purpose civic centers that suburban cities seemed to favor. You could get a library book, talk to your city councilman, apply for a building permit, have a barbecue in the adjoining park, let the kiddies romp in the playground and bail your white trash uncle Willard from the drunk tank in just one stop. I eased the Galaxie into a spot next to the adjoining strip of park, and as I stepped out of the car was immediately beset by a mongrel horde of honking geese and quacking ducks on the make for a handout from their home in a little weed-fouled canal that ran down the middle of the park. I reached back into the car for one of the (now very well-aged) Popeyes biscuits, broke it apart and tossed the pieces into the grass. A lot more honking and quacking, combined with a great deal of pecking and flapping of wings, quickly ensued.

The civic center building looked like it was designed by an underpaid assistant of Frank Lloyd Wright. It was a squat, bunker-like building with a red tile roof and a narrow slice of windows that ran around the circumference at a point just below the roof line. Below the windows was a strip of formed concrete bric-a-brac that gave the building its Frank Lloyd Wright feel. The police department had its offices in the back on the first floor, and its reception area was smaller than my dentist's. Either they didn't have a lot of business or they didn't feel the need to put up a front.

The reception desk wasn't staffed and I wasted about five minutes perusing the tiny trophy case—a crystal plaque for a fifth place finish in the law enforcement division of a relay race was the highlight—and reading the Union City Police Department Mission Statement—catching crooks was the main provision—before I noticed a sign directing me to press the white button for service. I pressed away and this produced a flinty-sounding buzz, followed several moments later by a flinty-looking desk sergeant. She had leathery skin with too-dark lipstick and too-dark rouge painted high on her cheekbones, and the marks on her belt indicated the buckle had been let out at least twice in the battle to contain her spreading waistline. She looked at my empty hands and then down to the untidy stack of forms in a tray on the counter and said, "You must fill out the Request for Police Report Form before I can process your request."

I forced a limp smile. "Actually, I'm not here for a copy of a report. I'm here to see an officer."

She straightened the stack of forms and then glared at me like I was the one who'd put them out of order. "Which one?"

I had left my notes from my interview with Ellen Stockwell at the office, so I said, "I'm interested in talking to the officer in charge of the Caroline Stockwell missing persons case. I can't remember her name, but I'm told she's a black female."

"Who told you?"

"Caroline's mother, Ellen Stockwell."

"And what's your involvement?"

"I've been hired by the family."

She looked down at the tray of forms and yanked it three inches further away from me. Apparently I was losing ground. "If you don't know the name of the officer, then I'm afraid I can't help you."

"Give me a break here. How many black female detectives can there be in a department this size?"

She smiled like a toad that swallowed a fly. "Sorry," she said, and started to walk away.

I was getting the idea that she would be perfect in the maitre d' role at Sam's, but just then a name swam to the front of my consciousness. "Wait," I blurted. "Ruth Washburn."

That snatched the toy from *her* Happy Meal. She blinked at me, opened her mouth, closed it and then slunk back the way she had come.

About fifteen minutes later, a sloppy-looking man came out from a door to the right of the reception counter. He had bug eyes, thin, straight hair flecked with dandruff and an odd manner of letting his head hang down over his chest. He looked up at me from under furry eyebrows that grew together in a single, arched line. "I'm Luke Calhoun," he said. "Captain of the Investigations and Communications Division." He put out his hand.

I took it warily. "I asked to speak with Ruth Washburn."

He nodded. "About the Caroline Stockwell case."

"Yes, that's right."

"I've taken responsibility."

"Since when do captains handle missing persons cases?"

Calhoun turned his head sideways like a bird eyeing a worm. "Around the same time private investigators do, Mr. Riordan."

"You know my name."

"And a good bit more. I just got off the phone with Mrs. Stockwell." He pulled open the door. "Let's go back to my office."

I followed him down a corridor with partitioned detective cubicles on either side to an office at the back. Apparently Union City thought the traditional "bullpen" arrangement was old fashioned: this could have been the layout of any other Silicon Valley office building. Calhoun's office was filled with modular Herman Miller furniture of the sort one would find in the offices of Silicon Valley executives, including an expensive-looking ergonomic chair behind the desk. There was also a computer and Palm Pilot sitting in a cradle next to it. The image of the high tech police captain would have been complete, except for the wide, quadruple-decker filing cabinets—presumably full of primitive paper case-folders—and the gumball machine on his desk that dispensed "jaw breaker" sized gumballs for a quarter.

"Would you close the door behind you, please?" said Calhoun just before I planted my butt in one of his two fully-adjustable, wheeled guest chairs.

I went back to close the door and was hovering over the chair again when he said, "May I see your pocket license and your photo ID card, please?"

California had recently mandated that private investigators carry a copy of their license *and* a photo ID. I fished both cards out of my wallet and passed them over. Hair that normally lay flat on Calhoun's forehead flopped forward while he gave the cards the old bird eye. He nodded when he was satisfied and passed them back. "Do you have a problem with authority, Mr. Riordan?"

I slid my wallet back into my hip pocket and dropped into one of the chairs. "Not really. It may be that authority occasionally has a problem with me." I smiled to show that I was joking. He didn't smile back.

"Apparently authority does have a problem with you," he said. "And as recently as last night. I spoke to a Detective Kittredge of the SFPD before I called Mrs. Stockwell."

"You've been busy."

"Since September 11th, I've made a point of reading all the felony bulletins issued in the area. And your name was mentioned prominently today in one from San Francisco."

I shrugged. "I don't know what Kittredge told you, but I'm cooperating fully with his investigation."

"He told me you were a showboating asshole who routinely circumvents and undermines police authority."

"Great. Did he also mention that he tried to intimidate me by dripping waste water from a sewer pipe on me?" I leaned forward in the chair and clasped my hands tightly in front of me. This wasn't working. I needed to cool down if I was going to get Calhoun's help. "Look," I said after a moment, "I think we're getting off on the wrong foot. Kittredge told me to butt out of his investigation and that's exactly what I'm doing. I'm here for an entirely different reason and it sounds like you've got a pretty good idea what it is. The Stockwells have hired me to look into their daughter's disappearance. I wanted to talk with you folks to see where you were with the case."

"Mrs. Stockwell told me that you hadn't actually accepted the case."

"That's right. I thought I should talk to her husband first."

"And us too, I gather."

"You got me on that one."

Calhoun gave a sarcastic smile. "Do you know anything about missing persons in California, Mr. Riordan?"

"I'd like to think so."

Calhoun picked up a thick binder from his desk. "This is the Missing Person Quarterly Bulletin produced by the California Department of Justice. It has sections for preschool children, primary school children, secondary school children, emancipated juveniles, adults and dependent adults. With the exception of dependent adults, each section averages about 150 pages, and each page has five individuals. That's about 4000 people." Calhoun paused to wriggle his furry brows. "But that's just the tip of the iceberg. The people in the bulletin are the featured cases. The actual number of open cases at any one time is about 26,000 and the total number of missing people reported each year is between 140,000 and 160,000."

"So your point is there are a lot of missing persons."

"Let me ask you another question. Do you know anything about the Stockwell family?"

"Golly, I feel like I'm not holding up my end of the conversation."

Calhoun stood up abruptly and marched out of the room with his head hanging at its odd angle and his torso bent well past the perpendicular, each step seeming just to save him from pitching forward on his face. When he returned, he held a stack of police folders in his hands. "You came to the right place to learn about the Stockwells. We've got all the information." He dropped one of the folders on the desk. "For starters, here's the case file on Caroline Stockwell. That's the one you came for, but I'm afraid you'll be disappointed. It's pretty skimpy."

He dropped another folder on the desk. "That one's thicker. That's the file on the Quentin Jr.'s suicide. Used his old man's service revolver to blow his brains out. I won't pretend that I was sorry to see him go, but it would have been better for all concerned if he had just crawled in a hole somewhere and ate the barrel. Instead, he went onto the high school campus one night, shot the lock off the principal's door and offed himself while sitting behind the principal's desk." He paused, wanting me to comment.

"Ellen Stockwell told me he died of a drug overdose. Did he leave a note?"

Calhoun snorted. "No, just an empty bottle of rum." He flipped more folders onto the desk. "Here are the files on Quentin Jr.'s previous brushes with the law. Let's see, we've got joy riding, vandalism, underage drinking, shoplifting." He was talking faster now, his face turning pink with emotion and his hair flopping forward once more. "Even a little cruelty to animals." He dropped the second-to-last folder. "Mind you, a lot of the charges were dropped in deference to Quentin senior. You know, fraternal order of police and all that."

He took the final folder—a thick red one—and held it up with two hands like it was a product he was about to endorse. "Then there's this file. A very special one. Any idea what's in it?"

"Weight loss secrets of Las Vegas showgirls?"

Calhoun slammed the folder down on his desk. "Bastard," he nearly shouted. "You're going to be sorry you said that. It's a report on an attempted rape. The perp was Quentin Jr. and the victim was—"

I finally understood. "Your daughter."

"That's right, smart guy." He plopped into his chair, breathing heavily. He tried to comb his hair back into place, but tendrils of it got mired in perspiration on his forehead. "Now you know about the Stockwell family."

I looked at him for a long moment, shifting my words carefully before I spoke. "Look, Calhoun, I am sorry about the Las Vegas crack. I can see how you wouldn't be a big fan of Stockwell junior—or Stockwell senior from what I heard of his remarks to Officer Washburn. But if you have a daughter, then you can certainly understand the anguish Mrs. Stockwell is feeling, and as a fellow parent and police officer, want to do everything you can to bring her home safely."

Calhoun shook his head, disbelieving. "Aren't you the little prig? Did you hear what I said about the statistics earlier? Given the volume of cases and the resources available to us, we are doing everything required of a small city police force to find her."

"Everything required and not a particle more."

Calhoun looked at me deliberately while he scratched his armpit. He said nothing.

"How about letting me take a look at the case file, then. You said it was skimpy, but there might be something I could work with."

He stopped scratching and moved to pull the folders out of my reach. "California state law does not require city police forces to cooperate with private investigators," he said. "Nor do Union City statutes. In fact, it's frowned upon."

I hauled myself to my feet and fished a quarter out of my pocket. I slipped it into the slot of his gumball machine and turned the handle. The gumballs rattled inside and a bright green one clattered down to appear at the opening at the base.

I held it up so he could see it. "Thanks for the gum, Captain. I hope my having it doesn't undermine the authority of the city charter."

CUERVO SPIT BATH

Captain Calhoun's gumball turned out to be as bad as his help. It was mostly hollow, and the part that wasn't lost its flavor after about two chews. I tossed the insipid remains out the window as I pulled to a stop on Rainer Street across from the Stockwells' house.

It was a modest rancher in a neighborhood made up of modest ranchers with two or—at most—three different floor plans. The Stockwells' looked pretty much like all the others except for wrought-iron bars that covered the windows and a red tile roof that had been substituted for the usual wood shake. A trailer home with a blue plastic tarp covering it loomed large behind the gate to the side yard, and an over-ripe T-Bird with a Landau top that was peeling like a bad sunburn stood spoiling in the driveway. I went up the walk, which had been warped and buckled by the roots of a silver maple, around a hose roller contraption that was parked in the way, and up to the front door.

The door swung open before I could even locate the buzzer. Ellen Stockwell stepped out and quickly pulled the door closed behind her. She was wearing an apron over her clothes from the morning and she held a small paring knife in her hand. I said:

"Et tu Brutus?"

"What?" she asked, flustered.

"I was talking about the knife—only I believe it was Julius, not Augustus who got stabbed."

"I'm sorry," she stammered, and slid the knife into an apron pocket. "I was making fruit salad."

"Fruit salad. That's nice. Are we going to eat it while we talk to your husband?"

She paled and took a sudden, intense interest in the welcome mat. "I called your office, but they said you were out," she said softly. "You were right about Quentin. He doesn't want to hire you."

"What'd he say?"

She brought the hem of her apron up to wipe her hands, then wadded the material into a ball. "It's not important. I should have listened to you this morning. Hiring you seemed the only thing left to us, but he can be so stubborn." She looked up from the mat and smiled. "I'm sorry to have taken your time. I'll pay you for your trouble—whatever you think is fair."

I licked my lips, thinking I should be glad to be shot of the mess, but recognizing what I actually felt was disappointment—whether from a sense of attraction to Ellen Stockwell or a desire to rub Captain Calhoun's nose in it. "There's no need to pay me," I started, but never finished the sentence.

A loud, inarticulate bellow issued from the house and suddenly the door whipped open and slammed into the interior wall. A shadowed figure cursed as the door rebounded, blocking the path to daylight. The figure struggled past the door, fumbled with the screen door latch and jostled us to one side to stand swaying and bleary-eyed on the tiny porch. It was Lieutenant Stockwell.

But it was a Stockwell that I'd never seen before. The one I knew was tall and ramrod straight with a hard, chiseled face that put the presidential pans on Mount Rushmore to shame.

This one was a walking meltdown.

His hair was a ruined bird's nest, his skin was sallow and sagging, and a great many five o'clocks had come and gone since the growth on his face could be called shadow. When he yanked Ellen out of the way to step in close, the tequila fumes that came to me were strong enough for a chemical peel.

"Junior G-Man on a pogo stick," he said in a voice like a shovel scraping asphalt.

"What?"

"You, Riordan. Junior G-Man on a pogo stick." He poked my chest with a sharp finger, punctuating each word. "You're the last person in the world I would hire to find my daughter."

Ellen made a mewling noise beside me. "Please, Quentin," she said. "I've already told him."

"I'm telling him again." He prodded my chest once more. "Riordan operates under the delusion that he's a professional investigator." He slurred the word delusion, giving it an extra syllable. "But he's just an overgrown teenager who bounces around the landscape like a pinball in an arcade game. Sure, he'll hit a bumper every once in a while and score a few points. But that's not skill. It's physics."

I brought my hand up and closed it over his finger. "If the booze isn't working to hold your conscience down, I guess making cracks about me might help."

He tried to jerk his hand out of my grasp, but succeeded only in overbalancing himself. I let go and he fell backward onto the screen door. "Get the hell out of here," he yelled. "Get off my property."

"Or what? You'll call the cops?"

He hoisted himself upright. "I don't need anyone's help to deal with you."

"That's good because you're not getting any. The Union City cops like you even less than I do."

Stockwell took hold of one of the porch posts and squeezed. "Keep going down that path and see what it gets you."

"You mean the bit about you and Calhoun almost being grand-parents?" I said nastily.

Ellen's breath caught in her throat and Stockwell's bloodshot eyes bulged out like double-hernias. He roared as he came at me. He hit me chest high and bowled us onto the grass. We landed with his full weight on top of me, knocking every cubic inch of breath from my lungs. Stockwell sat astride me and began going at my face and stomach with short jabs, but rage, alcohol and his awkward position made the punches ineffectual. I grabbed two handfuls of the sweat suit he was wearing and threw him to one side. I rolled the opposite direction and levered myself to my feet, just beside the hose roller dingus.

"Give it up, Stockwell," I said between gasping breaths. "I'm sorry about your son, but you do need someone's help."

Stockwell pried himself off the ground and took a tottering step forward. He let out another roar and the step became a lunge as he dove for my knees. I danced to the side, and instead of tackling me, he brought the hose roller down for a ten yard loss. There was a muted thud as his head hit the wound coil of hose, and then he bounced off and lay moaning on the ground.

Ellen yelled his name and came rushing over. She knelt beside him and gently pulled him onto his back. The rubber of the hose had been kinder to his skull than the metal edges of the roller would have been, and he didn't appear to be too badly hurt. He grimaced as he held his head with both hands. "Bastard," he spat.

"Oh, yeah? Now who's the pinball?"

Ellen glared at me. "Stop it. Both of you. You're both acting like overgrown teenagers." She took hold of Stockwell's arm. "Help me get him into the house."

We pulled him into a sitting position and each tried to hook an arm over a shoulder, but while not actively fighting us, Stockwell wasn't doing a great deal to help us either, and we ended up sprawled in the grass next to him. He laughed and called me a bastard again. I shooed Ellen to one side and got both my arms around his chest and heaved him upright. Ellen took an elbow and we half-walked, half-dragged him onto the porch. By the time we got there, I had decided that his incapacitation was mostly playacting and he was using the incident as an excuse to end the skirmish between us—which was fine by me.

Ellen held open the screen door and I guided him across the threshold. She nodded in the direction of a hallway. "Bedroom," she said.

We went through a room filled with laminated particleboard furniture from the Swedish clip joint where they tell you with a straight face, "some assembly may be required," down a short hall and into a good-sized master bedroom. The furniture here was older and more solid—dark mahogany from the 30s or 40s—which made me think it was passed down from one of their families. There was a half-empty bottle of Jose Cuervo on the nightstand and a copy of *911 Magazine* on the rumpled bedspread, so I was pretty certain this is where Stockwell had been when I came to the door. We sat him down on the edge of the bed and he lunged immediately for the Cuervo. He took a long pull, wiped his mouth with the back of his hand and gave a self-amused smile like a kid who'd just spray-painted a dirty word.

"Alcohol and concussions," I said. "That's a good combination."

"I don't have a concussion." He hit the bottle again, held the tequila in his mouth for a beat, then sprayed it over the front of my shirt.

He howled with laughter, "Oops. Guess it was my gag reflex—for you, not the liquor."

I jerked the bottle out of his hand and held it up like I was going to bean him. He twisted out of range and slumped onto the bed, shaking with poorly suppressed mirth. Ellen ran for a towel and did her best to pat me dry, but I'd been thoroughly strafed and the smell wicking off the cotton of my shirt brought bile to my throat.

Stockwell managed to control his laughing fit and glanced up at me with mock surprise. "What?" he said. "You still here?"

"Maybe it would be better if you waited in the kitchen, August," said Ellen. "I've got a pot of coffee going if you like."

I nodded curtly and passed the bottle over to her. As I went through the door, Stockwell shouted, "Oh, it's August, is it? Maybe you two would like *me* to leave so you can use the bedroom."

Just to keep my hand in, I made a rude gesture that nobody saw and continued up the hallway.

The kitchen hadn't been remodeled since the house was built and dated from that quaint period in American history when "all electric" was considered a good thing. The coffee pot was sitting on a chipped yellow formica counter with knife marks and a dull, hazy patina made by a lot of scrubbing with Bab-O powder. I poured myself three fingers' worth of coffee into an East Palo Alto Police Department mug and sat down at a butcher block table with a cutting board full of sliced orange, kiwi and pineapple and a *Sunset* magazine open to a recipe for "Katy's Tangy Poppy Seed Fruit Salad." Although I admired Katy for her tanginess, I flipped past her looking for something on home repair or, if I was forced to compromise, landscaping. I had settled on an article about the proper way to snake toilets when Ellen walked in.

"I am so sorry," she said, then caught a whiff of my new essence. She wrinkled her nose. "You absolutely reek of tequila. You must let me pay for the dry cleaning."

"That's three apologies and two offers to pay me in the last half hour. Let it go. None of it's your fault."

She nodded in a distracted way and let her eyes wander down to the table. "Oh, God," she said. She picked up the cutting board and took it over to the sink, where she unceremoniously dumped the entire harvest of sliced fruit into the garbage disposal. She ran it hard for a good minute, rinsed the cutting board and rammed it into the drain rack. She finished by shucking off her apron and collapsed into a chair across from me.

"Why'd you do that?" I asked.

"It just seems so pointless. I was only making it as a distraction. I don't even like fruit salad."

"Me neither. Especially that kind with the chopped coconut on top. Ambrosia, my mom used to call it."

"Yes, that recipe's on all the marshmallow bags."

"I guess they have to find some use for them besides S'mores." I took a sip of my coffee, which was good. "Look, it's none of my business, but what was that at the end there? About the bedroom."

Ellen took a deep breath and let it out in a ragged sigh. "He's just being melodramatic. One of the ways he's been punishing himself is by pushing me away. He was the one who moved out of the house. I never asked him. After losing his son and his daughter, losing me would be the penultimate tragedy."

"Penultimate? What would be the ultimate?"

"Killing himself, of course."

"You don't really think he's close to that, do you?"

She squeezed her eyes shut and then blinked them open, fighting off tears. "I don't know. They say if you joke about it, you're not really joking. You're giving everyone around you a warning."

"And he's been making jokes?"

She nodded mutely.

"Since I've already torn off the Band-Aid, do you mind telling me more about your son? You told me that he died of a drug overdose, but Captain Calhoun said it was suicide."

"Yes, it was."

"Why change the story?"

"I don't know. Maybe I'm trying to assuage my guilt. I didn't want to explain and drug overdose seemed less likely to provoke questions than the real story."

"What about the attempted rape? Is what Calhoun said true?"

"No," she said sharply. "And you shouldn't have brought that up with Quentin. The whole downward spiral began with that."

That didn't seem to jibe with what Calhoun had told me about the other arrest reports. "But there were other incidents. The joyriding and so on?"

"All that happened in the first year of junior high. He started hanging out with some older kids and lost his way. But when he got picked up for shoplifting, Quentin had Calhoun keep him in juvie for a week and that was enough to snap him out of it. He cleaned up his act. Calhoun would have never let him go out with his daughter if he hadn't."

"And the rape?"

" Quentin Jr. had broken it off with Frances—that's Calhoun's daughter. He was going out of state to college on a soccer scholarship and he felt that he and Frances had grown apart. I think that she made the accusation as a way of getting back at him." She looked down at the table. "I knew they were having sex when they were together. There would be no reason for him to rape her."

"You can't rape the willing, huh?"

She pursed her lips. "That's not a very PC way of putting it, but yes."

"Then why did he commit suicide? Would it have been that hard to clear himself?"

"I don't think so. They were together at a big graduation party and she claimed that he tried to rape her in an empty bedroom at the back of the house. But she didn't speak to anyone about it until days later. What we think—" She held herself rigid and blinked back the tears once more. "What we think is his suicide had something to do with the acne medicine he was taking. The drug has been linked to suicides in teens."

"Like the kid that flew the airplane into the building after September 11th."

"Yes, like that."

I made a deep study of the photographs in the plumbing snake article. It looked like a rotten job, but mine seemed infinitely worse. "Look," I said. "I don't care what your husband says. I'm going to look for your daughter. And I think you should help me."

Moisture welled at the corner of her eye, distended into a fat tear, then broke and ran down her cheek. "All right."

"It's going to mean me asking more uncomfortable questions."

"As you said, the Band-Aid is long gone."

I nodded and rolled the coffee cup between my hands. "Okay, then. When we spoke this morning I didn't know of your son's suicide.

CANDY FROM $TRANGERS   51

I have to ask if there's any reason to think Caroline might have done the same thing."

Ellen turned her head to one side and rubbed at the tear with her palm. It left a long, ragged streak of red on her skin. "I can hardly trust my instincts any longer, but I would say no. She has always been more even-tempered than Quentin Jr., and she was very excited about art school. I don't know for certain, but I also think she was seeing someone new."

"Do you know who?"

"No, she never mentioned him explicitly. This is more my impression. Lately she had been staying in the city after class, and from what she did say, it wasn't always to spend time with her friend Monica. Other friends from school was all she said."

"What about the acne medicine? Was she taking that too?"

"No, she's got my skin. She doesn't need it."

I raised my eyebrows and she flushed slightly. "What I mean to say is Quentin had a lot of trouble with acne as a teenager and unfortunately Quentin Jr. inherited it from him. Thank God neither of them got my rotten teeth." She brought her hand to her mouth self-consciously.

"I didn't mean to make you feel uncomfortable. You do have nice skin—and your teeth are fine."

She flushed even more and smiled for the first time since we talked on the porch. "Please, August. Now I *am* feeling uncomfortable."

"Sorry. Do you have the list of names I asked for this morning?"

"Yes, right here." She rose smoothly from the chair and took a sheet of yellow legal paper from a kitchen drawer. There were about twenty names on the list. Most had a phone number and address and a few had a notation to indicate a special relationship like "old boyfriend" or "best friend from grade school." A number of them were starred, so I asked what that meant.

"That's to indicate they are current friends," said Ellen. "Most of those are people she knows from art school."

Monica's name was in the middle of the list as a result of her last name of Mapa. She lived at an address on Folsom in the 2500 block, which meant her place was right in the middle of the Mission District. "Mapa?" I said. "What sort of name is that?"

"Monica's family is from the Philippines. But she was born and raised here."

"Okay. I've got one more question and then I'd like to look over Caroline's room if I may."

Ellen pushed the drawer closed and leaned her hip against the cabinet. "Of course. Whatever you want."

"Thanks. I'll be talking to the friends on the list you gave me, but I'd also like to talk to her teachers at school and her boss at work. Do you have those names too?"

She frowned. "You're making me feel like a bad mother. I don't know anything about her work except that it's the Starbuck's on the corner of 24th and Noe. As far as school, I only know the name of the school president—which is Julie Jaing—and Caroline's advisor, Robert Wesson. I'm afraid I haven't kept track of the other teachers."

The name Wesson seemed to ring a faint bell for me. "Wesson sounds familiar. Is that someone I should know?"

"Possibly, if you're into photography. He's a fairly big name on the West Coast. Mostly known for his work in black and white. Caroline told me he's going to have an exhibit at the MOMA this month."

"I take it Caroline is majoring in photography?"

"Yes, for this quarter anyway. Last quarter it was sculpture."

_____ ng abruptly. An odd expression formed on her features—mild surprise mixed with annoyance—and she brought her arms up to hug herself. "I forgot to tell you something."

"What?"

"You're going to think it's funny that I didn't mention it earlier: Caroline was seeing a psychiatrist."

I straightened in my chair and pushed the mug of coffee aside. "You said she was even-keeled. Why would she go to a shrink?"

"I'm sorry. She went through a rough patch after high school. Talking about the art school and her major made me remember that she had struggled with what she wanted to do with her life after graduation—she became just a little blue and depressed. Obviously, her brother's death had a lot to do with it. I never felt it was anything serious because we all go through something like that before or after college—and losing a sibling is hard on anyone. Anyway, she started seeing the doctor about eight months ago. At first it was weekly, but she only goes every other week now. Quite frankly, I expected her to stop very shortly."

I still didn't see how it could have slipped her mind so easily—especially after what happened to Quentin Jr.. I pulled a pen from my jacket to add the new names to the list. "Okay, we've got Jaing, Wesson and the shrink," I said with some irritation. "What's the shrink's name and his address if you have it?"

She pushed off from the kitchen cabinet. "Don't be angry with me. I wasn't trying to hide anything—I simply forgot. The doctor's name is Marvin Levin. I've got his card in my desk in the sewing room. Why don't I take you back to Caroline's room and I'll get it while you're looking there."

I nodded my agreement and she led me back down the hallway. The door to the master bedroom was closed and I didn't hear any sound from it as we passed. Ellen stopped at another door near the end. "This is it," she said as she twisted the knob. "That most exotic and alien of environments—the room of a teenage girl."

I smiled at her joke to signal we were still friends and stepped inside. The room was small, dark and cluttered, all the more dark because the walls were painted black and the window coverings were fashioned of black velvet. I flipped on the overhead light to find that the bulbs burned a dull crimson. A floor lamp next to a small computer desk gave the promise of more light, so I powered it on too. The rest of the space was taken by bookshelves, a metal chest of drawers with a Snap-on logo that was originally intended to hold tools, a Chinese screen and a black lacquered futon bed. A life-sized poster of Jim

Morrison in leather pants and a belt with conches the size of soap bars sneered at me from one wall and a montage of framed, black and white photographs hung on another. The photographs were all signed "Caroline Stockwell" in a tiny, cramped hand and all of them were close-ups of rather outlandish body art, including tattoos, piercings, and other miscellaneous manipulations—some of them located in places that were not typically open to the viewing pubic.

Past experience had told me that computers were a good place to start, so I went first to the desk. The machine on top was a Sony multi-media job with a video camera, a scanner and a portable MP3 player plugged into the back, but when I powered it on, I found it was password protected. I tried "Caroline," followed by "Morrison," followed by "TheDoors" but none of them worked. I gave up after my offer of "HelloILoveYou" earned me nothing more than an electronic Bronx cheer.

The closet at the back of the room drew my attention next. It was crammed full of clothes and shoes: black and red dominating the color palette, and clingy and tight or wispy and goth heading up the fashion parade. There was also a shelf for a small but expensive-looking stereo and a well-stocked rack of CD's. Littered around the floor and the shelving were a variety of shipping cartons from Amazon.com, some of which were empty and some of which remained unopened. Most had obviously contained CDs, but others were larger and appeared to have contained consumer electronics. I picked up one of the largest of the unopened packages and examined it closely. The first thing I noticed was that it was addressed to Caroline at her place of work. The second, that it had been shipped nearly two months ago. Both of these were suggestive of a problem with compulsive buying, but I hadn't been hired to investigate Caroline's spending habits, so I returned the package to its resting place on the floor next to a pair of lace-up platform boots with four-inch heels.

I tackled the metal cabinet next. I started—burglar-like—with the bottom drawer and found that it contained stockings and under-wear and, hidden beneath that, a small baggie of grass with rolling

papers and a roach clip. The only surprising thing was how casually
the dope had been concealed. I returned it to its place beneath a pile
of thong panties and moved up to the next drawer. It also contained
clothing, as did the next one and the one after that. It was only when I
arrived at the final pair of drawers that the story changed. Subdividing
the width of the cabinet in two, the top drawers were shallower and
had probably been intended to hold sockets for Snap-on wrenches.
The first drawer contained a disorganized jumble of magazines and
papers, including several bills. I thumbed through the pile, returning
the *Lenswork* and *ZYZZYVA* magazines and the course syllabus for
"Figure Drawing," and retained only a cell phone bill and a bank
statement for further study.

The final drawer turned out to be religious, or perhaps more
accurately, spiritual in nature. Inside was one-stop shopping for all
your metaphysical needs. There was a bible, a tarot deck, two packets
of sandalwood incense, a power crystal on a silk thread, a bottle of
"Ylang Ylang Pure Essential Oil"—prescribed for "nervous tension,
dry/oily skin and frigidity"—a Native American fetish in the form
of a stone bear with a feather tied to its back, and at the bottom, a
small book with a head shot of a goofy-looking guy with long greasy
hair and a high forehead wearing wooden beads and some sort of
leather undershirt. Although he looked like one of the white homeless
guys you see collecting aluminum cans under Highway 280 in San
Francisco's China Basin, his moniker was apparently Sri Atma Nidhi,
and his photo was floating in a field of orange poppies in soft focus
just below the title of the book: *Golden Dawn of the New Epiphany*.

The book seemed to be a collection of sayings, epigrams and
general directions for life by Mr. Nidhi, and I was thumbing through it
when Ellen returned. "Did you find something useful?" she asked.

"Maybe." I held up the book. "Recognize it?"

She gave a little chortle. "Oh, yes. I recognize it. That's the book
by Caroline's guru." She made little quote marks with her fingers as
she said the word guru.

"There's a sticker in the back that says it comes from an ashram in Berkeley. Is it possible she went there?"

The suggestion seemed to surprise her and she cupped her chin in her hand as she considered it. "I wouldn't have thought so. She got involved with them after high school, but she pretty quickly decided it was a bunch of malarkey. The man isn't even from India. He was born in Bisbee, Arizona, for goodness sake."

"When's the last time she went to the ashram do you suppose?"

"At least eight months ago."

"About the same time she started with the shrink."

She nodded. "She was probably motivated by the problems she was having at the time, but it really turned out to be a very casual infatuation. She laughed about it when she told me she was quitting."

I shoved the drawer closed. "All the same, I think I'll check them out. You mind if I keep the book?"

"No, of course not. Did you—did you find anything else?"

"Not very much. There are also a couple of bills I'd like to take with me. Do you know if she's used her phone or accessed her bank account since she left?"

Ellen took her lower lip between her teeth and chewed it white. When she spoke, it wasn't to answer my question. "I feel terrible. I should have remembered the ashram—and the psychiatrist too. I'm just not thinking straight about this, am I?"

I picked the envelopes up from the top of the cabinet where I'd left them and squared them in my hands. "You're too close to the situation. That's why you hired me." I held up the bills. "About the phone and the bank?"

She shook her head as if to clear it. "Yes, sorry. We checked her cell phone and the bank and she hasn't used either. And she didn't have any credit cards. Quentin took them away from her."

"Because of the Amazon.com stuff?"

"That's one reason. She did get carried away with on-line purchases."

"All right. Unless you have the password to her computer, I think I'm done here. Did you get the card for the shrink?"

Ellen nodded quickly and handed me another envelope. "The card's in there, along with a check for $2,000. Thank you again for everything. I feel like you've already made a difference." She reached for my hand and gripped it tightly.

I liked her touching me again, but I was more than a little surprised by her comment. I was trying to think of a tactful way to rein in her expectations when Stockwell demonstrated his talent once more for unplanned and unpleasant entrances. He ricocheted off the door frame into the room and shambled over to us, holding the now nearly empty tequila bottle by the neck. He went past Ellen as if she wasn't there, and instead of taking the swing I expected, came up to wrap me in a bear hug. The bottle thumped against the small of my back and dropped to the floor. I felt his hot breath in my ear as he blubbered, "Find my daughter for me, Riordan. Just find my daughter."

THEY EAT HORSES, DON'T THEY?

SHOULDERING THE HIGH EXPECTATIONS OF *both* THE Stockwells was something I hadn't planned on. Later that night, I sought guidance for the task in Sri Atma Nidhi's *Golden Dawn of the New Epiphany*, thumbing through the book while I imbibed a glass or three of Maker's Mark bourbon and listened to Miles Davis' *The Birth of the Cool*. The best advice Nidhi had for me was, "Once on the back of bounding tiger, it is hard to alight," but my biggest insight was the realization that the title of the book sounded a lot like the "Dawning of the Age of Aquarius." I suspected that a lot of the "new epiphanies" in *Golden Dawn* were repackaged from other sources too.

The next morning I went back to the office to finish a report for another case and pick up something I had promised to deliver to an old friend. The report wrapped up my investigation of a fellow musician who had been on temporary disability for eight months with acute Carpal Tunnel Syndrome, developed—he claimed—as result of his duties as a software tester. His employer had gotten fed up paying the disability benefits and had hired me to look into it. Once I found out that one of the symptoms of Carpal Tunnel is an inability to bring the thumb into opposition with the other fingers, and that he was a flatpicker in a bluegrass band, all I had to do to nail him was attend one of his gigs and video tape the session.

When I called Gretchen in to type up my scribbles, she skimmed through the report and asked me how in the world I could give up one of my own. "I was all set to let him go until he sped up the tempo like a runaway train during his one of his solos," I said. "Then he was a dead man."

"You bass players are a vindictive lot," she said, and went out with a flip of her hair.

I retrieved the item I was delivering from the office safe and then hailed a cab on Market Street to take me to my friend's place on Russian Hill. There was no point in getting the Galaxie out of the garage because—with the possible exception of the Marina—there wasn't a worse place to park in San Francisco, particularly when the person you were visiting lived on Lombard near the bottom of what souvenir postcards proclaimed to be "crookedest street in the world."

I exited the cab at Lombard and Leavenworth amidst a tourist expeditionary force of multiple nationalities. Standing at the forefront, shock troops from Japan aimed digital video cameras at the parade of cars coming down eight cobblestone switchbacks in the 40-degree slope from Hyde Street. Behind them stood Germans—dressed in khaki shorts and odd-looking sandals despite the cold weather—providing supporting fire with their Leicas. Overweight Americans, too diffident or lazy to claw their way to the front lines, brought up the rear, munching on corn dogs and taking the occasional pot shot with disposable cameras.

I threaded my way though the tourists and went farther down Lombard Street, past No. 953, which played host to MTV's infamous "Real World" show, and up to the door of a modest Victorian that had been segmented into three condominiums. I rang the buzzer for the flat on the ground floor and the door was opened almost immediately by an old black woman wearing a loose-fitting polka-dot dress and matching polka-dot hair band. Her limbs were thin and bony and riddled with twisted varicose veins, but she smiled when she saw me and twenty years dropped from her face. "August," she said. "You little villain." She took hold of my cheek with a bent, arthritic hand and pinched for all she was worth. "You've lost weight. What have you been doing with yourself?"

The right answer was recovering from being beat to within an inch of my life on the misadventure with the venture capitalist, but there was no way I was going to cop to that. "Ouch, Hilma, don't pinch off any more." I tugged her hand away from my face. "I've foresworn all animal products and become a vegan. This is the new healthy me."

"Sounds like the new cracked you." Hilma turned to walk back into the house, leaving me to close the door. "Besides which," she called over her shoulder, "no soy beans died for those wingtips. They look like cowhide to me."

I followed her down a short hall to the living room. "It's only a temporary situation," I said. "I've got hemp moccasins on order."

The old black man reclining on the leather Barcalounger in the middle of the room grinned big. His left pant leg was empty from the knee down and a shiny plastic prosthesis—dressed in a black wingtip of its own—was resting against the chair. "What are you babbling about *now*, boy?" he asked. "Did you bring my medal?"

I held up the gold, plaque-mounted medal that I had brought from downtown. The inscription said the medal came from the president's office of San Francisco State University and was awarded to "Victor Lane, 'Dean of Jazz,' for his long-lasting, widespread contributions to SFSU and the city of San Francisco." Since Victor had been too ill to attend the award ceremony he had asked me to go in his place and give his acceptance speech.

I passed the plaque over to him and he beamed down at it. "Ain't that fine."

"I don't know where we're going to put it," said Hilma, who had settled herself on the plaid sofa. "There isn't a square inch of wall that isn't covered with a picture or a medal or playbill or some damn thing."

I knew without checking that she was right. Victor had been a fixture in San Francisco's jazz scene since the 1930s and had played bass with Basie, Ellington and Gillespie among many others. He had autographed pictures from all of them, and as I glanced across to the fireplace mantel, I could see a photo of Billie Holiday adorned with a still bright-red lipstick kiss. Holiday had written, "Lover man, oh, where can you be?" beside it.

"We'll find a place for it," said Victor, and looked up to eye me skeptically. "I suppose you ruined my speech."

"How could I ruin it? I told them they could all kiss your ass—just like you said."

Victor laughed and leaned down to pick up his artificial leg. He waggled the foot in my direction. "Not my ass," he said. "My big toe."

"Guess I didn't bring the right props."

Hilma stood up with a grunt and snatched the leg out of his hands. "It's bad enough you won't wear the damn thing, Victor, but I will not have you roughhousing with it in the living room." She returned it to its place beside Victor's chair. "You know he ruined Thanksgiving at our daughter's house. Used the damn leg to bat dinner rolls across the table."

Victor winked at me. He had a been a big man once—over six feet and nearly 200 pounds—but time and a medical almanac of diseases had shrunk him to the point where a wink made him look like a naughty elf. "Lucky I didn't end up with a broken-bat single," he said, "the way Martha cooks."

"Hush up," hissed Hilma. "You want anything while I'm up, August? Tea, coffee or something stronger?"

"No, thanks. I should be—"

"I know what he wants," Victor put in. "He wants to play the bass."

He was right. I always wanted to play the bass when I came to Victor's. He had two: an old one, which he called "Baby," and a new one that he had purchased as backup. Baby had been with him for seven decades and he had played it everywhere and with everyone. Scratched and worn in many places, and quite probably inferior in tone, Baby was Victor's link to the heyday of San Francisco jazz and no one was touching it but him.

The backup bass, on the other hand, had no such heritage and was okay for friends to play. This was somewhat ironic as it was a beautiful instrument, crafted in Italy by the famous maker Alberto Begliomini, and worth about ten times as much as Baby. Victor had made a number of half-hearted attempts to sell the Begliomini bass over the years, and it was one such attempt that first brought me into contact with him. Even though the $30,000 price tag was well out of my league, I'd come by the house one day to kick the tires, and ended up not with a bass but with a good friend instead. Since my own bass had been destroyed in a brawl with some bad guys, playing the Begliomini was a still great treat during visits, and it was a standing joke between us that I would always try to negotiate Victor down from $30K, but neither of us took it seriously. I said:

"I might be persuaded to give it a try."

"Persuaded my ass," said Victor. "You've been stealing glances at it since you walked in the door. Go ahead. That's why Hilma took it out of the case."

The bass was on a stand next to the fireplace. I lifted it out carefully and took it to the center of the room. Someone once said that the perfect bass is like a tailored suit of clothes, good to look at and easy to wear. Victor's bass certainly fit the bill. The flamed Italian poplar gleamed invitingly, the Roman god Jupiter carved on the scroll was empowering and the ebony fret board felt just right under my fingers. My only complaint stemmed from the fact that I was taller than Victor, so the end pin on the bottom was not as long as I would have liked.

Hunching over slightly, I began to play the first thing that came to mind: a solo from French bassist Guy Pedersen. I had been listening to Stéphane Grappelli records from the 60s and Pedersen's solo on one of the tunes had stuck.

Victor nodded his head in time to the music. "Pretty good for a white boy, but I don't recognize the tune."

If I sounded good, it was more to do with the bass than me. It had a huge, deep sounding low end, a ton of sustain and a great upper register. "Grappelli," I said, reaching down the fret for a high note. "Guy Pedersen solo."

"A Frenchman," said Hilma, surprised. She had always had a soft spot for the French. "What does a no-account like you know about the French?"

I finished the measure and straightened up. "They eat horses, don't they?"

"Very funny. Victor and I went to Paris once. Stayed at the Ritz and everything. They gave Victor another damn medal, the Chevalier in the Order of Arts and Letters."

Victor laughed. "That's right. Me and Jerry Lewis. But this one means a lot more." He hefted the SFSU plaque, then watched as I returned the bass to the stand. "Well, August, what do you think?"

I rubbed a smudge off the gleaming poplar. "I'll take it—assuming you have ten year layaway."

Victor gave a bittersweet smile and shook his head. "Sorry, boy. I don't think I've got ten year anything."

I kicked myself on the cab ride back for bringing up anything to do with age. Victor was philosophical about his situation, but his recent bout with peripheral vascular disease had cost him his leg, and I knew that mortality was weighing heavier on his mind than ever before.

I paid the cabbie off in front of the Turk Street garage. I woke the Galaxie from a fitful sleep, then pointed it south to the neighborhood of Noe Valley. It was time to check out Caroline Stockwell's place of employment.

Originally home to working class immigrants, Noe Valley had evolved to a 21st Century enclave for Internet geeks, dog walkers, luthiers, aromatherapists, AIDS activists, lawyers, doctors, documentary filmmakers, organic farmers and lesbian moms. The main drag through the district was 24th Street, and judging from the people and paraphernalia in evidence that day, you couldn't fling a mango smoothie from your SUV without splattering a passing golden retriever, a baby in a stroller or a rolled yoga mat. You might also have nailed an Earth First! petition ghoulie.

I orbited in a three block radius for about ten minutes until I found a parking space big enough for the Galaxie. Unfortunately, it was in a yellow loading zone in front of the health foods market. Since there was a sign explicitly forbidding all but those with store business to park there, I put a scrap of cardboard with a scrawled, "Tofu Salesman" in the car window. I almost wrote "*Traveling* Tofu Salesman," but I figured that was pushing it.

The Noe Valley rendition of Starbucks was a partially converted Victorian with retail on the bottom and three floors of apartments above. Not counting the Irish Setter and the Rottweiler panting by the door, there were two benches' worth of khaki and fleece-clad patrons out front. Inside, the preference for khaki and fleece was maintained and even amplified, including one stroller-bound infant dressed in a hooded fleece jumper. It struck me that there was nothing more all-American than swaddling your child from head to foot in a substance made from recycled six-pack rings.

Most of the tables were taken by 20- and 30-somethings enjoying a late breakfast while chatting, highlighting textbooks with yellow markers, reading the newspaper or working on computers. A second infant could be seen breast-feeding in the lap of its young mother as she sat on a bench by the window. Since mom herself was sucking on a straw buried deep in a Vente Mocha Frappuccino, it was difficult not to have thoughts about cutting out the middleman—or woman.

I went up to the counter where two of the baristas were in the midst of a conversation. The first was a Chinese girl with bangs so long that she was constantly blinking to keep the hair from her eyes. "I went to Modesto for the weekend," she said, "and I stopped in at the local Starfucks for a laugh."

"How was it?" asked her compatriot, a reedy, fair-skinned kid with a blue bandana covering dreadlocks like coils of Spanish moss.

"You wouldn't believe it. They're such hicks down there—they don't even know to call decaf first on the orders."

"Oh my God," was the breathy response.

I decided to stick my beak in before they went off on the way Modesto steamed the milk. "Excuse me," I said in a voice that sounded grown-up and pompous, even to me. "I'd like to speak to the manager."

The Chinese girl came up to the register, still glowing from her crack about the yokels in Modesto. "And how do you know *I'm* not the manager."

"Because I'm guessing the manager doesn't refer to the business as Starfucks."

The glow faded and she blinked her eyes all the more furiously. "It's not because—I mean you don't want to see him because of that, do you?"

"No, it's about something else entirely."

The kid with the dreadlocks came around from behind the espresso machine. His expression, too, was suddenly downcast and serious. "The manager is on his break," he said. "He should be back in about ten minutes if you'd like to wait. Or you could leave your number."

I told him I'd wait and ordered a cup of plain black coffee without any Indian spices or soy additives and took it over to the last open table in the place. I sipped my coffee and let my glance wonder around the room.

A couple to my right were trading barbs across a demilitarized zone of newspapers held open at reading height. "Take this so-called advantage in spatial reasoning," she said tartly. "That's just another bullshit argument to stop women from advancing in the workforce. I mean, what the hell *is* spatial reasoning anyway?"

The man poked his head over the sports page. "One definition might be knowing which way to curb your tires on a hill."

She threw down the real estate section. "I told you not to bring that up anymore. The hydrant stopped it before it got half a block."

The table in front of me was host to two young women with a pile of books and backpacks large enough to provision an assault on Everest. The blonde, who sported a multi-colored Peruvian beanie and polished fingernails of at least three other colors, looked up from her dog-eared copy of *The Great Gatsby*. "You know what I just realized? Zelda Fitzgerald was the Yoko Ono of the 1920s."

Her brunette companion paused with her highlighter mid-paragraph to give this thought due consideration. "But Yoko broke up the Beatles. Who did Zelda break up?"

"Her husband, of course. Remember he wrote that essay, *The Crack-Up*?"

"Oh yeah. She also broke up Hemingway and Fitzgerald."

The blonde snapped her fingers. "That's right. She called them fairies."

"But you'd have to say Yoko Ono was the Zelda Fitzgerald of the 1970s. Zelda came first."

This seemed to ruin it for the blonde. "I suppose," she said listlessly. "It sounded better the other way, though."

I made eye contact with the fleece baby, who was parked in his stroller several tables over. I raised my cup in a silent toast and he responded with a frothy saliva bubble. This seemed the most profound thing to come out of anyone's mouth since I walked in the door.

I downed the rest of my coffee, and still lacking anything in the way of a managerial presence, turned to examine the community art exhibit hanging on the wall behind me. I realized with a mild jolt that the photographs were similar to those I had seen in Caroline's room. I stood up to get a closer look and confirmed her cramped signature on a gritty, black and white shot of a woman's navel pierced with a silver stud. "Self-Portrait," it was titled.

"How do you like the art work?" said a voice behind me.

I turned to find a tall, well-muscled guy with fair skin and very short blond hair. He had a way of making even the green Starbucks apron look snappy and I guessed that Chris Duckworth would be pleased to make his acquaintance. "Oh, it's a little recherché for me," I said.

He smiled. "Yeah, I saw that in this morning's Word-A-Day column too. You're one up on me—I haven't managed to work it into a sentence yet." He held out his hand. "I'm Dave Sands, the manager here. Leila said you wanted to talk to me."

"I'm actually here about the artist." I nodded at the photographs. "I understand she works here."

Sands got the sort of look of mild strain you get when you want to be polite, but are worried about where the conversation is headed. "Yes, she works here. She hasn't been in for a while, though."

"I know. She's gone missing." He watched with increasing strain as I pulled out my wallet and showed him my investigator's license. "I've been hired by the family to find her," I said. "I'd appreciate it if you would spare me a few minutes of your time."

Sands started to say something, then stopped himself. He ran his hand through his hair. "Okay," he said finally.

"You got somewhere we can talk?"

"This is it—unless you want to sit on coffee bags in the store-room."

I gestured at the table I had come from and returned to my seat. "You knew that she was missing, right?"

Sands settled into the chair across from me and glanced around the store a little nervously. "Yes, someone called, but I didn't know whether to believe him. He sounded drunk. At first I thought he said he was her father and then I thought he said he was the police. To tell you the truth, I wasn't sure if I should have talked to him about Caroline and I'm not sure … " His voice trailed off.

"If you should talk to me either."

He nodded.

"I realize it seems odd, but it's all on the level. Her father *is* a police detective. He's been hitting the bottle pretty hard since she went, so it's very likely he was drunk when he spoke to you."

Sands twisted his mouth into a dissatisfied pout. "But if he's with the police, why would he hire someone to look for her?"

"It's a long story. The short version is he's burned a lot of bridges. If you're still concerned about talking to me, you're welcome to call her mother and get confirmation."

Sands glanced at his watch and then crossed his arms. He gave me a level stare. "No, that's okay. I don't have anything earth-shattering to tell you, anyway. I was just being cautious."

"All right. Maybe you could start by telling me about her last day at work. When was that? Do you recall?"

"It was September 24th—a Wednesday. I know because I had to cover for her on the 25th, and after that, we put someone else in her spot in the staff rotation. But as for the day itself, there was nothing special. On Wednesdays she worked a full shift. She came in at 8:30 and worked until 5:30, just like usual. She didn't mention anything about missing the next day."

"Did she say if she was going somewhere that evening?"

"Not to me. If I had to guess, I'd say she went out with her friend Monica. Monica often met her after work on Wednesdays."

"But you didn't actually see Monica that evening?"

Sands unfolded his arms and reoriented the watch on his wrist. I noticed for the first time that it was a silver Oyster Rolex. "Are you in a hurry?" I asked.

He flashed a perfect smile of blinding white teeth. "No—I mean I am a little, but I just got the watch as a gift and I can't stop looking at it."

"Nice gift."

"Yes, it is." He pulled his shirt sleeve over the watch self-consciously. "To answer your question, no, I didn't remember seeing Monica. I might have been in the back when Caroline left, though."

"Did anyone else ever meet her after work? A boyfriend, say?"

Sands looked up to the ceiling to think for a moment, then shook his head. "No, I don't recall anyone else coming in to meet her."

"How about here at work? Did she have any friends on the staff?"

"If I'm honest, I'd have to say no. Caroline's a bit of a loner. She always took her breaks by herself, usually to walk up and down 24th Street snapping photos. I was probably as close to her as anyone in the store, and that's not saying much."

I looked over to the fleece baby, who obliged me by blowing another bubble. Sands was right: he wasn't telling me anything earth shattering. "Did she seem out of sorts in any way during the period before she left?" I asked. "Complain of any problems in her personal life?"

"No, she was actually very upbeat. She was excited to finally get her turn at the exhibit wall and was very pleased by the response she got when she hung her photos. I caught her a number of times just staring at people while they admired them. Since most people in the store didn't know she was the artist, it was kind of a voyeuristic thrill for her."

A strident beeping began at the back of the store, behind the register. Sands looked up in annoyance. From the flashing lights that accompanied the noise, it was apparent that one of the coffee brewers needed attention, but both of the baristas were busy with customers. "Are we done here?" asked Sands. "I really need to get that."

"Sure," I said. "We're done."

Sands jumped up and ran behind the counter to deal with the alarm. I lingered a moment at the table and then went back to the photo exhibit. I found an artist statement tacked up in one corner by the stand with the coffee stirrers and cream and was plowing through the turgid prose—which included quotes from Plato, Carl Jung and the obligatory reference to Joseph Campbell—when Sands' voice interrupted me from behind once more.

"Say, Mr.—Mr. Riordan, was it? If you're going to Caroline's house, can you deliver these for me? There's no room for them in the back and she really shouldn't have them sent here anyway."

When I turned, he pressed an armful of Amazon.com boxes into my chest. I grabbed at them, but one of the smaller ones dropped off the pile and fell to the floor. Sands bent to pick it up and stacked it on top once more. "There you go," he said with more than a trace of satisfaction. "I'll hold the door open for you."

Apparently, if I didn't want to become a human merchandise display rack, this was my cue to leave the store. I trudged after him, threading a careful path through the tables and strollers and giving the fleece baby a final wink as I passed.

"Thanks for taking these off my hands," he said as he twisted the door knob. "And good luck in finding Caroline. Tell her I'll be happy to hire her back when she returns."

"What if she's not returning?"

Sands fogged the crystal of his Rolex with his breath and polished it with his sleeve. "Oh, I've got a feeling about that. I think she's just taking a little sabbatical."

SHRINK RAP

BARELY ABLE TO SEE OVER THE TOP of the packages, I steered a diffident and tentative course up the crowded sidewalk to my car, where I shoveled the merchandise into the yawning space that used to contain the back seat. I'd removed the seat some time ago to make transporting my upright bass easier, and even though I'd lost the bass, I'd never reinstalled the seat—mainly because I had ditched it in the dumpster behind The Hob Nob Lounge on Geary one night around 2 am.

Thankfully, there were no tickets on the windshield, and after I settled myself behind the wheel, I paused a moment before pulling out to reflect on my conversation with Sands. At first, his parting remark about Caroline taking a sabbatical struck me as cavalier or somehow indicative of a fuller knowledge of Caroline's whereabouts than he let on. But after I thought about it, I decided that managing a business where you were constantly recruiting a stream of nine-dollar-an-hour baristas to keep the store running had probably jaded his view of employee commitment to the job.

Just then, I heard a tapping on glass and turned to find a red-headed beanpole with a Real Foods T-shirt glaring in at me from the passenger window. I hit the button for the electric window, but like usual, it got stuck part way down, leaving a four inch gap for him to shove his snout in like an angry dog.

"This is a loading zone. You can't park here," he snapped.

"I was just going."

"Well, make it sudden. I've got a truck-load of organic vegetables blocking traffic."

I turned to look behind me, and sure enough, there was a semi-truck with its blinkers on idling in the middle of the road.

"Sorry," I said. "Time to get my carnivorous ass out of the way of vegan progress." I gave him a cheery wave, fired up the Galaxie and pulled out on to 24th Street. Munching on the remains of an all-beef Slim Jim I scavenged from the glove box, I stayed on 24th until I came to Folsom and then turned left. Monica Mapa's apartment was three blocks down near the intersection with 21st. I parked kitty-corner in front of a greasy spoon with Spanish signage that advertised *tortas el primo*, which I thought had something to do with tasty cakes, but from the not-so-appealing pictures on the yellow awning were apparently gigantic ham sandwiches.

The building across the way was even less appealing. It had started life as one of San Francisco's ubiquitous Victorians, but now had all the adulterated charm and structural integrity of Michael Jackson's nose. Successive remodelling, repairs and simple neglect had stripped away the original aesthetics, leaving only a flat-sided plywood-sheathed hulk whose only unchipped paint had been applied by the neighborhood graffiti artists. I went up a staircase that had tread boards from five different sources—including a warped section of Ping-Pong table—and stood in front of a pair of pock-marked doors that led to the flats inside. The buzzer for Monica's flat wasn't working and neither was the tarnished turn-of-the-century—20th Century, that is—brass doorknob. In fact, the only things that appeared to be keeping the door from swinging open from the gusts of autumn wind rattling it in its frame were a cheap-looking deadbolt and a folded flyer for a check-cashing service wedged in next to the lock.

When I pounded on the door, the flyer came loose and swirled around the vestibule with a collection of leaves and dirt, but no one answered the knock and I couldn't hear movement inside. I tried the other door to see if I could roust Monica's neighbor, but got the same response.

Dr. Marvin Levin was next on my list, but it being almost lunch time, I decided to take my chances with the *tortas el primo* and found out that they were actually pretty good. I went for chorizo instead of ham and used a Negro Modelo beer and occasional toot from my flask to cut the garlic and chili powder.

As I sat in the Galaxie polishing off the last of the beer and licking chorizo grease from my fingers, my eye wondered to the back and I began to get curious about the Amazon.com packages. I picked up one that obviously contained a CD and found that it had been postmarked less than a week ago. That was interesting both because Caroline had disappeared a good two weeks prior and because she was not supposed to have any credit cards.

The CD turned out to be *Faceless* by Godsmack, featuring little ditties like *Releasing the Demons* and *I Fucking Hate You*. More interesting was the fact that it was gift-wrapped and came with a card. The card had been addressed to "Goth Angel" and was signed by "your secret admirer." The kicker was the message, which was all the more remarkable because it had to have been entered on a web form when the order was placed and was now reproduced in stark, impersonal laser print:

```
Paint your toenails carmine for me!
```

I stared at the message for a moment longer, carefully returned the card to its envelope and then leaned back to grab a handful of the remaining boxes and began tearing through them. By the time I finished, I had two more CDs, several books, and handful of DVDs, 128 megabytes worth of flash memory, a wireless network kit and a George Foreman Grill. All of the loot came as gifts and most of the boxes included a card of some kind. The addressee was always Goth Angel, and by and large her admirers tended to remain anonymous, but occasionally they signed with *nom de plumes* like "Blood Slave,"

"Skinner's Pigeon" or "Incubus". The theme of the messages was consistent—involving either a request for Caroline to wear certain clothes or do certain—fairly innocent—things like the toenail business or more cryptically, "fan me with the breeze from your beating wings."

A final item of particular interest was the fact that the shipments included packing lists, but the name of the purchaser was always "Private Buyer" and the address given was an obvious front: a P.O. box in New Jersey. If any of the people who'd sent the merchandise were involved in Caroline's disappearance, it seemed the only way to discover their real identities would be to get the information directly from Amazon.com.

I didn't know much about the Internet, but I was vaguely aware that Amazon had something called wish lists for their customers to request particular gifts and I was pretty certain this was the way Caroline had worked it. I decided I would talk to Chris Duckworth—the only Internet-ready drag queen I knew—and get some more background on wish lists and making online purchases anonymously.

I shoveled all the cards, goodies and packing materials into a messy pile in the back and hit the ignition. It was time to have my head examined.

Dr. Levin was a brave man. In a town where earthquakes visited destruction and debris on the populace as often as Hollywood revived the gangster movie, he put his office in a brick building—an old brick building at that. To be specific, it was a red-brick Edwardian on Gough Street across from Lafayette Park.

I'd called him first thing that morning to wheedle an appointment at 12 noon. I was ten minutes early, but since the therapist's hour was only 50 minutes—unlike the baker's dozen in that you get less, not more—I was hoping that he would be available to see me.

The name plate on the door said, "Dr. Levin and Associates," so I wasn't surprised to find a large, somberly-decorated waiting room with two other people cooling their heels on the burgundy-colored couches that ringed the room. There was a burnished metal sculpture that looked like the rib of an aluminum whale or wreckage from the Hindenberg in the middle of the floor and the artwork on the walls looked like Rorschach tests for violent criminals. I followed the directions for signalling my arrival by flipping a switch next to Dr. Levin's name and a small ruby light began to glow dully.

I settled myself on a couch and got halfway through an old *Reader's Digest* article on Joe's pancreas, when a bald guy in his late 40s with a tremendous forehead and a slight stoop came through one of the interior doors. "You must be August Riordan," he said. He smiled in an insincere way that displayed only upper teeth and compressed his salt-and-pepper mustache into a bristly three-inch caterpillar.

I copped to my identity and he led me back to gloomy office with two over-stuffed chairs and a small coffee table with a box of tissues on top. He waved me into the larger of the two chairs and perched himself on the other. "I hope you don't feel uncomfortable talking to me here," he said. "But there aren't any other rooms available."

"Why would I mind?"

"This is where I treat patients. I wouldn't want you to feel like I'm analyzing you."

"I'll raise my hand if start to get anxious. We didn't have much time on the phone this morning, but you understand my reason for coming?"

"Yes, I understand. Caroline is missing. But as I told you, there are limits to what we can discuss. I am bound by psychotherapist-patient privilege to protect the confidentiality of communications between me and my patients."

I squirmed around in the chair. My butt had sunk to a level lower than my knees, making me feel like I was looking up at Levin. I wondered if he'd engineered it that way on purpose. "I can still ask you for your opinions about where she might have gone or what she might do in a particular situation, can't I?"

"Yes. Yes, you can—if we are both very careful." He gave me one of his insincere smiles.

"All right. Let's start with the obvious question. Do you have any idea where she might be?"

"No, I don't."

"That's it? No elaboration?"

"I told you we both had to be very careful."

I grunted and pulled myself forward in the chair until I felt less in a hole. "Do you have any reason to believe she might want to harm herself or leave home?"

Levin pushed out his lips and ran the back of his hand along the skin below his chin. "I think it's very unlikely that Caroline would harm herself. I would certainly have taken a more aggressive approach in her treatment if I thought there was any real chance of that."

"Her mother said that she was going to stop seeing you soon. Would you agree that she was ready?"

"That's a decision that must be left to the patient. If you asked me if I felt she had made progress, I would say that she had. As to whether or not she felt confident enough to end the therapy, I couldn't say."

"What about leaving home? Do you think she might do that?"

"Here again, we must be careful. In general, one could say that almost all adolescents and young adults feel the urge to flee their family environment at one point or another. The question is whether they choose to act upon those urges."

I took a handful of the stuffing on the armchair and squeezed. "Yes, that is the question—and you didn't answer it. Would Caroline run away?"

Levin graced me with another of his phoney horse smiles. "The answer to that is multifaceted, Mr. Riordan. Even if I supplied it, I doubt you would understand."

"Multifaceted, huh? I know one thing that's multifaceted. Bug eyes. Is it like bug eyes?"

Levin looked like he'd swallowed a thistle. "Please. I realize you are frustrated, but there's no reason to be sarcastic."

I took a deep breath and tried again. "Look, doctor, setting aside whether I will understand what you have to tell me, I know a little something about this Jaffee privilege. The intent is to protect patients from having information in therapy sessions disclosed in court proceedings or other situations when it's not in their best interests. This is different. Caroline's family has hired me to help locate her and prevent potential harm to her. Given the circumstances, I think you could be a little more forthcoming."

Levin's eyes moved over my face while he fingered the bristles of his mustache. "I'm mildly impressed that you know the name of the Supreme Court case. And you're right about the intent of the ruling, so the question is whether helping you locate Caroline is in her best interests."

"Implying that there are good reasons for her to leave?"

Levin waved his hand in an impatient gesture. "I will say this. Her brother's suicide and her unhealthy relationship with her father have made her home life emotionally challenging. It wouldn't be beyond the pale for her to leave, but I wouldn't expect her to do it secretly and without warning. She's over 18 and could legally move out any time she chose."

"I get the part about her brother, but what are you saying about the father? That he abused her?"

Levin gave me a cool stare. "If true, I certainly wouldn't talk about it."

If he wanted to give me the impression that the answer was yes without saying so explicitly, he'd done a good job. "Okay," I said. "Assuming that she did go on her own power, I want to come back to the question of where she went. Her mother seemed to think she might have a new boyfriend. Did she mention that to you?"

Levin seemed surprised by the question—or more accurately, the assertion. "She didn't have a new boyfriend," he said flatly.

"You mean that you knew about."

"Caroline was always forthright with me. If there was someone new in her life, she would have told me."

"I see." I'd slipped back into the maw of the chair, so I hauled myself forward again. "Her mother also said that Caroline spent time at an ashram in Berkeley. Do you think she would go there?"

Levin smiled, and for the first time it seemed to be with genuine amusement. "I know the place. Sri Atma Nidhi's emporium of peace and enlightenment. I doubt you will find Caroline there. The man is a complete fraud and she saw through him quickly enough."

"With your help?"

"I like to give my patients credit for their own breakthroughs. I'm just the facilitator."

"That's swell." I reached for a tissue from the box on the coffee table and blew my nose with it, then leaned over to throw the tissue in a nearby waste can. Levin watched the whole operation with a faint air of disgust.

"Oops," I said, and held up my right hand. "Had a little break-through of my own." I reached for a second tissue. "You really ought to buy the triple-ply, Doctor. It doesn't make sense to skimp on the Kleenex in your line of business."

"Yes. Do you have any other questions for me, Mr. Riordan? If not, I'd like to get some lunch before my next appointment."

"I understand, but I've got to believe the more productive route would be for you to tell me the things you know about Caroline that could be useful in my search. Otherwise, I'm just groping in the dark."

"As I said at the outset, I don't know where Caroline is."

"You're her therapist. Aren't you concerned for her well-being?"

Levin drew himself up. "My ignorance of her location is not a measure of my concern." He sprang off the chair and gestured towards the door. "I think we're finished here."

I stood and looked at him across the table. "Just one more thing. Caroline had apparently been receiving some fairly expensive gifts from strangers. Quite a few of her admirers enclosed cards where they made little requests of her—like painting her toenails a particular color. Do you know anything about that?"

Levin's mouth went slack and his pupils vibrated back and forth, searching for something in my face. "No," he said. "Why would I know anything about that?"

"I guess because of how forthright she was with you."

He trotted out the patented phoney smile. "Yes, and that's exactly why I think you're mistaken. She mentioned no such gifts."

"All right, doctor. Thank you for your time." I put my hand out and he took it, eager to see me on my way. I gave him a good squeeze. "And don't forget about those Kleenex, huh?"

As I went through the door to the waiting room, I looked back to see him staring at his hand like it had suddenly become radioactive.

PUTTING THE GOO BACK IN GURU

JUDGING FROM THE SAMPLE I'D SEEN SO far, the male authority figures in Caroline's life were an unheroic lot. At best, her father was a hard-nosed bastard with a drinking problem, and at worst, he had abused her—either physically or sexually. Her psychiatrist came off like an arrogant, uncaring drip who seemed strangely proud of the confidences she gave him and was almost certainly suppressing information I could use. Her boss was the best of the group, but even he suffered from a bad case of Rolex worship.

As I pulled into a surprisingly convenient parking space in front of the Berkeley ashram, I wasn't expecting her guru to raise the grade point average any.

The building was a converted apartment house or hotel on the corner of Carleton and Telegraph. It was built in a sort of cheesy Mediterranean style, like a Dean Martin and Jerry Lewis movie version of a Tuscan villa. All the windows on the upper levels had their blinds closed or curtains drawn, but if this made it hard to look in, the people inside didn't have any trouble looking out. When I exited the car, I spotted four cameras sprouting from the pink awning and the red tile roof. I might have found more if the cop who was standing on the sidewalk hadn't interrupted me. He said:

"May I ask if you have business at the ashram, sir?"

A friendly-looking black guy with about two inches of blubber hanging over the top of his gun belt, he didn't seem particularly interested in the answer to my question. "More or less," I said. "Sure got a lot of cameras, don't they?"

He slid two thumbs past the blubber to hook them on his belt. "That's nothing. You should see the communication tower on the back of the roof and the razor wire that rings the property. Looks like the Berlin wall." His eyes drifted toward my jacket pocket. "Say, you're not a smoker, are you?"

"Not today. You looking to bum a cigarette?"

"Naw, I've got a pack, but I ran out of matches and I can't leave my post."

"I can help with that." I opened the passenger door to the Galaxie and punched the lighter down. "Give it a minute," I said, and straightened up. "You said you can't leave your post. What are you doing? Guarding the place?"

The cop grinned. "See that group across the street? I'm supposed to make sure they don't get within 100 yards of the property. The guru's got an injunction against them."

I looked across Telegraph to a handful of protesters with crudely painted cardboard signs standing between a kick-boxing studio and a barber shop. They were so few and the traffic on Telegraph so heavy that I hadn't noticed them before. One of them saw me looking and shouted something our direction.

"What's their beef?"

"I don't know the particulars, but I understand they are all ex-disciples. The guru brainwashed them or abused their trust or some such." He unbuttoned his breast pocket to take out a hard pack of Camel filters. "Think it's ready?"

I nodded and reached back into the car for the lighter. The cop shook out a cigarette that was bent at a fifteen-degree angle despite the hard pack and put it against the glowing coil. "Thanks man," he said after a deep puff. "I needed that."

"Why the injunction, then?"

"Oh, nothing really serious, I guess. They were hassling people coming in and out of the ashram. Shouting at the guru when he drove up in his Porsche. Throwing eggs at his car. Stuff like that."

"He should drive a Galaxie. It's the best way to demonstrate an indifference to worldly possessions."

He gave me a thumbs up and took another drag. "And the lighter works good, too."

"Mind if I go over and talk to them?"

"Sure, just don't bring any of them back with you."

I jogged to the far sidewalk just in front of a wave of cars released from the traffic light. There were six protesters altogether—four women and two men. They were all in their 20s or 30s except for an older woman with gray hair, and while I wouldn't have noticed it if I'd seen them separately, as a group they projected a certain feeling of hollowness or dejection that was hard to describe. A short woman in a gingham dress broke off from the group and came up to meet me. She walked with a sturdy aluminum cane and had metal braces on both of her legs.

"Did the cop send you over here?" she asked.

"Not exactly. He did tell me you what you were up to."

"I'm up to about three joints a day is what I'm up to." She smiled in a disarming way and I saw that she had braces on her teeth as well.

"Is that to treat guru withdrawal?"

"Hardly. That's to deal with the pain from my automobile accident." She knocked her cane against the braces on her leg. "I'm not wearing these just because they're stylish, you know."

The traffic light turned red and a group of cars accumulated at the intersection. The other protestors took this as a signal to wave their signs and shout at the drivers. "Nidhi is a fraud," they yelled. "Nidhi preys on young girls."

I inclined my head towards them. "Is that true?"

"Sure it's true. Haven't you read our literature?" She took a flyer printed on orange stock from the pocket of her dress and passed it to me.

The headline at the top read, "**DID YOU KNOW?**" in bold capitals, and below that was a series of bullets:

- Sri Atma Nidhi's real name is Eugene Applegarth.
- He was born in Bisbee, Arizona.
- He has never been to India.
- "Golden Dawn of the New Epiphany" was plagiarized from traditional proverbs of many lands, the writings of Confucious, the bible and fortunes from Bazooka Bubblegum.
- He was charged with statutory rape in Arizona, but the case was dismissed when he bought the family off.
- He has a net worth of nearly $6 million and never pays taxes.
- He once bragged to a friend that he was going to have more followers than "Jesus, Mohammed and Martha Stewart combined."

"The bit about Martha Stewart is funny," I said.

"It's not funny when you've been abused, or given up your home and all your money—or you wake up from the dream after wasting years of your life and have nothing but an empty place inside."

I guessed my sense of the protestors' hollowness and dejection was not misplaced. "Did those things happen to you?"

She regarded me solemnly for a moment. "Not the abuse—only the pretty girls get that—but otherwise I got the full treatment. I was told my gift—my dakshina—of the money I got from my accident settlement would bless me with a portion of the guru's essence. I was told my constant pain was my best friend. That it would lead me to 'unfoldment' and keep me hungering for God, purifying me and raising my consciousness higher and higher." She rapped the sidewalk with her cane, breaking the cadence of her little speech. "I was an idiot is what I was. And it's ruined my life—even more than the accident."

I mumbled something lame in the "I'm sorry" line.

"What's it to you?" she said sharply. "You don't exactly look like the sort to don the robes."

"I'm a private investigator. I'm looking for a girl who used to go to the ashram. She's missing."

"Name?"

"Caroline Stockwell."

She nodded. "I knew her. I saw her at some of the chants before I quit."

"Do you know if she's been back recently?"

She smiled and her braces glinted in the sun. "I couldn't tell you. I'm prevented by court order from getting within 100 yards of the place."

"Right."

"But I haven't seen her go in or out lately, so my guess is she wised up. She seemed like a smart girl."

"How about Nidhi? You see him today?"

"Oh yeah. We nailed his Porsche with an egg when he pulled in the lot. He probably called the cops after that. Are you going to talk to him?"

"I'm going to try."

She thought for a moment and then waved her cane in the direction of the building as if placing a curse. "Greasy bastard. I'll give you a little hint. The best way to put him on the ropes is to threaten him with bad publicity."

"All right. I'll keep that in mind."

"And tell him Beth says his karma is to be reincarnated as a tiger in a waterless region."

"I'll do that. Thanks for all your help."

She turned without saying anything more and hobbled back to the group. Another group of cars braked to a stop at the intersection and she yelled, "Nidhi is the opiate of the people and the ashram is the crack house!"

I took advantage of the break in the traffic to hustle back across. The cop was talking to a pretty woman at a bus stop farther down Telegraph, so I gave him a quick wave and went directly up to the entrance.

The interior surprised me. I was expecting something like a hippie commune. What I got was the full veneer and polish of a three star hotel. Cherry wood paneling covered the walls, warm light glowed from elegant sconces and the carpeting was lush and thick enough to lose your mantra in.

Two smiling women behind a reception desk greeted me as I walked in the door. "Welcome," they said in unison. "God dwells within you as you."

I patted my chest where I felt an incipient heartburn. "I hope he doesn't mind the chorizo," I said.

That earned me a strangled look of disapproval from the older woman, who had long braided hair with a part down the middle like a knife cut in paraffin. The younger one didn't break stride. "Is this your first time to the ashram?" she asked. "Would you like a tour?"

"Maybe later. What I'd like most is to talk with Sri Atma Nidhi. Is he around?"

This was an even bigger indiscretion. They glanced at each other and the older one put on a pair of round, John Lennon-type glasses to give me a thorough inspection. "I'm sorry," she said. "The Guru is very busy. But there are other teachers available who can explain our beliefs."

"No, it has to be the big guy. Do you have a piece of paper and a pen? I'd like to write him a note."

After a pause dripping with unspoken calculation, the older one nodded and the younger one scurried behind the desk to locate the requested implements. I'm sure they figured it was an easy way to fob me off.

I decided to follow Beth's advice and threaten Nidhi with bad PR, but rather than something specific, I kept my saber-rattling vague. I've learned that people tend to fill in the blanks with their own worst-case scenario. I folded the paper in half when I was finished and wrote, "To Gene Applegarth" on top.

The woman with the braids grimaced when she saw the name, but she took the paper all the same. "All right, then," she said, trying to will me out the door. "We'll make sure he gets it."

"I want you to take it to him now."

"We told you he's busy."

I leaned over the counter, getting in their faces. "If you don't take the note to him immediately, I'm going to call my friend at Channel 2. I'll make sure he does a story about what's in the note, and I'll also make sure it features live interviews with the protestors from in front of the ashram."

They stared at me like I was a SARS patient who'd offered to French kiss them. "Go!" I yelled.

Ms. braids-with-round-glasses hurried out from behind the desk. "You stay here, Jenny," she said to her compatriot. "I'll be right back."

Jenny looked at me with a twitchy expression and then got busy filing index cards in a metal box behind the counter. She had only gotten as far as the M's when two strapping lads with shaved heads and flowing orange robes appeared at the far end of the lobby and ambled up to the desk. They looked like they would have been more at home in orange jumpers issued by the state. "You wanted to see the Guru?" said the one with an obvious knife scar on his throat.

"That's right."

He didn't waste any time. His hand darted over to my arm and he dug his fingers into my triceps like he was kneading Silly Putty. His partner moved in close to tromp on my foot and sling an uppercut at my midsection. I twisted around to avoid taking the full force of the blow in the gut, but still received a stinging shot to the ribs. I crumpled forward. The guy with the scar laughed and shoved me into a dive that force-fed me about two yards worth of carpet.

"You *still* wanna see the Guru?" he shouted.

I levered myself up on one elbow, but he piled on, rolled me over and got busy seeing how far he could push his forearm into my windpipe. Black spots were swimming in front of my eyes like drunken amoebas by the time I reached the knife on my ankle and laid the business end alongside the scar on his throat.

"Oh yeah," I croaked as he let up the pressure on my windpipe. "You've been here before."

There's an old gag about bringing a knife to a gunfight, but no one ever makes jokes about bringing a knife to a wrestling match. That was the second time in a year it had saved me from a lot of heartache.

I held him close with a handful of robe while I maintained the pressure with the knife. "Roll over," I said. "And stay the fuck away from us or I'll cut his head off," I yelled to his orange brother.

I forced him onto his back, got to my knees and then yanked him to his feet. I couldn't avoid sawing a little at the skin of his throat during the maneuver, and a thin trickle of blood ran down from the place where the blade made contact. I stood behind him, taking gasping breaths while I scoped the area. The girl had run away or was hiding behind the reception counter. The other guy was looming in front of us in a semi-squat position like a sumo wrestler. "What should I do, Jerry?" he said.

"N-nothing, Tom. Don't do nothing," said Jerry.

Tom and Jerry—that was cute. I risked a glance behind me and spotted a door to the side labeled "Temple." "Here's what you do, Tom," I said. "Get Applegarth and bring him to the Temple. Tell him that Jerry and I will be waiting—and that Jerry has a particular interest in his prompt arrival. Got it?"

Tom nodded his head but seemed to be waiting for affirmation from Jerry. I pressed the knife a little harder into his throat. "Do it," he shouted to Tom.

Tom edged by us warily and trotted off to the back of the lobby. I pushed Jerry toward the door. "Open it," I said.

"You're making the wrong play," he said.

"Just open the door."

Jerry reached for the knob and pulled the door open. I took the knife away and shoved him into the room. He tripped on a potted plant and landed in a heap beside a little shrine. The room was long and narrow with another, larger shrine at the far end and pews and kneeling rugs filling the space between. The walls were painted white and the ceiling was translucent glass and the whole thing had the feel of a greenhouse or a fancy screened porch. No one else was inside.

Jerry sat up and brought his hand to his throat. He stared at the blood on his fingers and cursed.

"Go sit in one of the pews," I said.

"And if I don't?"

"I'll let the guts out of you."

I was really flying blind now. I didn't know whether Tom would come back with a gun, more orange brethren, or the cops, but I was hoping the threat in the note would worry Nidhi enough to prevent that and I didn't want to walk away after all the trouble I'd gone to.

Jerry took a place in the nearest pew and I sat down beside him with the knife at his side. "Great spot to contemplate your mortality," I said.

"Go to hell."

I was dividing my attention between Jerry and the door, so what happened next surprised me—but it would have surprised me in any event. There was a rattling noise at the back of the room and a short guy with greasy hair appeared from behind the big shrine pushing a tea cart. Dressed in purple robes, he looked like an older, chubbier version of the guru on the book cover, and when Jerry stiffened at my side, I had no doubt it was Nidhi.

He rolled his little cart—which was in the shape of a fantastic swan—to a stop by a prayer rug. "Welcome weary pilgrim," he said, and proceeded to flop down on the rug. "Tom, please serve the tea and then you may leave us."

"I'm Jerry."

Nidhi smiled beneficently. "Of course you are."

Jerry got up to pour tea into earthenware bowls and put one in front of Nidhi and another on the rug across from him. He bowed to Nidhi when he was finished and went out the side door, flipping me off from the doorway when he was certain Nidhi wasn't looking.

"Cut yourself shaving, Tom?" I said to his back.

"Please join me, Mr. ... " said Nidhi, letting his voice trail off.

"Riordan."

"Yes, Mr. Riordan."

"What? On the rug?"

"Of course. A man who humbles himself before God, garnishes his soul." He spoke in a soothing, honeyed voice.

I resisted the urge to make a crack about parsley and went over to the rug to sit down. It was goofy as hell, but so was everything else I'd been doing for the last half hour. With my bum knee, I couldn't sit cross-legged like Nidhi, so I settled on an awkward position with both legs stretched out in front of me.

Nidhi sipped his tea and looked at me thoughtfully. Up close, he had an unexpected something: magnetism wasn't quite the right word—fascination was closer. His hair was pulled back to emphasize his high forehead and his eyes were wide-set, deep brown and vaguely troubling—like very good prosthetics that you somehow knew were artificial. "Are you afraid of me?" he asked at length.

I laughed. "Not that I'm aware of."

"Then put away the knife. This is a sacred place."

I had forgotten I was still holding it. I hiked up my pant leg and returned the blade to its harness, hoping I wasn't compounding my errors.

"Have some tea," he urged. "You'll find it refreshing."

I picked up the bowl and sniffed at it. "Are you sure I won't find it drugged—or worse?"

"A skeptic's heart is wizened by his suspicions."

I took a sip of the tea and immediately wished I hadn't. It tasted like last night's bong water. "A skeptic's heart may be shot, but I bet his palate fairs better."

A faint smile curled at the corners of Nidhi's mouth. Score one for him. "I'm sorry you did not enjoy it. But you have been very dogged in your pursuit of an audience, so let us move on to that. How may I serve you?"

"I thought my note was pretty clear."

"Your note was vague. You threatened to tell what you know about me and Caroline Stockwell to the police. There is nothing to know, so your threat is idle."

"Really? I know that she came to the ashram."

"Many girls come to the ashram."

"And many of them are molested."

He lifted his shoulders slightly. "You have been talking to the misguided souls across the street. No one here has been molested. Since I walked the path of enlightenment under the guidance of my own Guru, Bhagavan Sri Pradakshina, I have remained celibate."

"Did this Prada—" I stumbled over the word. "Did this other guru hang out with you in Bisbee, then?"

"I know what you are suggesting. You are suggesting that I have never visited India. That is another untruth promoted by those across the street. I spent many years travelling with Pradakshina in western and southern India. He died before he could select a successor, but his spirit visited me after death and passed on the full power and authority of the Guru lineage to me."

"Visited you how?"

Nidhi brought his hands together, prayer-like, in front of his chest. "In the form of a bird of paradise," he said reverently.

"He came to you as a tropical plant?"

Nidhi's eyes flashed and I got a look behind the veil. "No, you moron. A bird of paradise is a bird as well as a flower."

"My mistake. But didn't I read in your book that anger is like an egg lobbed at a Porsche 911? Seemed like you lobbed a big one just then."

Nidhi clenched his jaw. "I said that anger is as a stone cast into a wasp's nest." He took hold of the leather thong around his neck and pulled a crystal amulet from the folds of his robe. He closed his hand around it tightly. "Did you come here solely to provoke me?"

"No, I came to find Caroline Stockwell."

"And I told you I don't know her."

"But I didn't have to believe you." My leg was getting stiff so I brought my knee up under my arm. "For one thing, if you don't know her, why did you sic Tom and Jerry on me?"

"A man in my position needs to be careful. There are many who would seek to discredit me for their own wicked purposes. I have found it wiser to deal with the threat promptly and firmly than to run from it or ignore it."

"Sounds like you got another aphorism for your next book. But if you *do* know where Caroline Stockwell is, or if, for instance, she happens to be living at the ashram, the best thing you can do now is to tell me now before I involve the police."

Nidhi smiled at me and released the amulet. He had the situation under control again. "I assure you, Mr. Riordan. I have no knowledge of Ms. Stockwell's whereabouts. And even were you to bring the police with a search warrant, you would not find her here." He shifted his bare feet from his lap and moved to stand up. "I think we are finished."

I was missing something, but I couldn't think what it was. I flashed on the Amazon.com packages in the back of my car. "Goth Angel," I blurted.

Nidhi said nothing, but there was a smallest of hesitations as he rose from the floor. I stood to face him. "You sent her gifts, didn't you? You met her here and started sending her gifts anonymously like the rest of those sickos."

"You've no proof of that," he said tersely.

"I'll get it."

"I am just a humble Guru with very little knowledge of worldly things like the Internet and privacy policies, but I think you will find that hard to do." He smirked at me and then clapped his hands sharply. Tom and Jerry came running from the entrance behind the larger shrine.

"And now, Mr. Riordan, I must ask you to leave. Tom and Jerry are here to escort you, and I think it safe to say that they will not permit you to pull your knife again."

HELL'S WEB STUDIO

THE UPPER DECK OF THE BAY BRIDGE was already becoming ensnarled with evening commuters by the time I made my way back to the City from Berkeley. I was tempted to knock off for the day, but the significance of the Amazon.com packages jostling around in the back seemed to be growing, and if anyone could tell me more about them, I figured it would be Caroline's best friend Monica.

Her neighborhood was full of the dented, high mileage cars and pick-ups of returning breadwinners, so I was forced to park several blocks away on Capp Street. Walking back to Folsom, a guy pushing a freezer cart with a bell wanted to sell me an ice cream, and another guy pushing a shopping cart full of electronics from the vacuum tube era, a Philco TV. I gave him a buck for trying.

The sandwich joint across the street was deserted, but when I came up to the apartment I found a woman on the stoop. She was wearing low rise cargo pants made of translucent white nylon with a matching jacket and, just at that moment, was bent over a duffle bag, rummaging through the contents for her keys, her lipstick or her Smith & Wesson .38—I didn't know which. Her underwear was clearly visible beneath her translucent clothing, but as she hunched over the bag, the fabric of her thong stretched well above the waistline of her pants, showing a "T" of crimson silk over dusky brown skin that was enough to make a judge gnaw his gavel.

She must have heard my nerve synapses popping because she stood abruptly and turned to peer down at me. The zipper of her jacket was open at both ends, revealing the lush valley of skin between her breasts at the top and the plain of her flat stomach—punctuated by a pierced navel—at the bottom. Her hair was short and black, her eyes big, green and provocative and her lips like a first kiss. She walked down the steps on pair of flimsy red sandals and stopped within a foot of me. The scent of sandalwood and musk carried across the last few inches, and when she smiled, it felt like a jolt from a cardiac paddle.

"Would you like to have sex with me?" she said, her voice cool and soft as the other side of the pillow.

I stared at her goggle-eyed.

"Don't think about it too much. It keeps the blood from the parts where it can do some good."

"Who wouldn't?" I finally blurted.

"Just checking." She made a slow pirouette and began to glide up the stairs once more.

"Hold on a minute."

"I was kidding you," she said without looking back. "Don't get your hopes up—or anything else."

I charged the steps and grabbed hold of her arm. She let out a shriek that they probably heard in Oakland.

"God damn it," I said. "Forget about the sex. Are you Monica Mapa?"

"Who wants to know?"

"August Riordan. I'm a private investigator, hired by Caroline's mother."

"Oh. You might have said so at the beginning."

"And you might not have been such a prick tease. It's going to get you in trouble."

She reached for her bag, giving me the full view down her jacket. "I know my men. You just aren't the sort." She winked at me. "Besides, Mrs. Stockwell called yesterday."

"You mean you knew all along—"

"Sure."

I ground my teeth in frustration. "I need to talk with you—inside."

She laughed and pushed her bag into my chest. "If you can find my keys."

As it turned out, there was no Smith & Wesson .38 in her bag, just a lot of skimpy Lycra gym clothes and some tennis shoes. I found the keys inside one of the shoes and handed them over, but not before I noticed that the fob on her key ring said "Goth Succubus" and had the web address **www.gothic-heaven-hell.com** printed below it. At that point I was certain I had come to the right place.

Her flat was on the second floor at the top of a steep flight of rickety stairs. The first thing I noticed was the lack of partitioning walls and scarcity of furniture—it looked like one of the trendy live/work lofts that are so common in the South of Market area of the city. The second thing I noticed was the video camera. It was on a tripod with a pair of flood lights mounted on either side, standing in front of a backdrop painted to look like a fiery inferno. There was a heavy oak chair with a throne-like appearance sitting between the camera and the backdrop, and off to right, a table with a Macintosh computer and a variety of peripherals. The camera was connected to the back of the computer by a thin cable.

If I still hadn't been able to figure it out, the walls were splattered with large color photographs of Monica in a risque she-devil costume with a pair of horns and bat wings sprouting from her head and shoulders respectively. In several photos she was sitting, lounging or otherwise adorning the throne-like chair with a cute little pitch fork that she held like a scepter.

"So this is hell," I said.

Monica giggled. "More like hell's web studio. You have to go online for the full experience."

"And where do I find heaven?"

Monica tossed her keys on the computer table and laminated herself into the throne. She swiveled her butt around so that her legs were dangling over the armrest. "Right next to hell, of course." Gesturing languidly to a pair of folded director's chairs, she said, "Park your ass in one of those."

I took one from where it was leaning against the wall and unfolded it by her throne. "I gather that Caroline plays ying to your yang."

"That's right. She's the angel and I'm the devil. Guess which one of us has more fun?"

"If what happened downstairs is a sample, you've a strange idea of fun."

She kicked off a sandal and pointed her painted toes at the ceiling. "You know you loved it."

"Okay. So tell me how it works—this heaven and hell thing. You guys make a web site and then what? What do you do with it?"

"We put content on it, silly. Don't you know anything? The web is full of content."

"What kind of content?"

"Media-rich content." She made media-rich content sound like it was a naughty French phrase. "Pictures of us, videos of us, stories about us, a guestbook, blogs, that sort of thing."

"Blogs?"

"Web logs. They're like an on-line diary."

"And the people that come to the site give you gifts?"

She ducked her lovely little chin up and down. "Mainly they give those to Caroline. I usually prefer cash." Then, after a moment's consideration, "But if you want to give me a gift, I would certainly accept it."

"I'll get back to you on that. And these people that give you things, you don't know any of them. They're total strangers?"

She laced her hands behind her head and looked at me coyly. "They may start out as strangers, but we get to know some of them a little better. We might talk to them over e-mail or instant messenging. But if they want to remain anonymous, they can. We understand that some of our fans are a little shy."

"Guys sitting in a darkened rooms getting their jollies over the Internet, shy? Whatever for?"

"Please. Be nice."

"Do any of these fans of yours try to do more than communicate electronically?"

"Oh, sometimes one of them will want to meet in person." Monica parted her lips and ran a mischievous tongue over them. "And sometimes I'll even agree to it."

I gripped the arms of the director's chair and leaned it forward on two legs. "You realize the risk you're taking?"

"Don't char your chalupa. I told you I know my men. I only do it when I'm sure about their motives and when there's—"

"Something in it for you."

She swung a hand out from behind her head and flipped it over like a game show model introducing the grand prize. "Something good in it for me."

I let the chair fall back. "Did Caroline ever meet one her fans?"

"It's possible. She talked about it once in a while, but I don't think she ever got a proposal that she really liked."

"But you're not certain?"

"We made our own decisions about what we would and wouldn't do. Caroline isn't the angel for nothing. She's much more conservative than me. If you're suggesting that she's been abducted by some weirdo she met through the site, I don't see it. But she might have got an offer for a trip from someone nice and decided to take it."

"And she wouldn't have told you about it?"

Monica stopped trying to use the chair for a couch and squirmed around to face me. "Maybe. Maybe not." She pushed the fabric of her jacket off her shoulder, exposing new vistas of exquisite, coffee-colored skin. "This synthetic stuff sure is itchy," she said in all innocence.

Maybe it was the painted flames behind her, but suddenly the room was getting very hot—and more than my chalupa was getting charred. "Cut that out," I said in a parched voice. "We'll take it as a given that you're the sexiest creature on earth."

"I'm so lacking in self-confidence. I need reinforcement."

"The hell you do. What you need is a baggy, floor-length housecoat from Sears Roebuck. Now, let's stay on topic. I think you're lying. I think you know exactly where Caroline is."

"Then you're wrong. I don't have any idea."

"Then why on earth aren't you worried about her?"

"Not being worried is different than knowing where she is." She aimed her brilliant smile at me like a spotlight—or a deathray.

I still didn't believe her, but something that had been poking at the edge of my consciousness burst through. "Caroline's family doesn't have any idea that she's got a web site, do they?"

She giggled. "Are you kidding? Her dad belongs in one of those caves with the petroglyphs in France. Caroline says he still does his police reports on a typewriter."

I did mine longhand, but I wasn't going to mention it. "And her mother?"

"Her mother has more than she can handle dealing with her dad. Especially after Quentin Jr. died. She hasn't had the energy or the will—or whatever the right word is—to be part of Caroline's life since then."

"Is Caroline trying to get back at her by going off with someone?"

Monica shrugged elaborately and the jacket fell back over her shoulder. "Now you're getting Freudian. How would I know? But I never said she had gone with anyone."

"Did her dad molest her?"

"Whoa—where'd you get that idea?"

It was my turn to shrug. "It came up." I looked past her to the inferno backdrop and then let my eyes wander around the apartment. It seemed cold, empty and comfortless. "What about you? Do your parents know you're doing this?"

"My parents haven't cared what I did since I got my belly button pierced."

"How old are you?"

"I'm not telling. Worried I'm too young for you?"

"Worry doesn't enter into it. But if you won't tell me, I have a foolproof cultural history question I can use to determine."

She crossed her legs and wiggled her butt delightedly around in the seat. "Oh goody. What is it? Was Paul McCartney ever part of a band? If I found a piece of the Berlin Wall would I return it? I've got those covered."

"No, it's simpler. What's a Datsun?"

She frowned. "That's pronounced daks-hund and it's a little wiener dog. What does that prove?"

"It proves you're 20 at most— and too young to be ... " I waved my hand around vaguely.

"You make it sound like prostitution. It's not. It's just a means to pay for college. Lots of people work their way through school."

"Like Honest Abe Lincoln."

"Exactly." She leered at me. "Except he didn't look as good in the devil suit."

"No, I imagine the halter top made him look flat." I ran my hand over my face and tried to think. Little came to me except that the skin on my chin was tender from my encounter with the ashram carpet. "Assuming that Caroline did go with someone she met from the site, it's likely she would have communicated with him initially by e-mail, right?"

"That's right. We put our address on the site so people can mail us."

"Different addresses or the same one?"

"Different. Caroline is on AOL. I'm with another ISP."

"I tried to get onto her computer yesterday, but it was password protected. You don't happen to know the password, do you?"

She made a little kicking motion at me with her bare foot. "Listen to you. I wouldn't tell you if I knew. That's invasion of privacy."

I growled and stood up to pull my wallet from my hip pocket. I extracted a card that wasn't too badly dog-eared and held it out. "I think you know a lot more than you're telling. You're convinced nothing bad has happened to her, but what if you're wrong? What if she's hurt or is being held against her will? Think about it and give me a call when you wise up."

She giggled and rose to take the card. She waved it like she was going to do some hocus-pocus, then lowered the waistband of her pants and slid my name, address and telephone number under her thong, right next to the skin of her abdomen. She watched my eyes track the card to its destination, then said:

"And why don't you come and visit me when *you* wise up, August. The address is easy to remember: www.gothic-heaven-hell.com. You'll see a whole new side of me." She released the waistband of her pants. "And by the way, if you like the thong, you can bid on it tonight on eBay."

MAN FROM INTERNATIONAL MALE

10:45 THE NEXT MORNING FOUND ME MUNCHING on a bagel with designer cream cheese at Chris Duckworth's kitchen table. He had his laptop out and was busy booting it up.

The bagel was good, but I was troubled by the topping. "Why is this cream cheese pink?" I asked between bites.

"It's gay." Chris was dressed in a sage-colored pant and shirt combo made of crinkly linen that he proudly pointed out in the *International Male* catalog the moment I walked through the door. It looked like it had been kept between the mattress and box springs of his bed, but the catalog seemed to suggest that the "texturing" had been done on purpose.

"No really," I said. "What's in it?"

"It's low fat strawberry honey cinnamon, okay?" The swelling around Chris's eye had gone down, so I could see the sarcastic glint in it as he turned to smirk at me. "If I'd known you were coming, I would have bought a tub of plain with extra cholesterol."

The laptop finished booting and Chris logged in and did some fiddling to get to the Internet. "Thanks to my neighbor's unsecured network, we've got an excellent wireless connection," he said. "Now what was the address again?"

I gave him the address of Caroline and Monica's web site and he typed it into the browser. The real estate of the welcome page was subdivided through the middle by a diagonal line. The lower portion of the page was engulfed in flames and featured a smiling picture of Monica in her she-devil outfit. Words in a cartoon balloon above her head urged us to give into temptation and click on her jeweled belly button to enter hell.

That was consistent with my expectations, but what appeared on the upper portion wasn't. Instead of a conventional representation of heaven with clouds, halos, harps, etc., there was a gloomy picture of a cemetery monument with Caroline leaning up against it. She wore a shiny black bustier with black gauntlets trimmed in gold and a long black and gold ruffled skirt. An elaborate pair of wings made of black feathers emerged from her shoulders and the black wig on her head draped hair across the monument, her arms and the wings. Her face was heavily made up with a pale white foundation, sharply contrasted with rouge and lipstick the color of week-old blood. The cartoon balloon above her head told us to click on the monument epitaph to join the angels in heaven.

Running below all of this was a warning in red text that the site contained full nudity and adult themes not suitable for children. We were further informed that we must be 18 or older to enter.

"Well," said Chris. "I guess that clears up any lingering doubts about which is more fun. It appears that heaven is full of sullen dead people who wear a lot of black, whereas the folks in hell make creative use of color, are better at accessorizing and are more well adjusted."

"Cut out the runway commentary and let's go in."

"Basement or attic?"

"Basement first."

Chris clicked on Monica's navel and the browser loaded with her not-so-private version of hell. There was a large picture of her sitting on her throne in front of the backdrop of flames, and prostrate on the floor around her were several other images of her superimposed on the original photograph to resemble worshiping subjects and/or souls in torment. The caption over the photograph read, "Caution: Extremely Addictive," and the fact that she had jettisoned the halter top to her she-devil costume did a lot to reinforce the argument.

"Very nice Photoshop work," said Chris.

"Yeah," I said in a thick voice. "Exactly what I was thinking."

Chris laughed. "I guess I know what you felt like when I was drooling over the models in the *International Male* catalog."

Chris scrolled the page down and a menu along the bottom came into view with entries for a free photo gallery, a pay-for-view gallery, a web cam section, a "Make a Donation" button and a link to auctions on eBay.

"You want to check out some of the other photos?" asked Chris. "Or maybe the web cam would be more to your liking?"

"I don't think my heart could take any more photos. I am curious about the web cam, though. Doesn't she have to be live in front of the camera for that to work?"

"Sure, but she might have archived some of the videos from earlier sessions. Let's find out."

Chris clicked the web cam menu button. A sparse page came up with the following message:

```
Monica is not holding court at present.
Come back at 5 PM to see her one hour
performance of I Dream of Goth Succubus.
Admission: $75.
```

"Hey, that's more than I make an hour," I said.

"But it's good value for the money. The original show was only a half hour—and black and white at that."

"Speaking of money, she told me that she didn't accept gifts like Caroline does—only cash. I guess that's what the 'Make a Contribution' button's for."

"Yep. I'm sure it links to a form to accept credit cards. There are also online services that let you give money anonymously so your name and address aren't available to the recipient."

"That sounds about right. She said their customers were shy." I pushed the bagel plate to the side and swept the crumbs that remained off the table.

Chris flinched. "Not on the floor, you bum. I just vacuumed." He reached down for the crumbs and hurried them out to the kitchen like he was disposing of nuclear waste.

When he returned, I said, "Let's check the eBay auctions. She told me that she was going to auction off her underwear. But I didn't think you could sell used clothing."

Chris laughed and clapped his hands. "A friend of mine who works there told me about this. eBay doesn't allow it, but people go around the restrictions. They list it as new—wink, wink—and all the perverts who have a fetish about worn underwear know what to look for in the description of the item. It's a sort of code."

He clicked on the auctions link, which brought up a new window with a list of current auctions for eBay seller: **goth_succubus**. There were five items for sale, all of them with current bids over $20. The newest listing was titled "Sexy Red Thong - new/unused" and had been posted the previous night.

"I hesitate to suggest this," I said. "But let's take a look at the first one."

"I always knew you were a panty-sniffer," said Chis glibly. I raised my fist at him Ralph Kramden-like and he squawked and twisted away from me in his chair, turning the laptop monitor so I couldn't see it. His face split in a huge grin as he read the listing. "Not only are you a panty-sniffer, but you're a love slave too. Check it out."

He turned the monitor back into view. The listing had a picture of the thong underwear lying in the seat of Monica's throne, and below that, the item description:

```
Hi! My name is Monica and I'm a college
student looking to make some extra cash.
I am selling a very sexy pair of my cute
```

```
thong panties, unused and unworn per eBay's
regulations. ;-)
     This is a private auction so my love
slaves feel safer, especially you, August!
     Visit me at www.gothic-heaven-hell.com.
```

"Enough of hell," I said. "I'm ready for heaven."

Chris shut down the eBay window and returned to the welcome page of the site. He clicked the granite monument and gothic heaven materialized before us. We stared at the monitor for a long moment, then Chris said:

"Are you sure you're ready?"

The picture at the top of the page was ample reason for doubt. An open-walled mausoleum surrounded by a fence of wrought iron pikes, it was home to a marble sarcophagus with an elaborate sculpture of the interred. He had apparently been a young man in his early 20s when he died, and his marble likeness was laid out on top of the sarcophagus as if to rest. Bending over him with a hand to his forehead and an expression of reverent concern was a statue of an angel—and mirroring the angel's pose on the other side, Caroline. The caption below the picture read, "Only those who abandon themselves to darkness, open up to the light." It was creepy as all get out and I couldn't help but wonder if it was intended to be emblematic of her brother's death.

When I didn't say anything, Chris cleared his throat a little self-consciously and began clicking through the menu items. The site was decidedly less commercial than Monica's, and while the pictures were in some ways more disturbing than the ones we'd seen on hers, none of them would be rated higher than PG-13. Several would probably fit into the "fetish" category, including a series of Caroline washing her hair and another of her rubbing lotion on her feet. In addition to the photo galleries, Caroline had a guestbook for visitors to post comments and a journal, or blog, as Monica had called it. Since I was particularly interested in clues to her visitors identity, I pointed Chris to the guestbook.

The entries in the guestbook were all posted anonymously or signed with *noms de plume* like the cards from the Amazon.com packages. A lot of the names were new to me—Raven, December Knight and Nick Knack—but I recognized one from before: Skinner's Pigeon. Mr. Pigeon's writings were more articulate than the others, which consisted mainly of one sentence proclamations of how great the site was or requests to satisfy more fetishes. An entry of his the week before Caroline's disappearance caught my eye:

```
Goth Angel,
    Without you my spirit is caged and
tortured like an animal in a lab
experiment. Do not abandon me! Answer my
pleas and return to earth where we may
commune once more.
    Your loving servant,
    Skinner's Pigeon
```

"Wow," said Chris. "Wonder how he pecked all that out?"

"Guess it's all a matter of conditioning."

"Very funny. Is it a clue?"

"I don't know. The timing is interesting and so is the fact that he suggests that they've communed—whatever that means." I waved my hand at the monitor. "Keep going."

We made a quick tour of Caroline's blog, but far from being a collection of the profound utterings of an other-worldly creature, the majority of the journal entries were complaints about work, annoying teachers at school and a head cold that wouldn't go away. Interspersed among the complaints were acknowledgements of gifts and compliments received, and one day she used the entry to answer questions from an admirer:

```
    How old were you when you had your first
kiss?
```

The first REAL kiss, when I really really liked him - 12yo.

Do you want kids?

I would love to, but at the same time, its a cold world, Ya know?

Do you think you are beautiful?

On the inside, I think I am...I don't care if I am outside anymore.

Who is your ideal man and does he have to be rich?

Good hearted, funny, talented, hard working, knows how to fix my car when it breaks down. *gfete* I don't care if he is rich, could care less about his money really.

Ever been in love?

I AM in love ;-)

Someone tells you a secret. Do you blab or keep it hush-hush?

Very hush-hush

Would you ever go nude on cam?

Nope...

"GFETE?" I asked.

"Grinning from ear to ear," said Chris. "Anything useful here?"

"The bit about being in love is interesting. Her mother said she thought that Caroline had a new boyfriend."

The final thing we checked was the link to her Amazon.com wish list. There were about 30 things on the list, and nearly all of them had already been purchased. The most recent items added were a collection of *Buffy the Vampire Slayer* videos and a book on fetish photography. At my urging, we put the *Buffy* videos in our shopping cart so I could see what it was like to do a transaction from the buyer's perspective. When we got to the checkout page and it was apparent there was no way to send the gift anonymously, I asked Chris about all the packages Caroline had received from "Private Buyer" from the covering address in New Jersey. He flipped back to the original page on Caroline's site and pointed to another link beside the wish list. It was labeled, "ProxyBuy" and was introduced with the caption, "If you want to give anonymously … "

"ProxyBuy is one of the services I was talking about earlier," he said. "You tell them what you want to buy from Amazon or wherever, and they get the item for you without revealing your identity to the retailer."

"What's in it for them?"

"They take a few extra bucks for each transaction. More if you want them to receive the merchandise for you and ship it to you in a plain brown wrapper."

"Sounds like a good scam. But that means if I do need to track down people who've given gifts to Caroline, I'll need to get the information from these ProxyBuy people."

He shook his head. "Good luck. Their whole business is founded on keeping identities private—like a numbered Swiss bank account. You'll need a court order at least."

"Swell," I said and pushed my chair back. "You doing anything vital for the next few hours?"

"I was going to look for jobs on Craigslist, but that could wait."

"I should think so. It's waited about 15 months now."

Chris stuck his tongue out. "You menial types in the low tech sector have no idea how hard this recession has hit. What do you have?"

I stood and smiled down at him. "Your mission, Mr. Duckworth, is to hack the computer of a teenage girl in the East Bay metropolis of Union City. Your cover will be that of an *International Male* model who has slept overnight in his clothes."

He rose wearily from the table. "Sometimes you're about as funny as a busted condom."

YOU ONLY HURT THE ONES YOU HUG

THIS TIME THE WORDS "FRUIT SALAD" DID not cross Ellen Stockwell's lips when she greeted me at the door. That was just as well because I wasn't sure how she and Chris were going to get on and he might have taken it as a crack. As it turned out, I needn't have worried.

"Ellen," I said, "I'd like you to meet Chris Duckworth. He's the, ah, computer expert I mentioned on the phone."

Ellen gave Chris her friendly, gap-toothed smile and reached out to take his hand. "Thank you for coming. I love your suit, by the way. Is it textured linen?"

Chris glared at me from under his eyebrows. "Yes it is," he said. "Good of you to notice. A lot of people don't appreciate textured fabrics."

"I'm sure it's just ignorance." She led us into the living room and stood by the Swedish, complete-assembly-required entertainment center-cum-bookshelf that dominated the back wall. She was dressed casually in jeans and a pullover sweater, but still managed to project a slim elegance. A smell of steam and hot fabric came from the back of the house, where I guessed she had been ironing. "Can I get you anything?"

"No, thanks," I said. "I'm going to get Chris started on Caroline's computer and then you and I can talk about what I've found out so far."

She clasped her hands in front of her. "Good. I'm encouraged you have news for us so quickly."

I held my face in a neutral expression that felt stiff and phoney. The news wasn't going to be any too encouraging when they got it. "Is the Lieutenant here, then?"

"He's—he's taking a nap like before. But I think it's best if you and I talk separately. I can pass everything on."

"Works for me."

"Good. Please go on back. I'll be in the sewing room when you need me."

Chris and I went past her to Caroline's bedroom. He whistled in mock appreciation when he got a peek at the decor and the mood lighting. "Transylvania meets the Orient with a bit of auto repair shop thrown in." He pointed at the Jim Morrison poster. "I do like Jim's pants, though."

"There's a surprise."

He moved over to the computer desk and switched on the lamp. "And I recognize the Chinese screen from the pictures on her web site. She used it as a backdrop for a lot of the stills and web cam stuff."

I grunted my agreement. "What do you think about the computer? Are you going to be able to get around the password protection?"

"Let's see what OS she's got on it," He pressed the power button and the machine began to whir softly. A moment later, a Microsoft XP logo snapped onto the screen. "XP. It could be very easy if she hasn't set the administrator's password. We can log in as the admin and remove the password to her regular account. If she has set it, I'll just have to use some of the tools in my little bag of tricks." He held up a canvas bag of CDs and floppy disks he had brought. "Ten minutes tops, either way."

I sat on the futon and watched while Chris did his magic. It turned out to be as easy as predicted. Before the computer finished booting, he hit one of the function keys along the top of the keyboard. He put the computer into something called "safe mode" and logged on as the administrator—without having to enter a password.

After he removed the password for her regular account, he started the computer again.

"There you go. We're logged in as goth_angel and we have access to everything on the computer."

I stood to get a closer look. "Including e-mail?"

Chris clicked on the icon for Caroline's e-mail program. After a moment's pause, it loaded in the middle of the screen, partially obscuring the black-and-white photo of a cemetery angel on her desktop. The program said there were 157 messages in her in-box, but almost immediately another dialog box popped up to tell us the program was downloading 452 more.

I tapped the screen. "What's going on?"

"Cable modem. It gives her always-on access to the Internet. She'd need something like that for the web cam or it would be too slow. The program is getting all the mail she missed while she's been gone."

The in-box filled with messages the way a stopped-up sink fills with water. I recognized some of the names from her guestbook, but there were a lot of new ones and it was clear it was going to take a very long time to wade through them.

"We'll be here all day."

"Yep. Sounds like we should make our order to go." He reached into his bag to take out a package of CDs. "Let's burn some CDs with the stuff we want and I can look it over later at home."

"Great, but how do we know what's important?"

"Shouldn't be that hard. We'll get all the e-mail, including everything she's filed away in other folders. She must be staging the web site on this computer, so we'll take a copy of that—"

"Wouldn't it be the same as what's out on the Internet?"

"Probably. But there might be some new things she hasn't uploaded yet. We can also take any other interesting files I find, like word processing documents, bookmarks or Internet browsing history. And if I can find the password to her Internet account, we might also be able to get access to the web logs for her own site. They might tell us more about who's going there."

"I knew there was a reason I hired you."

Chris pressed a button on the front of the computer. The CD drawer opened and he dropped a blank disk onto the tray. "Now all you need is a reason to pay me."

"Wouldn't want to spoil your unemployment eligibility. I'm going to talk to Ellen."

I went back up the hall to the sewing room, which was between Caroline's and the master bedroom. It had obviously been Quentin Jr.'s when he was alive, and a number of the furnishings—the double bed, a bookcase full of comic books, a framed varsity letter in track and a Union City High School pennant—dated from his occupancy. Ellen had put a flouncy yellow comforter on the bed, added some matching throw pillows and moved in a small desk and a sewing machine. I had to duck beneath a tension rod full of perfectly ironed shirts and pants hanging in the doorway to enter. The ironing board was set up at the foot of the bed and Ellen looked up and smiled as she ran the iron over the back pockets of a pair of khaki pants.

"Sorry about the laundry," she said. "We could talk in the living room if you like."

"This is fine." I nodded at the ironing board. "I never can get the pockets right. They always look like the Shroud of Turin when I'm done."

She laughed. "The trick is to turn the pants pocket inside out. But I don't imagine that you spend much time ironing your pants."

"That bad?"

"No, I meant that you probably have them done."

I sat down on the edge of the bed. "You're right. There's a dry cleaners on the first floor of my building."

"There is one thing, though. If you don't mind my mentioning it."

"What?"

"You have grass stains on your suit coat from when you tussled with Quentin. You ought to have that cleaned soon or they may never come out."

I grinned. "At least I don't smell of tequila."

"Well … maybe a little. I think some of it must have gotten on your coat." She glanced quickly at me and then took a deep interest in aligning the inseams of the pants.

I held the lapel of my jacket up to sniff at it, but the odor eluded me. Ellen laughed. "I'm sorry. I didn't mean to make you feel uncomfortable."

"Don't worry about it." I took the suit coat off and laid it down on the bed. "Look, Ellen, speaking of uncomfortable, I need to tell you something about Caroline that I don't think you know."

She stopped with the iron mid-stroke. "What is it?"

I held my hands up. "It's nothing bad in and of itself. But I think it could be related to her disappearance. She has a web site."

"A web site?"

"Have you read those articles about teenage girls and young women who put up sites about themselves? They usually have pictures, diaries and sometimes live video. I think even Mike Doonesbury's daughter had one in the comic strip."

She set the iron down with exaggerated care. "Cam sites is what they call them. And most of them aren't as innocent as the one in the comic strip. What are you telling me? That Caroline was posing nude on the Internet?"

"No, she wasn't. But it's a little more complicated than that. There are actually two sites. Caroline's and Monica's. Caroline's is pretty tame, but —"

Without waiting for me to finish, she dodged out from behind the ironing board and shot under the laundry in the doorway. She was all the way to Caroline's room by the time I got up from the bed and poked my head out to look. I started to follow, but I heard her say, "Show me" to Chris in a sharp voice and I lost my nerve. It would be hard enough for her to look at it without me standing over her shoulder.

I went back into the room and shut off the iron. I didn't think laundry was going to be a priority any longer. I returned to my seat on the bed and sorted my fingers for what seemed like fifteen minutes. Then I saw her go past, toward the kitchen, and a minute later she came back into the room, dabbing at her red-rimmed eyes with a paper towel. She flopped down next to me and we sat side-by-side without saying anything—or even looking at each other. Suddenly the will seemed to drain out of her and she slumped back into the pillows, sobbing as she stared at the ceiling. I felt about as useless as a conductor on a museum train.

"I know it's a hard thing to discover about Caroline," I said finally. "But it does represent progress in the investigation. We may be able to find a link between her disappearance and someone—someone who visited the site."

There was a stirring beside me, but no other response.

"Ellen?"

"What do you want me to say? That I'm happy to hear that my daughter may have been abducted by some weirdo she met over the Internet?" Her voice was hard and raspy.

I patted the bed between us, still somehow reluctant to look at her and even more reluctant to touch her. "We don't know that. It could be that she went of her own volition. Or it could be the site has nothing to do with anything. I need to pursue it, though, and I need for you to be aware that I'm pursuing it."

"Consider me aware. Consider me painfully aware." She blew her nose quietly. "I've learned more about my daughter in the last few days than I learned in the last few years. And I'm starting to get a picture of myself as a mother that is not very flattering."

"Look, I only know as much about your life as you've told me. But it seems to me that you've had more than your share of crises. Given everything you've had to deal with, it's not surprising that you have less than perfect knowledge of your daughter's life. Besides, she's over 18. You can't control her any longer. She's going to do many things that you won't know about—much less approve of. That's all part of the package."

The silence that followed seemed to swallow up my rejoinder. I had the odd feeling that I hadn't spoken at all, merely thought the words. Then there was a little sniff beside me. "You're a very kind man, August," she said softly. "But you're a liar. I have ignored Caroline—and Quentin too. After our son died, I just went through the motions. I'm like one of those books you buy in stationary stores that are all blank inside. It's up to you to fill them in, but I no longer have the energy."

I finally turned to look at her, but as I did, I caught a blur of motion by the door. Chris had thrust his head between a cambric shirt and second pair of khaki pants. He mouthed the words, "I'll wait in the car," and pointed down the hallway. I nodded and waved him on.

Ellen sighed heavily and pushed herself up from the pillows. The yellow fabric was tinged dark with her tears. "How do you like the middle-aged melodramatics? You must rue the day I walked in your office."

"I might have rued it—to use your melodramatic term—the day it happened, but I haven't since." I smiled and reached over to smooth a strand of hair from her face. We looked at each other like we shared a guilty secret, then—impulsively—she put her arms around me. I pulled her to her feet, enfolding her in an embrace whose ardor surprised the both of us. Her head felt just right against my shoulder, her breasts warm and soft against my chest. It was like coming in from the storm.

She turned her face up to me. I kissed her tentatively. Then a long slow deliberate kiss that didn't fool around. Her mouth opened and she entwined a leg around my calf, pressing her pelvis against mine. We held the clench until I thought I would pass out or spontaneously combust and then a shiver ran through her and she drew her head away.

"What do I do, August?" she whispered.

I made a ssshing noise and pulled her closer, but suddenly her body went rigid in my arms. She pushed me away, a look of absolute despair in her eyes.

I forced myself to look up to the door, knowing all the while what I would see.

Stockwell peered at us from between the laundry. He cleared his throat wearily. "So that's the way it is." He disappeared from view and bumped his way down the hall. A moment later, the door to the master bedroom pulled shut with a dry click.

"Oh, Jesus," said Ellen. She stood stock-still, a terrified spectator to an automobile wreck.

I reached for her, but she twisted away. She put her hands out in a stay back gesture. "You've got to leave," she said. "Right now."

"But Ellen, I can't leave you alone with him. He might hurt you."

"That's his right—he's my husband. You're an employee." Her chest heaved in a panicked breath that bordered on hyperventilation. "Please leave us."

"Don't be ridiculous. A marriage license isn't carte blanche for abuse."

"Go," she wailed. "Just go."

I nodded without saying anything and dragged myself away from there. I felt like a rusty nail in a piece of scrap wood.

NO DEFENSE AGAINST A CROW BAR

CHRIS ASKED ME WHERE THE HELL MY jacket was when I returned to the car, but I didn't go back to the house for it and I didn't answer his question. I didn't do anything but drive. I drove to his apartment, I drove to a liquor store and I drove home.

Since I was going for volume not flavor, I decided at the liquor store that there was no use bothering with an expensive brand of bourbon. I picked one of the rotgut varieties named after an old southern gentleman—no doubt the guy whose name was on the Kentucky State Hospital liver ward—and for the first third of the bottle I did miss the smooth, mellow taste of my usual Maker's Mark, but after that the distinction seemed illusory.

When I woke up the next morning in the middle of my living room floor, however, the distinction reasserted itself with a passion. There's an old Russian saying that there's no defense against a crow bar, and I had to agree because I seemed to have about ten inches' worth wedged into a tender spot in my occipital lobe. The full inventory of complaints included the cold sweats, the whirlies and a taste in my mouth reminiscent of the collection tray of a bug zapper. All in all, I felt about as vigorous as a beached jellyfish.

I rasped into work at about a quarter before noon and found the first thing of the day I could be thankful for: Bonacker was not there to further torment me. Gretchen smiled knowingly as I navigated the path to my office by steadying myself against the furniture enroute like an eskimo jumping from ice floe to ice floe.

"Had a little too much fun last night, bright eyes?" she inquired with a brutal cheerfulness.

I wallowed past her to the relative comfort and stability of my desk chair. I set the super jumbo-sized cup of Saeed al-Sahhaf's coffee I was carrying on the blotter and then laid my head beside it. "Fun's not the right word," I said with my eyes pinched shut. "You could try penance or self-anesthesia. I'm not entirely sure which was the motivating factor at this point."

"I see. I've always admired the mature way you deal with personal problems."

"Thank you. Is there anything else before I set the room to spinning?"

"Yes, you have two phone messages." She put a couple of pink message slips down in front of my nose. "The first is from Ellen Stockwell and the second is from Victor Lane."

I pawed at the slips, but couldn't bring myself to lift my head off the desk to read them. "I'm having a little trouble focusing right now. Anything specific you can pass on?"

"Not really. Apart from the fact they both wanted you to call them as soon as you got in. Of course, that was several hours ago."

"Couldn't be helped. I was in conference with the living room floor. Would you be a pal and get Ellen Stockwell on the line for me? Might as well get that one over with before the full effects of the anesthesia wear off."

"Expecting bad news?" I felt her at my side and then I felt a gentle hand rubbing my forehead.

"Expecting to be fired—or worse. God that feels wonderful."

She quit with the rubbing and tweaked the tip of my nose. "When are you going to learn, August?"

I heard footsteps going away, and a moment later, the phone detonated near my ear. I lunged for it and after a bit of fumbling managed to sit upright with the receiver cradled in close proximity to the prescribed location. I didn't dare open my eyes, though.

"August? Are you there?"

"Yes, Ellen, I'm here."

"Are you okay? You sound ill."

"I'm fine. A little hungover is all."

She took a moment to absorb that. "Is every man in my life an alcoholic?"

"I think you made it pretty clear that I'm not in your life. Employee was the term you used."

"That was wrong of me, but given the circumstances, I hope you understand." She waited for me to say something, but I didn't oblige. "You left your jacket at the house."

"I know. Throw it out or donate it or something. It's not worth bothering about."

"I took it to the dry cleaners. I'll get it back to you once it's cleaned."

I covered the receiver and tried to clear the barnacles from my throat. The pressure only made my head hurt worse.

"Hello?" she prompted.

"Sorry. I was dispatching a pink elephant. Thank you for cleaning the jacket."

A long, thin sigh came over the line. "This is much harder than I thought it would be."

"Perhaps that wasn't a realistic expectation. How did it go after I left?"

"Okay. Quentin was very drunk. He was asleep on the bed when I got back to the room. I don't think he even remembers."

"I see."

"August," she said with a new exasperation. "We are not going to be involved. I'm not going to cheat on my husband. For you or any other man."

"Right. But you still want me to find your daughter."

"I think you are feeling awfully sorry for yourself this morning. You're acting as if I've manipulated you somehow. As it turns out, I don't need you to look for Caroline. That's why I'm calling. She came home last night."

I prized open my eyes and sat up in the chair. "Is she okay? Where was she?"

"She's fine. She came back late last night and we haven't had much time to talk. She said she went somewhere with a friend—a real friend. Not someone from … "

"The web site."

"Yes. I don't know all the details, but she said they decided to drive cross-country on a lark. A voyage of discovery, she called it."

The bright light from the ceiling fixture was burning a hole straight through my retina into my cerebral cortex, but I still had enough brain cells left to register skepticism. "Ellen, that sounds exactly like something she would say if she *had* been with someone from the web site. What did she use for spending money? Why didn't she tell you she was going on a trip? Why didn't she tell *anyone*?"

"I'm not going to debate this with you, but she mentioned that she had told Monica where she was going and she said that she didn't plan to be gone as long as she was. There's no excuse for it, of course, but I'm inclined to forgive her. If this whole experience has taught me anything, it's that I haven't understood the real impact her brother's death has had on her. I've got to get back into her life. This is a wake-up call for me and I'm going to treat it as such."

"If it's a wake-up call, then you need to start by finding out where she really was. She's lying to you."

"Stop it. I'm not going to talk about this anymore." She paused, and then continued in a calmer voice, "I want you to keep the retainer. You were very kind to take this on in the first place, and you've been a real friend to me, even in the short time I've known you. I feel I owe you that much at least."

"Are you buying me off?"

"You seem determined to paint everything in the worst possible light this morning. I told you it is not possible for us to have a romantic relationship. And now I don't think we should have any sort at all."

"It's not that, Ellen. You're right—I do feel an attraction to you. But there's something very fishy about Caroline's story. I think you should let me keep working it to find out what really happened. Otherwise, you're just putting your head in the—"

"August?"

"Yes."

"I'm going to hang up now. Goodbye. Goodbye and thank you."

The line clicked off. I slammed the receiver into the cradle and slumped back onto the blotter. It was a good half hour before I could work up the interest or the energy to return Victor's call. When I did, it was a very short conversation. Hilma came on the line to tell me that Victor had been beaten and robbed and would I get down there right away.

PROFESSOR HUBBA
AND THE POTATO PIE

"**Y**OU LOOK WORSE THAN ME, BOY," SAID Victor from atop a mountain of pillows stacked against the headboard of his bed. A butterfly closure held the edges of a shallow cut over his eyebrow and an Ace bandage circumnavigated his spindly wrist, but he seemed in good spirits and his color was certainly better than mine.

"That's not right, Victor," said Hilma. "You should thank the man for coming instead of antagonizing him." She plunked herself down in a birds-eye maple rocker at the foot of the bed. I stood frowning beside her.

The dresser and the bed were also birds-eye maple, and together with the braided oval rug and the pair of deco torchiere floor lamps that flanked the headboard, the furnishings betrayed the advancing age of their owners. I flashed on the disquieting image of the entire lot on display in an estate sale and my mood became even darker.

"What happened?" I said sharply.

Victor grimaced, misunderstanding the reason for my tone. "We don't want to be a bother, August. This seems to be in your line, so we thought you might be able to help. But if you're too busy or don't feel comfortable, just say so."

"I want to help, Victor. Just tell me what happened."

Victor glanced at Hilma, seeking support or approval. She waved her hand impatiently. "This was yesterday afternoon," he said. "Hilma had gone out to do the shopping, so I had the place to myself. I was watching TV in the living room when the doorbell rang. I got up to answer the door, and when I pulled it open, I found ... " His voice trailed off.

"Just tell the man, will you?" said Hilma.

"A guy in a ski mask."

"You didn't look through the peephole to see who was there?" I asked.

"I can't see through that fiddly little hole. Besides, I thought it was her, left her damn keys behind again."

"What next?"

"I tried to close the door, but of course he wasn't having any. He shoved it back in my face and knocked me over. Cut my forehead on the latchbolt and sprained my wrist, trying to break my fall. You know what the bastard did then?"

"What?"

"Trussed me up with duct tape and locked me in the closet. Pulled off my leg for good measure and taped it onto the good one. Said it wouldn't be so easy to lose that way."

"Did you recognize his voice—or anything else?"

Victor glanced at Hilma again. "That's going to take some explaining."

"All right. We'll get to that later. What'd he take?"

Up until this point, Victor had told the story in a breezy unaffected manner, but now his voice became thick with emotion. "Took my instruments—Baby and the other. Took most of my autographed pictures. Took my French medal and the one you brought from SF State."

Hilma eased herself out of the rocker and went over to sit on the edge of the bed. I could see that it wasn't a comfortable perch for her arthritic joints, but she made no complaint. She just took hold of

Victor's hand and clasped it tight to her breast. Victor's lower lip began to tremble. He stared down the bed quilt as he fought to control it.

Theft of the instruments—particularly the Begliomini bass—I could understand. Theft of the photographs and medals I could not. They would not fence well because of their tie to Victor and their low intrinsic value. Either the thief was very cruel or very stupid. Given the way the thing was handled, I was inclined to believe he was a lot of both.

I shifted my weight, making my old wingtips squeak. "I know how much those things mean to you, Victor, and I want to help in any way I can. But we're much better off going to the police with this. They have a whole system for recovering stolen goods. And they may know of other robberies in the area that are tied to this one."

"We can't go to the police," said Hilma.

"Why not?"

Victor kept his gaze locked on the snowflake pattern of the quilt, but Hilma looked me square in the eye. "Because our grandson did this, August," she said grimly. "Our grandson."

"He was the one in the ski mask?"

Victor swallowed hard, his adam's apple rising and falling like a creaky freight elevator. "No. But I'm certain it was his friend Jayson. I recognized his voice and his build. And I'm just as certain I heard him talking to my grandson after he locked me in the closet."

"Have you confronted him about it?"

"He's not exactly what you call accessible. He doesn't have a phone and the last address Martha—that's his mother—has for him is one of them residential hotels in the Tenderloin."

I took hold of the back of the rocker to steady myself. The cheap bourbon was still working its magic on my inner ear. "Martha's your daughter?"

"That's right," said Hilma.

"What does she say about it?"

Hilma placed Victor's hand in her lap and stroked the back of it. "Sorry is what she says, and not much else. She hasn't had control of that boy for years. Not since he joined the gang and got into drugs."

"You think he took the stuff to get money for drugs?"

"Of course."

"And you'd like me find him and get everything back—without involving the police."

Victor nodded. "That's about the size of it. I know it's hard to believe, August, but he's fundamentally a good boy. I don't want him getting into any more trouble. I think if you knew him, you'd feel the same way. He's one of us."

"One of us?" There was no hiding the puzzlement in my voice.

Victor laughed. "A jazz musician. One of the best young horn players I ever heard." He gave me a sly smile. "Now just exactly what did you think I meant?"

It hurt my head to grin, but I did it anyway. "Stamp collector," I said. "I thought you meant he was a stamp collector. What's his name?"

"Reggie Lane. His father never married Martha, so ... "

"I understand. Do you have a picture I can borrow?"

Hilma pointed to the highboy dresser. "There's one of him in the gold frame there. You can take that."

I took the picture down from the dresser and examined it. It wasn't the best shot in the world for my purposes. In the first place, it had been taken from the side, and in the second, part of Reggie's face was covered by the hooded sweatshirt he wore. In spite of all that, he looked to be a handsome devil. Chestnut brown eyes with long lashes, brilliant white teeth beneath a trumpeter's soulful lips and Victor's high cheekbones added up to the sort of face that would launch a thousand schoolgirl fantasies. I dropped the photo into my jacket pocket.

"How about the name of the hotel. Do you know that?"

"It's the Galt," said Victor, and there was something funny in his voice as he said it.

"Not the one—"

"Yes," said Hilma. "That one."

"Swell."

Hilma offered to pay me then, but I told them that I'd just been gifted $2,000 for two days' work, and besides, their money was no good with me. I left after assuring them I would do the best for them that I could, and Victor—at least—seemed comforted by that. I think Hilma shared my unspoken concern that the money from his basses had already gone up Reggie's crack pipe.

When the restored version of *Vertigo* premiered in San Francisco several years back, the audience laughed when Jimmy Stewart's character referred to the Mission District as "skid row." There are certainly some unsavory places in the Mission—such as the apartment building Monica Mapa lived in—but for good or ill, the dot-com boom brought gentrification to the area and there are many more clubs, swank eateries, software factories and restored Victorians owned by yuppies with BMWs.

No, when your modern day San Franciscan refers to skid row, he is almost always talking about the Tenderloin. And when he talks about residential hotels in the Tenderloin—particularly notorious residential hotels—he is almost always talking about the Galt. The Galt was the scene a of multiple-murder-suicide when a long-time resident went postal after being jostled in the hallway. He gunned down the jostler and three other tenants who had the misfortune to be handy. He finished the business by going into his room and turning the gun on himself.

The hotel had been "under renovation" for years. The awning over the entrance had been stripped down to rusty metal I-beams that stuck out from the building like the skeleton of a hand. Plywood sheeting boxed off the front doors and someone had used orange spray paint to draw a long, wavering arrow that pointed to a ragged gap in the sheeting that looked like a human-sized mouse hole. "Enter" was sprayed next to it.

I ducked into the gap and followed a series of switchbacks in a plywood tunnel until I was deposited into the space they used for a lobby. The carpet had been ripped up, exposing a bare concrete floor pockmarked with six-inch craters. The only furniture was a pair of saw horses with a two-by-four laying across it, the only light fixture a low watt bulb hanging from the ceiling by a frayed wire. The Pine-Sol and mildew smell in the air was as stifling as dust beat from a rug. I went up to the reception desk and nodded to a fat guy in a Hawaiian shirt who sat behind a reinforced Plexiglas window.

"Can you tell me what room Reggie Lane is in?" I asked.

He put down the tattered Matt Helm paperback he was reading and pushed up the brim of his porkpie hat with a plump forefinger. "If I could," he said into the speaker hole, "it wouldn't be a room in this hotel."

"How long ago did he check out?"

He made a wheezy-sounding chuckle. "The only thing he checked out was the sidewalk. We evicted his ass last week."

"You got a forwarding address?"

He reached below the counter for one of those ersatz apple pies from McDonalds, shook it part way out of its cardboard sleeve and took a bite. He munched thoughtfully while he looked me over. "Who wants to know exactly?"

"A friend."

"The only friends Reggie has are drug dealers and gang-bangers. You don't exactly fit the profile."

"Okay, then I'm a private investigator hired by his family."

"And you're just trying to find him to let him know about his big inheritance."

I grinned. "I read somewhere that those McDonalds pies are actually filled with potatoes."

"Fine by me. Think I'd eat these things if I actually liked apples? But that's kinda beside the point, isn't it? You were going to tell me what your interest in Reggie is."

I took a twenty dollar bill from my wallet and slipped it part way into the metal tray beneath the Plexiglas. "How about I just make a contribution to the apple pie fund? Assuming, that is, that you have something helpful to tell me about his whereabouts."

He glanced at the money and then inhaled another third of the pie. "You're not going to do anything serious are you?" he said with his mouth full. "Just roust him a little maybe?"

"I wasn't kidding about the family. He stole some valuable stuff from his grandfather. All I want to do is get it back."

"Okay. I don't have an address for him. Mail forwarding is not one of the many services we offer here at the Galt. But I can tell you the most likely place to find him."

"Where?"

"Sooner or later you'll find him with his dealer. Dude by the name of Professor Hubba. He lives in the projects on The Point."

"Hunters Point?"

"That's right. He's in one of the units on the hill behind the PG&E plant, somewhere along Middle Point Road."

I pulled the twenty back. "That's not very useful. There's at least a dozen complexes out there. I'm not going to get very far knocking on doors asking for Professor Hubba."

He snorted. "Drop the professor if that's too formal for you. Just say you're looking for hubba."

Hubba was a slang term for crack cocaine, and I was quite sure the predominantly African American residents of The Point would not take kindly to a pasty-faced Irish detective going door-to-door asking for crack. I got my wallet out and went through the motions of putting the twenty back. "Guess you'd rather make jokes than money."

"Hold on. I can give you more than that."

"What?"

"I can describe him for you. He's a tall, well-built guy with a goatee. He usually wears a gold chain with gold dog tags and a red floppy hat with the brim folded up. And he's got a glass eye."

"Better. But what's his real name?"

"Don't know it. I do know his ride, though. Stands out from three blocks away. It's a Boss Mustang from '69 or '70. It's in cherry condition and it's painted bright yellow. And get this: he's got a pair of stuffed yellow tigers in the rear window of the car. You can't miss it."

I took the twenty out of my wallet again and flipped it through the slot. He palmed it immediately and it disappeared into the breast pocket of his Hawaiian shirt. "You got anything else on him?" I asked.

He smiled and dispatched the final segment of the pie. The red cardboard sleeve went into a trash can behind him that was already overflowing with red cardboard sleeves. "Nope. You pumped me dry."

I stared at him for a moment, trying to decide if I'd just thrown my money away the way he'd thrown away the sleeve. "All right," I said. "Say hello to Matt for me."

He nodded and picked up the paperback. "Watch your back now," he said.

CLAIM JUMPING
AT THE GOLDEN STATE

THE SUGGESTION TO WATCH MY BACK DID not fall on deaf ears, but upon reflection, I decided that it had fallen on under-armed and under-medicated ones. Before venturing out to The Point I went back to my apartment to get my 9mm Glock auto-matic—and swallow half the remaining aspirins in my medicine cabinet.

I had a permit to carry a concealed weapon—a CCW in police parlance—but it had not come easy. San Francisco is the toughest city in California—if not America—in which to be granted a CCW permit. There were only five permits issued to non-law enforcement personnel in the city, and I was not one of them. I had "worked around" the problem by finding a more accommodating sheriff in a rural county, contributing to his reelection campaign and renting a P.O. box to establish some semblance of legal residence.

I washed the aspirins down with a toot of Maker's Mark, filled my hip flask with more of the "hair of the dog" and also equipped myself with a can of SpaghettiO's with franks. There's nothing like American comfort food on a stakeout.

I got the Galaxie out of the garage and went down 6th Street to the on-ramp for Highway 280 South. I jumped off at the Caesar Chavez exit, turned on 3rd Street and cruised through an industrial area of warehouses, machine yards and abandoned grain elevators. At Evans I went east and crossed the border into the Hunters Point neighborhood.

Surrounded by water on three sides, Hunters Point is an inflamed appendix of land that juts out into the Bay from the southeast corner of San Francisco. But more than just water surrounds it. Thanks to the EPA superfund site at the old Hunters Point Naval Shipyard and the belching smokestacks and wastewater of the local PG&E plant, it's surrounded by toxic pollutants as well. Residents are warned not to eat fish caught in the area due to dangerously high levels of DDT, dioxin, PCB and mercury, and the rates of asthma, heart disease and cancer in the community are among the highest in the state. Add to that a long-running gang war between the West Point Mob—who controlled the area around Middle Point and West Point Roads where Professor Hubba apparently made his home—and the Big Block Gang—who claimed the rest of the district—and you had a particularly unhealthy place to live.

I turned on Middle Point Road, just before the squat, medieval-looking buildings and corroded metal smokestacks that comprised the PG&E facilities. The road climbed steeply, affording an excellent view of the Bay to the east that was obstructed only by the high-tension power lines running out from the plant. I passed the first of the San Francisco Housing Authority complexes—a plank wood bunker painted industrial green—and almost immediately spotted the Professor's car parked along the other side of the road. It was everything the guy at the Galt had said it would be, right down to the pair of stuffed tigers crouching in the back window.

I kept going until I came to West Point road and did an awkward three-point turnaround in front of a group of young black men who scowled at me and the sound of the Galaxie's growling power steering motor. I coasted down the hill again to a spot about three car lengths in front of the Boss Mustang and pulled to the side. My strategy was to wait for the Professor to come back to his car and brace him if circumstances permitted; if not, I would tail him to wherever he was going. Assuming, of course, that he ever came out to the car in the first place.

I tuned the radio to the one remaining jazz station in the area and opened the SpaghettiO's. I had decided some time ago that they, like English ale, taste best when served at room temperature. I was about a third of the way through the can, and feeling about the best I had all day, when a diesel bus came groaning up the hill and deposited two men at the stop across the way.

They were dressed nearly identically in oversized 49ers jerseys, baggy pants and unlaced Air Jordans the size and shape of moon boots. Neither of them fit the description of Professor Hubba. They started up the hill, but the taller of the two spotted me in the car and elbowed his buddy. He nodded in my direction. They ambled across the street in a negligent walk that came straight out of Akira Kurosawa's *Seven Samurai*. The shorter guy, who was wearing a baseball cap with the bill twisted back to about 4 o'clock, rapped on the window. I pressed the electric window button, and for once the window rolled all the way down without stopping. I wasn't sure that was a good thing.

"What you doing here, Buster Brown?" said the taller one. When he spoke, I could see his uppers were capped in gold.

"Eating lunch."

They exchanged looks. "Eating lunch?" said gold teeth. "Don't you have no place better to go?"

"I'm on a break." I gestured with my spoon. "From the plant."

The lie might have made my presence seem more plausible, but it didn't do anything to improve my popularity. The PG&E plant was universally despised in the neighborhood. "That plant is racist," said the guy with the cap.

"That's right," said gold teeth. "Don't you know better than to come up here, eating your Skettios, admiring the damn view? This here is Hunters Point." He leaned into the window. "And Hunters Point got the most notorious niggers that *is* in Frisco."

"San Francisco," I said automatically.

"Who are you? Herb Fucking Cain?"

"No. He's dead."

Gold teeth took hold of the door handle and jiggled it open. "Maybe you'd like to keep his cracker ass company?"

I put the can of SpaghettiO's down on the dashboard and pondered my options. If I pulled out the Glock, it was as good as driving through the neighborhood with a bull horn announcing my presence. But these guys weren't going to let me stay without a fight—which would be just as bad—so the only choice seemed to be to pack it in. I reached for the keys and turned the engine over. "Guess I'll be leaving then," I said cheerfully.

Gold teeth gave me a gleaming smile. "Guess you will be." He shoved the door closed.

They stepped back from the car, expecting me to put it in drive and slink away, but what they didn't expect was the San Francisco Police cruiser that pulled up behind them. That gave me something to smile about—which I did—and then I pointed at the car behind them.

The guy with the baseball cap figured it out first. He tugged at gold teeth's jersey and the two of them ducked behind the Galaxie and melted quickly up the hill. I caught a glance of gold teeth flipping me off in the rear view mirror as they went.

The surprising thing was that the cop in the cruiser seemed not to have noticed. He was looking down the hill at another cruiser that was coming around the wide curve in front of the PG&E plant. I rolled up my window, shut the motor off and went back to my lunch. After a moment, the other cruiser came up the hill and pulled to a stop beside the first, effectively blocking the traffic in either direction. Both cops rolled their windows down and started gabbing across the narrow space that separated them. Cop car 69 was what I called the maneuver.

They stayed locked in their embrace for about 15 minutes until another bus came down from the hill. The driver honked at them, and after a last few vital words were exchanged, they rolled in opposite directions. The SpaghettiO's were long since gone, so I took a snort from the flask. Then I played with the buttons on the radio, pressing them randomly in the middle of ads to see if I could splice together two commercials in humorous ways. The best I managed was a combination of a dating service spot and a pitch for the SPCA: "Want to spice up your love life? ... adopt a homeless animal!"

Eventually, I tired of that and let my head fall back against the rest. I strained to keep an eye propped open and focused on the rear view mirror, but the car was pleasantly warm, my stomach was full and the prior night's overindulgence had sapped my energy. I drifted off to sleep.

The only thing that saved me was Professor Hubba's aftermarket car alarm. I don't know how long I was out, but the next thing I remember was the sound of a loud chirp. Coming down the hill, the Professor had evidently used his remote to disable the alarm. I sat up in my seat with a start and blinked the crust out of my eyes in time to see a well-built guy with a floppy red hat yank open the door to the Mustang. Before he got into the car, he made a stealthy move behind his back to produce a gleaming automatic, which he slipped under the driver's seat.

The Boss Mustang switched like a light bulb and idled with a deep rumble that I could feel 20 yards away. The Professor gunned the motor once and then pulled out from the curb to rocket down the hill, the car's distinctive triple-bar taillights glowing bright red almost immediately as he braked at the intersection with Evans. He turned left and barrelled out of sight before I had even brought my hand to the ignition.

Fortunately, that part of Evans has a number of stop signs at intersections with private industrial roads, so by doing rolling stops through all of them, I was able to catch up with him in time to see him go right on 3rd. After that, I was pretty sure he was retracing my steps to Highway 280 and I could follow from a comfortable distance. With the bright yellow paint and the twin tigers in back, it was hard to miss the car.

As expected, we got on 280. He took it north back into town and exited on the flyway that dumped onto 6th Street. As we fought traffic towards Market Street, I decided that it was all a big joke and he was headed back to the Galt. He fooled me, though, when he made a sharp right onto Jessie Street in front of Gold Rush Pawn and pulled to a stop on the side of the narrow alley. I went a quarter block more and turned onto a parallel alley, nosing the car in behind a dumpster where I could look across an open parking lot to where he sat in the Mustang.

If he noticed me at all, he gave no indication of it. He had the car stereo going full blast with a rap tune, and apart from mouthing the lyrics and gesturing with his fist in time to the music, the only thing that seemed to draw his attention was the street behind him. I thought briefly about confronting him while I had him alone on neutral turf, but the pawn shop seemed too promising a development to jeopardize by not giving it time to play out.

I hunkered down to wait. At the far end of the alley, lights and reflectors were set up for a photo shoot in front of a scarred brick warehouse. The model appeared—a waifish blond with a heavily made-up face—and her handler immediately set to dabbing more goo around her eyes while the photographer leaned against the building looking impatient as he burned a cigarette. Two guys in orange vests and hard hats walked by carrying bags of donuts. One of them tossed an empty coffee cup at the dumpster. It bounced off the closed lid and skittered to a stop on the hood of my car, dribbling brown sludge into the opening for the wiper blades. Neither of them even looked my way.

The photographer finally got going with the model, but it was slow work. He would look through the camera at her pose, gesture excitedly for her to change some aspect of it, and when she didn't comply as desired, jump out from behind the camera to move her arm a quarter inch or push a tendril of hair behind her ear.

Half an hour and several glamour shots later, I heard a grinding of gears behind me. I twisted back to see a beat up cargo van with a restaurant supply logo turning off 6th. It jolted past me and swept into the parking lot behind the pawn shop. The driver tried to back up close to the door, but other cars in the lot made it challenging and he couldn't steer a clear path between them. After several tries he gave up, leaving the truck stranded in the middle of the lot at a thirty degree angle to the building. I lowered the passenger window a crack to catch anything that might be said.

Cab doors on both sides of the truck opened to disgorge a pair of black men. The driver I'd never seen before, but I was pretty certain that the shorter, slighter man was Reggie Lane. Professor Hubba popped the door to the Mustang, reached for the gun below the seat and then stood, tucking the automatic in the small of his back. He met the other men behind the truck, pointing and laughing at the driver. The driver smiled, said, "What the fuck I know about driving no truck." Reggie stood apart, staring down at the asphalt.

"Go get Myron," said the Professor. "And tell him to get his scrilla on."

The driver nodded and ran around to the front of the pawn shop. The Professor looked over to Reggie, who would not make eye contact. "Quit your moping. You brought it on yourself, Reggie boy. The Professor give you two zips of krypt to sell, he expects to get paid—even if you decide to flush it down the shitter for some crazy reason of your own."

Reggie kicked at the asphalt with his tennis shoe. "I told you. Jayson said the cops were at the front door. I had to get rid of it. And you didn't give it to me to sell. You said to hold it."

The Professor laughed. "And a fine job you did. Open up the truck."

Reggie undid the latch to the cargo door. He pushed the roller door part way open, and then stood on the bumper to shove it all the way up. Given the angle the truck was parked, I couldn't see very far into the cargo space, but I could see the scroll and fingerboard of a bass strapped to the truck wall.

Reggie jumped down and the Professor stepped forward to peer inside. "You sure this junk will pawn for a thousand?"

"A thousand? That's a Begliomini bass. It's worth—" Reggie bit off his sentence.

The Professor crowded in close. "How much is it worth, Reggie?"

Reggie brought his eyes up slowly to meet the Professor's. "A lot more than that anyway," he said meekly.

The Professor laughed again and slapped him on the shoulder. "Well, I guess you better hope you can raise the scratch before Myron sells it for the big money."

"Yeah. Guess so."

The back door to the pawn shop wheezed open and the driver and a scrawny guy with red hair I assumed to be Myron came outside. "Brought you some fine merchandise, Myron," said the Professor. "Quality goods."

"We'll see," said Myron. With some difficulty, he hoisted himself into the bed of the van. He glanced at the bass and began tugging at the straps that held it to the truck wall.

"Careful with that," bleated Reggie.

"Jayson," said the Professor to the guy who had driven the truck. "Go up there and help the man."

Jayson leapt up onto the cargo bed, knelt by the bass and began fiddling with something. Reggie watched for a few anxious moments and then scrambled up after them. "Not that way," I heard him say. "Let me do it."

I decided it was now or never. I took out my wallet and extracted all the money I had: over seven hundred bucks. It was the portion of Ellen Stockwell's retainer I had taken in cash when I deposited the check—and I needed it now for the play I was going to make. I returned the wallet to my hip pocket, urged the Glock from my shoulder holster and snicked open the car door.

I slid out of the car and ducked behind the dumpster. Holding the Glock to my side, I stepped out from behind it and walked casually, but quietly, up to the truck. Everyone inside was still engaged in getting the bass unstrapped. The Professor stood watching a foot or two from the tailgate, and when I was as close to him as he was to the truck and still hadn't been detected, I knew he had his glass eye to my side. I said:

"Daddy, tell me again about the time you got the drop on Professor Hubba."

He didn't quite reach escape velocity. He jumped, twisted in the air and tried to grope his hand around his back for the automatic. I raised the Glock to his forehead. "None of that," I said, and pulled the gun from his waistband.

There was no doubt who had the floor now. Three pairs of eyes and the Professor's lonely orb were locked on me as I dropped the heavy automatic into my coat pocket.

"Put your hands on the tailgate, Professor. Everyone else—lock your hands behind your heads and sit down."

Reggie and Myron dropped like two stillborn calves. Jayson and the Professor hesitated, exchanging scheming looks.

I put the muzzle of the Glock right up to the Professor's temple. "Do not try to scoop the moon from the bottom of the sea," I said cozily.

The Professor became very still. No one likes to deal with a nut—especially a nut with a gun. "What the fuck's that supposed to mean?"

"It's from a book I've been reading. I think it's got something to do with accepting the futility of a situation. Like now."

The Professor breathed in and out. He brought his hands up slowly and then dropped forward to lean on the tailgate.

"Now tell Jayson to put his hands on his head and sit down."

The Professor cleared his throat and spat on the asphalt. "Jay-Jay. Do what he say, man."

Jayson lowered himself to the truck floor, looking about as sullen as a cat dunked in dishwater. He locked his hands behind his head.

"Hope you thought farther ahead than this," said the Professor. "Because you ain't going to be able to hold four guys at gunpoint in the middle of San Francisco for long. Somebody'll see you and call the cops, regardless of your scooping the moon in June shit."

"I've thought about it," I said. "Put out your hand."

The Professor twisted his head to the right, straining to see me out of his good eye. I prodded him with the Glock once more and he took his hand off the tailgate and held it out.

"Turn up your palm."

The Professor complied and I slapped the seven-hundred-some-odd bucks from my wallet into it. "What the fuck?" he said. "Usually the man with the gun takes the money. He don't give it."

"It's the money Reggie owes you."

Reggie stirred at the mention of his name. He frowned and made a little strangled noise in his throat. "What's going on?" he managed to say.

"I'm sure Reggie appreciates your covering for him and all that," said the Professor. "But this here looks a little light. Reggie is into me for twelve hundred."

"Nice try. I believe the stated figure was a grand. Of course, that was under the assumption that the stuff you gave Reggie was real, instead of the chunks of drywall or pieces of dried potato that you actually fobbed off on him. It also supposed that you hadn't told Jayson to stampede Reggie into flushing the counterfeit crack down the toilet. And then there's the side deal you've probably got with Myron to take a cut from the sale of the instruments when Reggie loses the pawn."

The Professor was silent for a moment. "I'm going to stand up."

"Okay."

I stepped back from him. He rose from the tailgate and turned back to look at me. "If you think that, then why are you giving me the money at all?"

"Because I want it to end here. You take the cash and let the rest of it go. And that goes for any future harassment of Reggie."

"Who are you? His long-lost cracker relative?"

"I'm working for his grandparents, the people who own the stuff in the truck."

The Professor brought a hand up to rub his goatee. He squinted at me through his good eye. "And what if I don't go for your little proposal. What are you going to do then?"

I laughed. "You want me to start quoting proverbs again? I'll start by taking the money back. After that I'll get the cops on you for receiving stolen merchandise—or better yet—I'll just give you and Jayson to them for the burglary and assault. I'm sure Victor Lane won't have any trouble picking you both out of a lineup. If you want more, I know some guys in the Big Block Gang who owe me a favor. Maybe I'll redeem it in on your ass."

"Sh-e-e-t. You were going good there until you looped in the brothers from the Big Block. Don't expect me to believe that."

"You never know."

The Professor took hold of the gold dog tags around his neck. He jangled them absently while contemplating the deal. "All right. Bird in the hand. Jayson and I will be on our way—after you give me back my piece."

I smiled and shook my head. "I'll give it to Myron to hold for you. He's used to taking good care of other people's property."

"You better give it to him and he better take damn good care of it. Worth way more than this stack o' scratch you gave me." He glanced up into the truck. "Come on, Jay-Jay. Time to get sideways."

Jayson rose from the truck bed, slapped Reggie on the back of the head as he went around him and then dropped into the parking lot. I backed up to keep him and the Professor in front of the Glock. He sneered at me. "Ho cake," he said under his breath.

"I'm going to assume that's a synonym for cutie pie." I flicked the muzzle of the Glock in the direction of the Mustang. "Happy trails, gentlemen."

The Professor shrugged his shoulders elaborately and sauntered back to the car. Jayson followed on his heels, also doing his damnedest not to look hurried or rushed. They siphoned themselves into the front seats, fired up the motor and squealed down the alley, a thin cloud of burnt rubber lingering over the asphalt after they had gone.

I shoved the Glock back into my shoulder holster and gave my attention to the two left in the truck. "You can put your arms down, guys."

Reggie let his arms drop and jumped to his feet. "What the hell was that?"

"Mainly that was me recovering your grandfather's property. Property, by the way, that would devastate him to lose, especially if he knew that his own flesh and blood had a hand in it. That was also me saving your ass, but that I would rate as more of a side effect."

"Saving my ass? You don't know the Professor if you think that's the end of it."

"Then maybe it's time to clean up your act and stop playing the patsy for drug dealers. Now, do me a favor and tie down the bass again. And what happened to the cover? You shouldn't be transporting it anywhere without it."

Reggie looked away from me. "We couldn't find it."

"Great. I just hope for your sake the bass isn't scratched." I pulled out the Professor's automatic, which on closer inspection turned out to be a collector's edition of the Colt .45 called the "El Presidente." Chrome-plated with a gold trigger, pearl handle grips and the El Presidente moniker engraved on the barrel, it was the small arms equivalent of a spangled Elvis suit.

"Get your butt down here," I called to Myron.

Myron crawled dog-like out from the cargo area and came to rest twitching and sniffing by the tailgate. I ejected the magazine of the Colt, pocketed it, and then racked the slide back to eject the round in the chamber. It went sailing into the parking lot.

"What are you doing?" asked Myron, horrified.

"Did you think I was going to trust you with a loaded gun?"

"Professor Hubba will croak me for certain if I don't return the magazine with the gun. The magazine is specially matched on those El Presidentes."

I regarded him for a moment. He was 130 pounds of hay fever and halitosis. It was hard to picture him pulling a fast one, but he was more afraid of the Professor than he was of me and that made him untrustworthy. "Turn around," I said.

Myron dutifully turned and I shoved the Colt underneath the waistband of his corduroy trousers. "Face me again," I said. "Now open wide."

I put the magazine between his teeth and pushed his lower jaw closed. "Now walk back to your shop, and if I see you reach for the magazine or the pistol, I'm not even going to say a word. I'm just going to treat you like a human shooting gallery target. Once you get there, you stay there and don't come out until closing time. You got me?"

Myron made a gagging sound that could have been, "I got you," and nodded his head. I gave him a shove in the direction of the store. He stumbled forward, ran over to where the ejected round lay on the parking lot, scooped that up and then trotted towards 6th Street. He dodged a street person rolling a shopping cart down the sidewalk and then disappeared behind the front of the building.

"You're kind of an asshole, you know that?" said Reggie. He had secured the bass and was busy pulling down the roller door.

"Thanks. I get by."

He jumped off the tailgate. "Guess I'll be seeing you then, huh?"

"Not so fast, Reggie. You and I are taking this stuff back to your grandfather."

"No way. I can't face him now."

"Now's the only chance you got. If it comes back without you, he'll harden his heart to you now and forever. The only way to set it right is to take it back yourself."

Reggie turned away from me and picked at a hangnail on his thumb. It started to bleed. He wiped the blood on his pants and squeezed the thumb cruelly between two fingers. "All right," he said softly. "I'll go."

I didn't trust Reggie to drive by himself, so I left the Galaxie where it was and got in the truck with him. We drove to the Lombard Street address, speaking just enough for me to ascertain that the truck was borrowed from a friend who worked at the restaurant supply business whose logo was painted on the side. I had been worried that it was stolen.

The sun was dropping behind the hill at Hyde Street when we arrived and most of the tourists were gone for the day. Reggie got lucky and found a head-in parking space directly across from Victor's condo. He shut off the motor and sat with his hands clenched on the wheel. I said:

"You're doing the right thing. He'll be so happy to have Baby back that everything else will be forgiven."

"I hope so, man."

I pulled out my wallet.

"Put that away," said Reggie. "I don't want none of your money."

"That's good because I don't have any." I passed him a card. "Victor tells me you play trumpet."

"Yeah. What of it?"

"I play bass. Give me a call and I'll get you a gig."

Reggie blew air from his lips. "With who? Little Whitie and the Miracle Whips?"

I unlatched the door and climbed down from the cab. "Try Cornelius Crawford," I said, naming one of the hottest black saxophonists in the city. "Assuming you're good enough."

I slammed the door closed on his surprised expression and wandered down the hill towards Columbus. From there, I caught a ride on a cable car back downtown using an old souvenir ticket I had found on the sidewalk near my office.

I figured my having saved the ticket was a sign of good fortune—until I found a ticket of another sort under the wiper blade of the Galaxie.

ONE HOUR MARTINIZING

MORE UNPLEASANT SURPRISES WERE WAITING FOR ME when I got home. I was standing in the lobby of my building sorting through my mail—a discount coupon for bikini waxing, a CD with software for 50,000 hours of free Internet time and an offer for a "titanium" credit card—when the elevator clanged to a stop on the ground floor. I glanced up from the picture on the bikini waxing coupon just as the doors lurched open to reveal my old pals from the ashram, Tom and Jerry. They had exchanged their robes for more conventional garb, but their bald heads and their identical denim shirts gave them the same matched set look they had in Oakland.

I was slower off the mark than they were. Jerry charged out of the elevator and pushed me aside, while Tom rushed the door. Jerry followed on his heels, and by the time I made it out to the sidewalk in front of my building, they were sprinting down Post towards Leavenworth. I started after them, but after a few jolting strides, I decided that my hangover and I had had more than enough adventures for one day. I trudged back to the building and rode the elevator to my apartment on the fourth floor, knowing exactly what I would find.

The door was standing wide open. The living room wasn't too badly tossed because there weren't many obvious places to hide things. Some of the records in my jazz collection had been pulled off the shelves, the card table had been overturned and all the cushions on the sofa had been thrown on the floor. I was thankful they hadn't mucked with my turntable or any of the delicate electronics in my stereo system, and my sixty-pound Altec Lansing "Voice of the Theater" speakers were large and heavy enough to take care of themselves.

The kitchen looked bad—but it always looked bad. All the drawers were pulled out and all the cabinets were yawning open with my meager collection of pots and pans strewn over the landscape. The good news was I didn't have to worry about broken plates because I'd long ago switched to paper. The refrigerator door was also left open and there was a smashed bottle of mustard on the floor in front of it. That depleted the inventory inside by one-third, leaving only the ketchup and container of tartar sauce whose "best if used by date" was probably celebrated as independence day by certain former Soviet Republics.

There was nothing in the bathroom that couldn't be cleaned up with a firehose and 100 pounds of water pressure. The bedroom was another story. The bed was completely destroyed: the mattress separated from the box spring, the sheets torn off and the pillows eviscerated. The closet looked like it had been host to an indoor rugby match and the dresser drawers and their contents were dispersed across the room in a manner calculated to demonstrate the effects of maximum entropy. The only thing that wasn't upended or trashed was the magazine rack by the door. It was perfectly fine. So I aimed a vicious kick at it that sent it gyrating across the room like a disabled satellite.

I had no doubt that Tom and Jerry had been sent to the apartment by the guru to search for something. The only question was what. They didn't have anything in their hands as they exited the building, so either it was something small or they had failed to locate it.

I was tired and my head hurt. I decided to get the bedroom into a semblance of order and let the other rooms slide until the next day. I had just shoved the mattress on top of the box spring when I heard hesitant tapping at the apartment door. It was followed by a weak, "Anybody home?"

"No," I shouted. "The Tupperware party just broke up."

"August, is that you?"

I threw a wad of bedsheets to one side and strode into the living room. Ellen Stockwell stood in the doorway holding a hanger with a suit coat wrapped in plastic—my suit coat. She gawked at the overturned card table, the spilled sofa cushions and the jumbled LPs. "What happened?"

"Everyone wanted the cereal storer and I only had one. There was a riot."

"Please. Don't joke with me."

I took the card table by one of its legs and flipped it upright. "A couple of guys from your daughter's ashram broke in and tossed the place."

Her eyes flashed at the mention of her daughter, then she pressed a knuckle into her lower lip and nodded vaguely. She walked zombie-like over to the couch and flopped down into the cavity where the cushions went. She laid the suit coat on the arm of the sofa, but it slipped to the floor. "Caroline tried to kill herself," she said.

I couldn't summon any feeling of surprise. The story Ellen had told me that morning was too pat and simple for the truth. I didn't know what had happened to Caroline while she was gone, but there was no doubt in my mind that it was tied to the suicide attempt. Thinking these thoughts took too much time. Ellen glared up at me and stamped her foot. "Don't you dare say I told you so."

"I wasn't going to. Is she okay?"

"She's all right now, but she lost a lot of blood. I found her in the bathroom just after I got off the phone with you. Quentin has an old straight razor he inherited from his grandfather. She used that to cut her wrist. I would never have found her if her blood hadn't seeped under the bathroom door into the hallway carpet. As it was, I barely had time to jimmy open the door, bandage her wrist and get her to the hospital. They told me she was very lucky. She was wearing this crazy unitard thing and it actually slowed the flow of blood from the wound because it was so tight in the arms. In another minute or two she would have been gone."

I didn't say anything for a moment. "You were very brave, Ellen. Few people would have had the presence of mind to do all of that."

She ran a trembling hand through her hair. "Do you think so? I was on the edge of hysteria the whole time." Her hand closed around a bunch of hair at the nape of her neck and pulled at it savagely. "I need a drink or heroin or something."

"I've got alcohol, but it's not exactly wine coolers."

"I don't care what it is. I just want to lay waste to all conscious thought."

I nodded and walked over to the sofa to shake her hand loose from the death grip on her hair. "Relax. I'll be back in a minute."

I found the Maker's Mark bottle intact under a pile of canned food that had been pulled from the pantry cabinets. My collection of jelly glasses was unmolested, so I poured three fingers' worth into a glass featuring Archie and another three into a glass with Veronica and carried them and the bottle out to the living room.

"Here you go," I said, handing her the Veronica glass. "Kentucky's finest."

She downed about half of the bourbon in one go, then held up the glass to examine the picture. "Wasn't she the spoiled rich one?"

I sat down next to her in the cushionless sofa, placing the bottle on the floor in front of us. "That's right. I think Betty was Archie's main squeeze, but I always had a thing for Veronica."

She smiled into the glass as she took another sip. "And they say women always go for the bad boy."

I shrugged. "Only in comic books. I've had my fill of bad girls in real life."

"Why is it we always end up talking about silly things like fruit salad and comic books?"

"We're mental midgets, we're flirting or we're trying to avoid the painful topics."

"I wish it were the second, but I'm afraid it's the third."

I nodded and took a drink of bourbon. "Did Caroline write a note or say anything to indicate why she might want to kill herself?"

Ellen braced her forearms on her knees, cradling the glass with two hands as she stared down into it. "She didn't write a note. Afterwards—I mean after I got her to the hospital—she was resting and I didn't want to disturb her. In any case, she's in the ICU and they only let you visit for a few minutes at a time."

"And there wasn't anything more to her story about where she went than what you told me this morning?"

"No, that was it. She drove across the country with a friend."

"A male friend?"

"Yes, someone she met at school. I assumed he was the new boyfriend she had been hinting about."

I slumped back into the sofa and studied her profile. She felt my eyes on her and turned to look at me. "You've got that I-told-you-so look again," she said. "I realize now I should never have taken what she told me at face value, but I was just so happy to have her home that I didn't want to question things. Besides, I thought I would have more time to tease the story out of her. She didn't come home until around two that morning. We talked for about 20 minutes and then she said she was tired and could she go to bed. The next time I saw her she was on the bathroom floor."

"Do you think she really went to bed? Or did she wait for you to go to your room and then sneak into the bathroom to—to do it?"

"She was wearing the same clothes she had on when she arrived. But I don't think she went straight to the bathroom after I went to bed. If she had done it that early, I think she would have bled to death by the time I found her. Why? Is it important?"

"I don't know. Where was Quentin for all this?"

She frowned. "There's something else I should mention. But to answer your question, Quentin had his usual quart of tequila for dinner and passed out at about 8 PM. He made a brief appearance when Caroline came home—but he was still drunk and I don't think he quite registered what was going on—and he was completely useless this morning during the crisis. He just sat on the hallway floor by the bathroom and blubbered the whole time. The only thing he did was help me carry her to the car. He's at the hospital now, taking his turn at watching her. And I've never seen a paler, sorrier creature than the one who's sitting with his head in his hands in that waiting room."

I felt my face go flush, somehow embarrassed for Stockwell at the bitter description she gave. "I see. And what was the other thing you wanted to tell me?"

She gunned the last quarter inch of her drink and held out the glass for more. "Hit me again bartender."

I passed my glass over and took the empty one from her hand. She swallowed most of the contents before she spoke. "When I got back from the first trip to the hospital, Quentin told me that someone had tried to break into our house."

"When?"

"Sometime last night I guess."

"How did he know?"

"Quentin's always been very security conscious. He won't install an alarm—says they don't prevent break-ins and he doesn't trust the Union City police to respond in a timely manner anyway—but he has put in the best locks and other security devices he can find. That includes wrought-iron bars on all the windows."

"I noticed."

She smiled faintly. "They do make the house look like some kind of western jail, don't they? Anyway, he said someone tried to come in through one the back windows, but they couldn't get past the bars. He said they tried to pry them out of the wall."

"Which window?"

"The one to Caroline's bedroom."

"Was he certain that nobody got in? That whoever it was wasn't responsible for hurting Caroline?"

Ellen sat still and quiet for a long moment. "I never thought of that, but Quentin said nobody got in. They barely loosened one of the bolts on the bars."

I looked down at the floor and nudged the bourbon bottle with the toe of my shoe. "Might have been the same guys who redecorated my apartment."

"That's what struck me when you explained what happened. You said they were from the ashram? What's the point in breaking into either of our places?"

"When I went to check out the ashram, I was thinking that Caroline might be staying there. I'm pretty convinced now that she wasn't. But I do think that the guru had some interest in her—probably through her web site. It's got to be connected to that."

"Could he be responsible for her going missing?"

"Possibly. But as I said, I didn't really get the sense that he had seen her in some time."

Ellen nodded vaguely and swirled the remaining bourbon in her glass. She brought the glass to her lips in an almost guilty fashion and drained it quickly. "Hit me again?" she said with a false insouciance.

I shook my head and pulled the Archie glass from her hand. "No."

"Aren't you being the tiniest bit hypocritical?"

"You bet I am. As the guru says, 'A man with butter on his head should not walk in the sun.' Which is to say I've drowned my sorrows on plenty of occasions—as recently as last night even—and I'm the last person to pass judgment. But I'm not going to sit and watch you do it. Not here and not now."

She looked at me levelly. "Why ever not? You might get lucky."

"I wouldn't want that kind of luck, Ellen."

She turned her head to one side. "I have to ask you something I've no right to ask."

I knew what was coming, but I'm as human as the next guy. I wasn't going to make it any easier for her. "What is it?"

"I want you to find out where Caroline went—I mean where she really went. Not the crazy story she told me about driving across country. I've got to believe that whatever happened to her while she was gone is what drove her to try to kill herself. If I know more about it, maybe I can help her cope with it or prevent it from coming back for her—or I don't know what. It may be a complete waste of time, but I feel I have to make some sort of effort to find out."

"Why not just ask her?"

She brought her lips together in a tight line. "Because I don't believe she'll tell me. Six months ago I might have fooled myself into thinking that she would, but now I know different. She doesn't trust me any longer. And she certainly doesn't trust Quentin. She's been living her whole life apart from us."

I was still holding the glasses in my hands. I stacked Veronica on top of Archie and set them down on the floor next to the Maker's Mark. "All right, Ellen. I'll keep at it. But at some point I'll need to talk to her—even if you don't want to. And I think you need to be clear on one thing: if I find out what happened to her, just knowing what it is may make no difference at all. There may be nothing you can do to make things better. I've lived long enough to know that airing out the wound doesn't always make it heal faster."

"I understand." She broke across the space separating us and put her arms around me. She put her lips to mine and kissed me with a surprising urgency. I felt her hands grip my sides, her nails almost galvanic against my ribs. "This isn't the bourbon talking," she said.

I didn't need a second invitation. I picked her up from the sofa and carried her to the demolished bedroom where we made a desperate, precarious sort of love, like refugees in a war zone.

A PRIZE IN EVERY BOX

I WANTED ELLEN TO SPEND THE NIGHT—AND I think she did too—but she felt guilty about not being with Caroline at the hospital. I walked her to the elevator and then returned to the apartment. The place suddenly felt like a deserted bus terminal without her. I rescued my jacket from the living room floor, and that was the last bit of clean-up I did before I collapsed onto the partially made bed, not even bothering to kick off my shoes. I fell asleep with her scent on the pillow beside me.

I slept until 10 the next morning, but found I still lacked the motivation to do anything else in the way of clean-up. I threaded my way around the debris to shower and shave and then rescued some clothes from the heap at the bottom of the closet. Taking things as I found them, I paired a blue striped shirt with a red paisley tie—a combination I'd never tried before. Maybe the silver lining to the upheaval Tom and Jerry had visited on my life was a new freedom and flexibility in wardrobe, or maybe I was just rationalizing. I took the jacket from underneath the dry cleaner's plastic and shrugged it on. It smelled of cleaning solvent, but no tequila.

After a quick stop at Saeed's to pick up the needful in terms of coffee and donuts, I walked all the way down Post to Market, went a few blocks north towards the Ferry Building and then crossed over at Beale. I knew I was getting close to my destination when I passed a young woman carrying a bulky leather portfolio case, and a moment later walked by a guy at a bus stop sketching away on a pad with a charcoal pencil.

The San Francisco Lyceum of Art was housed in a building at the corner of Beale and Mission that looked like a vanilla sheet cake at a poor man's wedding. No ornate cornices or elaborate facades embellished it. It was just six layers of pedestrian cake with very little frosting. I wondered if the building was supposed to be representative of the school's design philosophies, but what I saw next convinced me otherwise.

The entrance to the school led through a substantial gallery of student work. There were mural-sized oil paintings of naked women painted in a bleary style as if the artist had been looking through glasses smeared with Vaseline. There were sculptures labelled as "installations" that included a random pile of weather-beaten boat oars and a gigantic set of severed finger tips that sprouted from the floor like so many toadstools. There were harsh color photos of unattractive people doing unattractive things that were priced so high that you knew they had to be good, even if your pitiful sensibilities failed to discern the quality. Twelve-hundred dollars, for instance, would net you a digital print of a pimply, shirtless teenager with fantastic Elton John glasses sitting on the toilet while he smoked a cigarette down to the filter and perused a Hustler magazine. I didn't see any samples of Caroline's or Monica's work, but it would have been difficult to take in anything else as I ran though the rest of the gallery shrieking with my eyes covered.

I came to a modest lobby with a bank of elevators along one wall. The directory informed me that the president's office was on the sixth floor, but a guard behind a reception desk stopped me from getting on an elevator until I'd signed in. "That's quite the collection you've got back there," I said to him as I put my name and time of day in the log.

He looked at me carefully, as if gauging my sincerity. "Yeah," he said. "I always come in the back door myself."

I rode the elevator with a couple of Japanese girls and a hulking blond kid who could have bench-pressed a Frigidaire. "The modes of conventional art are as recycled as story ideas for women's magazines," he said to the girls, who were hanging on every word. "The only way to achieve new heights is to break radically with tradition, as the impressionists did in the late 19th century and the cubists did in the early 20th. That's what I'm doing in my work."

All four of them—the girls, the kid and his ego—got off on a lower floor while I continued all the way to the top floor, which was much better appointed than the lobby. Carpet replaced tired gray linoleum and dark wood paneling supplanted plaster painted a cheerless steel blue. I followed a sign pointing down a hallway to the right and presented myself to a white-haired sourpuss sitting at a small desk in a cutout section of the hall, just beside a tall oak door with an embossed plaque that read, "Julie Jaing, President."

I put a card on the desk and told the white-haired woman I'd like to speak to Ms. Jaing. She looked at me like I was selling colonoscopies door to door. Taking her reading glasses from where they hung around her neck on a gold chain, she settled them on the tip of an anemic-looking nose. "It's Dr. Jaing, Mr. Riordan," she said after she read the card.

"My mistake. I'd like to speak to Dr. Jaing, then."

"And you don't have an appointment."

It was a statement, not a question, but I answered it anyway. "No."

She let the glasses fall back around her neck and picked up the card to return to me. "May I ask what the purpose of your visit is?"

"I've been hired by the family of Caroline Stockwell. She's one of your students. She's gone missing and I'm trying to locate her." I had decided it would be simpler to stick to the story that she was missing than explain the current situation. "I'm hoping that I can glean some information from the school administration and staff that will help in my search."

She frowned. "Have you spoken to anyone else?"

"At the school?"

"Yes, at the school."

"No, I figured it would be best to get permission first. That's why I came here." I gave her my winningest smile.

She nodded, but I'd clearly disappointed her. She was expecting to catch me out. "Very well. I'll inform Dr. Jaing that you're here and find out if she has time to speak with you."

She rose from the chair and knocked lightly at the tall door. Without waiting for a response, she pushed it open less than two feet and slid through, blocking the view to the interior with her body.

I loitered in the hallway for a moment, but when it became apparent a papal conclave was in progress, I lifted a notebook and pen from her desk. I wrote, "Note to self, take broomstick in for 25,000 mile tune-up" in block letters on the top sheet and returned both items where I found them.

Presently the door opened again and the white-haired woman stepped out. She pushed her sharp little chin out in a gesture of reproach. "Dr. Jaing will see you now—for fifteen minutes only."

"Can I walk right in or are there some Swiss Guards I need to salute?"

I didn't wait for a response, but stepped quickly around her, though the tall door and into an office with a lot of modern, swoopy-doopy looking furniture made of bent chromium and shiny plastic. A bank of square windows with semi-translucent glass covered the rear wall, and a woman was standing with her back to the door, looking out. Although what exactly she could see through the frosted glass was beyond me.

"Dr. Jaing?" I asked politely.

She turned to face me and I found that she looked oddly familiar. If Bob's Big Boy were Chinese and female, she would have been the spitting image. She had a large head with a helmet of black hair that was sculpted and formed into a wavy peak like Bob's. She was short and chunky, and if she wasn't wearing Bob's red and white checkered overalls, she was wearing a red dress with wide straps that fastened in front with buttons. When she smiled in greeting, she arched her eyebrows and plumped out already plump cheeks in a delirious expression that exactly mirrored Bob's. The only thing she was missing was the plate held over her head with a double-decker hamburger.

"Call me Julie," she said. "I've never met a real private eye before."

I felt my eyebrows go up in sympathy with hers. "And I've never met an art school president."

"I'm sure you'll be disappointed. Please have a seat." She moved behind her desk with the waddling swagger of a pro tackle in a locker room.

Her chair was the standard issue high-backed padded leather affair. Mine looked like the crash landing of NASA's Martian lander. I eased my butt onto a strip of formed black plastic and watched as the bent chromium bars that made up the superstructure flexed ominously under my weight. I felt certain it was either going to snap closed on me like a mouse trap or launch me into the air like a catapult.

"How do you like the chair?" asked Dr. Jaing. She grunted as she pulled herself closer to her desk, which itself looked like a chromium dissection table.

I figured this was a trick question. "Very innovative," I allowed.

"I designed it myself—along with several other pieces in the room."

"Let me guess—the desk is yours too?"

This earned me another Bob's Big Boy grin. "Exactly. I've yet to do a chair for myself, but that's my next project. Now, how can I help you? Leonora mentioned that you were inquiring after one of our students. Caroline Stockwell, I believe."

"That's right. She's been missing for nearly four weeks now. Her parents have hired me to look for her."

Dr. Jaing adjusted the flat screen monitor on her desk and typed something on a computer keyboard. "Yes, that's consistent with our records. She has incompletes for all of her midterms this quarter and her advisor put an alert in her file."

"I wonder if you could tell me what sort of student she's been. Is there any indication of a drop-off in her work recently?"

"You're looking to see if problems outside of school were affecting her work here?"

I shrugged. "Something like that."

"Let me see." She twitched a mouse across a pad and clicked on it several times. "I would say that Caroline has been a consistent, if average, student in most of her course work. The exception would be the classes she has taken in photography. She has received some outstanding marks—and special recognition in terms of school exhibits—for many of her courses, particularly the required ones, but she's also had some low marks in elective classes."

I leaned forward in my chair and felt the tension in the bars shift in what seemed like a capricious fashion. I clutched at the plastic seat. "The classes she received low marks in—when did she take those?"

"She took 'Advanced B&W Printing Techniques' during the summer session and received a C-. She also took 'Introduction to the View Camera' during the same quarter and received a D."

"Who taught those?"

"They were both taught by her advisor, George Wesson."

"That's a little surprising, isn't it?"

She folded her arms under her ample bosom and frowned ever so slightly. She didn't look as much like Bob now. "Why would you say that?"

"I don't know. I guess I would have expected her advisor to go a little easier on her. Or looking at it from her perspective, I would have expected her to gravitate to an advisor with whom she felt a little more simpatico."

"George Wesson is a nationally known artist. All the students who work with him consider the opportunity to be a great privilege. He is a demanding teacher, however. I assume he gave her the low marks because he felt her work was not up to the standard he expected. I'm sure the fact he is her advisor had no bearing on his decision."

"I wonder how she took it," I said to myself as much as to her.

"I don't know. You'd have to ask George." She paused a moment and her frown changed into an outright scowl. This was definitely not the jolly slinger of double-decker hamburgers I'd met at the outset. "In any case, I seriously doubt bad grades for classes taken several months ago would be the motive for Caroline to run away now. I hope that's not the story you're going to give her parents." She made little chopping motions in the air as she spoke to emphasize her point.

I held up my hands, risking the stability of my perch on the chair. "I never said anything like that. I just need to consider all the factors." That didn't seem to do it for her, so I sweetened the pot. "And I'm sure we'll find the school bears no responsibility for her departure when all is said and done."

"Thank you," she said, and put on her happy face.

I smiled back at her—a wary smile like the lion tamer gave the lion. "You mentioned talking to George Wesson. I'd like to do that, as well as speak to her other instructors. Would it be possible to get a list of them along with an introduction or some sort of indication from you that they can speak freely?"

She nodded. "I thought you might ask for that." She maneuvered the mouse to double click on something on her screen. A printer sitting on a pedestal beside her desk began making noise and soon two sheets of paper appeared in the output tray. She passed them over to me. "That's a list of her courses and instructors for this quarter. I'll have Leonora notify everyone that you'll be coming by to talk with them."

"Thank you." I stared down at the list without really seeing it. "Let me ask you another question. Have any of your other students dropped out this quarter?"

She frowned again. "Don't make this into something it's not. We have a very high course completion rate at the Lyceum. We did have one expulsion this quarter, but that involved an entirely different set of circumstances."

"May I—"

She stood and walked around to the front of the desk in that curious waddle of hers. I was being dismissed. I escaped the clutches of the guest chair in time to take her outstretched hand. "That's all, Mr. Riordan. I hope you have found your first meeting with an art school president useful." She squeezed my hand with a surprising strength. "Please don't cause me to regret my first meeting with a private eye."

I spent the next few hours running up and down the six floors of the building, talking to the instructors on the list Dr. Jaing had given me. I also managed to speak to several of the classmates from the list Ellen had provided. The general impression I formed was that Caroline was a quiet, loner type with only a few close friendships, but none of the people I spoke to felt that she had been particularly depressed or out of sorts during the time immediately prior to her departure. Nor had she made mention of a new boyfriend or an intention to leave town on a trip. Her instructors felt her to be talented, but said that she only really applied herself when she enjoyed the medium in which she was working—photography being her favorite. Another consistent comment was that her work was "dark."

By 2:30 all precincts had been heard from except her advisor, George Wesson. In my several visits to his office I was alternatively informed that he was in class, working in the darkroom or engaged in a private consultation. Now the department secretary—a friendly British woman named Cleo—told me that he was working in the studio on the fifth floor, but had specifically left instructions not to be disturbed. When I asked her if she had told him I was interested in meeting with him, she said, "Of course, luv. But as you may have divined by now, the interest apparently isn't mutual."

Getting into the now familiar elevator, I rode up to the fifth floor, and after wandering the halls for a time, found the double doors that opened into the studio. They were locked. A sign-up sheet taped to one of the doors indicated that Wesson had the studio booked from 2 to 4 PM and an annotation to the side said, "DO NOT DISTURB" in block capitals with a couple of underlines thrown in for good measure. Just as I raised my fist to pound on the door in the most disturbing fashion I could manage, the door to an adjacent office opened and the blond kid I'd ridden the elevator with slipped through. His gaze flitted my direction, then he broke eye contact and hurried down the hallway in a near trot.

He seemed so guilty-looking that I thought about going after him, but I decided that the office he came out of was more interesting—especially since it bordered on the studio. I walked over to the door and pulled it open as quietly as possible. Inside was a large space with workstations for cutting mats and for drying, trimming and mounting prints. Along the common wall with the studio was a door, and crouching beside that with the door pulled open a crack were two more young men. Whatever it was they were looking at had them completely engrossed. If Norman Rockwell had painted the scene, "Mouth-Breathers with Flushed Faces" would have been an excellent title.

I walked all the way up to the studio door before they noticed me and then pressed it closed. "You shouldn't be in here," I said sternly.

They gaped at me for a long moment and then one with tortoise shell sunglasses and a haircut like Julius Caesar finally sputtered, "No sir."

"Then get the hell out."

They fell over themselves like dogs trying to run on waxed parquet. I locked the outer door behind them and returned to the studio door. I pulled it open a crack, peered through—and then became a full-fledged member of the mouth-breathers' club.

The studio was a large, blank room with scuffed white walls. Clustered in the center, about 15 feet from my vantage point, was a set of photographic lights, a neutral-colored backdrop hanging from a scaffolding of metal tubing and a man with his head under a black cloth peering through the lens of a big camera on a tripod. It was what he was peering at that had prompted all the heavy breathing.

Monica Mapa lay naked on her back inside a rectangular cardboard box that was open to the camera. Her legs were bent beneath her and one arm was wrapped above her head, reaching out and around the top of the box. Her head was nestled next to her arm and she appeared to be gazing back—languidly—at her torso. The image was incredibly erotic of course, but there was something more to it. Somehow she had transcended the persona of slutty she-devil to become a Rodin sculpture in elegant repose.

The photographer came out from under the cloth and threw it to one side. He took a film holder from a case and slid it into the back of the camera. After pulling the dark slide out, he grasped the cable release for the camera and pressed the plunger home. The strobe lights flashed and I heard the shutter mechanism of the camera flip open and closed with a raspy sound like a grasshopper flying.

"Can I get out of the fucking box now, George?" said Monica in a peevish voice. "My legs are killing me."

The transformation to Rodin sculpture vanished in a poof. Monica was her old self again.

"Yeah, George," I said, stepping through the door. "How about a little break? I need to talk to you."

George Wesson turned to look at me with a surprisingly mild expression. He was a slight man with a mustache and a high, domed forehead. He was balding in front, but the reddish brown hair he did have was mussed from the black cloth. He didn't say anything.

Monica rolled out of the box and scrambled to her feet. She struck a pose with her arms akimbo and her chest thrown out like a Greek goddess getting ready to punish some mortals. "Riordan," she said, not unpleasantly. "What are you doing here?"

"I'm here to talk to Dr. Wesson about Caroline."

She strode up to me—her breasts bobbing gently as she came—and stopped within six inches of me. I rubbed my hands on the back of my pants, suddenly uncertain about what to do with them. I struggled to keep my eyes on her face. "I found out what a Datsun is," she said huskily.

"It wasn't an open book test," I mumbled. My mouth seemed very dry.

She took hold of my paisley tie and stroked the fabric like she was stroking something else. She paused at my collar to grasp the knot and cinched the tie tighter around my throat. "Are you feeling a little constricted, August?"

"For God's sake, Monica, stop tormenting the man," said Wesson.

Monica laughed and flipped the tie over my shoulder. She pirouetted in front of me and walked slowly toward the backdrop. The silent samba of her hips and ass was a major distraction, but I noticed for the first time that she had the tattoo of an aquamarine butterfly over her right shoulder blade. She ducked behind the fabric and emerged a moment later wearing a silk kimono. "I'm going, George. It doesn't look as though we're going to do any more today. But—" She waggled her finger at him. "You still owe me for the full two hours."

"Fine, fine," he said. "I'll talk to you later."

We both watched wordlessly as she sashayed out the front door. When she was gone, I let go of a breath I didn't know I'd been holding and loosened my tie.

"Nice work if you can get it, doctor," I said.

Wesson went behind the camera and pushed the dark slide back into the film holder. "I'm not a doctor. I don't have a Ph.D."

"Whatever. Everyone says you're the Big Kahuna around here."

"Thank you so very much, I'm sure."

"Look," I said. "Sorry to barge in on you. But I do need to talk to you about Caroline Stockwell."

Wesson nodded and pulled the film holder from the camera. He returned it to the case. "I suppose it can't be avoided."

His demeanor of long-suffering patience was annoying. "Take a lot of naked pictures of your students, do you Wesson?" I said to rattle him.

Wesson had picked up his piece of black cloth and was starting to fold it. He stopped to glare at me. "This is an art school. We do figure studies in all media, including photography. These figure studies require models, and the models come from a variety of places, including the student body. All the models are treated professionally, on a completely nonsexual basis."

I chuckled. "Student body. That's a good one, doc."

"I told you I don't have a Ph.D."

"Yes, you did, didn't you?" I walked up to his camera to examine it more closely. It was big and ungainly and had a long leather bellows. The lens seemed unusually large and I was surprised to find ground glass in the back rather than a traditional view finder. "This is kind of a funny camera to use, isn't it? Looks like something from the 1800s."

"It's called a view camera and it's perfectly modern. They even have digital backs for them now."

"Didn't you give Caroline Stockwell a D in a view camera class?"

"Yes, what of it?"

"You don't think that might have had some bearing on her disappearance?"

"A bad grade? I hardly think so. Caroline simply wasn't interested in large format photography. She realized that early on, but decided to stay in the class because she wanted the units. She was perfectly aware of the likely outcome given the amount of work she was willing to invest."

"Then what's your theory about where she went?"

Wesson put the now folded cloth in the case and brushed me aside to get to the front of the camera. He fiddled with something near the lens. "I don't have a theory about where she went. She said or did nothing that would lead me to believe she was going away."

"Did you take naked pictures of her too?"

"If you mean did I use her as a model for figure studies, I wouldn't tell you if I had. I don't give out the names of my models."

"Did you know she had a web site?"

He fiddled some more with a lever near the lens, but it appeared to be stuck. He straightened up with an exasperated sigh. "Yes, I knew she had a web site. The whole school knew that. She and Monica posted adverts on the school bulletin boards."

"Why would they do that?"

"To get more visitors obviously. Why else would they do it?"

"I wouldn't have thought they would want visitors from the school. Who at a school would have money to make donations or buy them gifts—unless you're talking about faculty members, of course."

"If you're trying to suggest that I was a visitor to their site, you're mistaken. In the first place, instructors are not so well-compensated here that they have money to throw around like that. In the second, I'm not the least bit interested in that sort of thing."

"Really? What's the difference between Monica half-naked in a devil outfit and Monica fully naked in a box?"

Wesson made a growling noise and bent to work on the lever again. "Spare me, Mr. Riordan. If you really can't perceive the difference, then there's nothing I can say now that would transform your aesthetic sensibilities."

I nodded to myself. "Maybe I was kidding you a bit, Wesson. But haven't I seen a picture very much like what you were taking today? A black and white photo of a nude woman in a cardboard box?"

Wesson looked up at me. He seemed a little surprised. "That's right. It's by Ruth Bernhard. It's called *In The Box Horizontal*. We were recreating the shot."

"Recreating it? I thought the whole idea was to do something original."

"It's called an homage. Monica and I wanted—" Wesson stopped short. In his annoyance with me, he had pushed the lever on the camera with more force than he had employed to that point and the lens simply flopped out. He tried to catch it, but he succeeded only in batting it into the floor harder. It hit with a thud and a sharp cracking noise.

He snatched it up like a Barry Bonds home run ball. From the expression in his face when he looked through the glass, you would have thought he had lost a child. "God damn it," he shouted. "Look what you made me do. This is a Schneider APO-Symmar L. It's worth more than I make in a month."

"I don't think—"

"Get out of here. Right now." His forehead and cheeks were mottled with purple and spittle flew from his lips. "I'm calling campus security." He strode towards the office door I had come through.

I watched him disappear through the doorway, looked around the room a little dispiritedly, loosened my tie still further and then got out of there. Riordan concludes another interview with finesse and aplomb.

I had just stepped out onto Beale Street when the hulking blond kid made another appearance. He pressed a wadded piece of notepaper into my hand and took off on a dead run. I shouted after him, but he pounded around the corner at Mission and was gone. I opened the paper. "SF MOMA" was all it said.

GAY FUEL

IF THE BUILDING THAT HOUSED THE ART school looked like a sheet cake, the home of the San Francisco Modern Museum of Art (SFMOMA) looked like a food processor. A gigantic zebra-striped food processor at that. In fairness to the architect, it was the building's tower of two-toned marble that gave it the food processor-like appearance. The edifice as a whole had been praised consistently by more astute critics than I since the day of its opening.

I forked over my ten dollar entry fee at the door and made a quick study of the catalog that the clerk handed me in return. Although the note I'd been passed at the art school had been enigmatic enough, I wasn't really surprised to find an exhibit titled, "Articulated Bodies: The Nudes of George Wesson."

The photos—about 60 of them—were displayed in a starkly lit gallery on the third floor. The majority were studies of female torsos posed in unorthodox ways. Spindled, folded and manipulated, the flesh in the photographs belied the definition of conventional beauty with twisted bellies, jutting hips and flattened breasts. There was an earthy voluptuousness to the images that somehow reminded me of African fertility idols. I wasn't sure if I liked them, but there was no denying their originality and power.

Since most of the photos lacked limbs and heads, and since all their titles were designations like "Nude #23" without reference to models' names, I was hard pressed to identify any of the subjects.

However, I noticed that the model in several of the photographs was slimmer—and presumably younger—than the other subjects and that her belly button was pierced. I took out the snapshot of Caroline that Ellen had given me and compared the stud and the general "lay of the land" in and around the belly button in Caroline's picture and the others. The snapshot wasn't as clear as Wesson's photos, but the stud in all the pictures had the same distinctive look—a curved steel post with a shiny metal ball on one end and a tiny jeweled star on the other—and the belly button itself looked identical: a cute innie that was little more than a dimple in a sea of smooth, taut flesh. It had to be Caroline.

Wesson may have been right when he said all of his models were treated professionally on a nonsexual basis, but it was hard to ignore that his and Caroline's was a teacher/student relationship first and photographer/model second. It seemed like a situation ripe for abuse.

I rode the elevator to the first floor lobby and used the pay phone to check in at the office. Gretchen told me that Chris had called and wanted me to call him back as soon as possible. When I got him on the line, he said that "a little bird" had given him some interesting insights about one of Caroline's admirers from the web site. The little bird's name was Skinner's Pigeon. I arranged to meet him at my apartment in an hour—he was bicycling over from the Castro—and used the time before the meeting to further my career as a patron of the arts by patronizing the museum cafeteria for a pastrami on rye. I don't know much about art, but I know what I like.

I beat Chris to my building by no more than five minutes. After I buzzed him in downstairs, he waltzed through the apartment door without knocking, wearing a pair of those ridiculous spandex bicycle shorts with a matching jersey of neon green. The cleats on his equally ridiculous bike shoes clanked on my hardwood floor and caused him to hobble around like he was walking on hot coals. He had a helmet under his arm and leather satchel slung over his shoulder.

"What the hell happened to this place?" he asked after he took in Tom and Jerry's handiwork.

"Maid's day off," I said.

"Right. This and every other day." He flung his satchel and helmet down on the couch. "Wait until you see what I've got."

"Information, is what you said."

"Yeah, I'll get to that. But that's not what I meant. Look." He thrust his rump out at me like he was doing the conga. There was a large pocket in his jersey where the fabric stretched over his butt. Something long and roughly cylindrical filled it.

"Is that a potato in your pants or are you just incontinent?"

"Very amusing, I'm sure. Pull it out for me, will you? It's hard to reach back there."

I reached daintily into the pocket. "If you're filming this with a secret camera," I said, "you're a dead man." The object felt cold and wet in my hand, and once fully exposed to the light, proved to be a bottle of something called "Gay Fuel," with the tag line, "Power food for the gay man on the go." The contents were a viscous green liquid that looked like pureed fungus. I hastily passed the bottle to Chris and surreptitiously wiped my hand on the arm of the sofa.

"What the hell is that?" I asked. "And does it have to be green?"

Chris shook the bottle vigorously. "It's got spirulina and open cell chlorella. They are both excellent sources of antioxidants and give Gay Fuel its green color." He stopped and twisted off the cap to sniff inside. "Mmm ... smells like good health. I'm part of a prerelease focus group the manufacturer has going in the Castro. It's great that companies are finally marketing to gay consumers."

"If it's got cholera in it, it sounds more like they are trying to kill them than market to them."

"Not cholera, *chlorella*. It's a kind of algae. Now, do me a favor and crush me some ice in the blender. Gay Fuel tastes best over crushed ice. I'll get the laptop booting so I can show you what I found on Caroline's computer."

I was thinking it was no surprise at all that Gay Fuel tasted best over ice—because it froze your taste buds—but when I got to the kitchen, I realized I was going to have difficulty supplying the requested commodity. The blender motor was already on its last legs before Tom and Jerry paid their visit, but they had finished it completely when they smashed up the glass jar. I pulled a couple of warped aluminium ice cube trays from the freezer and looked around the room for a means to crush the cubes. I was just about to tell Chris that he was going to have to have his Gay Fuel on the rocks and like it when my eye settled on the switch to the garbage disposal. Grinning with what may well have been devilish delight, I shoveled the contents of both trays into the drain and flipped the switch.

The disposal made a hell of a racket and the ice was far from uniformly crushed, but when all was said and done, I salvaged a tall glass of chips from the process. I did my best to rinse them off before placing them in the glass, but I figured that someone who would be willing to drink algae might actually welcome a taste of a little kitchen sink flora and fauna.

When I returned to the living room, Chris was sitting at the card table with his laptop going. I set the glass down next to him with a flourish and took a seat across the table.

He eyed the glass skeptically. "You need a new blender, August."

"You're more right than you know. Now, what have you got for me?"

"Well, I haven't made it through all the material from Caroline's computer—there's gigabytes of it—but I have found that she had three or four regulars that she corresponded with frequently. They e-mailed her so often that she had created special folders to file their messages. This guy Skinner's Pigeon is one of them."

"And?"

"And I'm pretty sure that they knew each other outside of the web site. By that I mean they had some connection other than that of anonymous pervert e-mailing and buying gifts for attractive cam girl." Chris smiled in a self-satisfied way, and I could tell he was pleased with the way he'd figured this out.

"Okay, bright boy, how do you know that?"

He picked up the Gay Fuel and poured half the bottle over the ice in his glass. It was disgusting. It looked like a pond scum snow cone. "Because he knew that she disappeared. He wrote her an e-mail after she'd gone and told her that he was afraid she'd run away and he hoped she was taking care of herself and wasn't involved with anyone who would hurt her. He seemed to think she had a new boyfriend or something and he wasn't exactly pleased about it."

"When did he write her?"

Chris used the built-in mouse on his laptop keyboard to retrieve something and gave me a date two days previous. He took a big sip of the Gay Fuel and smacked his lips provocatively. The drink left a green moustache on his upper lip.

"Wipe your face. It looks like you kissed a compost heap. Did he say anything else?"

"Yeah, he said he'd sent her another gift and he hoped she would take a picture of herself wearing it and post it on the web site."

I picked at a callous on my palm. "That's interesting. He thinks she's gone, but he doesn't think she's gone so far that she can't stop by the Starbuck's and pick up the package."

"Yeah, but don't forget—people who buy gifts from Amazon Wish Lists don't know where they are sent. Which means, I suppose, it's even more likely he has some connection with her outside of the web site. He knew that she didn't have the gifts delivered at home." Chris pushed the laptop aside and leaned over the table. "Do you think that she spent some time with this Skinner's Pigeon guy and he did something to harm her or scare her and she ran away? That would explain how he knew she had gone."

I was pretty sure I knew who Skinner's Pigeon was now and Chris's scenario didn't seemed too far fetched, but I didn't say that. What I said was, "The kicker is she's not gone any more. She came back yesterday."

Chris had his beak deep in the glass of Gay Fuel. He almost did a spit-take. "Why didn't you tell me before I came over here?"

"Because I had a hankering to see you in your bicycle shorts?"

"Try again."

"Because she tried to kill herself less than eight hours later. Ellen thinks something happened to her while she was gone and she wants me to find out what it is."

"Why don't you just ask Caroline? I mean, assuming she's okay. She is okay, isn't she?"

I filled him in on the suicide attempt, including the things Caroline had told Ellen the night she came home and the fact that Caroline was in the ICU at present.

Chris shook his head when I was finished and poured the rest of the drink into his glass. "So where are you? Do you have any idea what happened?"

"No, not really. When we discovered the web site, I thought there was a strong possibility her disappearance was tied to that in some way. I still believe that, but what you learned with Skinner's Pigeon and what I've learned in talking with people at the school and elsewhere is that—with the exception of her parents—a lot of people she knew from other contexts seemed to be aware of the site."

Chris stared at me over his glass, waiting for me to say something else. "Yeah, so? Does that surprise you?"

"No. I mean, yes, it surprises me. But it also just plain worries me. It surprises me because she was so careful about not letting her parents know about the site that I would have thought she would be more circumspect in revealing it to others. Silly me. Turns out she put a flyer up on the God damn school bulletin board."

"Do you know how many web sites there are on the Internet?"

"No."

"The number I read the other day is 80 million. I also read that the number increases between one and three million each month. But anyway, guess how many visitors per day those 80 million sites get, on average."

"No idea."

"Less than one."

"So your point is she had to advertise to build up traffic."

Chris chugged the last of the Gay Fuel and licked a film of green slime off his lips. I couldn't help but make a gagging gesture, but Chris pretended not to see it. "That's right," he said. "There may be a lot of perverts on the Internet, but to attract them you're going to have to do something to stand out because there are a heck of a lot of sites catering to them. Advertising your site via the web takes money and a lot of time to build up name recognition. Advertising with your friends is free and you already have the name recognition."

"Okay, makes sense. Then here's the troubling part—if her disappearance and suicide attempt were caused or motivated by someone from the web site, then it's just as likely that person was someone she already knew, rather than an anonymous weirdo who found her site by happenstance. And you have to wonder how seeing her on the site influenced his behavior."

Chris frowned. "But you already had to consider that possibility. Aren't nine out of ten murder victims killed by someone they know? This isn't murder, but you get the point. You were already looking at people close to her and in some ways this makes it simpler. As you said, it *is* less likely to be an anonymous weirdo—who presumably would be a lot harder to track down."

I shook my head. "I'm not making myself clear. I'm not talking easier or harder. I'm talking creepier. If it's someone she knows, my guess is he wouldn't have acted if he hadn't seen her pictured in that way on the site. If someone close to her did kidnap her or molest her, then the site may have acted as a catalyst to cause him to act out a fantasy with Caroline that otherwise would have been suppressed."

Chris stared at me for a long moment, then held up his hands like he was pushing something away. "That is creepy, August. And a little abstruse for my favorite happy-go-lucky private eye. Since when were you an expert on the dark side of human nature?"

"Since I observed my friends using words like abstruse as a means to poke fun at my limited vocabulary and intellect."

"Touché. But we are getting pretty far afield with this, aren't we? There could be a very simple explanation for Caroline's behavior. Plain old depression for one. It might have nothing to do with the web site or anyone else for that matter."

I nodded and went back to work on my calluses. "That's true. I won't really know until I talk with her. In the meantime, your news about Skinner's Pigeon has given me a few ideas to run down." I looked up from my hand. "But there is one other thing."

"What?"

I had never told Chris about finding the body of the Japanese girl after our gig, but seeing the butterfly on Monica's shoulder put me in mind of it again. I took a deep breath and launched into the story of stumbling over the girl on the way to my car. I finished with a description of my visit to the school and my interview with Monica and Wesson.

To say Chris was agitated was putting it mildly. "Why didn't you tell me the next morning?"

"The police detective—Kittredge—warned me off the case, and for once, I really didn't want to get involved. I just decided the less said about it the better."

Chris looked hurt. "That's ridiculous. I'm one of your best friends."

"That's right. That's why I'm telling you now— before anyone else."

He tilted his head to acknowledge the point. "Okay. But you suggested that the tattoo on the Japanese girl looked like the one you saw on Monica. You're not thinking there's some significance to that?"

"Sounds crazy, huh?"

"Yes and no. Butterflies have got to be one of the most common kinds of tattoos for women, so it doesn't seem surprising they both would have one. If the very same artist was responsible, I suppose that would be something of a coincidence, but my understanding is that artists get hot for a time and everyone goes to them. Maybe that's the case here."

"How do you know so much about this? You and Hambert didn't get his and his tattoos, did you?"

The mention of Hambert seemed to startle him. He glanced at his watch. "Not yet, but that reminds me. I need to get going. I'm meeting Hambert for a Pilates session."

I laughed. "If there was ever a drink to go with Pilates, it would have to be Gay Fuel. How are you two doing, anyway?"

Chris stood with his glass and walked towards the kitchen. "Hambert and I are doing swimmingly, thank you," he said over his shoulder. "The only bad thing is he ships out at the end of next week."

He disappeared through the kitchen door and I heard a muttered, "Jesus Christ—what went off in here?" Then came a rattling of crockery.

"August," he called out with a new note of strain in his voice. "What happened to the blender?"

PIGEONHOLING THE PIGEON

I'D NO SOONER GOT CHRIS CALMED DOWN and on the way to his Pilates class when the phone rang. I hurried to the kitchen extension to take it.

"Did you know in Chaucer's time that women with a gap in their teeth were considered highly amorous?" said Ellen without preamble.

I laughed. "No, but that's certainly consistent with my field research."

"Is it? It's been so long that I've been with another man—with any man—that I don't remember what it means to be amorous." Her words trailed off, then she blurted, "I've been thinking about you."

"What a coincidence. I've been—"

"Don't say it, August. I feel very guilty about what we did. And I feel even more guilty when I'm sitting with Caroline. At the time she needs me most, I'm daydreaming about you like some moonstruck teenager."

I pushed spilt coffee grounds to one side and leaned my hip against the edge of the kitchen counter. "You're being too hard on yourself, Ellen."

"I don't think so. I wish we'd met at a different time in our lives—or in a different life entirely."

"I'm not big on that Shirley MacLaine reincarnation stuff. I'm glad I got to know you now—however difficult a time it may be for both of us."

I heard a ragged sigh come over the line. "I shouldn't have called. I guess I just wanted to hear your voice." She paused, and a hospital PA droned in the background. "Have you made any headway on the investigation?"

"I was going out to follow up on a lead Chris Duckworth brought me. Nothing solid yet, though."

"I won't keep you, then. You'll call me later?"

"Yes, of course."

She hung up abruptly and I was left standing in the kitchen with the dial tone buzzing mockingly in my ear. I tugged on my lower lip and thought about what it meant when a woman asked you to call after telling you she shouldn't have called in the first place.

I finally gave it up as imponderable and went out to retrieve the Galaxie for the drive back to the Noe Valley Starbuck's. The manager didn't seem to be in, but I didn't have much trouble convincing the reedy kid with dreadlocks to check in back for more of Caroline's packages. Sure enough, three new boxes from Amazon.com had arrived and —more to the point—one of them came from Skinner's Pigeon. Given that he had requested Caroline to take a picture of herself wearing his latest gift, I had prepared myself for the possibility that the item would be inappropriate, risqué or both, but I still wasn't ready for the "Hello Kitty Leopard Pink Cyber-Goth Corset" with convenient Velcro fastener I found inside.

As with the other shipments I'd opened, the packing list obscured the identity of the purchaser as "Private Buyer," but Mr. Pigeon had been kind enough to accompany his gift with a note signed with his pet name for easy identification:

```
Goth Angel,
    Think of me when you wear this and be
reminded of the support, comfort and—dare
```

I say it—discipline I provide. If you were
to post a photograph of yourself in the
garment, I would be most gratified.
    Your loving servant,
    Skinner's Pigeon

As with the e-mail Chris had found, the note hinted at a relationship outside the context of the web site and, more specifically, seemed
to suggest that the relationship involved mentorship or counseling.
I'd had my suspicions about Dr. Levin since I first talked to him, but
this pushed me over the edge. I barreled across town to his office on
Gough, hoping to catch him before he went home for the day.

It was 5:45 when I arrived, and I found the glass paneled door
to the Edwardian locked. A sign on the door advised that the office
closed at 5 PM, which seemed early for most businesses, but entirely
consistent with the 50-minutes-to-an-hour approach that therapists
take to other timekeeping matters. In a snit, I pounded on the door
for a good five minutes with no results. I had stopped to massage
the reddened skin on the heel of my palm when a woman carrying
a heavily laden cardboard box appeared on the other side. Juggling
the box, she reached awkwardly for the door knob and just managed
to twist it open. I put my foot up against it to block it from closing,
waited while she stepped back and then held it wide open for her to
come through.

I'm not the sort of person who believes in fate, karma or any of
the new age terms for predestination, but when we both got a good
look at each other, I did believe in revenge. She started to thank me
for holding the door, then registered who I was and shouted, "You!" in
an angry voice with a heavy French accent. She hurled the box down
at my outstretched foot, where the thirty-plus pounds of books, file
folders and other office miscellanea eventually caused my big toe to
turn the shape, color and consistency of an overripe fig.

I immediately bent to shove the box aside and render whatever aid
I could to my tenderized appendage. She took this as an invitation to

pound on my back with both fists while shouting a string of obsceni-
ties at me in French, the only one of which I recognized was *merde*.

I knew at least three things about her. The first was her name,
which was Odile. The second was the reason for her anger: I had once
bound her with duct tape and locked her in the trunk of the Galaxie.
The fact that she had been holding a French-made Beretta in her lap,
waiting to ambush my client when I surprised her did not—apparently—qualify as a mitigating circumstance in her mind. The final
thing I knew about her was that she was a beautiful woman with a
lush figure and long black hair who had been in been in love with a
woman whom my client—a man—had made the mistake of getting
involved with. That had led to her stalking him, which in turn had
led to my putting her in my trunk.

I stood to face her and wrestled to take hold of both her wrists.
"Cut it out," I said. "Don't you know it's not healthy to hold a
grudge?"

"And don't you know that it's not healthy to be locked in the
trunk of a jalopy?" The way she pronounced jalopy made it sound
like a decadent French dessert.

I pushed her out of striking range and released her, still holding
my hands in a defensive gesture in case she went on the attack again.
"I locked you up, you mashed my toe. Let's call it even, okay?"

She ignored the question. "You must be a harbinger of evil," she
said with a kind of awe in her voice. "You show up every time my
life turns to shit."

I stood a little straighter, somehow honored by the recognition.
"What's wrong now?"

"I lost my job is what is wrong. Why do you think I'm carrying
this box with everything from my office?"

"Wait a minute. You work here?"

She yanked at the fabric of her black turtleneck, pulling it down
over her hips. A matching wool skirt and a loose belt of gold-colored
rings completed the ensemble. "No, you idiot," she said. "I just keep
my office things here. I do the actual therapy at the bus stop."

I remembered now that she had been in residency at Stanford at the time of our run-in. "Sorry. I'm a little slow today. Then you know Dr. Levin."

"Yes. He's my boss—or my ex-boss. He fired me today after I declined to fuck him. Are you seeing him? That would be perfect. The vile snake treating the grasping jackal."

"If I can pick, I'd rather be the wascally wabbit. And, no, I'm not seeing him, but I do want to talk. Is he in?"

She gave a grim little smile. "He left hours ago—right after he fired me. I am to be out by the time he returns."

"I see. You don't happen to have his home address, do you?"

She pushed her lips out the way the French sometimes do and made a little puffing noise. "If I knew, why should I tell you?"

"How does revenge sound? The grasping jackal is not the harbinger of evil for nothing. I'm trying to nail his ass."

"I am bitter, but not so bitter that I would inflict *you* on him. Perhaps, after all, it is best that I do not work here. Find his address some other way." She moved to pick up the box.

"How would you feel if you knew he'd been sexually harassing his patients? His young female patients. Would you give me his address then?"

She squinted up at me for a long moment, then took a notebook out of the box. She flipped open to a tabbed section and tore out a page. "Here. This is his address. I hope what you say is not true, but if it is, then he deserves every misery you are so very capable of inflicting."

She picked up the box with a grunt and charged down the sidewalk to the street. "Thanks for your confidence," I called after her.

Dr. Levin's house was on Washington Street in the tony neighborhood of Pacific Heights. His wasn't the most desirable address in the district, being too far down the slope of the hill that crested at Pacific Avenue, but the building itself—a former firehouse—more than made up for the lack. It was an imposing, churchlike affair with a hose-tower steeple and double doors wide enough to emit horse-drawn fire engines. I went up to the smaller, human-sized door to one side and twisted the old-timey door chime. I heard nothing for a long minute, and then the sound of someone clattering down a metal staircase came through the oak door.

It was opened by a woman with short auburn hair that was swept dramatically over her ears to emphasize earrings with diamonds the size of horse molars. Her face—and forehead in particular—were smooth and serene, but the skin of her throat was lined and sagging, which made me think she was probably the hostess with the mostest when it came to the Pacific Heights botox parties I'd been reading so much about lately. She wore a simple pink cotton shirt with jeans, but covered her shoulders with a fringed shawl made of pink silk.

"Yes," she said with an imperiousness that made damn clear I better not be selling anything.

"I'm here to see Dr. Levin."

"Is he expecting you?"

I quoted from *Golden Dawn of the New Epiphany*, "He who gathers thistles, may expect pricks."

She would have arched her eyebrows if her facial muscles permitted. As it was, she made a sort of protracted flinching motion with her head. "Is that supposed to be clever? I suggest you leave our property before I call the police." She moved to close the door, but I shoved my foot against it—damaged toe and all.

"Hold on. Dr. Levin will positively want to see me. Please give him this and tell him that there is a crisis with the patient involved." I passed over a plastic bag containing the gift from Skinner's Pigeon. I had the accompanying card in my breast pocket.

She hesitated, then snatched the bag out of my hand. "I'll take it to him, but I'm not making any promises. Now get your foot out of the way." I pulled my foot back and she slammed the door in my face. Two deadbolts snapped into place.

I heard the sound of steps going up the metal staircase and then I heard nothing. I walked away from the door and looked down the street. A woman in her early twenties with her hair in a scrunchy jogged down the sidewalk, the sound from her MP3 player leaking out of her earphones like singing munchkins as she went by. A silver Mercedes pulled into the driveway of a sprawling mansion across the way. The driver stepped out and caught sight of me loitering on the Levin's sidewalk. He eyed me suspiciously over the roof of the car. "Aluminum siding," I shouted. "Be over to your house in a jiffy." He ducked back into the car to get his suitcase and then hurried up the drive to sanctuary.

I heard the sound of feet on the metal stairway again and turned toward the firehouse. The deadbolts snicked back and the door pulled open to reveal Dr. Levin. He looked as stooped as before, but he had decided to do something about his hair. Through the miracle of combing, he'd moved the crown of his head to a point one inch northeast of his left ear and in the process managed to shunt a few strands of hair over his bald pate. He held up the bag I'd given his wife and flashed one of his insincere smiles. "I'm afraid you have the advantage over me with this, Mr. Riordan. I'm not quite sure what I'm supposed to make of it."

"Then why'd you come to the door?"

He smiled again. "Well, naturally I didn't want to be rude. I know that you are looking for Caroline, and as I told you, I want to do what I can to help—within the limits of the therapist-patient privilege."

"I never told your wife who I was. How'd you know it was me—or that it had anything to do with Caroline?"

The smile dropped from his face like a dried scab. He looked involuntarily to the thing in his hands, then forced his eyes back to my face. "Well, I—I saw you come up the walk from the living room window of course. And I knew you'd been hired to find Caroline from our previous conversation."

I leaned into him. "I think if you'd seen me, you would have answered the door yourself—or stopped your wife from answering it at all. But let's skip the cat and mouse bullshit. You sent Caroline the corset. You've been sexually harassing your own patient. That's the minimum charge. What I came to find out is if you kidnapped and molested her too."

Levin backed away from the door and I could see into a narrow, tiled entryway. Further back was a spiral wrought iron staircase. "What are you talking about?" he said. "I would never engage in that kind of behavior. I'm a licensed, ethical professional. I have three degrees from Harvard. I was elected to Phi Beta Kappa in my junior year."

"What? You didn't get a bid after freshman rush?"

Levin's face reddened and he sputtered inarticulately. "Good God," he said finally. "You are the most ignorant man I've ever met."

"You can shove your Phi Beta Kappa key right up your ass, Levin. Academics and state licenses don't have a thing to do with it. This is an issue of ethics and character, not intellect or learning."

The pupils of Levin's eyes vibrated like black BB's. "You've no proof of any of this. Has Caroline said I sexually harassed her? No. I'm certain that she hasn't. I never once said or did anything during our sessions that could be interpreted as harassment."

I stepped over the threshold, causing Levin to give more ground. "Drop it. You know that Caroline isn't available to say anything and this isn't about your therapy sessions. I wouldn't be here if I hadn't determined that you are Skinner's Pigeon."

"Skinner's Pigeon? What are you babbling about now?"

"Caroline has a web site with another girl where they post pictures of themselves and encourage visitors to give them gifts and money. Most of the visitors use code names to hide their identity when they send e-mails or gifts. You picked Skinner's Pigeon. I suppose you thought the connection to B.F. Skinner's operant conditioning experiments with pigeons was a clever, veiled reference to your profession, although it sounds like a cry for help to me. Are you having issues with self-esteem?"

Levin snorted and fixed me with another of his phoney smiles. He'd pulled himself off the ropes. "That's it? That's your proof? The fact that someone happened to use a name associated with research in my field?" He threw the bag containing the corset at me and it bounced off my chest. "Take that ... *thing* and get out of here—or I'm calling the cops."

I moved like I was going to pick up the bag and then pivoted towards him. I grabbed a handful of his shirt and shoved him against the wall. He reeked of a citrus-based cologne. "Skinner's Pigeon wrote to Caroline the day after I visited you in your office," I said into his ear. "He knew that she had run away and he knew that she was rumored to have new boyfriend—although he was clearly jealous about it. You're the only one who could have known those things."

"Don't be ridiculous. Any of Caroline's friends could have known that. You haven't proved anything."

I tightened my grip on the wad of expensive Egyptian cotton I held in my hand. "Do you know anything about the Internet, Levin?"

"What does that have to—"

"I don't either, but my associate Chris Duckworth does. He's traced the origin of the e-mails to your computer. We've got you nailed."

It was pure bluff, but Levin wasn't quite sure what to make of it. Tiny beads of sweat appeared between the strands of his barcode hairdo. He licked his lips, but then managed another smile. "I don't think that's possible. But what if it were? Let's do a little thought experiment. If I were one of Caroline's many admirers—if I corresponded with her and sent her gifts—there's still nothing you could do about it. She's advertising herself on the web, for God's sake. She's *inviting* people to make her an object of fantasy. In that scenario, in our little thought experiment, I would merely be a subscriber to a freely available web service."

I grit my teeth and hissed through them, "You're her fucking therapist, Levin. You're supposed to be helping her, not feeding your sick perversions. If I find out you're the reason she ran away, I'll ... "

He laughed. "You'll do what? Feed me a knuckle sandwich?"

That tore it. I let go of his shirt and popped him right in the mouth.

"Over 999 served," I said.

Levin slid down the wall and collapsed in a heap on the floor. He was more shocked than hurt, but his lip was split and blood was oozing from the wound. "What kind of troglodyte are you?" he said wonderingly.

"The kind that will kick you until I stave in every last one of your ribs. Now what do you know about Caroline's disappearance?"

He brought the back of his hand up to blot the blood on his lip, staring at me all the while. "I told you everything I knew at the office."

I moved a step closer to him and drew my foot back. "You didn't tell me about visiting her web site."

He scuttled like a silverfish along the baseboard. "Okay, okay," he said. "I did go to the site and I did send her gifts. But I never saw her outside of the therapy sessions and most of the time she never even responded to the e-mails and gifts I sent. I didn't have anything to do with her running away."

"Did she know Skinner's Pigeon was you?"

"No, I don't think so. I mean, one time I thought so, but I decided not."

I stared down at him, trying to decide what to do next. I halfway believed what he was telling me, but my threat to beat him further was idle and I knew that I would never get the advantage of him like this again. "I want your files," I finally said.

"What?"

"I want all the files you have on Caroline."

"Those are privileged documents. And you wouldn't know how to interpret them anyway."

"Don't tell me about privileged after what you've done. Give me all the files or I'm reporting you to the AMA—whatever oversight board you shrinks have—and Caroline's parents. And if you think I'm a troglodyte, you haven't met Quentin Stockwell. Police Lieutenant Quentin Stockwell, that is."

Levin looked down at the floor and shook his head. "I know all about him. All right, I'll messenger you the files tomorrow."

I reached down to yank him to his feet. "I want them tonight."

Levin started to argue, but the sound of someone on the spiral staircase came to us. We both turned to watch as Mrs. Levin wound her way down from the floor above. "What's going on here? I thought I heard something fall."

"We were just having a little therapy session," I said. "Pick up the bag, Dr. Levin."

Levin reached dutifully for the corset and I gave him a shove towards the front door.

"Where are you going?" demanded Mrs. Levin. "We have the opera."

"Tell them to start the screaming without you," I said. "He's going to be late."

BUTTERFLIES AREN'T FREE

I DROVE LEVIN TO HIS OFFICE IN MY car to minimize any chance of him slipping away. He sulked quietly on the ride over, huddled in a malevolent ball as far away from me as possible on the big bench seat of the Galaxie. By the time we got to his office, though, he had gotten his courage back and refused to get out of the car. He threatened to report me to the police and demanded to be driven home immediately. I sighed in a bored way and said:

"You can get out and walk home if you like. But in addition to everything else I promised, I'm going straight back to your house to give your wife a copy of every single e-mail you sent to Caroline, along with a full explanation of what you've been up to." I paused to rub my chin. "In fact, if you're not going to give me the files, maybe you should just check into a hotel. You won't be getting won't get much of a welcome at home after your wife gets the news."

Levin caved completely after that. He let me into the building and unlocked the door to his office, where I liberated a fat file on Caroline and about a half dozen audio cassette tapes. When I asked him whether Caroline knew that he had taped their sessions, he coughed in a self-important way and mumbled something about "standard practice."

The last I saw of him was a look of squinted hatred that seemed to hang in the evening air long after his taxi had pulled away. I walked back to the Galaxie to thumb through the file and I realized he had been right about one thing: I couldn't make heads or tails of it. There were weekly entries going back nine months. They were handwritten in a sort of abbreviated shorthand that was illegible and full of jargon and abbreviations that made no sense to me. I was running through my mental Rolodex to locate someone I knew who would be willing to help me decipher the contents when my eye fell upon the sheet of paper Odile had torn from her notebook. Written above Levin's address was an entry for "Odile Laroche" complete with address and phone number. I figured it was worth a try: I still had nine good toes at my disposal.

I jogged across the street to Lafayette Park to look for a pay phone, and for once my search was rewarded with a functioning machine. Mind you, I had to chip bubble gum out of the coin slot and the broken pieces of the receiver were barely connected by a slimy red wire with half the insulation missing. Odile answered on the first ring, then promptly hung up at the mention of my name. I managed to squeeze in a succinct explanation of my request on the second attempt, and after a long pause that almost convinced me she'd set the phone down and walked away, she relented and agreed to review the materials—if only to get back at "that sick little wienie puller."

I drove over to her apartment in the Bernal Heights neighborhood, dropped the file, tapes, and my card on her doorstep, rang the bell and slipped away before she answered. I didn't relish the idea of more face time with her and needed to get a move on if I wanted to see Caroline at the hospital before visiting hours were over.

Ellen had told me that she had taken Caroline to Washington Hospital in the neighboring town of Fremont. Running the Galaxie hard on the six of eight cylinders that still had compression, I covered the 40-some miles across the Bay Bridge to the hospital's location in the northern part of town in about 50 minutes. It was 8:15 when I arrived.

The lights in the visitors lot were burned out or broken, making the area in front of the entrance unusually dark. The nearly deserted reception area and the eerie fluorescent glow that came through the

windows as I approached put me in mind of Hopper's famous painting of a New York diner, *Nighthawks*. In place of the busboy in the
painting was a middle-aged woman wearing a white uniform. Her
hair was black and cut in a short Cleopatra style and she had a lot of
dark makeup around her eyes. She tracked me as I came up to the
reception desk the way a bored feline tracks a mouse.

I told her I wanted to visit Caroline Stockwell.

"Visiting hours are 11 AM to 8 PM," she said. I started to protest,
but she rode right over me. "However, in special cases those hours
may be extended. Is yours a special case?"

She seemed to have every expectation that it was because she
was already reaching for an adhesive name badge from a box on her
desk. Applying the full power of the native Riordan intellect, I lied,
"Yes, it is a special case. I'm her uncle and I've just flown in from out
of state to see her."

The receptionist didn't bother acknowledging the response. She
didn't even bother looking up. "Name?"

"August Riordan."

She wrote that in block caps on the badge, peeled off the backing
and handed it to me. "Put that on and go up to the nurses station on
floor ... " She typed something rapidly on the computer on her desk.
"Six. Check in there and they will let you know if Ms. Stockwell can
see visitors."

"Does that mean she's out of the ICU?"

The receptionist smiled reflexively. "We call it the critical care
unit now. But, that's right. She been moved to a regular ward."

I thanked her, received a blank, thousand mile stare in return
and walked towards the elevators. On my way, I passed a refrigerator
with glass doors containing fresh cut flowers. There was a metal box
for honor system payments on top. I selected a bouquet of carnations
and stuffed my ten dollars in the box. I figured it would help my story
if the nurses on the sixth floor were a tougher screen.

The sixth floor was almost as quiet and deserted as the receiving
area had been. A guy wearing a paper hat and pushing a towering

cart of hospital trays full of uneaten servings of lime Jello and tapioca pudding and he directed me to the nurses station. The nurse on duty there had a lot more enthusiasm than the woman downstairs. She also had chewing gum, breasts that could only come from a request to the plastic surgeon to "supersize" her order and nails the size, shape and color of Chili Cheese Flavored Fritos.

"How can we help you tonight, Mr., ah, Riordan?" she said warmly with more than a trace of Texas.

"I'm her to see Caroline Stockwell."

"Well, as I'm sure they told you downstairs, this *is* outside of normal visiting hours, but I think Caroline is still awake. Do you have a special reason to see her tonight?"

"I'm her uncle ... " I said, then feeling that this was somehow insufficient, added, "and her godfather."

The nurse smiled. "And you've brought an arrangement of flowers from the stand downstairs." She reached across the counter with her orange Frito claw to reshuffle the carnations in their vase. She sighed when she was finished and brought her hand up to his mouth like she was going to share a confidence. "Next time I'd go for the gladiolas. No one likes carnations. They're for floats and funerals."

"Er, thanks for the tip," I said.

"Come on, then. I'll take you to Caroline's room."

We went back towards the elevators, turned left at an adjoining corridor and stopped in front of room 624. The nurse tapped lightly on the door, then opened it without waiting for a response. "Caroline," she said brightly. "Your godfather is here."

I grimaced at the mention of godfathers but stepped gamely into the room, holding the now discredited carnations discreetly at my side. Dark eyes framed in a mess of purple hair glared at me from the bed. Pale, sardonic lips moved to form words that I was certain would be, "I've never seen this guy in my life," but what came out instead was a dispirited, "Oh, goody."

The nurse nodded as if that was the prescribed response and moved to leave the room. "I'll let you two visit now. But don't stay too long, Mr. Riordan. Caroline needs her rest."

I waited until the door closed behind her, and then placed the vase of flowers on a table along the wall. Another, larger arrangement with no connection to floats or funerals was already there. I stood a little uncomfortably by the foot of the bed and looked at the occupant. Her face—like her lips—was pale. The paleness accentuated her cheek bones, making the resemblance to her mother even more pronounced. She had a cuff of thick bandages around her left wrist and an IV going into her right hand. She was wearing a paisley blue and white hospital gown, but was tucked so far into the covers that they nearly came to her chin. I said:

"Thanks for letting me get away with the godfather business back there."

She shrugged microscopically. "My mother said you were coming." A beat went by. "So, are you doing her or what?"

That one hit a little too close to home. I struggled to hold my face in a neutral expression. "Where'd you get that idea?"

"All she talks about is you. The last time I saw her so obsessed was with Julio Iglesias. She used to keep a *People* magazine with pictures of him in her bed stand drawer, right next her vibrator."

"I don't need to know that."

"Sure you do. At least you know she's not frigid—in the off chance you haven't nailed her yet. But then, you're no Julio Iglesias."

"Praise be to Allah for that. But she can't have said that much about me. From what I understand, you've only had a few hours with her since you've, ah, returned."

Caroline smirked and pushed a strand of hair off her cheek. She moved very slowly, as if she was very tired or very drugged. My guess was both. "That's right, and all she could do was drone on about this private eye she hired. About how you and my old man got in a fight and how you had found out about my web site."

"That doesn't sound like it was about me. That sounds like she was expressing concern about you and the effort it took to find you. Most people go their whole lives without ever once having to hire an investigator."

"Yeah, and she didn't need to do it either. I came back on my own power, and as far as I can tell, you didn't have a fucking clue as to where I was."

I undid the button of my collar and loosed the knot of my tie, suddenly feeling very tired myself. "Could be. But I know where you weren't—on a cross-country car trip. My guess is you were with someone—someone you trusted—and they abused that trust. You might have been on a trip, but I'm betting you were in the Bay Area the whole time."

She smirked at me again. "You sound like a newspaper horoscope or a bad palm reader. You don't know diddly, and you're trying to bluff me with a bullshit scenario that would fit a million situations. Hell, if my car broke down and I was ripped off by a bad auto mechanic, it still would fit your story."

"All right, let's get specific. I know about Skinner's Pigeon. He must have made an inappropriate advance or—"

She barked a derisive laugh. "What would have been an appropriate one? I would never let him get within six feet of my precious alabaster flesh. Sure, I knew he was visiting the web site and sending me gifts—and I did everything I could to steam him up during our sessions—but there's no way I would fall under his sway." She raised her arms and waggled her fingers threateningly like a villain in a silent movie.

I was more than a little relieved not to have misread the situation with Levin. "Why make such a mystery of it, then?" I said. "Why don't you just tell everyone what really happened."

"I did. I went for a cross-country trip with a friend."

"And came home and promptly sliced open your wrist."

She shrugged her microscopic shrug. "You ought to be more sensitive to my situation. I'm on a suicide watch here. You want me to ring for the nurse and tell her you're causing me mental trauma?"

"You're causing everyone who cares for you trauma by the truck-load. I think you're shielding someone. Is it Nidhi? He was almost certainly visiting your web site, and two of his disciples tore my apartment apart looking for something. Or how about Wesson? Those aren't exactly studio portraits down at the MOMA. He may also be a stalker from the web site. He definitely knows about it."

That got a rise out of her. She thrust herself further out of the covers, wincing as she put weight on her damaged wrist. "You really are a shit-stirrer, aren't you?" She glowered at me while hugging her wrist to her body.

"That pretty much sums up the job description for a private investigator. You didn't answer my question, though."

"I didn't answer it because it's crazy," she said, but there was thought behind her voice. "I haven't seen the guru or been to the ashram in months. And Wesson isn't like that. Besides, he's ... "

"He's what?"

"He's a teacher at the school."

I didn't think that was what she intended to say. I nodded, but didn't respond. She picked at the tape that secured the IV to her wrist and then let her gaze wander over to the carnations I'd brought. She smirked and shook her head. Then a funny thing happened: tears welled at the corners of her eyes. When I still didn't say anything, she beat on the covers with her fist.

"What do you want from me?"

"I want a chance to help. But until you tell me what happened— and who made it happen—I can't do anything."

"Don't flatter yourself, Riordan. You couldn't do anything if you did know." Her voice quivered as she said this last bit.

I moved a little closer to the bed, hoping she was finally going to open up. "Why don't you try me?"

Her movements became jerky. She wiped at her eyes with the back of her hand and then reached across her body to grab the bed covers. "Okay," she said frantically. "Okay. I'll try you." She swept the covers off, revealing her torso wrapped in the paisley gown.

"Wait," I bleated. "Don't."

She ignored me, twitching the hand up to her shoulder where she yanked at the cloth. The knots in back tore or came undone and soon she was naked to her waist. She squirmed and kicked and the gown ended up in a wad at the bottom of the bed. Tears streamed down her face as she pressed both hands to her sides—just below her breasts—like she was framing a piece of art. Her chest heaved. "What about this, Riordan? How you're going to help with this?"

The "this" was a savage-looking tattoo of a Komodo dragon that covered her entire torso. The thick tail wrapped around her mons pubis, the scaly body followed a line across her stomach and chest—with each of the foreclaws seeming to seize a breast—the ugly, blunt head with its speckled snout nestled near her throat and the slimy pink tongue flicked out to ensnare an iridescent butterfly that floated along her shoulder. The butterfly looked identical to the one I'd seen on the dead girl in the alley. The compelling depravity of the image—which was tattooed in deep, vibrant colors and seemingly executed with a high degree of skill—managed to simultaneously repulse and allure. But that was from the perspective of the viewer. From the perspective of the human canvas, it was a horrific thing to have permanently etched on your body. The scar from a third degree burn would have been infinitely preferable.

I stood and stared and could not think of a single comforting or helpful thing to say. It was inevitable, somehow, that the nurse chose that precise moment to return to the room. I don't know if she heard the hysteria in Caroline's voice or simply decided that visiting time was over.

"Oh my God," she said hoarsely. "What are you doing?"

I turned to gape at her. She looked back at Caroline and then glared at me and launched a right hand claw that seemed to come from miles and miles away. I watched it come and I knew that I could easily block it or duck out of the way. But I couldn't. It hit me square on the face.

My partial upper flew out of my mouth and went skittering to the far corner of the room. The nurse shrieked and cringed from the gap-toothed monster in front of her. "Get out of here," she screamed. She ran to the nightstand on the near side of the bed and picked up the phone. "I'm calling security."

I felt like a humiliated teenager. Blood rushed to my cheeks and made the places where her nails hit me throb all the more. I managed an inarticulate grunt and stepped over to the corner to pick up the plate. I didn't attempt to put it back in. "I'm leaving now," I said with as much dignity as I could muster. "But you're wrong about what happened."

I speared the edge of the covers as I went by and yanked them over Caroline, who looked up at me with the savage expression of someone who has lost so much that they can only take comfort in the humbling of others.

"That's right," she yelled at my back. "Get the fuck out of here. And go back and tell my mother what a damaged piece of goods her daughter is."

THRONE DOWN

I HOPED THAT WHEN CAROLINE CALMED DOWN SHE would explain matters to the nurse, but just in case she didn't, I found the stairs and snuck down them to avoid any unpleasant encounters with hospital security. When I got out of the building, I aimed the Galaxie at the nearest gas station and filled the 1960s-sized gas tank to the tune of $46.25. Then I went inside the mini-mart and—holding a hand over my missing teeth—bought my first pack of cigarettes in about three months, surprised to find that the price had gone up considerably. I tore open the pack with shaking fingers and chain-smoked three on the curb in front of the store before my jangled nerves settled down. As I stood there watching mothers in mini-vans work the pumps, it occurred to me that if I was ever to develop an economic theory it would be that the price of a gallon of gas and the cost of a pack of cigarettes seek the same level.

I went next to the rest room where I washed off the denture and put it back in my mouth. It went in fine, but I immediately noticed a very sharp edge with my tongue. I pulled the plate out again to examine it in the gritty yellow light and found that one of the wire clips that secured it in place had broken, creating a needle-like point. I shoved the plate back in my mouth, vowing this time to go through the trauma of getting implants rather than putting up with the damn denture any longer.

My last stop was the pay phone, where I intended to call Ellen to let her know what I had found at the hospital. I guessed that the unitard Caroline had been wearing the night she came home was intended to hide the tattoo. I assumed the hospital staff were aware of it, and while they probably thought it was a horrible desecration of a young woman's body, they didn't realize that it was a recent addition or that it was the cause of Caroline's suicide attempt. Caroline might even have told them to keep quiet about it. I dropped two quarters in the pay phone slot and dialed Ellen's number. It rang three times and I heard her answer, "Stockwell residence," in a hushed voice.

I opened my mouth to speak, and then panicked. I suddenly realized this wasn't something I wanted to tell her over the phone. I slapped down the toggle on the receiver cradle and listened as my quarters fell into the coin box.

I needed to talk to someone—if not to Ellen. I dialed Gretchen's cell number from memory. Since I refused to use the voice mail system at work, I sometimes called her after hours to ask her about messages I might have missed during the day. It was mainly an excuse to talk to her away from the office and she knew it, but she played along with it anyway.

"This is the neighborhood video store," I said when she picked up. "I'm calling because you turned in a personal tape by mistake. I loved you in the Catholic school girl outfit, but you really need to lose the dork in the urologist getup."

"Nice try, August."

"Didn't fool you for a minute, huh?"

"No. I always play the naughty nurse."

"You almost make me wish there was a video tape, but I'm done with naughty nurses for the foreseeable future." I told her about my visit to see Caroline.

"How awful, August. Did she say how she got the tattoo?"

"No, I didn't get the chance to inquire." I winced as I inadvertently ran my tongue over the sharp point on the denture. "I'm afraid it was something she *asked* to have done, perhaps not realizing how truly hideous it would turn out to be."

"Hmm," said Gretchen. "It must take a long time to get a tattoo like that. I think she would have realized what she was getting and cut her losses before it was finished."

"Depends on whether she was conscious for all of it—and which end of the tattoo they started with. The butterfly itself is very pretty." I thought again about the girl in the alley, and then I remembered the tattoo I'd seen on Monica Mapa's shoulder.

"August," said Gretchen. "Are you there?"

"Yes, sorry. I was thinking."

Gretchen laughed. "I thought I smelled wood burning."

"Watch it."

"What are you going to do now?"

"I need to tell Caroline's mother about the tattoo. I just don't have the heart to do it tonight. I'm bushed—physically and emotionally."

"Then you probably won't want to play the ... "

A Japanese sedan with loud glass packs and about 12 teenagers came bounding off the street and passed close to the phone booth. "I didn't catch that last part," I said. "What'd you say?"

"I said then you won't want to play the gig at Bruno's. Sol Hodges called late at the office. His bass player showed up drunk, had a few more drinks on the house and promptly passed out. Sol's got two more shows at 10 and 12 and the owner is threatening to boot him unless he finds a sober bass."

I thought about it. Playing with Hodge's band, Distant Opposition, was always a treat because of the caliber of the musicians. The request to join them on such short notice was a backhanded complement: Hodges thought enough of me to let me jump in cold, but also knew that I wasn't likely to have something already. "I don't know," I said. "It would be hard to make the logistics work. I'm down in Fremont. I'd have to get home and then drive across town to the Mission to get to Bruno's."

"Forget going home," said Gretchen, and there was a smile in her voice as she spoke. "Hodges says you can use the other guy's bass. Sounds like it would be good for you August. I think you should go for it."

I didn't take much convincing. "Okay, doll, you sold me. Would you call Hodges for me and let him know I'm coming?"

"Will do. By the way, he said to bring a trumpet along if you knew one."

"Dundee's not playing?"

"That's what he said. Hodges said his lip wasn't healed from that bar fight of yours."

I felt bad for Dundee, but I thought I knew someone who would fit the bill. "Gretchen, one last favor. See if you can get hold of Vic Lane and have him tell his grandson to meet me at Bruno's. The kid's supposed to be good."

"All right, Auggie," she said with cheerful resignation. "Just promise me there won't be any more urologist jokes."

I committed to banish them from my repertoire—with fingers crossed—and jumped into the Galaxie. I played Coleman Hawkins's *Desafinado* full blast on the ride back to the city, letting the bassa nova beat transport me much faster than the car could ever do.

The gig at Bruno's turned out to be a success in every respect. The owner was happy, I played well enough that Hodges let me take a couple of very creditable solos and Reggie more than proved his chops. He and Cornelius Crawford—the band's outstanding alto sax player—absolutely caught fire on an uptempo version of Tad Dameron's *Good Bait* during the encore.

The last I saw of Reggie, he was having a drink at the bar with Hodges. I heard Hodges promise to put in a good word with another band leader who was looking for a trumpet and the kid's face lit up like night baseball. As I went through the upholstered red leather door onto Mission street, he shouted at my back, "August, you're the bomb!"

The euphoria from the gig seemed to fade as soon as I got outside. Maybe I was jealous of Hodge's interest in the kid or maybe I was depressed about the turn of events at the hospital. Probably it was some of both. I stood under the sign that trumpeted the supper club's name in large, red 1950s-style letters and fingered the pack of smokes in my pocket, resisting the urge to light up. The street was dark and a palpable cottony fog hung in the air. The few lights visible glowed diffusely like the blotchy yellow stars in a Van Gogh painting. I crushed the package of cigarettes, threw them into an overflowing garbage can and took a few meandering steps up Mission towards 21st Street, away from my car.

I kidded myself that I was walking to clear my head before driving back to my apartment, but since Bruno's was only about three blocks from Monica Mapa's, I knew the real reason for my little gallivant was to check out her place. It was too late to have any reasonable expectation that she would be up, but if she was, I felt certain that she'd have more to tell me about Caroline's misadventures than she'd admitted so far. The journey took all of ten minutes and the only signs of life I passed on the way were a growling street sweeper with flashing lights that materialized out of the fog like an alien space craft and the mounded blankets and flimsy cardboard screens of the homeless sleeping in doorways.

I prowled around the side of her building that fronted 21st and turned the corner onto Folsom. My pulse moved a little quicker when I saw that the lights were on in the second floor apartment. I trudged up the mismatched tread boards of the staircase to the entryway and stopped short. It was very dark in the vestibule, but a piece of white tape glowed faintly on the door to the flat. It appeared to be holding something small that protruded slightly from the pitted wood surface. I dug my fingernail under the edge of the tape and peeled it back. Stuck to the tape was a tiny metal bar or post of some kind, but in the bad light I couldn't make out exactly what it was. I ran my thumb over the metal and I felt a wet slickness. A flutter of dread ran through me.

I bolted down the steps to the streetlamp on the corner, and holding my thumb to the light, saw a smudge of dark blood.

The item in the tape proved to be a stud like the one I had seen in the pictures of Caroline. It seemed to me that the blood on it could only mean one thing. It had been removed forcibly from someone's belly button—and the someone was likely Monica. I rushed back up the steps to the vestibule and pounded on the door. It rattled in its frame as it did the first time I came to the apartment, but there was no response from within. I aimed my foot at the place where the cheap deadbolt met the jamb and gave a sharp kick. The door flew open and a foot-long splinter went sailing into the darkened entryway.

I wasn't carrying my gun, but I paused to draw the knife on my ankle and then took the interior stairs two steps at a time. Light stabbed out from a crack beneath the apartment door onto the landing. I reached for the knob and twisted. It turned in my hand.

I pushed the door open and watched as it proscribed a lazy arc across the entryway. It had just enough momentum to kiss the far wall and bounce back an inch or so. I looked across the wide open room and saw what I'd seen before: the camera, the fiery backdrop, the computer table and the throne. The only thing different was the throne—it was occupied. Monica sat in a stiffly erect pose with her hands on the arms of the chair and her knees pressed together. She looked like a sculpture from an Egyptian tomb, if you ignored the fact she was naked. Her limbs appeared to be held in place by tape and her head flopped onto her chest like it was hinged.

I moved slowly into the flat, alert for movement from the back, but thinking all the while that there was only me and Monica—and only I was still breathing. When I came up to her I could see that I had been right about the tape. It was a white surgical tape like I'd taken from the front door and it was wrapped tight around her wrists to bind her to the chair, and around her ankles and knees to hold her legs together. I returned my knife to its harness and carefully cupped my hands underneath her chin to lift her head. I found more tape around her neck where it bound her to an ornate wooden baluster on the back of the chair. There were dark bruises on her throat that didn't seem to have anything to do with the tape and I felt absolutely no trace of a pulse. Her skin was cool to the touch, but I couldn't begin to judge how long she had been dead.

I had been right about the source of the stud taped to the door. There was a jagged half-inch rip in the flesh above her belly button, but there seemed to be very little blood around the wound. I guessed that the stud had been yanked out after she died. In fact, it seemed as if everything from the stud to taping her to the throne was something the killer had done after she was dead—probably from strangulation.

I let her head back down to her chest as gently as I could and stepped back, my hands trembling. Finding young women dead was getting to be a habit with me, and finding them in ritualistic poses with mutilations was a particularly nasty turn for the habit to take. I sat down in a chair in from of the computer table to get myself under control and figure out what to do next.

I propped my elbows on my knees and held my head in my hands, staring down at my feet. My brain was a howling maelstrom of conflicting thoughts and impulses. I pushed back from the table, trying to get more space to think and jiggled the mouse attached to the computer in the process. A screen saver of crackling flames had been running on the monitor and now it cleared to reveal Monica's section of the heaven and hell web site. But someone had been at work on the site. In place of the original picture of Monica, a photo of her in the chair as she appeared now had been inserted. Somehow her head had been propped upright, giving the image a ghastly zombie-like appearance. "Unreliable Medium!" had been written in dark red letters underneath. There was nothing erotic or enticing about the page any longer: it truly looked like hell.

The caption beneath the photograph sparked a vague suspicion. The instructors at the art school had all used the term "medium" to refer to the means of artistic expression, like photography or sculpture. I stood and squeezed behind the throne to examine the skin above

Monica's shoulder blade. The butterfly tattoo I'd seen when she posed for Wesson in the art school studio was different. The skin in and around it was reddened, and the butterfly itself had faded. I had never seen the "before" and "after" of laser tattoo removal, but I had to believe the after looked a whole lot like this.

One of the impulses I'd had earlier was to ransack the apartment for clues to Monica's killer and—I now assumed—Caroline's tormentor. The alteration to the web site and Monica's faded tattoo seemed to confirm the connection between the violence done to both women, but their discovery left me feeling even more shaken. I was getting in over my head with this and didn't want to risk muddling things up more for the police. Monkeying with the computer, in particular, could well obliterate any chance of finding the killer's fingerprints on the keyboard and mouse.

I crab-walked my way out from behind the throne and went further back into the flat where the kitchen and bedroom were. Using a tea towel I found hanging on the refrigerator, I picked up the phone in the kitchen and dialed 911. I gave the woman who answered with basso profundo voice the address and told her that they could find the body of a dead woman if they hurried—or even if they didn't. She wanted me to stay on the line until the police arrived. I said I would wait on the stoop.

I dropped the connection in the middle of her protests and walked back into the main room. Monica still hung in the chair by strips of cruel white tape, seemingly contemplating her tortured belly button. I walked to the place in front of her throne for the last time and laid my hands softly on the crown of her head as I remembered my parish priest did when he blessed children who were too young to take communion. "Bless you, Monica," I whispered.

The interview room at the Mission Street Police Station was newer and nicer than the grimy old one at police headquarters on Bryant. Detective Kittredge's suit was nicer too. I caught sight of the of the Brioni label when he shucked off the coat to hang it on the hook by the door. I said:

"I heard the last mayor donated a bunch of his Brioni's to Goodwill when he left office. Did you pick up a bargain, Kittredge?"

He yanked out a chair and sat down across from me at the tiny metal table. "Bite me, Riordan. He's a 44 regular. I'm a 46 long."

"But you know his size. You must have checked."

Kittredge shot his cuffs, annoyed. Gold links in the shape of little golf bags flashed under the humming fluorescent light. "If anyone here has been shopping at Goodwill, it's you. Look at that piece of shit you have on. The lapels won't even lay flat because the seams are so puckered."

I glanced down at my lapels. He was right: the seams were puckered. I'd never noticed it before. "They were fine when I came in here," I said. "It must have to do with the long term effects of exposure to police station air. I've already given my statement twice. How much longer do you plan to keep me here?"

Kittredge nodded like he was hoping I'd ask that. "You know, I was reading an interview with that new action movie star the other day. What's his name? The Mountain? Something like that—he used to be a professional wrestler."

I frowned. "No idea."

"Anyway, he said he looks for two things when he gets a script to review these days. Consistency and believability. I'm kinda like that guy. I'll be happy to let you go once I get a little consistency and believability out of you."

I slumped back into my chair. "I only got one version of the story to tell, Kittredge. I can't help it if you don't think it would make a good script for The Mountain."

"Yeah? Well, tell me again when you left the supper club."

"I left around closing time. About 1:45."

"And you decided to go see this Monica Mapa at 1:45 in the morning because?"

"Because I found out that she had misrepresented some things about Caroline Stockwell when I last interviewed her. For instance, she told me she didn't know where Caroline had gone. But Caroline indicated Monica knew all along where she was."

Kittredge picked up the end of his silk tie and examined the abstract deco pattern of circles and squares printed on the fabric. "That tells me why you went to talk to her," he said in a bored tone. "It doesn't tell me why you picked 1:45 in the morning to do it."

"I went over there simply because it was convenient. And because I was concerned about what Caroline had told me at the hospital. I wouldn't have even gone to the door if I hadn't seen the lights."

He dropped the silk tie and his eyes came up to meet mine. "She was quite a nice piece of Filipino pie. Are you sure didn't go over for a taste? Maybe she didn't want to make it with a loser in a Goodwill suit and you ended up with your hands around her throat."

I snorted. "That's right. Then I taught myself the Internet so I could update her web site and did some voodoo with the forensics so it would look like she died much earlier. I thought you said something about believability."

Kittredge cocked his head, pretending to consider it. "All right. Let's shift gears then."

"Let's. But pick one that goes forward."

Kittredge ignored the jibe. "You said you think what happened to both girls is linked. Why is that?"

"It's obvious, isn't it? They were friends. They shared a web site where they both solicited money and gifts from visitors. They were attending art school together. And they both had what appeared to be very similar butterfly tattoos. The only difference is Monica's was on her shoulder blade and Caroline's is in front. I think the butterfly was a sort of trojan horse that the tattoo artist did first. After the girls agreed to it, he gained their confidence enough to trick or force them into having the other thing done. At least that's what happened with Caroline. Monica got wise to him or decided she didn't like the butterfly and went to have it removed. And—"

"And he killed her for it. I understand. And the business with the web site and the 'unreliable medium' is his way of expressing his outrage that she denied him a canvas for his work. Is that it?"

"Yes. That's the only way it fits together."

He shrugged, not agreeing, but not disagreeing either. "What about the belly button stud on the door? What was that supposed to mean?"

"I can't say for sure, but if I were you I'd be checking to identify the manufacturer. Because if you can't identify one and it turns out to be a custom piece, then I'd say the killer made it and gave it to Monica. He ripped it out because she betrayed him."

Kittredge gave a deep sigh. "At least you're getting better on the consistency front—if not the believability. But you're forgetting something, aren't you?"

"You mean the girl I found in the alley?"

"That's right."

"It was dark and I didn't see the tattoo very well, but it looked like the same sort of butterfly. And the thing that I thought was a pink band or a ribbon ... "

"Could have been the tongue of a dragon."

I brought the palms of my hands up to my temples and mashed them into my head, suddenly feeling a throb of pain behind my eyes. I could guess where this was going and I didn't like it. "Yes, the start of dragon's tongue. Only the girl must have seen it and decided it wasn't what she'd signed up for, so she got killed too."

Kittredge nodded. "And there's something a little funny about that tongue. I researched it. Turns out most tattoo artists do an outline of the tattoo before they ink it in. This guy was filled in as he went—which is unusual. Maybe he was self-taught." He paused and then gave me one of his searching looks. "Don't you think it's a little odd that you found the first girl and almost immediately got involved with the Stockwell and Mapa girls?"

I ran my own tongue over dry lips. "Sure, but that doesn't mean I'm the killer. Apart from not knowing anything about the Internet, I also lack any ability to draw and know nothing about tattoos—including whether you outline or fill in as you go."

He surprised me by smiling. "So that's your defense? Ignorance and no talent? That would probably stand up in court. But I'll give you a hand out of the hole. We identified the first girl. It took us a long time because she's in the US on a visa. A student visa. She arrived at the beginning of the month and was going to start at the art school in the winter semester. And in case you don't remember, the art school is about three blocks from where you found her."

I put my elbows on the table and levered myself forward in the chair. "Had she been hanging out there before she started?"

"No, not really. She was too busy seeing the sights and going out with American men—including some sailors she met during Fleet Week. Apparently a lot of foreign students register simply to get the visa and take an extended vacation in the US. But she had been assigned an advisor and had had a few meetings with him." Kittredge stopped, but he seemed to have more to say.

"Well," I said. "Who is it?"

"Even a no-talent like you should be able to figure that one out. I've already told you more than I should."

I blinked at him. "Wesson. That would tie a lot of things together. He's an artist and he's the only one who had a connection to all three girls. But what about the tattoo angle?"

He waved his hand. "I'm not having this conversation with you. Just be thankful we had other avenues to explore because you keep forgetting: he's not the only one with a connection. You have one too."

"You already used your thunder on that one. Besides, with Monica dead, Caroline is bound to be more forthcoming. She can point you directly to the murderer."

Kittredge's face took on a rigidly neutral expression. "That would be the ideal scenario."

"What's that supposed to mean?"

Kittredge got up and pushed his chair under the table. He put his hands on the back and leaned over it. "It means just what I said. If we can get her to talk, that would be ideal. Let me ask you another question. Did you look at any other pages on the web site?"

"Sure. I looked at most of them when we found it."

"How about in the apartment last night—or I should say—this morning."

"No, I didn't touch the computer at all. I didn't want to smudge any prints the killer might have left behind."

Kittredge looked at me for a long moment and pushed off the chair without saying anything. He turned to take his jacket off the hook, shrugged it on and then yanked open the door to the interview room. Cooler air from the hallway flowed in, making me realize for the first time how hot and stuffy it had gotten in the room.

"There weren't any prints," said Kittredge stolidly. "Whole place was wiped clean. You're free to go."

I frowned at him. "That's it? What were you getting at with the web site?"

He jerked his chin in the direction of the door. "You're free to go."

I stood on weary legs and walked past him. I was halfway across the squad room—which was already filling with detectives from the morning shift—when I heard his voice behind me. "Do yourself a favor, Riordan. Keep a cool head and steer clear of this from now on."

I turned back to look at him.

"But mostly," he said, "keep a cool head."

TANGLED WEB

TRUDGING BACK TO WHERE I PARKED MY car in the Mission, I felt like a shipwrecked sailor fighting his way through the surf to dry land. All my body wanted to do was curl up and sleep in the back of the Galaxie. But my head wanted to locate the nearest Internet browser and find out why Kittredge had advised me to keep it so cool. My head won out. I assuaged my body with a scalding cup of mini-mart coffee that tasted like boiled corn pads and then drove to a 24-hour copy center on the corner of Market and Dolores.

The only other customer in the place was a smiling homeless guy with about three teeth and long wispy chin hairs like the anemic roots of a plant. He had a big plastic garbage bag of papers, curios and other oddments sitting on the floor next to him and he was carefully taking them out one at a time and placing them on the glass of a self-service copier. He would put the lid down and press the copy button, but since he hadn't put a credit card in the pay slot, nothing would happen. This didn't seem to bother him. He went through the motions of removing an imaginary copy from the out tray, stacked it neatly on top of his other imaginary copies, and continued on with the next artifact from his bag. One of the copy center employees caught me staring at him and said, "That's Ralph. Comes in every morning and does the whole routine with a new bag of stuff."

I nodded and said, "At least it saves on toner."

I walked over to the area where they had PCs you could rent by the minute and selected a likely looking Windows machine. I'd gotten into the habit of having Chris or Gretchen help me with almost everything to do with computers, but I figured I could at least handle bringing up a browser and typing in the address for Caroline and Monica's web site.

Getting through the procedure the copy center had for renting the computer turned out to be the bigger challenge. I eventually convinced the credit card reader beside the computer to take my card, but almost immediately ran into another roadblock when I tried to click through the "terms of use" agreement that popped up on the PC screen. For some reason, the "accept" button was not active, and no matter how many times I clicked on it, the pop-up would not go away. In a desperate act, I actually started reading the five pages of all-capitals boilerplate in the dialog box and realized that the process of scrolling through it was the thing that caused the accept button to become active. I was ready to agree to anything at that point and almost broke the mouse button when I mashed it down.

I brought the browser up with comparative ease and typed in the URL for Caroline and Monica's site. The home page painted in segments, and what I saw suddenly made me very nostalgic for the boilerplate. The diagonal line on the page dividing heaven and hell was still there, but the pictures above and below the line had been replaced. The picture of Monica in hell was now a smaller version of the macabre pose from the apartment. Clicking on it brought up the larger rendition that I had seen when I discovered her body. As to the change in heaven, someone smarter than me might have anticipated it—but I didn't. In place of the tableau with the cemetery monument, there was a bleary picture of Caroline's naked torso showing the dragon tattoo. I clicked on it and was treated to a much enlarged version that took up nearly the whole page. Written below the picture was the following caption:

The Dragon and the Butterfly
(Ink on human canvas)

The picture had been taken in a darkened room with a bright flash and a lot of the detail in the highlights had been lost due to overexposure. Caroline appeared to be lying in bed, but it was impossible to say whether she had posed for the picture willingly because her head and her wrists and ankles—where she might have been bound—were cropped out of the picture. I leaned into the monitor to study what showed of the room's furnishings, looking for some clue as to the location. There wasn't much to go on—a sliver of blank wall, a fragment of bedspread and a portion of the headboard. The bedspread was a bright turquoise and the headboard a flossy, white enamel, so Caroline's bedroom was out of the running, but that was as much as I could determine. I put my nose to the screen, straining to identify the odd-looking metal stand or rack that gleamed faintly the corner when I heard a step behind me.

"That's disgusting. You shouldn't be looking at that in a copy center."

A kid in a conservative blue suit with a crisp white shirt and a tie made for bankers or morticians hovered over me. He looked all of about 20. He had a black leather case on his shoulder and held what appeared to be a bible.

I twisted out of my chair. "Nobody should be looking at it anywhere," I said. I reached for the computer mouse and closed the browser. I clicked on the button to log off and the reader spat out my credit card with a metallic raspberry. "But maybe you should go back to making flyers for the 'Up with People' concert and keep your suggestions to yourself."

I went past his startled face to the front entrance. There was a pay phone by the door. I dropped in a couple of quarters and dialed the number for Mr. Duckworth's residence. He lived all of three blocks from here, but I didn't feel like walking.

"Who dares to disturb the glamorous one before 9 AM?" he answered.

"Who dares, wins," I said tartly.

"What's that, August? The motto for the Hitler youth?"

"Not unless the nun who taught Latin at my grade school had a big secret. *Qui audet adipiscitur.* Never mind that. I called because I want to know if there's a way to make a local copy of a web site."

"You mean copy the contents of a site to a personal computer?"

"Exactly."

"Sure, there are utilities for that. Or you can just go through and save each page to your disk from the browser."

I told him briefly about the discovery of Monica's body and what I'd found out about Caroline. "Whoever's responsible decided to post his handiwork on their web site. The cops are bound to take the site down as soon as they figure out where it's running so I wanted you to make a copy before it's gone."

There was no sound on the other end of the line. Then there was a little throat-clearing noise. "Jesus, August. You're creeping me out. Didn't the Japanese girl you found after our gig at the House of Shields have a butterfly tattoo?"

"Yeah, she did. She was also enrolled at the art school. The cops think that's the link between the three of them." The homeless guy with the wispy chin hairs smiled and nodded at me as he left with his bag of treasures. I waved goodbye and turned my back to the door.

"Did she have a web site?"

"Who?"

"The Japanese girl."

"I've no idea, but we're getting off point."

There was another long pause.

"Chris?"

"Yeah, I'm here. I was just thinking about another idea I had for helping you."

"Thanks, but no thanks. I don't need you pulling another one of your unauthorized plumber's squad tricks and getting us in both in trouble. If you'll recall, the last time you did that I found you trussed up with duct tape in the basement of a house in Daly City."

"This is different."

"Sure it is. Now will you do what I asked?"

"Yes, I'll copy the site."

"Okay, then, goodbye."

"Goodbye," he parroted back, but he didn't sound like he meant it.

I hung up the phone and went out into the feverish amalgam of people, cars and clanging antique trolleys that was upper Market Street on a weekday morning.

The good housekeeping fairies hadn't sprinkled any of their magic pixie dust on my apartment while I was gone. It was still the same jumbled mess it had been when I'd left the morning before. It was depressing, but that wasn't what made me spend the next two hours working like the crazed broomsticks in *The Sorcerer's Apprentice* to clean the place up. It was avoidance, plain and simple.

After I dropped the last Hefty bag full of broken crockery down the garbage chute and treated myself to the last few sips in the Maker's Mark bottle, I knew I didn't have any more excuses: I had to call Ellen Stockwell. I picked up the phone and dialed her number.

There is a certain tone to a man's voice when he sobers up after a drinking spree. It's partly physical—dehydrated sinuses give him an adenoidal timbre—and it's partly emotional—the resonance of a world-weary resignation. Lieutenant Stockwell's voice had that tone.

"Is Ellen there?" I asked after he had muttered hello.

"She's at the hospital."

I hesitated. Dropping this on Ellen was bad enough, but giving the news to Stockwell was an order of magnitude worse. "This is

Riordan," I said finally. "I found out something about what happened to Caroline that I need to pass on."

"Save it," said Stockwell. "We heard about your after hours visit. You're lucky the nurse walked in on you instead of me. I would have taken you apart with my bare hands." There was a soft, sighing sound like the air going out of a beach ball at the end of summer vacation. The line went quiet, then I heard Stockwell sniff back what I guessed were tears. "You know, there was another guy in the department who had a daughter Caroline's age. His name was Frank Ballou and he was in Vice. He used to joke that his only job as a father was keeping his kid off the brass pole."

"Brass pole?"

"Yeah, as in the brass pole that strippers swing from. Right now, if I could trade Caroline's situation for the brass pole, I'd do it in a heart beat."

"Maybe it's better we can't make Faustian bargains like that. It's true the tattoo is bad, but laser—"

"Fuck the tattoo and the laser and your dime store metaphysics. Caroline tried to kill herself again. Swallowed a bunch of pills or something. She's in a coma and they're not sure she's coming out."

I switched the receiver from one ear to the other to no real purpose and slumped down on the arm of my living room sofa. "When did this happen?" I asked quietly.

"They don't know for sure, but they're guessing sometime in the early morning."

"Do they know what she took?"

"Not really. They're guessing some kind of tranquilizer."

"Had they prescribed any for her?"

Stockwell growled into the line. "Yeah, they gave her a big bottle to put on her bed stand and told her to swallow a handful whenever she felt blue. Think I didn't already ask all these questions?"

"Sorry," I said. "I forgot what you do for a living. I've got to tell you something else, though."

A beat went by. "What else can there be?"

"I found Caroline's friend Monica dead in her apartment last night. She was murdered. She had the beginnings of a tattoo like Caroline's on her shoulder, but she'd tried to have it taken off. Whoever killed her updated the girls' heaven and hell web site with new pictures of both girls. The one of Caroline showed a close-up of her tattoo. The one of Monica was a ritualistic pose taken after she died."

"Who did it?"

"I don't know. The SFPD thinks it was one of the teachers at the art school."

"The detective a guy named Kittredge?"

"That's him."

"He left a message on the machine, but there hasn't been time to call back. You saying you don't like the guy he tapped?"

"I really don't know," I said slowly. "It could be him. He's Caroline's advisor—and he took pictures of both girls."

"You mean like … naked pictures?"

"Like that."

There was an outright sob and Stockwell went away for a moment. "You don't have any conception, do you Riordan?" he said when he came back. "Holding a job as a cop and keeping a marriage and a family together have always been almost irreconcilable goals. But to get kicked off the force, have both of my children kill themselves and lose my wife to a clown like you leaves me with bupkis. I've failed at all the things that matter most."

"Listen, Stockwell, I—"

"Shove it, Riordan," he said in a flat, emotionless tone. "You're off the case. Don't ever call here again."

DARKROOM DEVELOPMENTS

I FELT A HOLLOW, CRAVEN FEELING INSIDE, LIKE I'd I filched from the church offering basket, and while I wasn't going to consider myself off the case until I heard it directly from Ellen, that didn't mean I had a clue about what to do next. I paced around the apartment for the next twenty minutes trying to decide—twice ignoring the phone when it rang—and eventually concluded that I could be just as rudderless and guilt-ridden at work as I could at home.

When I walked through the door to the outer office, I found Bonacker standing next to his desk, gabbing away on his cell phone. He wore a meatball brown running suit with a tight collar and elastic at the wrists and ankles. It fit like a fumigation tent. "I just get the gastrointestinal sense that you don't have sufficient coverage, Larry," I heard him say into the phone. He smiled at me and rubbed his fingers together like he was already fondling the commission check.

I went past him to Gretchen's cubicle. She looked up with a strained expression. "When are you going to get a cell phone, August?"

I glanced back at Bonacker. "As soon as I start selling insurance or hell freezes over—whichever comes first. Why?"

"Because I've been trying to reach you all morning. You've got to get with the program. Private investigators in the 21st century have cell phones."

"I'll take it under advisement. What's up?"

She crossed her arms, being careful not to wrinkle the flouncy, black silk blouse she had selected for today. "You have a crying man in your office is what's up." Her eyes ran over my face and her expression softened. "And you look like shit."

"That's good because I feel like shit. Spending the night in a police station can often have that effect. So who's the man and why is he crying?"

She nodded towards my office door. "Better see for yourself. I couldn't get anything out of him but saline."

She watched as I twisted the knob and pushed through to the office. George Wesson sat with his head in his hands in one of the clients' chairs. If I looked like I'd spent the night in a police station, he looked like he'd spent it in a tumbling clothes dryer. Everything about him was rumpled and rent, from his disheveled hair to the mud-stained and abraded leather clogs on his feet.

"Dr. Wesson?" I asked.

He looked up. Tears had scored his face like hot wax and his eyes were red-rimmed. "I told you I don't have a Ph.D.," he said quietly.

"Sorry. I really did forget this time. May I ask why you're here?"

"You of all people should know. You found her."

I nodded carefully and thought a long moment before I spoke. The last thing I wanted was to derail him from saying whatever it was he'd come to say. "You're talking about Monica. Yes, I did find her. Do you know anything about what happened?"

He half turned his head and worked his features into a bitter, distorted smile, fighting off more tears. "I know she's dead and I know the papers say I'm a 'person of interest' in the case. I gather that's the new politically correct way of saying I'm a suspect."

"But you didn't have anything to do with her death?"

He sniffed and ran the cuff of his rumbled white shirt under his nose. "I did. But not in the way you think. I would never have done anything purposefully to harm her. I was in love with her."

I heard the door to the office pull closed behind me. Gretchen had rightly determined this was an interview better conducted in private. I chewed my lip for a moment and then went around my desk to my chair and eased into it. It still managed a subdued squeak like whimpering dog. "Maybe you better explain how you were involved, then."

Wesson focused on a spot on the floor and talked in an emotionless drone. "We were having a love affair. You know something about Monica and her commercial endeavours, so you might conclude the love was all on my side and the only thing on Monica's was money. But it wasn't." His eyes came up to mine, daring me to challenge his statement.

"Okay."

He nodded to himself. "She cared for me as much as I cared for her. I never gave her money or expensive gifts—only photographs I had taken. She, on the other hand, would often buy expensive things for me. For instance, that lens you made me break in the studio was a gift from her."

I didn't know what Wesson photos were going for, but the cynic in me wondered if she wasn't treating the relationship as a long-term investment: funding his photographic equipment needs in return for valuable artwork. I didn't say that, however. What I said was:

"If this was a relationship of equals, then why keep it a secret? Are you married?"

"Now you're being disingenuous. No, I'm not married, but Monica was a very young woman. And although she never took any courses from me, she was also a student at a school where I was an instructor. Maybe you've met our school president, Julie Jaing. She's about as sympathetic as—"

"A spiked mace?"

"Yes, exactly. I would have been out on my ear in an instant."

"The last time I spoke to you, you gave me the big speech about treating all your models professionally on a nonsexual basis. Sounds like that was just so much chewing gum. Were you having an affair with Caroline Stockwell too?"

Wesson flung a heated look at me, stood up, clawed his fingers into his thighs while teetering on his feet, and then abruptly sat down. "I had my doubts about coming here. You're not giving me much in the way of reassurance."

I thought of at least three smart remarks to make to that, but bit them off. I leaned forward in my chair to run my hands over the tattered cardboard on the desk blotter, smoothing it down. "Look. I'm not sure why you *are* here, but if you're expecting my help in some way, shape or form, you've got to realize that my interest in this thing has always been about finding out what happened to Caroline. It's clear to me that you know much more about both girls than you admitted to before. Give me what I want and I'll do my best to help you—within the limits of the law. Otherwise, you're wasting both of our time."

He pinched at the whiskers of his mustache with a thumb and forefinger and nodded slightly. "I wasn't lying before. My relationship with Caroline has always been that of artist and model or teacher and student. She only comes into it to the extent that she was friends with Monica—and friends with the person who ... " His voice trailed off and he looked down at the floor again.

"Killed Monica," I prompted.

"Yes, that's my strong suspicion, but I was going to say the person who did Monica's tattoo."

I sat up straight with a loud squeak. "And who was that?"

"I don't know. Monica never said exactly. She told me it was someone Caroline was seeing and suggested that she met him through the web site. But that was it."

"Suggested how exactly?"

"Oh, nothing explicit. She just said that he was one of Caroline's many admirers. I assumed he had come through the web site because they both had so many admirers from there."

I mulled that over, trying to imagine the conversation between Wesson and Monica. "How did Monica refer to him?" I asked. "She must have used his name. She can't have always referred to him as Caroline's boyfriend."

Wesson looked up at me, pressing his palm to his forehead like he was in pain. "She didn't even call him her boyfriend exactly. Just somebody she was involved with. I've thought a lot about it and I don't remember her ever mentioning a name."

"Did she mention what he did for a living, how old he was—anything specific?"

"The only thing I remember her saying about him was that he knew all about Tantric sex—the Kama Sutra and that sort of thing. I half-kiddingly asked her where the guy had learned all that. She just laughed at me, and then—and then we didn't talk about it anymore."

"What did you talk about?"

Wesson reddened. "We were in bed. We had sex."

I tilted my head back and blew air through my lips. "Okay. Let me ask you another question. Caroline took a lot of photographs of body art. I saw them in her bedroom and in a coffee shop exhibition. Did you see those photographs, and did you ever hear her talk about the artist responsible for the tattoos?"

Wesson gave me a bleak little smile. "Your thoughts are paralleling my own. When I read about Monica's death this morning, I remembered Caroline's photos—she had taken a number for my classes—and I tried to recall if she ever mentioned an artist. I don't think she did. I asked her one time how she found the models, and she told me she had placed a flyer on the school bulletin board—like many of us do. I think she took the subjects as they came, rather than seeking out people who had gotten tattoos from a particular artist."

"All right. So we've got someone Caroline met through the web site who studied the Kama Sutra. But you said you were somehow responsible for Monica's death. I haven't heard anything that ties with that."

His eyes welled with moisture again and he rubbed at them with the back of his hand. "I meant that I encouraged her in something that may have led to her death. Not that I was directly responsible."

"Let's have it then."

"It has to do with the tattoo on her shoulder. The first time I saw it was the day you intruded on us in the studio. I told her I didn't like it. That it detracted from her natural beauty."

"What did she say?"

"She said it was her body and she could do what she wanted. She also said that it was exquisitely executed and that I was a snob about photographic arts and wasn't willing to admit that a tattoo could be art as well. I got angry then. I told her that was hitting below the belt because she knew that many of the other artists in the school—and the world at large—still don't consider photography to be an art. I told her she could keep the tattoo, but that I would never take a picture of her where it was visible. That I didn't want something so cheap and artificial-looking appearing in my images."

"But I've seen pictures you took of Caroline that showed the stud in her belly button. How was this different?"

"It wasn't. I asked Caroline to take the stud out when we began our sessions in the studio, but I found the hole it left to be more distracting than the stud itself. And I certainly didn't approve of Monica's, but she'd gotten it long before we met."

There were bits of pencil erasure scattered about my desk. I began herding them together with the edge of a memo pad. "Then you must not have cared very much for Caroline's shots of body art," I said idly.

"Yes and no. Her artistic motivations for those images were coming from a different place. It wouldn't have been a subject I would have selected, but I respected her choice, nonetheless."

I got annoyed with the erasure bits—and all the gabble about aesthetics—and swept them off the desk. "We're chewing around the edges here. What's the punch line? It looked to me like Monica had tried to have the tattoo removed when I found her body. What happened?"

Wesson nodded solemnly. "We met after I kicked you out of the studio. She had thought about the tattoo in the meantime and admitted that she didn't feel as strongly about it as she had suggested, and if I wanted her to get rid of it, she would. The only thing she felt bad about was betraying Caroline's friend. She said he was struggling to find acceptance for his art and this would be upsetting to him."

"So she went to a doctor to have it removed, and when Caroline's friend found out, he killed her."

He brought his head down to rest in the palm of his hand. "Yes," he said to the floor. "That must have been what happened."

"When's the last time you saw her?"

"We had lunch together yesterday. She had just gotten back from the first laser treatment. The doctor told her she would need three to four more to remove the tattoo completely."

"How was her mood?"

Still looking down, he brought his shoulders up in tiny shrug. "She was upbeat. She said she felt good about the decision to have the tattoo taken off and she told me she had just sold some things on eBay for a lot of money."

I was tired and the strain of thinking up the right questions to ask Wesson was turning my brain into so much stir-fried tofu. Something was bothering me about the time line. "Caroline had come home by then. Had Monica heard from her?"

"Not that she mentioned to me."

"But if Monica got the tattoo while Caroline was gone, then that means Caroline's friend was still in the area while she was missing."

Wesson sat up in the chair, letting his head loll wearily against his shoulder. "Monica had given me the impression that they had gone on a trip to Mexico. Apparently they came back sometime sooner than Caroline returned home, but Monica didn't say anything about seeing her or talking with her."

"Do you know where they were staying?"

"No. I told you I didn't even know the guy's name."

"Then what about you? Where were you when Monica was killed?"

He snapped his head around to stare at me. "I don't know when she was killed."

"Neither do I, but tell me what you did after you had lunch."

"We went back to my apartment in North Beach for several hours. We had more s—"

"Okay, okay, I get the picture, Wesson. What did you do after she left?"

"I went into the darkroom. I was way behind on my printing. I worked all night and then went to a little place on Columbus to get some breakfast before I crashed. That was when I saw the article about her death in the paper."

"What did you do then?"

"I've been wandering the streets trying to decide what to do. I already knew from the article that the police wanted to talk to me, and I knew that they would find my semen in her body ... and that would only make it worse."

"Swell. Did anyone see you after Monica left your apartment?"

He closed his eyes and shook his head. "No. I was in the darkroom by myself until I stopped for breakfast. No one saw me between the time she left and the time I walked into the restaurant."

"Did you have a new Japanese student who was matriculating at the school next year?"

He frowned. "What does that have to do with this?"

"Humor me and answer the question."

"We get a lot of foreign students who enroll at the school. Most of them never finish the course work. It's mainly a dodge to get a long-term visa."

"And?"

"And, yes, I got assigned advising duties for a Japanese girl who is starting in January. Her name is Mika something. I met with her a couple of times. She can barely put two English words together. I don't expect her to last long."

"She already washed out. She was found dead a block from the school with a butterfly tattoo on her shoulder. It didn't get much play in the papers because no one knew who she was until recently."

Wesson's face became very pale. A look of raw fear crystallized in his eyes. "I do remember reading about that. I noticed it because it was so close to the school, but I never … They're going to think I killed her too, aren't they?"

"Based on my conversation with the cops this morning, it's pretty clear they already do. I guess it's time to get it out on the table. What do you want from me?"

"My god, it's obvious isn't it? I want you to keep me out of jail."

"I don't think anyone can do that. You'll have to go in for at least a day or two until you make bail. I can recommend a bail bondsman and a good criminal lawyer if you like."

He jumped to his feet and put both hands on the edge of the desk to lean into my face. I noticed for the first time that his fingernails were stained black and that a faint aroma of vinegar and ammonia emanated from his person. "You're not getting me," he sharply. "I want to hire you to find Monica's killer. Her real killer."

I put my hand on his shoulder and pushed him gently back. "You're the one who isn't getting it. At this point, there's nothing you could do to stop me from finding her killer. I just hope for your sake that you're telling the truth."

"I said I loved her," Wesson began, but three sharp raps on the pebble glass of the office door interrupted his thought.

"Come in," I shouted.

Jack Kittredge came through the door, grinning like he was there to pick up a new suit. Behind him stood another cop, and behind him, Gretchen with her arms held rigid at her side looking as mad as I'd ever seen her. "I told him to stay out," she snapped.

"And that's exactly what I told your boss this morning," said Kittredge. He stepped forward, pulling a pair of handcuffs off his belt as he came. "Dr. Wesson, you're under arrest for the murder of Monica Mapa."

Wesson dissolved against the desk. "I don't have a Ph.D.," he said miserably.

TANTRIC TWISTER

Twenty minutes later I was sitting in front of Gretchen's
desk trying to assess how I felt about Wesson and what he told
me. Gretchen was devoting half her attention to baby-sitting me
and the other half to her computer.

"I guess I believe him," I said finally.

"Why wouldn't you? He hardly seems like the murdering
kind."

"I don't care for his relationship with Monica—or Caroline for
that matter. He told me he would be bounced from the college if it
were discovered, and I've no doubt that's true."

Gretchen smirked. "Are you sure you aren't just jealous of his
success with younger women? All these brooding artist types have to
beat them off with sticks. How many girlfriends and wives did Picasso
have? Anyway, it sounds like Monica was exploiting him more than
he was exploiting her."

"Maybe," I said, and reached over to toy with her Rolodex. It
fell open to the letter K, where a good half inch of her boyfriend's
cards were stacked. "By the way," I said, "is there such a thing as a
brooding urologist type?"

Gretchen pointed the business end of a letter opener in my direction. "No, but I'd watch out for the maiming administrative assistant
type if I were you."

I held up my hands in mock submission and pushed the Rolodex out of reach. A soft chime came from Gretchen's computer and she worked the mouse to click on something on the screen. She gave a crooked smile—just like what you'd see in one of Picasso's cubist paintings. "Check this out."

She swung the monitor around to show a picture of a gas-guzzling, 1960s convertible filled with dirt, parked in front of a car dealership. A crop of pink and violet pansies sprouted from the soil and a message beneath the picture read, "Next stop for the Galaxie 500?"

"Where'd that come from?"

She laughed. "Chris sent it. Ever since he got his picture phone, he's become a regular photo journalist. You should have seen the shots he took at the zoo. There was a great one of a baboon hanging from a branch that he captioned, 'Riordan family tree.'"

"Oh yeah? And why exactly didn't I see it?"

"Because you need a *cell phone* or a *computer* to get them."

"Right," I said. "I knew that. I just hope he's not doing a running shtick on me and my luddite lifestyle behind my back."

Gretchen rolled her eyes and expertly threaded a stray lock of hair behind her ear. She began pounding away on the computer keyboard. "Taking ourselves a little too seriously, are we?" she said as she typed.

I continued as if I hadn't heard her. "The Galaxie, for example, is a very practical car. Safe, not likely to be stolen, plenty of storage space ... "

"Makes an excellent planter when filled with dirt."

I blinked at her—not really registering the gibe—and then stood abruptly and headed for the door. The mention of storage space had triggered a thought that I felt I had to act on immediately. "Gotta go," I tossed over my shoulder.

"Jesus," I heard Gretchen say to my back. "You can sure dish it out, but you're a wuss when it comes to taking it."

The Galaxie was in my parking space at the Tenderloin garage where I'd left it—and so were the Amazon.com packages for Caroline that I'd picked up at the Noe Valley Starbucks. Ellen had told me that someone had tried to break into Caroline's room the night she came home, and I had speculated it was the same people who ransacked my apartment—Tom and Jerry, the orange Popsicle twins from the ashram—looking for something that tied the guru to Caroline.

There were plenty of packages in Caroline's closet that I hadn't looked through, but when I was talking with Gretchen I realized that just as many remained in the back seat of my car. Given that Wesson had said Caroline's admirer knew about eastern sexual techniques, there seemed to be a lot more urgency in determining if the greasy little fakir really was sending her gifts.

I shoved the packages into a big pile and sorted through them all again, looking for something I'd missed in the merchandise or the accompanying notes that hinted at Sri Atma Nidhi, eastern religions or the Karma Sutra. I had just reacquainted myself with the patented grooves and unique sloped surface of the George Foreman grill and had thrown both the grill and the warped little note that accompanied it aside ("Think of me as you warm your meat.") when the jostling caused a CD on the top of the pile to slide out of its package to the floor.

There was no title or other text visible on the CD, and the note in the package—while patently crass—was opaque enough without context, so it was easy to see how I'd skipped by the CD before. The thing that made it stand out now was the picture of a green and yellow butterfly done in a folk art style on the cover. I tore off the cellophane wrapping and flipped open the jewel box. The disk inside was titled, "Becoming God of Your Body," and was billed as containing:

Ground breaking discourses by Sri Atma Nidhi on the
Tantra, a spiritual sexual science that not only expands

consciousness, but liberates it. These meditations are guaranteed to challenge, stimulate, and enrich your life in ways you would never expect.

The note read:

```
                Caroline,
     I got what you need, babe.
                A.N.
```

I tossed the note and CD on the front seat and fired up the Galaxie. For once, it started on the first crank. Maybe I was personifying three tons of rusty scrap metal destined to be somebody's planter, but I decided the car was as eager as I to get to Berkeley.

After my last adventure at the ashram, I knew there was no way I would be able to waltz in the front door without getting arrested, beaten or worse, so I took up a post on Telegraph Avenue near the automatic gate that opened onto the lot behind the building. I could see the guru's black Porsche 911 through the chain link fence, gleaming in the autumn sunlight, and across the way, that same autumn sunlight gleamed off the leg braces of Beth, the ex-disciple who had given me the dirt on Nidhi in the first place. She and the other ragtag protestors in her group maintained their vigil, waving signs and shouting slogans at the cars stopped at the intersection with Carleton. I put on Cannonball Adderley's *Cannonball Takes Charge* CD and slumped behind the wheel, contemplating the metal fire door at the back of the ashram that I imagined Nidhi would have to come through when he punched the clock after a hard day's work of enlightenment and consciousness raising.

A class at a nearby karate studio let out, and a passel of teenaged board breakers dressed in cotton pajamas boiled out onto the sidewalk, shouting and laughing and karate-chopping the air as they went by. The rear view mirror showed the bus stop behind me, a pair of white-haired Asian men sharing the bench and a bag of lichee nuts with a pile of peeled skins and discarded pits between them.

I made it through the Adderley CD and another from Benny Carter, and the only thing remotely interesting that happened was a Frisbee came sailing over the fence that separated the parking lot from the backyard of a tumble-down cottage. A moment passed, the fence shook and ten fingers appeared at the top—below the coil of razor wire that crowned the wooden planks—followed by the hair, forehead and sad eyes of a hispanic kid who glanced wistfully at his lost disk and then dropped abruptly from sight.

It was almost 5 PM when the back door of the ashram finally swung open. A blonde with a pixie cut and upturned nose who looked as wholesome as white gloves on Easter Sunday came skipping out. She glanced expectantly behind her and wonder of wonders—Sri Atma Nidhi himself materialized in the doorway. He wore a flowing, long-sleeved purple shirt, his crystal amulet, chinos and a pair of sandals. If he'd come within spitting distance of a shampoo bottle since the last time I'd seen him, there was no evidence of it in his greasy coiffure.

Nidhi's appearance caused two things. The first was a pronounced increase in the energy associated with the shouts and gesticulations coming from the protestors. The second was a fumbled preparation on my part to tail him wherever he might be going. I managed to get the car started and the shift indicator in drive before the automatic gate pulled open to emit the Porsche, but Nidhi surprised me by launching out of the parking lot at near racetrack speed. I hadn't even rolled past the gate by the time he was through the intersection, the blond girl's hand dangling out the passenger window as if she were trailing it in the water on a canoe ride. Two eggs intended by the protestors for the Porsche exploded on the windshield of the Galaxie, putting me at an even further disadvantage as I groped after him on Telegraph with the wipers smearing the yoke into a near impenetrable haze.

I stayed with him for about three blocks, then he zipped through a corner service station onto Dwight Way while we were stopped at a light and I was preoccupied wiping my windshield clean with the fat end of my tie. The tie was ruined and so was the tail job by the time I realized Nidhi had given me the slip. With horns blaring behind me, I watched the letters on his "MY CARMA" vanity plate grow small as he zoomed toward the Berkeley hills, and then I slowly and reluctantly pulled into the service station to hose down my window.

After I washed off the egg, I gave the station more of my business to the extent of using their men's room. When I came out, a kid on a scooter with a pony tail sticking out the bottom of his helmet was parked in front of my car, looking annoyed at the way I'd blocked access to the air and water spigots. I held up my hand to forestall any smart remarks, piled into the car and cut across Telegraph, heading back to the ashram. I didn't have any particular motive in mind except a lukewarm desire to look the place over once more, but when I caught sight of Beth standing at the corner, a new thought occurred to me.

I made an illegal U-turn at the next light and swung back around to park by the curb. Beth and the rest of the protesters were stacking their signs, boxing their flyers and giving each other hugs, preparatory to knocking off for the day. I tooted the horn to get her attention and then waved her towards the car. She trundled down the sidewalk to the passenger door of the Galaxie, leaning heavily on her aluminum cane and shaking her head as I struggled to get the electric window to come down.

"What a gentleman," she said when the window finally receded. "Make the cripple come to you."

"Sorry," I said. "I didn't think."

She shrugged. "We'll pretend I needed the exercise. Did you find Caroline Stockwell?"

"Not exactly. She came home on her own, but she's had a very bad experience. I still think Nidhi's involved and I'm trying to get leverage on him."

"So?"

"So I wondered if you knew where he lived."

She grinned like Christmas morning and made a show of examining the nails of one hand. They were chewed painfully short and painted a purplish black. "You going to invite me in?" she asked without looking up. "Or you going to keep me standing on the sidewalk?"

I reached across the Galaxie's bench seat and popped the latch. She pulled the door open wide, threw her cane on the floor, positioned herself to drop back and did a free-fall onto the seat. I pulled Nidhi's CD and note out of the way just before her hefty gingham-clad cheeks hit the vinyl. She hoisted her legs around to the front and turned to me to smile. "Now that's more like it."

"Welcome aboard," I said. "I think you were just about to tell me where Nidhi lives."

"That's what you were hoping, anyway. Assuming I do know his address, what exactly are you going to do if I tell you?"

"Mail him a Whitman sampler?"

"Try again."

I'd been holding the CD and note at my side and I now slid them into a pouch on the driver's door. I wasn't sure why, but I didn't want Beth to see them. "The idea is to pay him a visit," I said vaguely, "and ask him a few questions."

"Questions about Caroline Stockwell?"

"Yes, and other things."

Beth put her index and forefinger down on the vinyl seat and walked them across the space between us. She stopped about an inch from my leg. "And would any of these things concern illegal or otherwise scandalous activities?"

"You could say that."

"Goodie," she said and tweaked my thigh with her forefinger. "Then I'm coming too."

I pulled my leg out of range and rubbed the spot she'd nailed. "Didn't your mother teach you to keep your hands at home? And what makes you think I'd want you along?"

She laughed. "Oh, I'm sure you wouldn't—unless there were no other way I'd tell you how to get there."

I twisted in the seat to look at her straight on. She laced her fingers together and rested her chin on them, batting her eyelashes at me in a coquettish fashion. I stood about five seconds of the display and then growled, "All right, but keep a low profile and let me do the talking."

"Whatever you say, Chief."

I turned the ignition key sharply and brought the Galaxie coughing to life. "Pull the door closed and let's roll."

"Hold on a minute. Give another toot on the horn. I want to get Ronnie's attention."

Although the protestors on the corner had dwindled, Ronnie was apparently one of the two remaining men. Beth waved at him after I honked and he came pounding down the sidewalk. He was short and chubby, and when he peered into the car in an unself-conscious way, I could see from the distinctive look of his flattened features that he had been born with Down's syndrome. "Hi Beth," he said a little too loudly. "Whatcha doing?"

"I'm taking a little ride with August here. You'll have to catch the bus home by yourself."

"No problem," he said good-naturedly. "Is this the wicked handsome dude you were telling me about?" He pronounced the last syllable of the word handsome like it rhymed with boom.

Beth reddened and gave a shy, up from under look at me. "No," she mumbled. "That was a different guy. But there is one other thing, Ronnie."

"What's that?"

"I'd like to borrow your digital camera."

"Of course, Beth. You're one of my best friends." He unhooked a small leather case from his belt and passed it through the window. "I just changed the battery so you can take lots of pictures."

"Thanks, Ronnie. I probably won't take that many but it's good to know I can."

Ronnie nodded and thrust his hand into the car. "Nice to meet you, dude."

I took his hand, which was soft and slightly damp. He gave mine two pronounced pumps and then released it. "See you guys later."

"Bye Ronnie," said Beth, and watched as he slammed the door closed a little too hard.

I put the car in gear and pulled out from the curb. "Wicked handsome dude?" I said out of the side of my mouth.

"Don't even wave the opener at that can of worms."

"All right. But the camera?"

She ignored the question and pointed down the street. "We could do with more driving and less talking."

She directed me onto Dwight Way in the direction that Nidhi had gone and we stuck with it until it dead-ended into Panoramic. We went right on Panoramic, snaking our way further up into the foothills with the road getting narrower and the houses more palatial with each switchback that we traversed. When we came to a T intersection where Dwight Way picked up again, I was more than a little annoyed to find that our route required us to turn back onto it. Apparently, all I would have had to do to find Nidhi on my own was fumble along the first street I'd seen him go down.

Beth didn't make me feel any better. After a half block, she smiled and tugged at my sleeve. "There," she said, pointing at a house on the left. "How about that? Turns out he's not that far from the ashram."

"Yeah," I allowed, "how about that." The house was made of rough-hewn timber stained a tobacco juice brown and was built on stilts that projected up from the hillside. It was massive, blocky and ugly, looking like an overgrown Lincoln Log cabin, but I didn't haven't any doubts that it was worth a good $4-5 million in the Bay Area's overheated real estate market. A grooved concrete driveway rose steeper than a ski jump from street level to a garage. From our vantage point, the swooping tail fin of Nidhi's Porsche could just be made out at the edge of the open garage, and beyond that—looming in the shadows—a monstrous refrigerated case for wine storage took up the entire back wall.

Deflated helium balloons hung like shrunken heads from a pair of granite posts that flanked the drive. I nodded towards them. "Looks like we missed the party."

"Wait a few days. Nidhi's always got some kind of love feast, open house, feel good orgy scheduled. That's when he nails the girls."

"Oh yeah?"

Beth nodded and chewed thoughtfully on her blackened pinky fingernail. It was slim pickings. "He gets them high on hashish and takes them down to his basement 'fun room' for the fun and games. It used to be his wine cellar, but when he figured out it was the perfect place to molest people in isolation while the party kept rolling upstairs, he moved out all the wine and filled the room with bean bags, mood lighting and hidden lubricant dispensers."

I grimaced, and made a mental note to take a scalding hot shower when I got home. "You seem to know an awful lot about this," I said. "Have you been down there?"

"Not with him. I think I told you that he never molested me. But I've been in every room in the house at one time or another. I even have the blueprints for it."

"Blueprints? Why would you have the blueprints?"

Beth reached down to tap one of the metal slats on her leg braces. "Me and my crippled legs paid for the house. With the settlement I got from the automobile accident."

I whistled softly. "How much are we talking about?"

"My shyster lawyer took 40 percent, but I still ended up with half a million. That was enough for the architect and the construction. Some other fool donated the land. I lived in the house with Nidhi for a time after it was built, but it didn't take long for him to con me into leaving. He said he needed my room for an indigent ashram member. The next time I saw it, he'd filled it with his collection of Fender guitars. He's got about fifteen vintage Stratocasters and he can't even put three chords together."

An edge of strain crept into her voice as she said this last bit. I watched as her chin began to tremble. She turned away from me to sniff and rub at her eyes. "I'm sorry, Beth," I said, and reached to comfort her.

She pushed my hand away. "It's only money. What matters now is preventing him from ruining other lives. That's why I'm here."

I nodded and let my gaze wander back up the hill. "Stopping him from ruining other lives is a tall order, kiddo. I'm on board for causing him as much trouble as possible, but all we can do today is ring the doorbell and roust him when he comes to the door. If he doesn't answer or his bodyguards show up, there's not much else to do short of pulling a gun."

"Fuck ringing the door bell." She yanked on a gold chain around her neck and produced a house key from beneath her peasant blouse. "It's a master. Works on all the doors."

I smiled. "I love a woman with resources." I wrestled the Galaxie over to the side of the road and killed the motor. "I have to ask this, even though I'm almost certain of the answer. Are you sure you want to go in with me? It's still breaking and entering, even if you have a key."

Beth stared at me levelly for a moment. "Next question."

"Silly me. Next question. Any alarms?"

"There's an alarm, but he never turns it on. It really doesn't matter, though, because I know the code."

I opened the door to the Galaxie and stepped outside. Leaning back into the car, I said, "I wish you'd stop bogging us down with all these trivial concerns. Let's get to it."

Beth sniffed fiercely and blinked away her remaining tears. "Damn straight," she said.

Given the house's hillside location and Beth's disability, there was no opportunity to sneak up on it, so we decided to simply brazen it out. We made our way up the concrete drive—Beth taking slow and deliberate steps up the steep incline—and then followed a flagstone path through a terraced and carefully landscaped garden to the front door. If Nidhi had been watching from a window, he would have had a good five minutes to get ready.

Beth's key worked like a champ. The door opened on a foyer with rounded plaster walls painted in an orange-colored wash. There was an octagonal skylight in the ceiling at the center of the space and the light from it shone on a near poster-size photograph of Nidhi hanging in a gilded frame. The top of the picture was canted forward from the wall so that Nidhi seemed to be looking down on you, and there was a rough stone ledge or altar underneath and a small silk rug on the floor below. The whole thing had a sort of shrine-like appearance, so when I lifted the lid of the earthenware jar on the alter, I wasn't surprised to find it filled with currency. I dropped in the bikini wax coupon I had received in the mail—and fortuitously retained in my wallet—and set the lid back down.

Beth snorted. "You should have scooped out the cash."

I put my finger to my lips. "Maybe on the way out," I said in an undertone. I stood with my head cocked, listening for the sound of other people in the house, but the only thing I heard was the distant sigh of a refrigerator compressor shutting down. "What's the plan?"

Beth pointed to a hallway that opened on the left. "Through the living room to the kitchen, and then down the stairs."

"To where?"

"To the fun room, of course."

"You're certain?"

"Come on—he didn't bring that Ice-Capades Barbie here to meditate."

I held my hand out in an "after you" gesture and fell in step behind her. We went through a large room that was five laps to the mile with low couches, wrought iron tables and intricately patterned Agra rugs scattered on top of an ebony tile floor. Above us, an ugly hammered-metal lantern hung from a chain like a grotesque chrysalis.

At the far end of the room was a swinging door that Beth indicated led to the kitchen. I cracked it a few inches to reconnoitre before blundering through. From what I could see, there was nothing in the way of people, but plenty in the way of expensive, restaurant-quality appliances, cookware, cutlery and assorted gizmos and gadgets. I doubted Nidhi cooked much for himself, but when he did, he wouldn't be warming his food in the can like I did.

We pushed though and came up to yet another door, this one situated between Nidhi's gleaming Wolf range and his oversize Sub-Zero freezer. Beth nodded towards it and whispered, "Down one level for the fun."

I nodded and pulled open the door quietly to poke my head into the dimly lit space beyond. The acrid smell of marijuana hit me almost immediately. A staircase dropped precipitously to a basement room painted in the same orange wash as the foyer. Black bean bag chairs were sprinkled around like raisins in a pudding, and in the middle, like a plum, sat a padded ottoman covered in black leather. A hookah with two smoking hoses was set up in the center of that, and just beyond the cobra snake-shaped mouthpieces lolled the head of the blond girl from the Porsche. She was staring blankly into space with an expression of anticipation or dread, the way you might look if a dentist was tapping on your back molars to locate a bad tooth.

The reality was much worse. She lay naked on the ottoman with her legs propped on Nidhi's bare shoulders. He crouched on the floor like a pudgy gargoyle with his fingers clutched around her ankles and his loins pressed against hers. The scene was revolting with a capital "R", but there was also an undeniable element of absurdity. Nidhi's eyes were rolled up to the ceiling and he looked as if he was in some sort of trance. Neither member of the copulating couple was moving or thrusting and they seemed to have no interest in starting.

"Did you hear something?" said the girl. She sounded doped.

"Hush my dear," said Nidhi. "Uniting of the male energy of Shiva with the feminine principle of Shakti requires intense concentration. Do not be distracted by ambient sounds."

"Whatever," said the girl, and shifted her narrow hips slightly.

"Don't do that," said Nidhi. He made a grunting sound.

A beat went by, then the girl gasped. She propped herself up on her elbows. "What is that?" she demanded.

"Nothing."

"You said you could last for hours—that you weren't going to come."

"I—I told you not to move."

"You shot your wad, didn't you?" The girl was almost screaming now. "You said no rubber because gurus don't ejaculate. You said they retain their semen to conserve the—the something or other."

"The kundalini energy."

"Well, you must be one dead Energizer Bunny now. I'm absolutely swimming in spunk. I can already feel it dripping out."

"Please, Kira, there is no need to be crude."

I hated to agree with Nidhi, but I was certainly beginning to question the "wholesome" label I'd given to the girl earlier. Behind me, I felt Beth press in close, jamming me in the thigh with the handle of her cane. "Get out of the way," she whispered.

"What are you doing?"

"Watch and see."

She elbowed past me to the first step on the stairs, where she pulled Ronnie's camera from the big pocket in the front of her dress. She aimed it at the couple on the ottoman—who were still entwined in tantric bliss—and pressed the shutter. The flash went off with a paralytic light, and after a few seconds of stunned silence, Kira let go with a teenage-slasher-movie shriek. She twisted out of the coupling with Nidhi, catching him in the jaw with her foot, and tried to claw her way off the ottoman.

Beth's camera recharged and she fired off a second picture. It turned out to be the money shot because it showed Nidhi in all his naked glory, holding Kira by the foot as she struggled to get away. When later uploaded to the protestors' web site—and dozens of other sites across the Internet—it gave the impression that Nidhi was forcing himself on a beautiful blond girl one third his age, when in reality all he was doing at that point was trying to save himself a second kick to the jaw.

Not that I was shedding any crocodile tears for Nidhi. What I was doing was hustling past Beth to the bottom of the stairs. By the time I got there, Kira was scuttling towards me on her hands and knees while Nidhi stood hunched beside the ottoman, trying to cover himself with one hand while he rubbed the point of his jaw with the other.

Kira stopped when she saw my feet. I reached down to gave her a little nudge. "Get up, Kira. You look like a Shih Tzu."

She came to her feet in a smooth motion, hugging her small breasts while she looked me over sourly. I saw that her shoulders and chest were sprinkled with sliver glitter. "Who are you?" she said.

"Just a fellow who wants to talk to the Guru."

"Couldn't you have picked a time when everyone had a few more clothes on?"

I grinned in spite of myself. "Good point. Why don't you go throw yours on and have a seat on the ottoman."

Nidhi looked at me with real fear in his eyes. He wasn't the same guru without his robes and his bodyguards "What about me?" he asked.

Beth came clunking down the stairs behind me. "Don't let him get dressed. He needs to be humbled and humiliated."

"He may need to be humbled," I said. "But I also need to keep my lunch down." I jerked my chin towards the ottoman. "Go sit with Kira and drape your shirt over your privates."

Nidhi retrieved his shirt from the floor with an air of fractured dignity and dropped onto the ottoman, rearranging the purple cloth several times before he achieved satisfactory coverage. After injecting herself into her hip-hugger jeans, Kira flopped next to him and crossed her legs with a big sigh. She was already bored with the whole thing.

"Beth," said Nidhi, "I would have expected better of you." He fixed us with a trenchant stare. "But you are both going to jail for breaking and entering."

"I wouldn't push the B&E thing too hard if I were you," I said. "I caught your goons red-handed as they came out of my apartment. And I'd lay odds they attempted the same thing at Caroline Stockwell's house the night before. Of course, breaking and entering is nothing once you graduate to maiming young women—and murder."

Nidhi frowned slightly, then went through the motions of brushing at glitter from Kira that had adhered to his ample gut. "If you're referring to Tom and Jerry, I'm sure they had nothing to do with a burglary at your apartment—or anywhere else. As to the maiming and murder, I can't imagine what you are frothing on about."

The hookah made an odd gurgling noise, like motor oil being poured down a drain. No one paid any attention to it but Kira, who leaned back to fiddle with it. I came up to stand in front of Nidhi. "Caroline Stockwell was kidnapped and forcibly tattooed with a grotesque picture of a long-tongued dragon ensnaring a butterfly. Now she's in a coma after a suicide attempt. Her best friend Monica was killed when she had a similar butterfly removed. You were visiting their web site and mailing them gifts—and you sent Tom and Jerry to my apartment and Caroline's house to recover them. The only place they didn't look was my car. And that's where I had a package you sent to her containing your tantric sex CD. A CD that has a picture of a butterfly on the cover."

Kira had turned back from the hookah about halfway through my little speech. "Jesus," she said. "You're creeping me out."

"Quiet, you little cunt," snapped Nidhi. "You don't know the first thing about this."

"I know you gave me a tantric CD with a butterfly on the cover," she snapped back.

"That's a coincidence. There's nothing significant about the butterfly. We don't even know that what he is saying about the tattoos and the other girls is true. It's probably something he made up to pressure me."

"The San Francisco Police don't think I made it up," I said. "They've already got someone under arrest. I just happen to think they've got the wrong man. We know that the killer has done this before and I've learned that he's studied tantric sex. You've got a history of sexually abusing young woman, you're a so-called expert on tantric sex—"

"You got that so-called part right," put in Kira.

"And you chose a butterfly to illustrate your CD. There's way more piled up against you already than the guy they've got in jail."

Nidhi smacked his hand against the leather of the ottoman. "Will you stop with the butterfly already. It means nothing. I don't even know how it got on the cover. My staff at the ashram handle all that. You can't break into my house and threaten me on the basis of a freaking butterfly. It's ludicrous."

"He's right," said a voice behind me.

I twisted back to look at Beth. She shrugged. "I drew the butterfly. I did all the CD covers back then. It was the only thing that gave me any pleasure. I don't think he knew or cared anything about it."

Nidhi flung his hands up in the air. "You see."

I pulled my hand across my face and thought angry thoughts. "Then why did you send Tom and Jerry to ransack my apartment?"

"I never said I—"

I reached over to grab him by the ear, Three Stooges-style. "Cut the bullshit."

Nidhi winced and tried to levitate off the ottoman as I pulled on his ear. "I didn't know what happened to Caroline Stockwell," he said in a strained voice. "But whatever it was, I knew I couldn't afford to be linked to her through the gifts. I couldn't stand the bad publicity."

"And you sent Tom and Jerry to Caroline's house for the same reason?"

"Yes. To retrieve the gifts."

"Then where were you last night?"

Nidhi flicked a nervous glance over to Kira. "At the ashram—with her."

"Well?" I said.

Her mouth flopped open and she pressed her palms to the side of her head. "Christ," she said. "I can't believe I'm alibiing this bastard." She took him in with a contemptuous stare. "Yes, damn it. We got high and played Twister. He spent the whole time trying to get into my pants, but I told him, no, I wanted to wait for the right moment. And what a special moment it's turned out to be."

I grunted and turned back to him. "That's the whole story? You've had no recent contact with Caroline?"

"None."

I sighed. I felt like a magician who'd failed to make the elephant disappear. "Well," I said evenly, "you better get used to bad publicity. I've got an idea that Beth's photos aren't for her family album. But if you ever try to retaliate in any way against Beth or me—or Kira here—then I'm going straight to the San Francisco police. There's a certain knuckle-dragging police detective there I'll have no trouble convincing that you are a good suspect after all. You on the same plane of enlightenment with me?"

I gave his earlobe an extra twist. "Yes, damn it," he said. "I'm with you."

I released him and stepped back. "Fine. Let me just leave you with a favorite quote from your own book:

'Desire nothing that would bring disgrace.'"

Beth snapped one more picture of him then—"Disgraced sect leader caught with pants down" would have been an excellent caption—and she and I headed back up the staircase. Kira hesitated, but then came bounding off the ottoman to join us, which was probably wise since Nidhi starting cursing all of us at the top of his lungs once we made it to the kitchen. When we got outside, we piled into the Galaxie and drove to the Berkeley Youth Hostel where Kira was staying.

"What will you do now?" I asked in the driveway.

"Shower, take a morning after pill and catch the Greyhound back to Barstow—in that order."

"Smart girl," said Beth.

I dropped Beth at her apartment in the Potereo Hill district of San Francisco. "Thanks for your everything, kiddo," I said when I'd helped her out of the car.

She smiled—avoiding eye contact—and waggled her cane idly in the air. "Yeah. Sorry I ruined it for you there with Nidhi."

"That's okay. I wanted the truth and that's what I got. At least I can eliminate him and move on."

She curled her finger at me like she was going to whisper a secret. I leaned down and she surprised me by planting a big sloppy one on my lips.

"You *are* the wicked handsome dude," she said.

A WALK ON THE WILD SIDE

I WAS ITCHING TO GET HOME TO MEMORIALIZE Beth's compliment in my diary, but I decided it would be a good idea to check in with Gretchen before I knocked off for the day. For one thing, it would be nice to hear her voice, and for another, I was feeling at loose ends. With Nidhi and Levin out of the running—and Wesson tacitly accepted as not guilty—I wasn't quite sure where to turn. I hoped Gretchen would have some advice or news of a development that would get me started again. She did, but it took me a long time to appreciate a big part of it.

I coasted down Pennsylvania Avenue to 22nd Street and got out to use a pay phone near the train station. It was a funny area. Ultra-modern artists' lofts rubbed shoulders with warehouses and industrial yards from businesses founded in the early 1900s, which in turn played footsie with homeless encampments in the parking areas near the station. The dwellings ranged from cardboard and tarp paper tents on the low end to abandoned camper vans and RVs on the high end. Overhead was the massive Highway 280 skyway—rumbling ominously with traffic like a distant bombardment—and down an embankment reachable only via a steep set of rickety wooden stairs lay the roadbed of the commuter train. The station itself was nothing more than a wide spot along the tracks, shielded from the elements by the skyway.

The phone was off the street near the top of the stairs. I dropped my 50 cents just as the engine from a northbound train poked through a tunnel a few hundred yards from the station. The line rang a long time before Gretchen picked up. "It's your favorite PI," I said when she finally answered.

"What I figured," she said. "You usually manage to call when I'm halfway to the elevator."

"Where you off to at—" I glanced at my watch. "5:20?"

"I'll have you know I got in at 7:30 this morning. But since you asked, Dennis is taking me to dinner and a show. I'm leaving a little early so I can get my nails done."

I stared at a gigantic peace sign some graffiti artist had done on one of the skyway pillars. "Well, I'll have *you* know that a woman called me a wicked handsome dude today."

"What does that have to do with the price of yak dung in Pakistan? Your appearance was never the issue."

The train came squealing to a stop at the station and the doors slid open. Commuters tumbled out and broke towards the stairs like players in a home team introduction. "All right. I don't know why I brought it up. Any messages for me?"

"You brought it up because you're still jealous of Dennis—and I think it's cute. Yes, you've got two messages. Chris called and said if you get the chance before this evening, you should stop by and see him. He's got something to show you."

"Something to show me? What exactly?"

Gretchen gave a little giggle. "He told me, but I really do think you need to see it for yourself. Mere words do not suffice."

"Swell. It better not be another bottle of green microorganisms. What else you got?"

"A woman with a French accent called. Odile something. And speaking of interest from the opposite sex, she sounded pretty damn sexy."

"It pains me to admit this, but I think it's safe to say that she doesn't care for me in that way."

"Are you sure? She wants you to meet her at six at a bar called the Wild Side West on Cortland Avenue."

The first of the commuters came pounding to the top of the stairs: a guy in a black turtleneck with a ten speed bike balanced on one shoulder and a leather satchel slung over the other. He set the bike down smoothly and peddled past me in an annoyingly competent maneuver. "You think she still expects me?" I asked. "It's almost six and I didn't confirm."

"She said she was going to be there anyway. You're to stop by if you're free."

"All right, then I will." I cleared my throat a little awkwardly. "I'll let you go so you can get to your nail appointment. Have a good time at the show."

"How nice, August," Gretchen said brightly. "Thank you for not making any jokes about Dennis. Have a good time with your French friend."

"Don't bet on it," I grumbled.

Cortland Avenue ran through the middle of the Bernal Heights district, and the Wild Side West bar was about halfway between Mission Street and Highway 101, the east/west delimiters of the neighborhood. The exterior was made up like a Western saloon with a hanging shingle sign by the door. Inside were a high wooden ceiling, a bar that could have come off the set of *The Good, The Bad and the Ugly,* a random collection of scarred wooden tables and chairs that could—and probably did—come from the Salvation Army and a pool table with blood-red felt. The candelabras and the silk throw pillows hadn't arrived—and no one was looking for them either.

Over the bar, a TV was running an episode of *Xena, Warrior Princess* on mute, but to make up for the lack of sound, speakers at all four corners of the room blared the song *Bring Me Some Water* by Melissa Etheridge. There were about a dozen women in the bar, and all of them whose lips I could see were mouthing the words to the song. A few of them were also stabbing the air with clenched fists in time to the beat. I was beginning to get a certain idea about the place.

Odile was sitting with her back to me at a big round table next to a fireplace whose mantle was decorated with pairs of antique shoes. Her companion across the table was wearing mirrored sunglasses that reflected and distorted my wavering form when she looked up at my approach. Her close-cropped black hair was secured under a blue bandana and she wore a set of heavy metal chains around her neck—one of them with curved, thorn-like spikes—on top of a grease-stained wife beater. She was smoking a cigarette with a good half-inch of ash clinging to the end in spite of the state smoking ban.

"Odile?" I squeaked like a bad ventriloquist.

Etheridge's plaintive lyric raged over the speakers, "Can't you see I'm burning alive?" and the woman in the bandana sneered, "What do you want?"

Odile glanced back. "It is okay, Gina, I invited him." She smiled thinly. "I was not sure you would receive my message."

"Well, I did."

She gave a Gallic shrug. "Come sit with us."

I hesitated, not certain exactly where to sit. I started toward Gina, then thought better of it and settled on a chair part way between the two women.

Gina laughed as I sat down. "Feeling a little out of place, are we?"

"Maybe just a little."

Gina nodded and took a deep drag on her cigarette. The tip of it glowed red and the long ash plopped onto the table. She blew a blue-gray plume of smoke into the air. "I remember when I was in eighth grade I used to ask the boys in the lower grades if they knew that their epidermis was showing. They'd get this squirrelly look on their face—kinda like you have now—and glance down nervously to see if their fly was open. Then I'd laugh, and most of the time they'd run away in tears."

"Children can be very cruel," said Odile.

"They sure can," said Gina. "And so can adults. So here's the question I ask now. What's the most useless appendage in the world?"

She leaned back in her chair, smiling, and I noticed for the first time that she had a stud in her tongue.

"I don't know," I said slowly. "Trailer hitch on a Yugo?"

Odile made a little snorting noise and covered her mouth in her hand. "Gina, I think it is time for Mr. Riordan and I to do our business. Would you give us a few minutes? I will come and get you for another game of pool when we are finished."

Gina stood up and walked round to give Odile a kiss on the cheek. "I love the way you French chicks say pool."

"Looks like you've got yourself a live one," I said after she had gone.

"Yes, she is very alive, and as you can realize, she is also very protective of me. But we are only friends."

"I see. Well, I'm sure you didn't ask me down here to talk about your love life. Did you get a chance to look at the files I left?"

Odile took a sip from a glass of dark beer at her elbow and shook her head. "Yes, I examined them. But I would know more about what happened to the girl before I speak of the files."

I gave her a run down of Caroline's history, including what I knew about her family life and what had happened to her, Monica and the Japanese girl. I concluded with the story of Caroline's second suicide attempt.

Odile frowned. "I am a little surprised that she should try again."

"Why?"

"The first attempt—well, that was probably a dramatic way to get the attention of her parents and communicate her shame with what had happened. The thing she said to you at the hospital, 'Go back and tell my mother what a damaged piece of goods I am,' is very consistent with that. She wished for her parents to take her back into their lives and reaffirm her value. To deny that she was damaged."

"But the second?"

"The second attempt would seem to come from a more genuine sense of despair. By that time, I would hope that she had received the reassurance from her parents that she craved—at least from her mother. If not, or if there was some new setback, she might have tried again. But still … " Her voice trailed off.

A new Etheridge song came over the speakers, seemingly louder than the first—if that was possible. I pulled my chair closer to the table. "But still what?"

She blew air through her lips. "My impression of Caroline from reading Levin's files is that she is, at core, a very strong person. She does not fit my model of someone who would actually kill herself."

"Her brother did."

"Yes, but the mother told you he was taking the acne medicine that has been linked to suicide in teens." She held up her hands. "In truth, it is all speculation. No one can ever tell you why someone kills herself—especially a shrink who has been fired less than six months after she finishes her residency."

"I'll take your speculations over Dr. Levin's pronouncements in a heartbeat. Speaking of which, he hinted that Caroline's father abused her. Did you see any evidence to support that?"

"No, she made no mention of it to Levin. But it is certain that their relationship was strained. Like many fathers, he did not know how to talk to her once she reached puberty. And once the son died, the fracture between them grew larger. He made some clumsy attempts to draw her closer—by buying her expensive gifts, for instance—but by then he was drinking heavily and she had lost respect for him."

A waitress appeared at my left elbow and set a large schooner of dark beer in front of me. "Compliments of the lady at the pool table," she said.

I looked over to table to find Gina squinting at me without her shades as she inhaled another cigarette. I held the schooner up in salute and she did the same with her cue.

"There," said Odile, "you have made a new friend."

I nodded as I took a big gulp of the beer. "I'm just glad I didn't meet her in grade school. Listen, the main thing I'm interested to learn is if there is any indication of who might have done this to Caroline."

Odile pushed down the sleeve of the black sweater she was wearing and rearranged the thin silver bracelets at her wrist. "I think it likely that she knew the person who—who disfigured her. Perhaps knew him very well."

"Why?"

"The level of humiliation she evidently felt. When you are betrayed by someone you know, it is much worse than being taken advantage of by a stranger. If by a stranger, it is easier to admit what happened and seek the help of parents or the authorities. But having a friend do this would be very ... how do you say it? De—"

"Degrading?"

"*Exactement.*"

"Then you don't think the web site had anything to do with it?"

Odile placed four elegant fingers along her cheek and shook her head. "I did not say that. It may have had everything to do with it. If a friend or acquaintance saw Caroline and Monica on the web site, partially disrobed and catering to the fetishes of admirers—as he would never see the girls in real life—he may have felt emboldened to treat them *as* sexual fetishes. From what you say, this is exactly how Dr. Levin behaved."

I took another sip of beer and relaxed back into my chair. Mercifully, the Etheridge CD had ended, leaving only the background murmur of conversation, the clinking of bar glasses and the occasional kiss of pool balls. "I'm a little surprised you would say that because I suggested something very similar to a friend recently. I speculated that the web site had somehow been a catalyst for the killer to act out a fantasy."

Odile stared at me for a moment, then smiled and shook her head. "Now I am the one to be surprised. What we are talking about, in effect, is the objectification of women. To create a something out of a someone. It is a topic for which feminist scholars have much passion. I would not expect a—a man like you to have entertained such thoughts."

"Thank you for using the word 'man' instead of 'Neanderthal.' But if the killer is a friend who acted because of the web site, how do you explain the Japanese girl? She doesn't have a web site and she had only been in the country a few months. Presumably not long enough to have made many friends."

"How do you know that she does not have a web site? It may be a Japanese site, but she could still have it. And friends do not take so long to make. It seems clear from what you say that the killer is associated with the art school. She must have met him there."

I tugged on my earlobe, thinking. "Everything you say points back to Wesson. I had pretty much decided that he was innocent."

"He may well be. Caroline never mentioned him to Levin. This I know."

"What friends did she mention? There seems to be no one left."

Odile shrugged her Gallic shrug. "There is her boyfriend of course."

I reached for the edge of the table and pulled myself forward. "Levin said she didn't have a boyfriend. When I told him that Caroline's mother thought she did, he bristled at the suggestion. In fact, he later chastised Caroline in an e-mail for getting involved with someone."

"Dumb shit," she said matter of factly. "That is very much like him. Caroline talked several times of a new friend she had made at school, never actually calling him her boyfriend, but it was clear enough to me from the things she said. Levin wouldn't want her to be involved with anyone else, so he naturally would ignore or misinterpret what she was saying."

"He put all of this in his notes?"

"No, he only wrote his conclusions there. This is from sessions I heard from the tapes."

It was frustrating to know that Levin could have pointed me in the right direction if only he'd unplugged his ears. "What can you tell me about the boyfriend, then?"

"Not a great deal. Levin did not let her speak of him for very long. Caroline said he was a talented artist whose work was misunderstood. I have the impression that he was a student at the school at one point, but was no longer registered. It was clear she admired him very much."

"What about a name? Did she mention a name?"

Odile smiled almost coyly, causing the skin around her eyes to crinkle. "You are going to think me very silly or very clever. Caroline never mentioned his name while she was in session, but one time Levin's receptionist pulled him out of the room to deal with some emergency. You have the picture? Caroline was alone, but the tape continued while Levin was gone."

"And?"

"And she made a cell phone call. It was very short. She said, 'Cricket, it's me. I'm almost done with the witch doctor. Meet me on Haight in 30 minutes?' The other person must have agreed and then I heard her put the phone back in her purse."

"Cricket? That's not much to go on. It might not even be the person you think was her boyfriend."

"As I said, you may think me very silly or very clever."

I rubbed my face and glanced around the bar. Gina was lounging against the pool table with a cue in her hands, watching our conversation intently. She nodded fractionally when I caught her eye.

I looked back to Odile. "I should let you get back to your pool game. Thank you for taking the time to look through the files. You've given me some new things to go on."

"You are welcome. I feel, perhaps, I have misjudged you the tiniest bit. I am sorry I threw the box on your foot when we met at the office."

"That's okay. I probably deserved it. One last question: if you were me, what would do next?"

Odile looked at me soberly and pushed her lips into a little pout. "If I were you, I would look for other art school students who have web sites—and find out if they know anyone named Cricket."

A SCANDAL IN SCANDINAVIA

THE SAN FRANCISCO MUNICIPAL RAILWAY—OR MUNI FOR short—is justifiably proud of its fleet of cable cars, but its boast of having "the largest trolley-bus fleet of any transit agency in the U.S. and Canada" is a more dubious distinction. As you might guess, trolley-buses are the bastard offspring of buses and trolleys: rubber-tired vehicles with motors powered by electricity from over-head wires. This sounds fine in concept until the pair of hinged poles that connect the bus to the wires jump off track—something that never seems to happen to the trolleys that run on rails—leaving the trolley-bus stranded in the middle of the street.

A #24 bus was stranded exactly this way in front of the Castro Street Victorian that housed Chris Duckworth's apartment. The long trolley poles bounced, disconnected on their springs, making the bus look like a confused insect with its antennae waving feebly in the air. I jogged across the street, past the cursing Muni driver who was just climbing out to reattach the poles, and up to the entrance of Chris' apartment. He buzzed me in without responding to the crack I made about selling *Boy's Life* subscriptions on the speaker dingus, and I hiked up the three flights of stairs to his cramped little garret.

The door was standing open. "I'm in the back," shouted a voice from the interior. "Check out the laptop on the coffee table."

The couch next to the coffee table was upholstered in a shiny blue material, had a lot of swoopy-doopy lines and generally gave the impression of a daybed in a harem. I sat down gingerly on one corner and hefted the computer from the table. Its screen saver cleared immediately to reveal the web site of another young woman. She was an attractive blonde who appeared to have a lot of the same interests as Caroline—art, photography, gifts from strangers—but she seemed more mature, and certainly appeared to have a better facility for web design. The menu structure of her site was easier to navigate and the layout was cleaner and more stylish. The colors were a little wild—a lot of DayGlo greens and yellows from the 1960s—but I could forgive her this after the gloomy goth coloration of Caroline's and Monica's efforts. The one thing that troubled me was that the girl seemed faintly familiar. But as often as I might have wished for it, I knew that I hadn't run across any art students named Brita visiting from Sweden.

"How did you find her?" I shouted in the direction of Chris' bedroom.

I heard a scraping of closet hangers, then, "She's a perfect match, isn't she?" came the muffled response. "She's into art, photography and she's even here on a visa like the Japanese girl."

I put the laptop back on the table and tried to find a comfortable perch on the couch without getting prone. "If you mean a match like a bull's-eye painted on her back, I agree. It'd probably be a very good idea to warn her. But back to my question. How did you find her? Some magical incantation you typed in a search engine?"

"No," said Chris, sounding a little less muffled. "There are lots of web directories for cam girls. It would be very easy for the killer to search for art students with cam girl sites in the Bay Area—or San Francisco for that matter. As it happens, the only one extant is Brita." I heard a long zipper going up. "But that's more by design than by happenstance. ... "

Chris—or should I say Brita—stepped out from behind the bedroom door. He wore an orange cowl-neck sweater over a turquoise mini-skirt and matching turquoise tights. Soft leather boots that just came over the ankle filled the bill in the footwear department, and in the wig department, a short muff of blond hair styled in an artfully haphazard urchin cut. His makeup was dramatic without being over the top, and all in all he looked like a shorter, younger Sharon Stone out for a romp in 60s garb.

I was hopping mad.

"What the hell is this?" I demanded.

"It's last year's Marc Jacobs. I got it at Loehmann's for a hundred bucks."

"I'm not talking about the fucking designer fashions. I'm talking about you interfering in my investigation after I told you to stay out of it."

He made a little pshaw gesture. "Don't be silly. I've been helping you every step of the way. Who hacked Caroline's computer for you? Who tracked down Skinner's Pigeon? Me. Your faithful Indian companion."

My tongue strayed to the sharp point on my partial plate, enraging me further. "I asked you explicitly to help me with those things. I did *not* ask you to set up a web site to lure sickos. The idea is ridiculous. No one—least of all the killer—is going to go for it. If you accomplish anything, it will just be to warn him off."

He spun on his boot heel and marched out of the room. When he came back, he was cradling two arms full of Amazon.com boxes. He flung them onto the couch, where three-quarters of them tumbled onto the floor and the remainder piled to a stop against my leg. "Where do you think these came from?" he said. "Publishers Clearing House?"

I looked at him levelly for a moment, not saying anything. I sighed and picked up the box closest to me. It had been opened and then folded closed again. Inside was a cylindrical bottle of frosted glass with a silver top that was meant to look like it contained something pretty special. The something was "Cellular Retexturizing Booster," which I guessed was another name for skin cream. "How much does this gunk sell for?" I asked.

Chris gave a smile that would have been seductive if I hadn't known a little too much about what he had under his designer togs.

"150 bucks a bottle—and worth every penny, big boy. You don't want your Swedish cutie getting wrinkles."

"No, I suppose not. So these gifts have been coming from visitors to your site—just like with Caroline?"

"Yep."

"How long have you have you been engaged in this little enterprise?"

"Just a few days. I tried to tell you about it when you called to ask me to copy Caroline's site."

"And you're sure your visitors have no idea that you're a man?"

He laughed. "Not unless they're fantasizing about some very unusual things involving my cat. For instance, one of them made a suggestion about shaving my p—"

I waved my hands. "Okay, stop right there. I get it. Has anybody written anything that suggests he could be responsible for what happened to Caroline and Monica? Asked you to get together with him maybe? Talked about tattoos?"

Chris sat down on the far end of the couch and smoothed his skirt over his legs. He plunked his elbows on his knees and rested his chin between his fists. "Not so far. I've been looking for that, of course. The fact of the matter is, I've been surprised how mundane and repetitive most of the correspondence is. There appears to be very little that's unique or creative in the way of depravity these days."

"Anyone named Cricket or something similar contacted you?"

"No. No crickets, grasshoppers or locusts have e-mailed or sent gifts. Why do you ask?"

I recapped my session with Odile, ending with the reference to Cricket she had heard in Caroline's recorded phone conversation. "But even if Cricket's not the one," I said, "Odile seemed pretty convinced that the killer would turn out to be someone who knew Caroline and Monica from before."

"Which is what you thought."

"Yes, and while I'll grant you that I underestimated your ability to entice heterosexual perverts into sending you gifts, it does make me think that you're wasting your time trying to flush out the killer this way. You won't have any personal connection to him."

Chris straightened and swung one leg smartly over the other. "Well, it's not a complete waste of time. I'm absolutely cleaning up when it comes to makeup and lingerie."

"Yes, but—"

"And more to the point, I found something else that suggests the web site is more likely to succeed than you think. The Japanese girl had one too."

"She did? How did you find out?"

"It wasn't hard once I had the idea to look for it. I was backing up Caroline's site to my hard drive like you asked and it struck me that the girl—Mika is her name—might have had a site too. As I said, there are a lot of directories for cam girl sites and it was relatively easy to find one for a Japanese art student going to school in the US."

"Was it in English?"

"Part was, and the rest was in Japanese. I couldn't read anything in the Japanese section of course, but there were some pretty racy photos there. The English section was tamer." Chris pulled the laptop across the table and typed something on the keyboard. "Anything else about the site that occurs to you to ask?"

I looked down at one of the Amazon.com boxes on the floor and nudged it idly with my toe. A squat amber bottle of perfume flopped out and fell with a clunk to the floor. "Not particularly. I assume she was soliciting gifts?"

"Yes, but her wish list was on the Amazon Japanese storefront so it was harder to figure out what she was requesting. But that's not what you should have asked. What you should have asked is whether the site had been defaced."

Chris spun the computer around so that I could see the screen. On it was a depressingly familiar image: the bare shoulder of the Japanese girl with the tattoo of a butterfly and the start of the dragon's tongue. There was a label in Japanese beneath the photograph.

"What's it say?"

Chris bit his tangerine-glossed lip. "It took a while to find somebody to translate it, but I did. It says, 'Unfinished Work.'"

I slumped back against the crazy curved back of the couch, half of my spine against the upholstery and half against the wall. "So he did the same thing to all of them. I wonder if the cops know about this."

"My guess is not—or they would have had the site taken down like they did Caroline's and Monica's. I spent a little time trying to analyze the HTML that he changed on both sites to see if there was anything distinctive we could trace back to him, but I didn't have much luck."

"What do you mean, analyze the HTML? What you see in the browser is what you get, isn't it?"

"Not really. HTML stands for Hypertext Markup Language. Its a sort of code for the browser to render when you type in the address of a web page. You never see the HTML directly unless you select View Source from the menu. Anyway, the thing about HTML is that it's very flexible. There are many different ways to code a page to achieve the same final appearance. Most people use an editor—like Microsoft FrontPage—to develop their HTML, and each of the editors has a distinct style of HTML coding that you can often trace back to them. Some of them also leave comments in the HTML with the editor name and version."

"Seems a little thin. What would we do even if we could tell what editor he'd used? It's not quite the same as finding the typewriter somebody used to type a ransom note. There must be thousands—or maybe millions—of copies of any editor."

"Yeah, I guess it was a stretch," said Chris, and then got a sort of pinched look on his face. I thought maybe one of his garters had popped, but he said, "There was one thing … " and spun the laptop back around. He did some more typing, muttered, "I thought so," and then said loudly, "It's there too."

He pushed the computer back at me. "Take a look at that."

There wasn't much to see. A couple of windows with some gibberish between angle brackets was all I could get out of it. The interesting bit was apparently an identical line that was highlighted in each:

```
<!-- chirp, chirp -->
```

"If that's important," I said, "then you're going to have to explain it. It means about as much to me as the Japanese caption."

Chris reached over to pat me on the leg. "Don't worry. I like you for your strong back, not your brains. That's an HTML comment. Web page developers insert it into the HTML when they want to explain something about the code to people who are going to maintain or modify the page later. The words between the dashes comprise the actual comment text, but it never actually shows up in the browser when the page is rendered."

"So?"

"So the person who defaced Caroline's and Monica's site, as well as the Japanese girl's, went out of their way to put that in the updated HTML. And guess what kind of animal makes a chirp?"

"A cricket?" I unpeeled myself from the back of the couch. "He signed his work?"

Chris nodded. "In effect. Now at least you know your French psychiatrist friend was right. It's the guy Caroline was talking to on the phone."

I pushed the Amazon.com boxes on the couch to one side, stood and waded through the ones on the floor to a spot in front of the coffee table. "Well, thank you for that. That's the kind of help I can use. I still think you're wasting your time with the web site, though, and please don't do anything else without clearing it with me first. Okay?"

Chris looked down at his skirt and picked at the fringe on the hem. "Okay. It's just that I've been a little at loose ends. Hambert and I broke up."

"I thought he didn't ship out for another week."

"He doesn't, but he said he was afraid of being outed. Said I was too flamboyant for him." Chris bit his lip again and moisture collected at the corner of one eye. "I've got hat boxes that are further out of the closet than he is."

I was tired and I wanted to get home, but I walked back over to Chris and punched him lightly in the shoulder. "Come on, Brita. Hitch up your girdle and I'll take you out for dinner. Maybe you can meet a new sailor boy."

We went to AsiaSF, a restaurant where "gender illusionists"—who double as the waitstaff—perform on a platform runway. Chris didn't meet any sailors, but he did exchange phone numbers with our waiter/waitress: a blushing Chinese lotus blossom in a high-collared silk dress with long slits up the sides.

All I exchanged was a large pile of cash for the bill.

FLASH POINT

I DREAMED I WAS IN AN ALL-NIGHT DINER eating a solitary meal when the rest of my teeth fell out. They tumbled from my mouth to the table like so many thrown dice. The waitress, who was Monica Mapa in a stained and faded uniform, appeared at the booth. She swept the teeth up without comment and brought them back in a doggie bag. "For later," she said, and gave me a knowing look.

I was spared further psycho-trauma by the jarring ring of the telephone. I hadn't replaced the phone on the nightstand after Tom and Jerry ransacked the place, so I slithered off the bed to the floor, tracing the phone line from the wall to a place mid-way under the bed frame before I located the handset. I rolled onto my back and fumbled the receiver to my ear. "Hello," I lisped, missing the two teeth that really were out of my mouth soaking in a glass in the bathroom.

"I hope I didn't wake you," said a tough male voice.

"Not at all. Morning yoga. I just finished with 'upward facing dog' when you called."

Lieutenant Jack Kittredge chuckled derisively. "Is that the position where you get on all fours and lift your leg in the air?"

"Something like that. What can I do for you, Lieutenant?"

"It's more what I can do for you. I'm calling to let you know you lost another client."

I pressed the clammy plastic of the receiver closer to my ear. "I wasn't aware that I had another client to lose."

"That's what he told us, anyway. I'm talking about Wesson."

"You're calling to tell me he gave you the slip between my office and the station?"

Kittredge chuckled again. "No, but he lawyered up immediately. Got that shyster Schwartz involved, who had a special bail hearing set that afternoon. We ended up having to kick him on $50,000 bail and didn't get a word out of him—except that you were on the case and were going to prove him innocent."

"I told you, I never signed him as a client. And the judge must not have thought much of your charges if he let him go for 50K."

"Yeah, that's true. But when we woke his honor up at four this morning to get a warrant to search Wesson's house, he seemed to have changed his mind."

"Maybe you should have got the search warrant first to build a better case."

He grunted noncommittally. "It doesn't matter now. Wesson did a swan dive off the east tower of Saints Peter and Paul Church in Washington square. The pastor found him smeared across the concrete steps in front at about 1:20. Seems the good Father was making final rounds after midnight mass and he stumbled over the body."

I felt my jaw hinge open. "You're saying he's dead?"

"No, I'm saying he has to carry around his brains around in a jelly jar. Of course he's dead."

I levered myself off the floor and sat on the edge of the mattress. "Let me get this straight, Kittredge. He committed suicide by jumping off a church tower in the middle of the night."

"That's right. Turns out he lives about two blocks away."

I squeezed my eyes shut and rubbed the sleep from them. "There's more to this, isn't there? You're leaving something out."

"You mean about the note?"

"What about it?"

"It was pretty simple. All it said was 'I'm sorry.' The interesting bit was that it was tattooed on his left arm. And when we got the warrant to go through his house—surprise, surprise—we found a full set of tattoo equipment, sketches of the butterfly tattoo he'd done on Caroline Stockwell, Monica Mapa and the Japanese girl, digital pictures of all the finished tattoos on his computer and copies of the defaced web pages from Caroline's and Monica's site."

"I'll bet you found more than the pages from Caroline and Monica's site."

Kittredge made a growling noise. "That's right, smart guy. He also had the Japanese girl's. And if you know that, it means you been sticking your nose further into this in spite of my earlier warnings. Well, it all stops now. I'm calling the Stockwells to let them know we found their daughter's kidnapper and then I'm filing the paperwork."

"Is that before or after your call the paper to come and take your picture?"

"Screw you, Riordan. Just be sure you don't do any talking of your own to the media."

"That's the real reason for this call, isn't it? To keep me from contradicting your story."

"It's not a story and there's nothing to contradict. We've got Wesson dead to rights, and it's not in your interest or anyone else's to say different."

"I just hope Caroline Stockwell confirms it all when she wakes up," I said, but I was talking to dead air.

I hung up the phone and got showered and dressed. I wasn't sure what to make of Kittredge's news. If I could take what he said at face value, it sounded pretty compelling, but the mere fact he had called made me think that he was worried about something. I was pondering this while munching through a bowl of my favorite breakfast cereal—Captain Crunch with Crunch Berries—when someone knocked on the door. The someone hadn't bothered to buzz downstairs to be let in, which in my experience meant cops or salespeople.

It turned out to be cops—but not the one I expected. Standing at the threshold when I pulled the door open was Quentin Stockwell. The transformation was frightening. He looked sober, serious and motivated—every bit the old Stockwell I remembered.

"Did you hear that the San Francisco cops think they got the guy who hurt Caroline?" he said without preamble.

"Yeah," I said, "I got a call."

He bulled his way past me into the room. "They're full of crap."

I pushed the door closed and lounged against the arm of the sofa. "I'm not saying you're wrong, but what makes you so certain?"

Stockwell looked around like he was on the realtor's tour. "Jesus Christ, this place is every inch the dump it was the last time I was here. And you've still got that Fred Flintstone audio equipment."

"Emily Post says sharing your home with guests is one of life's greatest joys."

"And Ben Franklin says fish and guests stink after three days. I'm just getting a head start." He marched over to the card table and pulled out one of the folding chairs to sit down. "You got any coffee?"

I went to the kitchen to pour us two cups from the pot I had going. I set one in front of him and pulled up a chair across the table. "You were just about to explain why the SFPD is full of crap."

Stockwell looked down and squeezed the cup in his two hands like he was trying to crush it. "Let me tell you a little story," he said after a moment. "Late yesterday evening I was with Caroline in her room at the hospital. I'd fallen asleep in a chair. I heard a noise or sensed a movement that woke me up. I was pretty groggy and it was dark in the room, but I saw a figure approaching Caroline's bed. I shouted and the figure turned and ran out the door. I followed but he was already going down the stairwell by the time I got into the hallway. I called hospital security and the Union City cops. No dice. He got clean away."

"That doesn't surprise me. My impression of the security and visitors procedures at the hospital is that they are pretty lax. Did you get any kind of look at him?"

"Mainly from the back. He wasn't particularly tall—I'd say no more than five-foot-ten—but he was massively built. He's almost certainly some kind of weight lifter. He was wearing a watch cap, so I couldn't see his hair. But here's the scary part. There was just enough illumination from the status lights on the monitors connected to Caroline to see what was in his hands when he approached the bed. It looked like a hypodermic needle."

The room suddenly seemed very quiet. I heard the drip from a leaky faucet in the bathroom. "Do you think it's possible that he put Caroline in the coma?" I asked.

Bunches of muscles tightened into igneous lumps at the corners of his jaw, then with visible effort, he relaxed. "That's my guess. And when the drugs he gave her the first time didn't kill her, he came back to finish the job."

"What time of night was this?"

"It was a little after four o'clock. Well after this Wesson character took the dive off the church steeple—if that's what you're driving at."

"Yes, it was. That means the mystery man at the hospital could also have helped Wesson with his suicide—not to mention planting all the tattoo stuff that they found at his house. Did you tell your story to Kittredge when he called?"

He nodded and took a sip of the coffee. He grimaced. "Where'd this come from? A drip pan in a crematorium? Yes, I told Kittredge. He said if I really saw the guy it must be unrelated—and then he asked me if I'd been drinking."

"Had you?"

Stockwell reddened and started to point an accusatory finger at me. He checked himself and dropped his hand to the table. "No, I've been off the sauce since we last spoke. I realized I couldn't do anything for Caroline unless I stopped."

I nodded and took a slug of the coffee. It tasted fine to me. "How is she doing?"

Stockwell pressed his lips together and then spoke in a quiet voice:

"The doctors say it's 50-50. She might come out of the coma or she might not. The longer she stays in it, though, the less likely it is that she'll come out."

"Did they ever figure out what kind of drug it was?"

"GHB."

"One of the date rape drugs."

He nodded.

"Given what happened, are you—are you doing anything to prevent another midnight visit?"

Stockwell shifted angrily in the chair. "Don't tell me my business. I moved her and I've got her under 24-hour guard."

"Let me ask you another question then. Why are you here?"

"I'm here because we God damn hired you, that's why."

"Maybe you don't remember exactly what it was you told me the last time we spoke. You bounced me off the case."

"If I had anywhere else to go, Riordan, believe me, I would. But you're the only one who knows all the players and the full background. I don't have the time or the luxury of starting from scratch. Besides which, you took a big fat retainer from Ellen, and as far as I can tell, you've done very little to earn it."

I shrugged. "I haven't done so bad for you, Stockwell. I found out about the web site and the whole business with the tattoos. And yesterday I learned that Caroline definitely had a boyfriend."

"What do you mean?"

I explained what I'd learned from Odile and Chris about Cricket and his chirps on the web sites. "If Wesson was killed and then framed for the murders," I said, "it was probably this Cricket character, who was very likely the person who came to Caroline's room last night."

Stockwell shook his head. "I don't know how you do it. This is exactly what I meant when I said you bounce around the landscape like a pinball in an arcade game. You rely on gay computer hackers and lesbo shrinks, yet you still manage to find things and link them up."

"That comment says more about you than it does about me."

"Maybe. But there's a limit to how far your undisciplined, right-brain methods will go." He stood from the table. "You know what you should be doing now—what you should have been doing the moment you got a street name for this guy?"

"Going around to all the tattoo shops in the area asking if anyone's heard of him?"

"That's right—and checking to see if anyone recognizes the style of the tattoos wouldn't hurt either." He pushed the chair under the table. "Come on."

"What? Right now?"

"Yes, right now. Pin on your diaper and let's go."

I pushed back from the table and went to the bedroom to retrieve my jacket and a folder of web site printouts Chris had made for me. Stockwell stood by the door holding it open. As I came up to him—shrugging on the jacket—he wheeled and landed a punishing uppercut to my stomach. I folded like a canvas awning. He said:

"I may have lost my job, but I haven't given up on my family. Stay away from my wife."

If you want to be tattooed, pierced or otherwise manipulated in San Francisco, you'll do best to head to one of four parts of town: North Beach, the Mission, the Castro or the Haight. We started with North Beach and the Mission district because of their connections to Wesson and Monica Mapa, but struck out pretty quickly. None of the tattoo artists in the half dozen or so parlors we visited recognized Cricket or his work.

The Castro district was next, but Stockwell flat out refused to get out of the car. In truth, there was little point because the gay community appeared to prefer piercings to tattoos and neither of the two shops I visited even had a tattoo artist on call that day. I did ask one of the "body manipulation professionals" to inscribe a picture postcard of a pierced body part to Stockwell, but for some reason he didn't appreciate the gesture.

That left the Haight, or Haight-Ashbury as it's called whenever people speak nostalgically of hippies, flower power, the 1960s and the Summer of Love. The fact of the matter is, the Haight has as much to do with the 60s today as the Fantasyland castle in Disneyland has to do with the Bavarian castle on which it's modeled. The only remaining artifacts from the time when The Grateful Dead, Janis Joplin, Jefferson Airplane and Timothy Leary roved the landscape are the occasional head shop and the incidental Tibetan jewelry store. Far more common are boutiques, vintage-clothing shops, military surplus outlets, restaurants and women's shoe stores that all seem to feature wacky footwear created by gluing three-inch cork heels onto bowling shoes. And tattoo parlors. Plenty of tattoo parlors.

There were so many, in fact, that after parking Stockwell's SUV in the Kezar Stadium parking lot at the edge of Golden Gate Park, we decided to separate and divide the work between us. He took the parlors on the South side of Haight Street and I took the ones on the North.

I got lucky in the first one I walked into. It was called Skin Furniture and it was housed in a shotgun building with a neon sign in the window and hundreds of tattoo designs papering the walls inside. Standing behind a glass case of studs and other piercing jewelry was a rabbity-looking guy with a tentative goatee and a faint odor of fried egg emanating from his person. He was refilling the business card holder on the top of the case—a human skull painted bright red with its jaw prized open in a rictus of astonishment—when I came up. He gave me a tepid smile that was less a sign of welcome than an attempt to mask the confusion my presence had engendered. Apparently I didn't fit the profile of his usual clientele. I said:

"I'd like to get a tattoo."

He nodded. "Have you ever, um, gotten one before?"

"No," I said cheerfully. "Never have. But I've got a particular design I'd like to use." I pulled out the picture of the butterfly tattoo from Mika, the Japanese girl. "Can you do that for me? I'd like to get it on my butt."

His eyes made the round trip from the photo to my backside several times and then he reluctantly took the picture from my hands. He held it about two inches from his face. "This is good work. I don't know if any of the artists here could do something in exactly that style. We've got plenty of other butterfly flash, though."

"Flash?"

He waved at the designs covering the walls behind him. "Flash is what we call the patterns we use for common tattoos. We must have about fifty butterfly designs to pick from."

"I really had my heart set on that butterfly. Do you know where I might get somebody to do it for me?"

He set the photo down on the counter, then angrily pushed up the sleeves of his sweater. A tattoo of a winged eyeball peered at me from one forearm and a creature with a spider's body and a woman's head from the other. "Did Stan send you in here to hassle me, man?"

"Who's Stan?"

"Stan Zemler. The owner of Osiris."

I gave him my best befuddled tourist look. "I'm not following."

He sighed. "Okay, sorry. I guess I was being paranoid or territorial or something. Osiris is a tattoo shop down the street. Stan Zemler owns it and lately he's been churning out a lot of killer tattoos in a new style. This looks a lot like some of the new flash I've seen in his shop."

"Does Mr. Zemler ever go by the nickname Cricket?"

Now it was his turn to look befuddled. "No, man. And I wouldn't call him an insect to his face if I were you. He's a tough bastard. Rhino would be a better nickname for him."

I picked up the photo from the counter. "Thanks for the advice. Where did you say I could find his shop?"

He threw his hand up dismissively. "Northwest corner of Haight and Masonic. But don't be expecting Stan Zemler to draw any butterflies on your ass cheek."

Smiling, I turned from the counter and hurried out the door. I wanted to get to Stockwell before he went into Osiris so we could brace Zemler together. I crossed Haight and jogged up Stockwell's side of the street, ducking my head into two other parlors as I headed toward Masonic, but he must have been in and out of them already.

I spotted a sandwich sign on the sidewalk about a half block up with a picture of a squinting, mean-looking pharaoh holding a crook and flail crossed over his chest. I stepped up my pace and arrived at the sign just as the door of the tattoo parlor swung open.

Stockwell came sailing out onto the sidewalk, landing on all fours by the sign. The door slammed shut. Clutching his elbow with one hand and biting his lip in pain, he stood to look at me.

I quoted from *Golden Dawn of the New Epiphany*, "Falling hurts least those who fly low."

"Eat shit," he affirmed.

JIMINY CRICKET

W E WENT TO A COFFEE SHOP TWO doors down to regroup. Stockwell blotted a cut on his palm with a napkin while he explained that Zemler had taken one look at the picture of the Japanese girl's tattoo and called out to the back, "Hey Rita." He had assumed Zemler was enlisting Rita's help in identifying the tattoo artist, but what he was actually doing was summoning her to the front of the store with her shotgun. She pressed both barrels into Stockwell's forehead while Zemler came around the counter to grab him by his belt and collar.

"And you saw the rest," said Stockwell.

We were sitting at a table near the front of the coffee shop, annoying the guy behind the cash register because we hadn't bought anything. "So mentioning the name Rita was code for the woman to bring the gun," I said.

Stockwell grabbed another handful of free napkins from the dispenser. "Yeah, her real name's probably Heloise or something. Maybe the gun is called Rita."

"I take it you didn't flash your badge."

"No. I had to turn it in when they put me on suspension. I don't think an East Palo Alto badge would have carried much weight with this guy anyway. He looks like he's a charter member of the Hells Angels."

I had already told Stockwell what I'd found out at Skin Furniture, so I said, "Could he have been the guy you saw in Caroline's hospital room?"

"Maybe. He's certainly got the build for it. But I hope to Christ Caroline would have better sense than to get involved with a guy like that."

"You didn't get a chance to ask him about the Cricket moniker?"

Stockwell grimaced as he extracted a small pebble from the cut in his hand. "No, I didn't get a chance to do anything but eat sidewalk."

"So what do your methodical, left-brain methods dictate that we do now?"

Stockwell threw the pebble onto the floor and wadded up all the soiled napkins into a bloody ball. "Go back in and break the bastard."

I smiled. "Doesn't sound much different than my undisciplined, harum-scarum approach. You want me to go in first since he hasn't seen me?"

Stockwell stood up. "No, I want another crack at him. You go around back and take care of Rita."

"Okay, but I'm not carrying. You got something to even the odds a little?"

"No guns. I had to turn in my service revolver with my badge and I'm not giving the SFPD an excuse to jam me up on a weapons charge."

I barely managed a feeble, "Yeah, but—" by the time Stockwell strode out the door.

The tattoo parlor was housed in the first floor of a blue and white-trimmed Victorian. We found the entrance to an alley that ran behind the building and went down it, picking our way around potholes, glass from broken malt liquor bottles and puddles of a foul-smelling liquid that probably wasn't accumulated rainwater. There was a door and a window at the back of the Victorian. The door was treble-locked, but the window was an old sash job without a screen, and was open a crack. Stockwell propped a discarded wooden pallet against the side of the building and I used it as a ladder to climb the three or four feet necessary to reach the sill.

I eased the window up. It opened on a storeroom full of dusty cardboard boxes and oddly shaped equipment covered with sheets. A door at the back of the room stood propped open with a cinder block, but I couldn't see more than a few feet past it into a darkened hallway.

I twisted around to give Stockwell a thumbs up sign. "Give me five minutes before you go in," I whispered.

Stockwell nodded and I hoisted myself onto the sill of the window, pivoting awkwardly on my belly to swing my knee over the side. It cost me a painful testicle massage, but I eventually managed to thread my foot through the opening and find a toehold on a cardboard box inside. I got the other leg around and let my full weight onto the box. It crumpled at the edge, spilling me backward onto the floor. I rolled into a ball as I hit, damping the noise and avoiding any major injuries.

I scrambled up and crept to the edge of the interior door. Nothing was moving in the corridor beyond, but I heard a radio playing Janis Joplin's *Me and Bobby McGee* at full tilt. Maybe there was more left over from the old days of Haight-Ashbury than I realized. I soft-shoed it down the corridor, pausing to try a closed door on the right. It was locked. Light splashed into the hallway from an open doorway further down on the left, and that also appeared to be the source of the music. At the far end, a ratty brown curtain screened what I assumed was the front of the shop. I sidled up to the open doorway and craned my head around.

A large woman in bib overalls sat with her back to me at a decrepit rolltop desk that was missing all of its drawers. There was a bible open on the desktop and she was busy tearing tissue thin pages out of the good book and piling them up at her elbow. Next to the stack of bible pages was a baggie of pot, and beside that a rolling machine, so it was clear that her plan was to make the Old Testament story of the burning bush manifest in a different sort of way.

Janis Joplin was coming out of an old floor console radio with the speaker grill torn off, and lying on top of the console was the other "woman" I'd come for: Rita. She was a double-barreled, side-by-side gun, broken open to reveal a load of what looked like fat, no-nonsense 12-gauge shells. The rest of the room looked like someone had upended a dumpster in it. Remains of fast-food meals, discarded cartons of tattoo ink, crumpled papers and dust bunnies the size of dinosaur eggs were littered about. At the back was a small bathroom with what appeared to be a locking door that looked like it could come in handy.

I stepped across the threshold, aiming to snatch up the shotgun before the woman in the bib overalls could react. The warped linoleum floor had other ideas. It groaned like a living thing as I put my weight down and the woman twisted in her chair to look at me. I'm sure she was expecting Zemler, but when she got a look at me and the sheepish expression on my face, she launched out of her chair towards the shotgun, not bothering to even protest my presence.

I strode across the room. We collided a few feet from the radio and I gave her a body check that would have knocked the mouth guard out of an NHL forward, but I might as well have been body checking a hippo. She didn't lose a step. She reached the radio at the same time I did and grabbed the stock of the gun. I grabbed the barrels. We wrestled over the weapon for a frantic moment and the wrenching movement caused the breach to snap closed. Her hand crawled up the stock towards the double triggers. Just as she got her finger inside the trigger guard I did the only useful thing I could think of, and that was to twist the barrels over—hard. She yelped in pain as her finger got torqued by the metal loop of the guard.

I jerked the gun out of her grasp and fumbled it around to point at her. She drew in a breath to yell, but I cleared the safety and pushed the muzzle of the gun into the deep valley of her décolletage. "Keep quiet or I'll be making a bigger noise," I hissed.

She pushed her jaw out defiantly. "You're too late. The shit's not here."

I had no clue what she was talking about, but I nodded at the pot on the desk. "Looks like it's still here to me."

"That's not—" she started, then stopped herself. "Who *are* you?"

"Harry Merkin from Gideons International. I'm with the BDIU." I stepped back from her and gestured with the gun in the direction of the bathroom. "Get into the bathroom."

She stared at me like she was imagining the marks where the lobotomy incisions would go. "What the fuck is the BDIU?"

"Bible Defacement Investigation Unit. Now go." I stepped behind her and prodded her towards the powder room.

She lumbered like a trained bear into the dark, windowless room and then spun around to glower at me. Keys on a ring at her side jingled as she turned. "You won't get away with this, Merkin—or whatever your name is. Stan is going to settle your hash when he finds out."

Her repetition of the word "merkin" brought a juvenile smirk to my face that I couldn't quite squelch. "I'll take my chances. Throw out the keys."

She unsnapped the keys from a loop on her overalls and threw them out onto the floor at my feet. Keeping the gun trained on her, I took hold of the door and felt around the back of it to make sure that the lock didn't open from the inside. I had lucked out: it was a one-way deadbolt. I pulled the door closed and snapped the bolt over. I heard her flip on the light inside and the sound of rattling exhaust fan started a moment later. "I'm telling you, Merkin, you're a dead man," she shouted over the noise.

I reached down to pick up the keys and then bounded over to the radio. I didn't figure it would be long before the real yelling started, so I turned up the radio a couple of notches and hurried out into the corridor. I closed the office door and used a key from her ring to lock it as well.

I was due out in the front to help Stockwell, but now that I had the keys, I was curious about the locked door I had passed earlier. I prowled back down the corridor and went through four keys on the ring until I found one that fit. The room beyond smelled like paint thinner and rubber cement: *eau de* meth lab. The usual collection of glass jars, plastic tubing, pressurized cylinders and empty cartons of decongestants were scattered over a crude table built of thick plywood sheeting and saw horses. That explained the "shit" the woman in the overalls had been talking about.

All of this had taken too long. I heard a crash from the front of the store and a strangled shout of "Riordan!" I ran up the corridor to the ratty curtain and pushed it aside with the barrels of the shotgun. Stockwell was bent over the near side of a glass display case, being held down by a giant who was pounding him in the face with a fist the size of a mutant cantaloupe. I bolted past the curtain and came up behind the giant. He was wearing combat boots and cut-offs made from camouflage pants. I aimed a vicious kick at the bare skin at the back of his left knee. His leg buckled and he flopped backward, pulling Stockwell down on top of him. I shoved the muzzle of the shotgun into the stubbled skin of his cheek. "Don't move," I said, louder and more trembly than I intended.

Stockwell rolled off the giant's chest and scrambled to his feet. He held the side of his jaw and squinted at me, his face contorted in pain. "Think you could have cut it any closer?"

"Sorry. I got sidetracked."

Stockwell moved to the front of the store and turned the open/closed sign to display closed. Then he let down all the venetian blinds and locked the front door. He came back around behind the display case and prodded the big man on the floor with his toe. "Meet Mr. Zemler. He's the kind of guy who would rather fight than talk."

Zemler's head was large and round, his hair buzz-clipped short and his features clustered very close together like a bowling ball drilled for a small hand. The pupils of his eyes were dilated so wide that there was hardly any color to his irises. He sniffed violently. "I can talk. Exactly what the fuck is it that you clowns want?"

"Right now, all we want is for you to roll over," said Stockwell.

I ground the shotgun further into Zemler's cheek. "You heard the man."

Zemler rolled over with an ungainly grace, like an elephant seal on the beach. Stockwell reached behind his back and produced a pair of handcuffs, which he barely managed to lock around Zemler's outsized wrists.

"What's with the cuffs?" said Zemler into the floor. "Nobody said anything about the cops."

"That's right," said Stockwell. "Nobody said anything about the cops. Now stand up."

Zemler struggled to his feet, favoring the leg I had kicked. Stockwell shoved him in the direction of the tattoo station opposite the display case. "Have a seat, big man," he said.

The station had a reclining chair like you'd see in a dentist's office. Beside that was a stool and beside that was a wheeled stand with a tattoo machine and a tray to hold inks, needles and other paraphernalia. Zemler backed up to the chair and dropped into it, his cuffed hands making it hard to maneuver or get comfortable. He was wearing a black tank top with a German army eagle patch sewn in front, and I noticed that his arms had the eagle as a tattoo in several places, along with a couple of Iron Crosses. I was betting it wouldn't be hard to find a swastika if you knew where to look.

I took a post not too close to the chair, with the shotgun at port arms. Stockwell came up to the other side and stood by the wheeled stand. He picked up the tattoo machine and turned it over in his hands. "I showed you a photograph of a tattoo when I came in here the first time," he said. "I've since found out that tattoos very much like it have come out of this parlour." He looked up at Zemler. "Now I want to know who did them."

"What's it to you?"

Stockwell threw down the tattoo machine. He wound up and slapped Zemler across the face—hard—then lunged forward to grip both arms of the chair. "What's it to me?" he spat. "A lot. I'm going to kill whoever did them."

Although the skin of his cheek burned red where Stockwell had hit him, Zemler seemed to hardly notice the slap. He gave a dry chuckle. "You don't have the brass for it." But something made him glance at me and the filament of a very low wattage bulb began to glow. His jaw went slack. "What happened to Betty?"

"That's a good question," I said. "But whatever it was, let me assure you that I *do* have the brass for it." I laughed in a callous way and Zemler made a noise in his throat like rocks being poured down a rainspout. He struggled to get out of the chair. Stockwell took a handful of the German eagle on his chest and shoved him back.

I moved a step closer to him. "Your concern for Betty gives you something in common with my friend here, Stanley. He's also concerned about a loved one. The person who did the tattoo he showed you hurt his daughter very badly. Now, I don't happen to think that you did the tattoos. Frankly, the word on the street is that you're just not that good. I think someone else has been giving you the flash for tattoos in that style and you've been copying them."

Zemler worked his features into a tightly clustered pout. "What the hell do you know? Take a look at that tat on my arm. That's quality work."

I snorted. "You know how you're supposed to pick a barber, Stan? You avoid the guy with the best haircut and look for the one with the worst because they cut each other's hair. I think it must be the same for tattoo artists."

"Fuck you."

"I love you too. But neo-Nazi skinhead tattoo artists are from Mars and I'm from Venus. I feel like we're not communicating. There's no percentage in you protecting this guy. You could get hurt. Betty could get hurt. And, speaking of cops—who seemed to be on your mind a few minutes ago—they could find out about the meth lab you've got cooking in the back room. Right here in the heart of Haight-Ashbury. Wouldn't they be surprised to know that?"

Stockwell's eyes flashed at the mention of the meth lab. Zemler looked from me to Stockwell and then back again. "How do I know you guys aren't cops? He looks like one anyway."

"If you thought that," said Stockwell, "why'd you pull a gun on me when I came in the first time?"

Zemler looked down at the monstrous silver skull emblem on his belt buckle and licked his lips. "They're not my tats, okay? I bought the flash from a guy who said I could use them for tattoos in the shop without giving him credit. But I entered them in an industry contest under my name and I won. He found out. He put the word out in the community that I was taking credit for his work and sent a bunch of people over here to harass me—judges from the contest and people pretending to be customers. I thought you were another one and I was fed up. I've been doing a little crank, so maybe I didn't use the best judgement. I called Betty to put the shotgun on you, and that was that."

"So this guy who sold you the flash," I said, "is he named Cricket by any chance?"

Zemler snapped his eyes up to mine. "That's his street name, anyway. It's because a tattoo machine sort of looks like a cricket—and makes a chirp or a buzz like a cricket. That's why."

Stockwell picked up the tattoo machine again. "I guess I could see that," he said slowly. "But what's his real name?"

"Jimmy Schantz."

"Describe him."

"He's young—in his early 20s. He's a bodybuilder, but not as big as me."

"And what do you know about him?"

"Not a lot. He's an art student or something. He used to hang around here with his girlfriend, trying to get me to hire him full time. I told him I didn't have the business to justify it, but I finally bought some of his flash. Sorry I ever touched it."

Stockwell gripped the tattoo machine tightly. His finger slipped onto the trigger and the machine jumped to life with a sharp, buzzing noise, surprising all of us. "His girlfriend?" he stammered.

"Yeah," said Zemler, "a cute girl with purple hair. I think her name was Caroline or something. She really seemed stuck on the guy."

Stockwell dropped the tattoo machine into the tray with a loud clatter. He said nothing.

"You know where this guy lives?" I asked.

"No, not really. I've seen him a lot in the neighborhood, so he could be flopping around here, but I don't remember if he ever said." Zemler leaned forward in the chair. "I get it now. Caroline's his daughter, isn't she?"

"You're a quick one, Stan."

"Then you got what you wanted then, right?"

I looked over at Stockwell, who nodded slightly. "Yeah," I said. "We got what we wanted." I broke open the shotgun and removed the shells and then set it down on the glass display case. I dropped the ring of keys next to it.

Stockwell already had the front door unlocked. He jerked it open and went out onto the sidewalk. I moved to follow him.

"Hey," said Zemler, "What about Betty?"

I stopped in the doorway and turned to look back at him. "She's fine. You just need to let her out of the bathroom."

"And the handcuffs?"

"They're yours to keep. Thanks for playing our game."

COMMENCEMENT

THERE WERE TWO J. SCHANTZ'S IN THE San Francisco phone book, but neither of them was the one we wanted. We put what was left of our collective brains together and decided a better place to find Cricket's address was at the art school. Stockwell drove his Explorer so hard on the way downtown that he actually got airborne coming over the hill on Oak Street. I reminded him that Steve McQueen in *Bullitt* had a Mustang Fastback not a tipsy SUV, and he reminded me to keep my trap shut.

There was no security guard on duty in the art school lobby, so we skipped the sign-in ceremonies and rode the elevator straight up to the sixth floor. The hallway was deserted and the white-haired sourpuss in front of Dr. Jaing's office was also MIA. I came up to Jaing's imposing door and knocked lightly. Nothing. I tried again and got the same nonresponse.

Maybe it was all the people who weren't where they were supposed to be, but I was beginning to get a case of the heebie-jeebies. I looked over at Stockwell. He scowled and gestured impatiently. "You're a big boy. Open the door and go in."

I gripped the knob. I was almost relieved to find it locked, but while the lock had been set, the latch hadn't gone into the strike plate and I was able to push the door open. I was told later that the police photographer fainted when he saw what I saw then.

Julie Jaing lay on her desk. She was wearing a jumper like the one from the day before, but the material of the dress had been pushed well past her waist. Her pale, chubby legs were parted and a twisted chromium bar protruded from the middle of them. Another, shorter bar was sticking out of her mouth. Blood had pooled at her feet and then run off the edge of the desk to form a manhole-sized stain in the carpet. The chair that she'd designed was in pieces on the floor near the bloodstain. She'd been raped to death with her own artwork.

A frisson of revulsion ran through me. My brain seemed to shut down and I slumped against the doorframe. I didn't have a particularly favorable impression of Dr. Jaing, but whoever killed her had hated her with a depth of feeling I couldn't understand. Hers was a grisly, soul-crushing death. No one deserved it. No one deserved even the contemplation of it.

I heard Stockwell say, "What is it?" and felt him elbow past me into the room. He was silent for a moment, then he whispered, "Holy Jesus."

Something at the corner of my eye caught my attention and I jerked around to see the white-haired secretary spread out on the carpet along the near wall of the office. Her arms were crossed peacefully over her chest, but she didn't look any more alive than Jaing. I dropped to my knees and put a finger to the carotid artery. It was hard to tell, but I thought I felt a faint beat. I'd been told by a paramedic friend that blood flushing into the nail beds was an easier test. I pressed on her index finger and saw the nail go pink.

Stockwell had been watching from near the desk. His face was as pale as alkali. "She still with us?"

"Yeah," I croaked. "I think so." I took her arm from where it lay across her chest and put it by her side. There was a red mark like an ant bite in the crook of it. "She might have been drugged. I think I see a needle mark."

"You got a handkerchief?"

I stood and passed Stockwell one from my hip pocket. He went around the desk to where the phone was lying, next to Dr. Jaing's head.

Her lips were cut and swollen from assault with the metal bar, but, mercifully, her eyes were closed. Stockwell wrapped the handkerchief around the receiver and picked it up. He used a pen from his breast pocket to press the numbers on the dial pad, but stopped after he dialed 91. "Wait a minute," he said. He set the receiver down. "There's something in her mouth."

I looked at him with what must have been an incredulous expression and he turned even paler. "I mean something other than the bar." He wrapped the handkerchief carefully around the chromium metal and pulled out the bar. Dr. Jaing's mouth gaped open in a hideous parody of her Bob's Big Boy grin. There was a wadded up piece of stationery that filled almost the entire space.

"Are you sure that was a good idea?" I asked.

"No. And this one's even worse." He set the bar down on the desk and picked at a corner of the sodden paper. It tore off in his fingers. He grimaced, pulling her mouth open wider with one hand while taking a bigger pinch of paper with the other. This time he managed to extract the compressed ball. A piece of chipped tooth and a long string of saliva followed.

I bore down hard on the Captain Crunch I'd eaten this morning as it tried to circumnavigate my esophagus. Stockwell moved beyond pale to bilious green. He stared at the buff-colored paper he held daintily between two fingers. There was printing on it, but it was impossible to read without spreading it flat.

He placed the ball on the desk and teased it open. It was crinkled and soaked through with saliva and blood, but in the end it was clearly identifiable as a letter printed on school stationery. It was dated about a month earlier and had been sent by Dr. Jaing. The body of it read:

> This letter serves as official notice that you are expelled from the San Francisco Lyceum of Art—effective immediately. This expulsion is for physically assaulting a Lyceum instructor during the course of a conversation about the appropriateness of your submission for

an assignment in FND 112-OL: Figure Drawing. (The findings of our investigation into this incident have been supplied to you in previous correspondence.)

Due to the severity of the violation, there will be no appeal of this decision and no application for readmission will be accepted.

Enclosed please find a check for $523.47, which is a prorated refund of your tuition payment for this quarter.

The letter was addressed to James R. Schantz at a Masonic Avenue apartment in the Haight.

"At last, the smoking gun," said Stockwell. "What this whole thing has been about. Little Jimmy gets kicked out of art school, so he finds a new way to get his work noticed. And lashes out at the institution he holds responsible." Stockwell dug into his front pocket and pulled out his keys. "Take them."

"Why?"

"You've got to get over there. He wouldn't have left the letter as a calling card if he were staying in town, but there's a small chance you can still catch him. He can't have killed her very long ago."

I took the keys out of his hand. "Why don't you go—or come with me?"

"Someone's got to stay here with the secretary until the ambulance comes. And someone has to explain what happened and get the police after Schantz. That's the most important thing. Given the way we've tampered with the evidence—and you being the highly-respected keyhole peeper that you are—the first thing the San Francisco cops would do if they found you here is slam you down on the floor, handcuff you and toss you in the back of the cruiser. It'd be hours before they believed you enough to put out an arrest warrant for him."

He had a good point. I just wasn't sure how much more respect a suspended police officer from East Palo Alto was going to be given.

I borrowed his pen to scribble Schantz's address on my palm and hurried across the room.

"Riordan," said Stockwell just before I got through the door.

"What?"

"There's a Colt .44 Special in a lockbox under the backseat. Key's on the ring. Be careful—it's a single action."

Cricket's apartment was in a brown stucco sarcophagus from the 1960s about a block off of Haight. I got Stockwell's Colt out of the lockbox, and after checking that the hammer was down on an empty chamber, stuck it under my waistband. It was a heavy, awkward Western-style six-shooter with a seven and half inch barrel and it felt like it was going to drop down my pants at any minute. Having it was better than going after Cricket unarmed, but as a single action the gun had to be cocked before it was fired, which made it just that much more awkward to use.

I went up the walk to the front of the building. A high wooden fence protected the back of the property. A gate in the fence was propped open with a U-Haul moving box full of books and I could see through it to a door on the side of the building that was held open by yet another box. It looked like moving day for someone, and I had to wonder if the someone was Cricket. I scanned the street carefully for husky psychopaths lugging household items, but the only person extant was a chubby, teenaged female in skin-tight hip-huggers with a serious case of girl love handles. She caught me staring at her, sneered and popped her gum.

I went through the gate and up to the side door. It led into a dingy laundry room, crammed full of coin-operated machines and a folding table with a tangled pile of sheets and Bart Simpson boxer shorts on top. A dialog balloon above Bart's head urged, "Don't have a cow, man!" I didn't have a cow, but I did have the Colt, which I pulled from my waistband while I threaded my way to a door at the far end of the room that opened on an interior hallway. Here, there were numbered doors for apartments and a staircase.

Cricket's apartment was on the second floor, so I went up the stairs, hugging the outside wall to have a better chance of seeing anyone coming down. In spite of my precautions, I nearly ran into a girl carrying some flattened cardboard boxes on the second floor landing. I shifted the gun to my left hand and held it behind my back. The girl was short and thin and blond and looked all of about 20. She smiled and leaned her boxes against the baluster. "You must be Jimmy," she said. "I'm Cateland. We've just moved a load's worth into the kitchen and living room, but we haven't got to the bedroom. Feel free to go in and grab your stuff."

More wheels turned in my head than in a triple-decker hamster cage. "Right," I said finally. "Door's unlocked then?"

"Yes. Apartment 210." She laughed. "But you know that. I'm just running these down to the storage locker. I've got to move some laundry to the dryer as well, so pull the door closed if I'm not back when you're ready to leave." She started to pick up her boxes and then looked back at me with a worried expression. "Maybe I should … " Her voice trailed off.

I gave her the big, high wattage smile. "Don't worry, I won't take anything that's not mine. In fact, why don't I wait for you to come back? I can give you a few pointers on the cranky plumbing."

Her face cleared. "That would be great. See you in a few, then."

I smiled her down the first few steps and then turned to go up the hallway, holding the gun at my side. I didn't know what I was going to say when she got back, but I did know I was going to find a way to wait in the apartment until the real Jimmy Schantz showed up.

I didn't wait long. As I stepped through the door, a massive arm hooked over my throat and began ratcheting down like a pipefitter's wrench. I raised the Colt. It was slapped out of my hand. I clawed at the arm ineffectually, my fingers finding no purchase on the hairless

skin. I felt myself being dragged backward and then there was a stinging pain at my left shoulder. The bite of a hypodermic needle.

I twisted to the right, trying to shake off my attacker or at least
forestall the descent of the plunger. I succeeded only in cramping
my back. I reached over to find the hand holding the hypodermic. I
gripped the thumb and bent it back with everything I had left. I heard
a grunt and the needle was rammed even further into my arm.

My legs spasmed and I bit so hard on my partial plate that I
actually felt it crack. My vision went spotty—and then entirely dark.
I felt myself slumping to the ground.

My consciousness melted, puddled and dissolved through the
floor, an insentient black ooze like tar from some prehistoric pit.

To say that I came to would be an overstatement. I was aware of
pain, strange odors and the taste of iron in my mouth, but I didn't
really believe these things—or more accurately—think they had
anything to do with me. I was a thing apart. I was weightless and
transcendent, an incorporeal phantom hovering above the world of
physical sensation.

Seconds, minutes or possibly even hours went by—I had no way
to gauge. Gradually, there was a change. I began to grow heavy, to
get reconnected to my body. Sensations sharpened and grew more
real. I was able to move my arm and felt the pain that radiated from
my left shoulder as I did so. But there was no question of opening my
eyes. It was worth my life to keep them closed and avoid confronting
my situation.

More time passed. A feverish sweat formed on my brow. I ran a
rubber tongue over puffy, dry lips. A stink of rotten eggs or something
worse came into my nostrils. I gagged and then coughed, rubbing up
against a multitude of sharp points and protrusions, all along my legs,
back and head. I brought a shaking right hand up to my temples and
massaged them. I realized I was lying head down, and could no longer

suppress the desire to learn where I was and what had happened to me. I pried open my eyes. Seams of light glowed above me, but there was very little else to see. I was in a darkened box of some sort lying on an irregular surface. I reached below me and felt a stuffed plastic bag, then an eggshell and then something moist and grainy I thought might be coffee grounds.

I was in a dumpster.

I struggled to my knees, breaking through the trash bags I knelt on, and reached up to the lid of the dumpster. Its surface was slimed and corroded. I pushed with one hand and succeeded in raising it less than an inch. I got my feet under me and brought both hands to bear, driving upward with trembling legs. The lid flipped over on its hinge and slammed against the wall of a building. I clutched the lip of the dumpster to keep from falling back into it. My heart beat against my rib cage like a trapped animal. My head spun like a Tilt-A-Whirl.

My eyes and the faint glow of dawn light told me I was behind the apartment building, sometime in the early morning. My watch told me it was 5:46. I'd been out for nearly 18 hours. I didn't know if Cricket had intended to kill me or merely incapacitate me— or if he even cared —but I did know it had been a close call. I brought my hand up to my throat to rub the bruised skin and muscle, and in doing so, aggravated the pain in my left shoulder. I raised my arm to examine it. There was a circle of blood around a hole in the sleeve of my suit coat, and sticking out of the hole, the jagged spike of a broken needle. I took hold of the needle and yanked it out.

It hurt less than I expected, but that didn't mean it didn't hurt. I put the needle fragment in my breast pocket in hopes there was something to be learned by having it analyzed and then milked the wound, encouraging it to bleed to flush out any germs that might have been on the needle. Not that it would do me any good at this point.

From its rapid effects and the out-of-body feeling I'd had, my guess was that Cricket had injected me with Ketamine—or "Special K" as it is called on the streets. Stockwell had said Caroline had been drugged with GHB which—along with Special K and Rohypnol—were among the drugs favored by date rape practitioners. A preference for these drugs seemed to fit well with Cricket's need to knock his victims out for long periods of time to create his masterworks.

I took a couple of deep breaths to psyche myself up and then slithered over the edge of the dumpster. I stood beside it, shivering and feeble like a newborn bird that fell from its nest. I patted myself down. Thankfully, Stockwell's and my keys were still in my front pockets, but my wallet was missing and of course there was no sign of the Colt .44. I still had the shotgun shells from Zemler and my knife was still lying snug in its harness on my leg.

I trudged around the back of the building to the gate. I went through it and then across the front lawn where I spotted a garden hose. I turned on the spigot and drank what seemed like two aquarium's worth of water. My tongue strayed to the roof of my mouth while I drank and I found a new sharp edge. I remembered the cracking noise when Cricket attacked me and I pulled the plate out to examine it. Sure enough, the molded material at the back had split down the middle. The edge of the crack was extremely sharp, and coupled with the earlier damage, made wearing the plate like going around with a couple of razors in your mouth. Vanity made me return it. My hair was disheveled, my clothing bloodstained and I smelled of the dumpster, but damned if I was going to walk around without my front teeth.

I shut off the faucet and looked up at the building. It dawned on me suddenly that Cricket might have hurt the girl if she'd come back to the apartment before he got out. I hurried up to the entryway and pressed the buzzer for 210. I waited for less than 20 seconds and mashed it down again. A noise like an electronic cough came over the speaker dingus and a sleepy voice said, "Yes?"

"Cateland?"

"Yes. Who is this?"

Tension leeched out of my shoulders. "Never mind," I said, and released the talk button.

I went down the walk and across the street to Stockwell's Explorer. I figured it was more important to get hold of Stockwell and find out what had happened than it was to talk to the girl.

Early morning traffic was almost nonexistent going across the city. When I got to my neighborhood I found that there were no parking places in the immediate vicinity, but I wasn't in the mood to dick around with it—especially with someone else's car. I shoved the Explorer squarely into the bus stop in front the building and jumped out. I went up the stairs more by force of will than physical locomotion. I came panting up to my apartment and stopped short. A beautiful woman in a black crepe dress and designer shoes was curled up asleep in front of my door. She had a laptop computer under her head that she was using as a sort of pillow. It was Gretchen.

I reached down to rouse her. She woke with a start and her eyes fluttered open. "August," she said blearily. "Where have you been?"

"That's a long story, angel. A more relevant question is what are you doing here?"

She pushed herself upright, suddenly very awake. "It's Chris. Something's happened to him."

I stared at her, my thought processes verging on vapor lock. It seemed like there was more than enough already without this. "What exactly?" I said.

"I think he's been kidnapped."

ALL I WANT FOR CHRISTMAS

I OPENED THE DOOR AND HERDED GRETCHEN INSIDE. She fell on the couch and brought both arms up to wrap around her head. "Why don't you carry a cell phone, August? This never would have happened if Chris or I could have reached you."

I sat down beside her. I realized this was the first time she'd been back to my apartment since we broke up. It was a depressing thought. "I don't think it would have mattered, Gretchen," I said. "I've been unconscious for the last 18 hours."

She let her arms drop and turned to stare at me, a look of genuine concern in her eyes. She sniffed and wrinkled her nose. "You smell awful. Where in the world have you been?"

"It's not important. Tell me what makes you think Chris was kidnapped."

"He got an invitation from someone he met through his web site. They wanted to meet him."

I felt my face go stiff. "What happened?"

"The guy who wrote him—he said his name was Jimmy—he invited Chris for a drink. Chris called the office to tell you about it. He wanted you to be there to question him when he showed up."

"And when he couldn't get hold of me?"

Gretchen looked down to the laptop. She squared it carefully on her knees. "We talked about it. I told him it was too dangerous. He said I was being silly, that he didn't want to miss the opportunity or spook the guy. So we compromised. Chris told the guy he would meet him for coffee during the day. We figured that would be safe—much better than meeting him at some bar at night."

I nodded slowly, waiting for the punch line and knowing I was going to hate it. "And then?"

Gretchen slapped her hands down hard on the laptop. "I let him go. I should have gone with him, but Bonacker had an important policy rider he needed finished. I was home, changing for my date before I even thought of it again—and then I realized I hadn't heard back from Chris. I called him at all his numbers, but he didn't answer. I got desperate. Dennis came to pick me up and I made him drive me over to Chris' house. He wasn't there."

"But that by itself—"

"No, August, let me finish. We went over to the coffee shop where he was going to meet the guy. It's a little family-owned spot in the Marina. The owner remembered Chris. Said he was one of the best-looking women he'd ever seen in the place. He said Chris met a man there for a cappuccino, but Chris got ill. The owner helped the man walk Chris out to his van."

I looked at her for a long moment. The description fit the pattern I had hypothesized for Cricket. "Sounds like he was drugged."

"That's what we thought. Dennis said there are certain drugs that—"

"Yes, I know. I just had some firsthand experience with one. Did you get anything else to go on? Description of the guy who took Chris? Anything about the van?"

She looked hurt. "I knew you were going to blame me. I know I should have gone with him. But I really didn't think anything could happen in a public place."

I took hold of her hand. It was cold and trembly. "Gretchen, calm down. I'm not blaming you. I'm just looking for something to help find him."

She pulled her hand away. She flipped open the laptop and pressed the power button. "We didn't think to ask the owner for a description.

He did mention that the van was old and beat up. One of those VW camper buses. He thought it was funny that such a good-looking girl would be seeing a guy with that kind of car."

"All right. But why are you starting your laptop?"

"Because there's one other thing. You remember how Chris had been sending me pictures from his cell phone?"

I thought back to the car filled with dirt. "Yes."

"He sent me one at about five this afternoon. I didn't look at it until much later—after I started worrying about him."

"When was his date at the coffee shop?"

"2:30. He must have sent it after he'd been kidnapped. There was no message. Just the picture." She typed something on the keyboard and fiddled with the built-in mouse. She pushed the computer onto my lap. "Look. Does that mean anything to you?"

It was a picture taken inside a small room—or a camper van. No people were visible, but you could see through the windows to the outside. The profile and several supporting pillars of an elevated freeway were visible. One of the pillars had graffiti on it—a large peace sign. I picked up the laptop and held the screen close to my face. A thrill ran through me. "I know where this is."

Gretchen clutched her hands together. "Where?"

"It's near the train station at 22nd and Pennsylvania. A lot of homeless people camp out there. Some of them in RV's and camper vans." I handed the computer back.

I went into the bedroom and took the Glock and its holster off the bedpost. Gretchen came to stand in the doorway as I buckled it on. She bit her lip. "What can I do?"

"Call the cops. Get them to send a car over there. Make up a story if the truth sounds too goofy."

"Okay." She dodged out of the way as I passed back into the living room. I'd reached the apartment door by the time she spoke again. "August, please be careful. Don't let me lose two of the men I love most."

It was quiet when I got to 22nd and Pennsylvania—eerily quiet. It was too early for train commuters and the traffic on Highway 280 was so light that you could hear individual cars bumping over the seams in the roadway overhead. I had no way of knowing that the police car Gretchen had summoned had already come and gone.

Most of the homeless were camped about a block away from the train station in a distinctly ungated community directly beneath the freeway overpass. Keeping up with the Jones in this neighborhood meant having a lean-to, cardboard box or tarp to sleep under, a Safeway shopping cart to haul your possessions around in and a bottle of Thunderbird or Mad Dog 20/20 for recreation and use as a soporific. As I walked by the encampment after ditching Stockwell's Explorer near the station, it appeared that all the residents had self-medicated themselves into a sound stupor. There was so little stirring, in fact, that an evil-looking crow felt emboldened enough to perch on the handle of one of the shopping carts, surveying the grounds of the littered encampment for food. He held me in his beady black eye as I approached, and then took off with an irritated caw when I drew too near.

Across the street, parked along a chain link fence that surrounded a San Francisco Muni bus yard, were the upwardly mobile—or perhaps just mobile—domiciles of the community. There was an old Winnebago with crudely painted zebra strips and tires so bald that I could see the steel belt peeping through in patches. There were also a pair of 1970s vintage VW bus camper vans—the Westfalia model—parked nose to nose. The one on the left had its pop-top open, allowing the roof to hinge up several feet higher with a tent-like structure of canvas encasing the back and sides. The one on the right had a for sale sign. Both had sun shades blocking the front windows and curtains drawn on all the others, and again, there was no sign of life or activity within.

I crept up to bus on the left, figuring that if Cricket was in one of the vans with Chris, he would have opened the pop-top to provide more space. I unholstered the Glock and put my hand to the passenger door handle. Locked. I made a tour around the van, trying the driver's side door, the one in back and finally the big sliding door, and that didn't buy me anything either. I was pondering the trade-offs involved in smashing the passenger door window with a rock when a gust of wind caused the fabric in pop-top to flap, drawing my attention. I realized it was a weaker link than the window and getting through it would be a lot quieter too.

I walked back to the homeless encampment and liberated a plastic milk crate that was being used as a camp stool and set it down by the side of the van. Pulling my knife from the harness on my ankle, I stepped onto the crate. The fabric for the pop-top was secured to the roof with an aluminum molding and it was a relatively easy task to poke the knife through the canvas and slice cleanly along the molding, even while I held the Glock ready with my other hand. I had cut about a foot when I felt something move inside the van.

I stepped off the carton and crept up to the back of the van. I crouched there for a good two minutes, feeling foolish and exposed, but no one came out and I heard no further movements. I returned to my post on the crate. When the cut measured about two feet, it was long enough for me to peel the canvas up and peep into the interior. There was not much to see. The only signs of occupation were an empty bedroll, a candle in an old tuna can and a paperback book.

I spread the slit wider and canted my head along the roof to see further into the back. It was then that I heard the passenger side door latch pop open.

"Got yourself a new gun, I see. I like the old one better."

I twisted my head around to find Stockwell's Colt .44 Special being pointed squarely at my back. It was held by the husky kid who I'd seen coming out of the office door at the art school—the same one who'd passed me the note about Wesson's exhibit at the SF MOMA. He was in his stocking feet and was wearing sweat pants and a T-shirt. His well-muscled arms bulged out of the shirt, smooth and hairless as a marble statue. When I didn't say anything, he smiled. It made his face look almost cherubic. "I thought you'd be on your way to the landfill. I guess you were still breathing after all."

I moved my feet to turn towards him.

"None of that," he said sharply. "Why don't you drop the gun and the knife in the nice hole you cut in my camper top? That will keep them out of harm's way."

I pushed the Glock and the knife through the slit in the canvas. They clattered down the side of the sliding door. My mouth suddenly felt very dry and my hands were visibly shaking. "It seems like you've had a number of dosage problems, Cricket," I said as calmly as I could. "Not killing people when you wanted to. Killing others when you didn't. The Japanese girl was one you didn't mean to kill, wasn't she?"

"Shut up and step off the crate."

I hesitated. He came up to take hold of my beltline and yanked me to the ground. He stood just behind me now, with the gun to my left ear.

"What about Brita?" I said. "Did you get the dosage right with her?"

He laughed and I could feel his breath tickling the back of my neck. Suddenly his right arm was around my throat again, choking me like before. "You mean Chris, not Brita, don't you, Mr. Riordan?"

Maybe it was my weakened condition or maybe it was my panic at being caught in the very same situation as before, but my vision started to dim almost immediately. My legs and arms began to tingle and a ringing noise filled my ears. I felt myself being dragged backward again.

"No Special K this time, Mr. Riordan," said Cricket, almost gently. "Just the big squeeze."

I struggled again with the massive forearm locked around my neck, and again my fingers found no purchase. My tongue cleaved to the roof of my mouth. I felt the sharp edge of the cracked plate cut into it. And that was the seed of my salvation.

With only a vague idea of what I hoped to accomplish, I pried the plate out of my mouth. I spread it open along the crack like a wishbone, popping one of the fake teeth out and exposing the sharp edge of the molded material. I slashed with it over my shoulder. There was a howl in my right ear and the arm around my neck loosened slightly. I felt something warm run down my fingers. The arm fell away entirely.

I reeled against the van, turning to face Cricket. He was hunched over near the back tire, holding his hand to his right eye. Blood ran threw his fingers. "You fucking cut my eye," he wailed. He still held the Colt and he showed now that he hadn't forgotten it. He aimed at my chest, squeezed the trigger.

Neither of us got what we expected. I got a jolt of adrenaline. He got a whitened knuckle from pulling hard against the single action trigger without first cocking the revolver. He cursed and fumbled for the hammer. I bolted for the open van door, focused only on recovering the Glock.

I piled into the passenger seat and locked the door behind me. There was no one inside but me—if Chris was still at the encampment, he had to be in the other van. I slithered past the console and the gear shift, lunging to the spot below the slice in the pop-top. I snatched up the Glock from the carpet—and that's when the shooting started. There was a sharp report and a slug came tearing through the side door of the van about three feet above me. It passed through the driver's seat, embedding itself in the dashboard. While the Colt was an awkward gun, it was a powerful one. A bullet from it could easily penetrate multiple layers of the cheap sheet metal in the van. I doubted my 9mm would even go through one.

I raised my hand to window level and pumped several rounds through the glass toward the back of the van where I imagined Cricket must be, then rolled quickly to my right. A booming shot followed, bisecting the space I had occupied just a moment before. The angle of fire had changed: the shot followed a course almost perpendicular to the van, suggesting that Cricket had moved towards the front.

Returning fire now meant risking a shot straight into the homeless encampment. It seemed a losing proposition anyway, given my
position and the mismatch in firepower. My knife gleamed dully
on the carpet next to my face. I snatched it up and jumped on the
rickety built-in table against the far wall of the van. Another shot
crashed through the van, the slug passing just below the table and
hitting the back wall with a tremendous thump. I stabbed the knife
into the canvas of the pop-top, slicing an opening about three feet
long on the far side. Then I worked the Glock again. Two shots were
enough to vaporize the back windows, hopefully drawing Cricket's
attention that way.

I pushed myself through the slit in the canvas and flopped down
between the van and the chain link fence, hammering my shoulder
as I hit the asphalt. Another shot from Cricket's revolver covered the
noise of my fall. I couldn't tell where it went.

What I could tell was that he was standing opposite the right
rear tire. I scurried underneath the van, coming to rest about a foot
away from the plastic crate. Maybe Cricket thought he had hit me,
or maybe he was worried about using more bullets—I had counted
four shots so far—but he lingered at the back for a long moment and
then crept forward towards the crate. He put his foot on it, apparently
intending to risk a peek through the original hole I had made.

I put the Glock about an inch from his ankle and pulled the
trigger.

Blood and bone chips sprayed back on my hand. Cricket shrieked.
He reached down to clutch his ankle, lost his balance and toppled
to the asphalt. By reflex or design, his finger tightened again on the
trigger of the revolver. A shot went zinging over the roof of the van.
Clearly in tremendous pain and with blood still flowing from the
wound to his face, he struggled to level the revolver at my head.

I fired three shots in quick succession, tattooing him from his belly
button to his sternum. He sagged into the ground like a deflated pool
toy, Stockwell's Colt .44 sloughing out of his hand to the asphalt.

I found Chris hog-tied on the floor of the other VW van. He had been wearing a wig, which was lying in a wad on the floor, and a dress, which was peeled down to his waist. The iridescent wing of a butterfly tattoo had been started on his shoulder, but at that point Cricket evidently realized he had the wrong sex of canvas.

When I cut through Chris' bonds and removed the duct tape from his mouth, the first thing he said to me wasn't "Thank God" or "Boy, am I glad to see you," it was:

"What happened to your teeth?"

I had an overwhelming urge to tie him back up again, but the arrival of the SFPD prevented me from acting on it.

BLUE NOTE

"I DECIDED TO KEEP THE TATTOO," SAID CHRIS. "It's a good re-minder of lessons learned."

We were on a break at the House of Shields, sitting at a table in the balcony away from a large group of friends who had come to see us play. Chris was dressed in a strapless red sequin gown with what looked like a real diamond and ruby pendant centered over his fake décolletage. The pendant was probably as fake as his boobs.

Sitting across from him with a fake beer was Stockwell. He'd never seen Chris in drag and was clearly uncomfortable as hell about it, but he couldn't bring himself to diss a guy who had helped to bring his daughter's tormenter to justice— especially when it involved wearing women's clothes. He picked at the label of his nonalcoholic beer. "Yeah," he said, "Caroline's resigned to keeping hers too. She's going to try to have the tongue removed so it doesn't appear as if the dragon is eating the butterfly, but laser tattoo removal just isn't good enough to take off something as large as the dragon."

I rattled the ice cubes in my bourbon and soda. "She's doing okay, then?"

Stockwell pursed his lips. "Physically, she's in great shape. The doctor said there was no brain damage from the coma. Mentally, she's still a little shaky. She really was in love with that Cricket bastard— thought he was a misunderstood genius—and it's very hard for her to accept the betrayal." He cleared his throat. "That new shrink that you recommended seems to be helping. The, ah, French lady."

"Glad to hear it." I suppressed a grin. It was painfully clear how hard it was for Stockwell to accept help from the likes of frogs and fags. "Did you ever find out the story behind the coma? Did Cricket inject her with GHB at the hospital?"

Stockwell peeled off a big piece of the beer label and wadded it up into a little ball. "No. I learned GHB isn't usually injected. It's taken orally."

"So he slipped it into something she drank like he did with me," said Chris.

"Not exactly. He visited her the same night Riordan did and brought the drug along. He told her he didn't want her talking to the police. Then he told her—he told her it would be better for both of them if she swallowed the GHB. And she did."

"I see." Chris shifted his gaze to his Cosmopolitan glass and took a hurried gulp.

"Which makes it the second time he got his dosages wrong," I said. "The first time was with the Japanese girl—and the third time was with me."

"That's right," said Stockwell. "But he went for the Japanese girl only after Caroline split with him during their trip to Mexico. He drugged Caroline while they were down there and she woke up with the tattoo. Cricket was deluded enough to think that she was going to appreciate what he had done, but of course she was devastated and ran away. He came back to San Francisco and hooked up with the Japanese girl—and after he killed her with the overdose—Monica Mapa."

I took a sip of bourbon. "Monica must not have been in contact with Caroline at that point."

Stockwell nodded. "Caroline was still wandering between here and Mexico. She said that Monica had always been a little jealous of her relationship with Cricket, so she wasn't surprised that Monica found Cricket's attention flattering."

"But she was still loyal enough to Wesson to get the tattoo removed after he told her he didn't like it."

"Yeah, I guess. From what you told me about her, I'd say it was less loyalty and more a matter of knowing which side your bread was buttered on."

Chris edged his chair forward to the table. "What *about* Wesson? What really happened with him?"

"I finally got Kittredge to come clean with me about that," I said.

"Fucking bastard," put in Stockwell.

"Nice language. And him a brother officer—not that you'll get any disagreement from this side of the table. Anyway, after what went down at the train station, they did a full series of blood tests on Wesson. I guess they don't normally screen for Ketamine, but they found it in spades. It appears that Cricket broke into his apartment, drugged him, did the 'I'm sorry' tattoo and planted the equipment. The next stop was the church tower for involuntary diving lessons. Oh, and here's the kicker—Wesson is left handed so he could have never have put the tattoo on his own left arm."

Stockwell picked some more at the beer label. "I'll wager they found Special K in the art school president too."

"You'd win that one," I said. "They also found the place on her arm where he injected it. The secretary told them he attacked her when Jaing wasn't in the office, then apparently lay in wait for Jaing's return."

Chris shuddered. "At least the president was drugged during the rape. Hopefully she didn't feel anything."

I looked over at Stockwell, who met my gaze. We both knew that something that horrific would have to be felt. "I wouldn't spend too much time thinking about it if I were you," said Stockwell.

Chris brought his hand up to his throat in a girlish gesture. "Don't worry. I'm having enough trouble not thinking about what happened to me. I'd like to scoop out the part of my brain where that memory is stored with a spoon."

Stockwell grunted. "I *am* a little surprised he didn't kill you."

Chris blanched under his make up. "Way to sugar coat it, Lieutenant."

"I'm just saying it doesn't seem to fit the pattern."

I downed the rest of my bourbon and crunched on an ice cube. "I have a theory about that. I don't think he intended to kill anybody at the start. But once the Japanese girl died, the rules changed for him. He'd crossed the line and all the subsequent killings came easier. He went after Monica because she betrayed him, and Caroline because of her risk to him. He murdered Wesson to cover his tracks, and indirectly, to revenge himself on the school. But killing Wesson brought home the point that Jaing and the school were actually at the root of all his problems, so he killed Jaing in the most vicious and sensational way he could think of, no longer concerned about concealing his identity."

Stockwell shook his head. "That's a swell theory, but it doesn't explain why he let Duckworth here off the hook. If anything, it argues for him to continue the frenzy by finishing him off in an even more spectacular fashion."

"I don't think so. It was clear he was leaving town—his business was finished and the police would definitely be after him for Jaing's murder. I think he wanted to leave one more masterwork behind as a sort of calling card—a human canvas for the press to pick up on once the story broke. He obviously wanted that to be another pretty girl, but I think he was toying with the idea of going ahead and tattooing Chris anyway. He didn't have many options at that point."

Chris resettled the diamond and ruby pendant on his chest. "Well, he certainly didn't say anything about it to me. I met him in the coffee shop, drank half a cup of coffee, and the next thing I knew, I woke up in the van with my dress peeled off and him standing over me with a tattoo machine. He yelled and called me all sorts of names, but he never gave any indication of what he was going to do."

"What was the story with the two vans?" I asked. "Why were you in one and he in another?"

"He owned them both. One was a sort of mobile tattoo parlour with all his equipment and a gas generator—that's the one you found me in. I guess the other was just for getting around."

"And the picture Riordan used to find you," said Stockwell, "how did you send that?"

"Cricket went to the front of the van to do something with the equipment. My purse was nearby and I managed to fish out my phone, even though my hands were tied. I couldn't use it to call anyone without him hearing, so I took a picture and sent it to Gretchen. I would have done more, but he caught me right after."

Stockwell inclined his head slightly. "Clever boy. Or girl—or whatever you are."

Chris smiled. "Why thank you, Lieutenant. I'm happy to be whatever you'd want me to."

Stockwell reddened, but was saved from further repartee by the arrival of a waiter. "Phone for you, Cassandra," he said.

Chris stood and ran his hands over his hips to smooth his dress. "Excuse me, boys, my public calls. I'll see you downstairs in a few."

Stockwell watched him sashay down the staircase, then turned back to me. "Jesus," he said. "that's just a little too real. I better get out of here before I start liking it."

"You don't want to stay for the second set?"

"Sorry. Jazz just sounds like so many sick cats to me." He stood and put his hand out. I took it. "This is hard for me to say, but thank you for everything. I don't think Caroline would ever be able to get past this if Cricket had got away." He lowered his voice. "Or even if he'd lived to go to trial."

I nodded and shook his hand. I wasn't going to tell him that attraction to Ellen had more to do with my involvement—or that the belief that Cricket had murdered Chris was the real reason I fired those last three rounds. The truth of the matter was, I had been fairly certain Cricket was out of bullets. I knew for sure when I checked the still warm Colt by his outstretched fingers.

Stockwell left and I sat down again at the table, firing up an illicit cigarette and watching the smoke drift up to the rafters. I thought of resolute girls who hadn't let leg braces or loss of insurance settlements stop them from doing what they knew was right. I thought of pretty girls in she-devil outfits who knew the value of a dollar, but wouldn't be around now to make a quick buck on eBay or frazzle the nerves of men twice their age. I thought of slim, graceful women with gap-tooth smiles who did much more than frazzle nerves, but who couldn't—or wouldn't—change their lives in the way I wanted.

A yell from downstairs broke my reverie, "Riordan, get your butt down here."

I stubbed out my cigarette and shuffled down the stairs to rising applause from the audience. The tables in front of the bandstand were full and I caught sight of Victor Lane and his wife grinning at me as I made my way to the front. "Hey, August," he shouted. "Why is a bass solo like a sneeze?"

I knew the answer, but played along. "I don't know, Victor. Why is it?"

"Because you know it's coming, but there's not a damn thing you can do about it."

I smiled and waved him off with mock indignation. As I stepped onto the riser, Chris approached from where he'd been loitering near the microphone. "Turns out my call was really for you," he said into my ear. "Special delivery from a party who wishes she could be here." He pressed a small envelope into my palm.

Inside was a note from Ellen Stockwell. It read simply:

August,
In a future life . . .
all my love,
Ellen

Chris watched as I read the note. Something in my face made him squeeze my arm. I walked back to the Begliomini bass that Victor had given me and took it off the stand. I slipped the note from Ellen under the strings on the pegbox and carried the bass forward to the middle of the stage. Victor's grandson, Reggie, smiled at me as he limbered up the valves on his trumpet. Tristin Sinclair tipped his pork pie hat. Chris took a bow by the microphone and the applause reached a crescendo.

He looked back at us with a power-drunk expression that seemed dangerously familiar. He turned to Sinclair. "It's time," he yelled. "Play *Meat*."